CYBERSEX

CYBERSEX

MIRANDA REIGNS

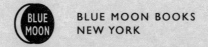

BLUE MOON BOOKS
NEW YORK

Cyberwebs
© 1999 by Miranda Reigns

Sweet Revenge: Cyber Webs II
© 1999 by Miranda Reigns

Obsessions: Cyber Webs III
© 2001 by Miranda Reigns

Published by
Blue Moon Books
An Imprint of Avalon Publishing Group Incorporated
161 William St., 16th Floor
New York, NY 10038

First Blue Moon Books edition 2003

ISBN 1-56201-351-3

9 8 7 6 5 4 3 2 1

Printed in the United States of America
Distributed by Publishers Group West

CHAPTER 1

■

THE MASTER

What compels a perfectly sane woman to throw away everything she has struggled thirty-four years to achieve?

What demons possess me that I could jeopardize a marriage of sixteen years and drive away the man I love? What powerful inner turmoil causes me to abandon my career just as it is about to peak?

Do all women go through this turbulence and confusion, this neverending downward spiral, spinning out of control, grasping for help and stability but finding none?

For many months I had been plagued by a restlessness, a total lack of purpose. I would spend hours at work daydreaming instead of meeting deadlines. Communication with my husband had all but stopped. I felt as if I had no identity. Try as I might to deny it, it was the pull of a powerful, unforeseen force, always beckoning, always demanding to be satisfied. It was addictive, and I had become addicted. Nothing else mattered.

I can't quite put my finger on when I became determined to find myself, but I do know when and where I began to act upon those feelings.

In a small studio apartment in Mission Viejo, I am miles away from anyone who knows me. My only companion is an overweight cat with an attitude. Thank God for Taz. He's here for me to cry on and hold onto. He never complains that I mat his fur, but rather licks himself clean of all the evils in the world and purrs contentedly.

I am basking in the sunshine of a gorgeous summer day, soaking in the rays that are as necessary to sustaining life as breathing. The sun has always been healing for me, and I react to it just as a wilting flower does. I blossom, coming totally alive yet remaining serene, accepting.

But that night, once again, the chaos courses through my body, continuing to torment me. I have held back long enough. It's time to give in to my obsession. I'm ready and I am alone, responsible to no one but myself.

I unplug my phone. With a few familiar mouse clicks, I'm in. Just in the nick of time.

All the usual boxes pop up. My responses are quick and automatic, until . . . my name? I've always used my own name, Miranda, but now I find myself hesitating. I want something different. I don't want to be Miranda anymore. Miranda is safe. I want to cross the threshold and enter a world that is not shielded, not protected. I want adventure and danger.

A new name? I want it to be eye-catching. Of course, it will also need to symbolize just exactly what I'm looking for, what I'm up to. It has to be seductive and mysterious and be intriguing to both men and women alike. Hmmmm . . . Aphrodite! Perfect! It's exactly what I'm looking for. Aphrodite, the Goddess of Love. It is my goal now to make *new* friends. And these new friends will be different. These will be Aphrodite's friends, and they will excite my soul.

I look up at the clock. Three PM. Plenty of time. Now, where to go? Who to look for? No one in the list of names stands out; how about a special room? Let's see, there's the "Kiss and don't tell" room, the "No men allowed" room, the "Domination/Submission (D/S)" room. . . . The Domination/Submission room . . . now that sounds intriguing. I bet I can find a whole slew of people to add to my "friends" in that room. Since this is my first time in such a taboo place, I decide to just eavesdrop for a while.

There is a lot of joking and playful banter, where "DarkKnights" threaten "Damsels" with a flogging for being impertinent and defying direct orders.

Beep, beep, beep. Oh, someone called "Big Man" is inviting me in. Stay idle long enough with a name like Aphrodite, and they'll come looking for you. I grin and open the window.

\<BigMan\>	So you like to watch?
\<Aphrodite\>	Busted, huh?
\<BigMan\>	Yes, you are, little lady. So what brings you here this evening?
\<Aphrodite\>	Honestly? I'm exploring.
\<BigMan\>	Exploring, huh? What exactly are you looking for?
\<Aphrodite\>	Well, I don't know for sure. Just looking for something different.
\<BigMan\>	Well, sweetheart, you came to the right place. Now, what attracted you to this room?
\<Aphrodite\>	Oh, I guess you could say the picture of a soft, fragile female being dominated by a "BigMan" might have had something to do with it. . . .

3

\<BigMan\>	So the thought of being dominated excites you?
\<Aphrodite\>	Well, I didn't realize that until just now, but I guess so. . . . Wow.
\<BigMan\>	Choose, Aphrodite, are you "Slave" or "Slut?"
\<Aphrodite\>	Well. . . .
\<BigMan\>	Be very careful of which you choose.

Ooooo, now I can tell, this is going to be fun!

\<Aphrodite\>	Okay then, "slave."
\<BigMan\>	Good choice . . . Now "slave," are you all alone right now?
\<Aphrodite\>	Yes.
\<BigMan\>	Ok, slave, take off your shirt, and I mean for real . . . no faking it, understand?
\<Aphrodite\>	Yes, I understand.

How far into this do I want to go? Do I want to just play, or do I want to . . . ?
I remove my shirt.

\<Aphrodite\>	Ok, my shirt is off.
\<BigMan\>	Good. Are you wearing a bra?
\<Aphrodite\>	No, I very rarely wear a bra.
\<BigMan\>	Ok, slave, touch yourself. Feel your breasts. Make your nipples hard. Pinch them. DO IT!!!
\<Aphrodite\>	Reaching down to pinch and pull at my nipples, feeling the soft mounds of my breasts. . . . Mmmmmmmmm
\<BigMan\>	What are you feeling, slave?
\<Aphrodite\>	Um, arousal. . . .

<BigMan> | Excellent. . . . Now stand up and face the computer screen.

<Aphrodite> | Ok. . . . Standing.

<BigMan> | I want you to go find a couple of things before we continue. . . . Do you have: A pair of high heels and any body jewelry?

<Aphrodite> | Yes, I have heels . . . and a belly chain.

<BigMan> | How tall are your highest heels?

<Aphrodite> | About 3 inches, why?

<BigMan> | Not big enough, but they'll have to do. What color are they?

<Aphrodite> | Beige.

<BigMan> | This is proving very disappointing, slave. They really should be either black or red and 6 inches high.

<Aphrodite> | Sorry . . . I wasn't expecting you to. . . .

<BigMan> | Go get them anyway, and the belly chain, too.

<Aphrodite> | Right away!

Thank goodness no one can see me scurrying around my tiny apartment topless, looking for a belly chain and some heels.

<Aphrodite> | Back, got them.

<BigMan> | Good, are you still standing?

<Aphrodite> | Am now. . . .

<BigMan> | Take off your pants, slave. Then remain standing.

<Aphrodite> | Okay, they are off, and I'm still standing.

Oh, this is so very wicked. I can't believe that I am actually getting turned on by this!

<BigMan> | Put the belly chain on, slave. . . .

<Aphrodite>	Belly chain is on. . . . The excess chain is dangling between my legs.
<BigMan>	It should. Put your heels on now.
<Aphrodite>	Heels are on too. . . .
<BigMan>	Now, slave, I want you to spread your legs as far as they will go, and bend over so that you are leaning on your computer desk (or table) still facing the screen
<Aphrodite>	Done, legs spread wide. . . . Leaning on desk.
<BigMan>	Now tell me slave, don't you feel ridiculous?
<Aphrodite>	Well, not really . . . I actually feel quite . . . sexy.
<BigMan>	There is hope for you yet. Do you know why a slave must wear 6-inch heels?
<Aphrodite>	Not really . . . why?
<BigMan>	To keep her off balance, making her even more vulnerable.
<Aphrodite>	Oh. . . .
<BigMan>	Do you have a favorite fantasy, slave?

That brings a serious blush. . . .

<Aphrodite>	Yes, as a matter of fact, I do.
<BigMan>	I want you to sit down now and tell it to me. Be graphic, slave.
<Aphrodite>	Um, well, it is kind of long. Do you have at least 2 hours?
<BigMan>	Well, even if I didn't, I do now. . . . This could prove well worth the wait.
<Aphrodite>	I'll do my best to keep your interest piqued.

"Ok. I am a "no nonsense" businesswoman. I am extremely attractive and sexy of course, but very cool and "off limits." I am happily married and have been so for many years. I rarely engage in personal chatter with co-workers, being way too busy attending meetings and trying to meet deadlines. I have been lovingly nicknamed the "Ice Princess." I work in a huge office building on the 15th floor.

It's your first day on a new job in this same office building. We work for the same company, but your office is on the 14th floor. You are being taken on a tour of the building. Your new co-worker, Dave, has been assigned to show you the ropes and make you feel comfortable in your new surroundings.

I am working diligently on a project in my office when I decide that I really need a break. I head off down the hall in search of a steaming hot cup of coffee. I am wearing my hair pulled back and piled up on top of my head in a very proper, business-style bun. Still, a few wisps have managed to escape and are falling freely about my face and neck, giving me a very soft and alluring look. I am wearing a pinstriped dress, buttoning up the front, with cuffs on the sleeves and a shirt-type collar. My incredibly long and shapely legs are accented by black stockings and high heels.

I must have been walking too fast, for I am suddenly taken off balance and almost fall. I look down and notice that one of my shoes has just lost a heel. Damn, I'm really lucky that I didn't break my ankle. I bend down to pick it up, and as I start to stand, I feel a heavy presence looming before me. I hesitate, and then notice I am staring directly at a pair of pant-clad legs. As I straighten up further, my eyes travel up an incredibly well-proportioned male body. Finally rising to my full height, I am quite alarmed to see that I am only face to chest with this person and just narrowly escaped colliding with him altogether. I look up and prepare to apologize to him, but my breath catches and the words are lost. Standing before me is the most magnetic, sexually potent man I have ever bumped into. It's you. I can feel your sexual energy as your eyes bore into mine and search my soul. It's like your hands have somehow entered my body and are pulling at me, gripping me. You don't smile, you don't say a word. You just look. I can't believe what is happening. I've never so much as given a man other than my husband a second glance, and here I stand unable to pull my gaze away from yours. God, you're handsome . . . and I can't keep my jaw from dropping as a surprised O involuntarily escapes my mouth.

You finally pull your eyes from mine and focus them on the provocative O shape currently formed by my lips, causing an instant response from your cock. You are as bewildered as I am. You have always been in control, always been sought after. You've had more women than you can count, yet you've never gotten such an intense response and an instant erection from just a look before. Your reaction angers you, and I notice your face change into a scowl. Dave finally decides to intervene and rescues us from further embarrassment by introducing us. "Chris, this is Miranda. Miranda, Chris." Still unable to speak, I just nod. You mumble a "pleased to meet you," and then are whisked away by Dave. When Dave gets you alone he tells you, "Don't even think about it. She's married and cold as ice."

"Funny, she didn't seem cold as ice," you say as you look back over your shoulder, one last time, at my retreating form.

It takes me minutes to recover. Coffee forgotten, I

8

seek refuge in my office. I hobble back down the hall, suddenly not caring that I am missing a heel, and close the door. I lean against the door and almost collapse, trying to figure out what had just happened. God, I am so overwhelmed. I can feel the heat rising from my core . . . feeling sexually ravaged without ever having been touched.

I close my eyes and relive the past few minutes over and over again. My hands subconsciously take over and my finger begins to trace the outline of my lips, around and around, finally dipping into my mouth. I suck on my finger, getting it wet, sliding it in and out, in and out, finally removing it. My lips stay parted, my eyes remain closed. I have forgotten where I am, what I am doing, my instincts taking over.

Still leaning against the door, my hands start to slide down my body . . . down my neck . . . over my breasts, feeling my nipples respond and awaken, thrusting outward . . . marveling at the feel of the silk of my dress . . . going lower . . . pressing against my stomach, pressing myself into the door . . . my breathing coming in ragged gasps . . . unaware . . . unaware . . . hands going lower until I no longer feel the silk of my dress, but rather the silk of my stockings. Lightly massaging my thighs, caressing them . . . moaning . . . moving upward . . . upward . . . up under my dress now . . . lost, lost in a world of my own making . . . past the tops of my stockings . . . touching bare skin now . . . the inside of my thighs . . . higher, going higher. . . . Oh God . . . feeling incredible wetness. I am soaked. Touching myself . . . whimpering now, sliding a wet finger across my clit, rubbing it in circles, while on the other hand, a finger easily slips inside my eagerly awaiting pussy . . . moaning louder now . . . breathing harder now . . . rubbing, thrusting, rubbing, thrusting, circles . . . in and out . . .

over and over. . . . Ohhh, Ohhhh. . . . A strangled sob escapes just before I let go and bring myself to a frenzied climax. As wave over wave crashes through me, I start to come back to reality. Finally, my eyes open. I focus, and am suddenly horrified that I am behaving like a wanton hussy. What is wrong with me!?! I guiltily look around, making sure that no one witnessed my shameless display, compose myself and return to my desk. Try as I might, I cannot concentrate on my work and decide to call it a day.

Time passes. I haven't seen hide nor hair of you for over three weeks. I am finally able to make it through the day without my thoughts straying back to our brief encounter. It feels good to be focused on my projects again. I have a very important project due tomorrow, and it doesn't look like I am going to get it done. Resigning myself to the fact that I will have to put in a long night, I call my husband to give him the bad news. Then I roll up my sleeves and settle back down at my desk.

When I next look up, it is 10:00 PM. With a big yawn and stretch, I am relieved that I have finally finished, and it's still not too terribly late. Looking slightly tired and disheveled, I lock up my office and head for the elevator. The entire building is dark and quiet, and I think to myself that I must be the only one here. I enter the elevator and press *P* for the parking garage, then lean back and relax against the mirrored interior. I catch a glimpse of myself and smile at my tired form, congratulating myself on a job well done. The elevator starts descending and I am surprised to see that it is stopping at the 14th floor. *Hmmmm*, I think to myself. Some other poor sap must have had to work late, too. The elevator door opens and there you stand. You are holding your suit jacket in your hands and are looking slightly tired and mussed up as well. Our eyes make contact again, and all those same overwhelming feelings I felt the first time I met you come rushing back with a vengeance. A sick feeling washes over me as I back as far into the corner as I can get.

You enter the elevator slowly . . . wondering if you will take advantage of such a situation. You take in my appearance, noticing how incredibly sexy I look, even fatigued. My hair is down, soft, framing my face. I have a white silk blouse on, first two buttons undone, revealing a nice section of cleavage. You are fairly certain that I am not even wearing a bra, barely making out the dark shape of my nipples in the dimly lit interior of the elevator. I have on a very short black suede skirt, black stockings, and of course, high heels. You greedily look me up and down then rest your gaze, once again, on my face. You notice my panicked look and smile at my obvious discomfort. The elevator again begins to descend. You continue to stare at me, and although I try to avoid your gaze, I can see your eyes at every angle, from every direction, surrounding me in the mirrors.

I look up at the floor indicator lights . . . *13, 12, 11* . . . come on, come on, just a little further . . . *10, 9* . . . when suddenly the lights start to flicker and go completely out. The elevator starts to screech and comes to a sudden halt somewhere between the 9th and 8th floors. . . . Oh, God, what's happening? . . . This can't possibly be happening. Just as suddenly as the lights flicker out, they come back on again, but the elevator stays still. What we don't know is that the entire city is experiencing a blackout, likely to last for hours, and the only reason we have lights in the elevator at all is because of the automated battery backup system.

I rush over to the buttons and maniacally pound on them. Worried that I will injure myself, you drop your coat and rush over to me, taking my arms in your hands. This slight contact inflames you, and you growl as you push me back into the elevator corner, my arms held way above my head. Your touch is sending electrical shocks throughout my body, and I roll my head from side to side as if to say . . . no . . . no . . . no. Holding both my arms in one of your hands now, you take your other hand and hold my chin still, making me look at you. The look in your eyes is dark, dangerous, promising, devouring. I know there is no stopping what is sure to transpire, but I give you one last pleading look. The air is so charged with sexual energy, it is suffocating. All the nerve endings on my body are tingling . . . responding, and I let out an anguished moan. Struggling with yourself as long as you can, you finally give in to your animalistic instincts and lower your head to mine, consuming my lips in punishing, passionate kisses. You are barely in control. . . . Your need to possess me is powerful and demanding. Your kisses are furious, your tongue probing, violating my mouth. I am so consumed by your fire, I am amazed that I remain conscious. Oh God . . . what you are making me feel . . . !

Your hand abandons my chin, only to sink into the silky softness of my hair and become entangled in it. You pull my head back, exposing the vulnerable flesh of my throat, and leave a trail of burning kisses, marking me forever. You finally release my arms, but your hand remains buried deep in my hair, immobilizing me. The other hand reaches for my blouse, and without a second thought savagely rips it apart, causing buttons to explode in every direction. A rush of air against my naked breasts causes my nipples to pucker and another agonized moan to be expelled. You take in the lovely shape of my breasts, not too big, not too small, and are extremely aroused by the sight of my nipples: dark brown, large and responsive. You let go of my hair so that you can kneel down and get eye level with them. I remain plastered flat to the elevator wall, an unseen force holding me in place.

Your hands are holding my sides, just under my arms . . . sliding up and down, sending shivers down to my toes. Your mouth has found one nipple, and you are greedily feasting upon it. I can feel your teeth raking and pulling at it, biting and nipping, then suddenly changing to softly sucking and kissing. The contrast in the sensations is playing havoc with me. I am losing my mind . . . mewling . . . whimpering . . . oh God . . . wanting . . . yearning . . . craving. My pussy is on fire . . . swelling. . . . throbbing . . . pulsing. God help me, but I want you to fuck me. . . . This is so wrong . . . so wrong. You find my other nipple, teasing it, devouring it . . . making it dance, making it grow. My shirt is still hanging open, no longer tucked into my skirt. You push it aside and continue your fiery assault down my belly. My stomach quivers and shakes with each kiss, going lower and lower. Your hands slide alongside my body until they are resting on my hips, your tongue probing my navel. God, I'm in anguish. . . . My hands brace themselves in *your* hair now.

You continue lavishing kisses on my stomach while your hands slowly move down the sides of my thighs. Then they start to inch back up, under my skirt, reminding myself of my own actions just three weeks earlier. I can feel your warm, strong hands on my skin, and they continue moving upward until they make contact with my bare ass. The fact that I am not wearing any panties drives you even more wild. You grip and squeeze my ass, roaming all over, your fervor renewed. You are getting impatient. You want to fuck me so badly. Your cock is straining in your pants, begging to be freed. Wasting no time, you yank my skirt up to my waist, baring my pussy to your view. Her lips are thick and glistening, pulsing with need. She is neatly trimmed and you find her the most tantalizing sight you've ever seen. Your mouth engulfs my clit, while you insert one of your fingers, deep, deep into my hot, hungry sheath. I scream out. . . . God, I'm going to cum in seconds. I am so turned on, so heightened. You devour me, taste me, ingest me, consume me . . . licking, sucking and thrusting your finger in and out. I can't hold back. . . . I don't want to hold back . . . and again I scream as earth-shattering convulsions wrack my body.

With a speed uncommon to a man of your size, you are once again standing erect, working furiously at undoing your belt. I stand helplessly by, watching you, attempting to catch my breath, trying desperately to remain standing. You finally get your pants undone and pushed down to your ankles, revealing a very large and powerful-looking cock. I gulp, worried that I cannot possibly handle such a monster. The decision is not left up to me. In one swift thrust, you bury yourself deep inside me, pushing me perilously close to unconsciousness from the intense pleasure. Growling, you stand up to your full height, impaling me, lifting me completely off the floor, and start to fuck me with all the force of three weeks of pent-up sexual frustration. You are pushing me back into the corner with every thrust, pounding into me. My legs wrap around your waist, creating deeper penetration. You thrust relentlessly . . . fucking me mindless, over and over . . . deeper and deeper. "Oh, yes. . . . oh, yes . . . oh God . . . oh God . . ." I keep repeating over and over. Finally, you feel your balls start to tighten. You know you are getting ready to explode. . . . *Thrust*. . . . *Thrust*. . . . *Thrust* . . . one final time. You kiss me ferociously as you unleash the

---

14

booming wail of a wounded animal, and erupt into one of the most powerful orgasms ever experienced, shooting load after load of steaming hot cum deep, deep, deep into my sweet, sexy body.

On the verge of collapse, you set me down, and we both slide down the elevator walls to the floor, panting heavily. I stare at the wanton creature gazing back at me from the mirrored walls, dismayed by my shameless appearance. Shirt ripped and hanging open, skirt wrapped around my waist, hair completely messed up, still wearing stockings and heels. I look over at you, and notice you are managing to bring your breathing under control without too much difficulty. I, on the other hand, fear I will never recover.

You are giving me a rather strange look, like you are trying to work out a solution to a problem. I'm not quite sure how to read it, but I notice that the longer I look at you, the more your cock seems to like it. It is miraculously beginning to twitch and revive itself. I'm amazed and look back at your face questioningly. You have a wolfish grin on your face as you say, "I'm not quite through with you yet." My eyes widen as you help yourself up, offering your hand to me. I refuse your hand, preferring to stay exactly where I am at for the moment. Not at all deterred by my lack of enthusiasm, you grab my wrists and haul me up in one fluid motion.

Now that the urgent need to *take* me has been satisfied, you renew your seduction much more slowly. Again, you search my eyes, your gaze still heated and smoldering. You take one of your hands and lightly caress my face with your thumb. I close my eyes and moan, unable to stop the fire that is beginning to reignite. This tender, slow torture may be even more difficult for me to handle. I feel both of your hands lightly graze my neck to rest on my shoulders, then skilfully manipulate the remainder of my blouse so that it falls, sliding down my arms into a heap on the elevator floor. With the removal of my blouse complete, I am overcome by a million tiny shivers prickling their way over every inch of my newly exposed flesh. Unable to ignore the feather-light sliding of the silk and the gust of warm air assaulting my skin, I am held spellbound.

Next, you straighten my skirt, slowly unzip it, and let it go, until it too settles into a heap at my feet. I step out from the center of my skirt and kick it aside, standing exposed, leaving little to your imagination, in garter belt, stockings, and high heels. I feel wickedly sexy standing before you this way. You step back to admire my scantily clad body, your eyes scorching every inch of my skin as they travel up and down. You come back over to me, place your hands on my arms, and slowly turn me around so that I am facing the mirrored wall. I can feel your hot breath as it pulses at the back of my neck. You push me up against the mirror until I am pressed flat against it. The cool surface instantly causes my nipples to tighten and pucker. You take my arms and raise them slightly above my head, spreading them about a foot apart to lie flat against the mirror, my palms and forearms also make contact. You turn my head to the side so that my right cheek is similarly pressed against the mirrored wall. My eyes close, my lips part, and my breathing becomes labored. My body is responding to the uncertainty of what you are going to do next, excitement and anticipation replacing my fear.

You whisper in my ear, "Don't you dare move. I want the entire top half of your body to remain flat against this wall. Is that understood?"

"Yes . . . yes. . . ."

Next, you commence to sexually assault my mind, whispering all kinds of lewd suggestions and statements

---

16

directly into my ear, asking me darkly intriguing questions, forcing me to answer you and admit my deepest, darkest secrets.

"Do you have any idea how incredibly sexy you are? Do you have any idea what I'm going to do to you next? Do you know that you are completely in my power and helpless to stop anything I choose to initiate?"

Oh God . . . oh God . . . stop the mind fuck, please. I can't take this. "Yes . . . yes . . . I know . . . please . . ."

"Please . . . what, Miranda?"

"Please . . . no more. . . ."

"I haven't even started yet, Miranda."

"Stop . . . stop talking . . . stop. . . ." I'm barely able to squeak out the words.

Your hands lightly graze a trail down the center of my back, invoking a mixture of involuntary tremors and shivers. God, I'm so hot . . . so turned on, on fire . . . your mental foreplay unleashing my most hidden and unacknowledged desires.

One of your hands stays firmly planted in the center of my back, keeping my chest pressed flat against the wall, while your other arm reaches around my waist and pulls it out toward you, causing my back to arch and giving you a delightful view of my ass. You also pull my legs and feet out about one foot from the wall.

"Spread your legs apart for me, Miranda."

"Stop it. . . . This is so degrading."

"One more time. . . . Spread your legs apart." This time your demand is accompanied by a stinging swat to my backside.

I gasp, "Okay, okay!" and spread my legs apart. Oh God, this is so humiliating . . .

"Wider."

With a stifled cry I spread my legs as wide as my wobbly heels will allow.

"Much better." Your hands start to caress and probe my fully exposed and vulnerable ass.

Again you whisper sinisterly, "Ever been fucked up the ass, Miranda?"

At this, I react in fright and try to move . . .

"I told you not to move. Not one inch. Not until I tell you that you can." And you press my chest back up against the wall with your palm remaining centered in the middle of my back.

"Well, have you? Answer me." Another stinging swat to my ass.

"*Yes!* Yes . . . once . . . once before . . . stop it, please. . . ." I sob.

"Did you like it? *Did you like it*?"

"Uh . . . uh . . . kind of . . . It was a little uncomfortable. . . ."

"I bet you weren't this turned on, though, were you? You know how I can tell you're turned on, Miranda?"

"No . . . no . . . how?"

"From this . . ." and with that you take two of your fingers and bury them to the hilt inside my pussy without the slightest resistance, causing me to gasp and cry out, startled. God. . . . What you are doing to me?

"Good God, Miranda . . . you are so wet . . . so fucking wet . . ."

You take the juices from my pussy and begin to spread them on my asshole, liberally covering it with moisture, slightly penetrating my ass with your finger, making sure that I am slick inside and out. Oh God . . . oh God . . . then the hand that has been around my waist travels lower and starts to stimulate my clit. Oh God, I want you . . . I want it . . . I don't care where. . . . At that thought, I feel the head of your cock teasing the en-

trance to my ass, slowly encircling it . . . slowly probing
. . . proceeding cautiously. I arch my back further, sticking my ass out more, wanting to feel you buried deep
in my ass . . . impatient now.

You slowly begin to penetrate me, entering inch by
inch. You groan, overcome by the sensation of such
tightness, and push on further. Unintelligible sounds,
originating from deep within my throat, are being driven
from me, torn from me. I am moaning uncontrollably
. . . feeling your entire shaft finally buried deep inside
me. Your hand is still working furiously on my clit. I
start to move and buck against you, wanting this . . .
wanting to be fucked up the ass, needing to be fucked
up the ass. "Fuck me! Fuck meeeeeeeeeee!" I cry, and
you need no more urging. You start to fuck my ass with
long, deep, steady strokes, over and over . . . getting as
deep as you possibly can. You're not going too fast, but
you don't need to. You are so close to losing control,
to releasing your tidal wave of cum . . . can't go any
faster. Stroke, stroke . . . in deep, pull out . . . in deep,
pull   out. . . . Ohhhhh. . . . Ohhhhhhhhhhh. . . . I   am
ready to explode . . . your fingers relentless on my aching, needing clit. Arching, thrusting . . . that's it . . .
that's it . . . feel it building. . . . peaking. . . . Oh God . . .
Oh God. . . . "Ahhhhhhhhhhhhhhhhhhhhhhhhhhhrg. . . ."
we both scream at the same, exact moment . . . throwing
ourselves into turbulent wave after turbulent wave, oscillating pulse after oscillating pulse of incredible,
mind-blowing ecstasy.

    <Aphrodite> I Well, how was that?
    <BigMan> I We need to meet, Aphrodite. Where are
                 you from?
    <Aphrodite> I Well, I can't make you any promises . . .

I am currently residing in sunny, Southern California.

<BigMan> I I am going to be conducting business in LA, a week from Monday. Let me take you out to dinner.

<Aphrodite> I Dinner, huh? I don't even know you.

<BigMan> I I am quite trustworthy. I can help you explore your fantasies in complete safety. You won't regret it.

<Aphrodite> I I don't know. You have to give me an "out." What if I'm not the least bit attracted to you?

<BigMan> I I don't believe that will be a problem, but at the very worst, you'll get a free dinner.

<Aphrodite> I Promise? Even. . . . seafood?

<BigMan> I Whatever you desire. And that "out" you were talking about. . . . I can give you a code word. Use it anytime during dinner. . . . or after, and we will part ways, no questions asked.

<Aphrodite> I Okay, I want you to know, up front, I'm going to tell several of my friends where I'll be that night, and if I don't come home, they'll find you. I've got your e-mail address. It won't be hard.

<BigMan> I I would expect nothing less. Now, your code word will be "taxi." Use it anytime, and I'll bow out gracefully. Just be certain that you truly mean it, because once it is uttered, I won't allow you to take it back. Deal?

<Aphrodite> I Deal. How well do you know Southern Cal?

<BigMan> I Well enough to know of an excellent

20

		seafood restaurant, situated right on the beach with a hotel, not more than a mile away. I'll make reservations.
<Aphrodite>	I	Who said anything about a hotel?
<BigMan>	I	Hey, *I'll* need someplace to sleep that night.
<Aphrodite>	I	Very true.
<BigMan>	I	Now, give me your address so I can have the limo pick you up.
<Aphrodite>	I	Oooo, the red carpet treatment. You certainly treat your *slaves* well.
<BigMan>	I	You don't know the half of it, Aphrodite. But you will . . . you will. Now, give me your address and I'll give you the names and addresses of both the restaurant where we will meet, and the hotel where I'll be staying.
<Aphrodite>	I	Well, I must say, I am quite apprehensive but curious. I'll look forward to meeting you. I just want you to know that this is something I've never done before and probably will never do again. It's a one-time, explorative type of thing. Understand?
<BigMan>	I	You're absolutely precious, you know that? Of course I understand. Until Monday. . . .
<Aphrodite>	I	Until Monday, then. Good night, Mr. Big.
<BigMan>	I	Nite, Slave.

After adding <BigMan> to my list of *friends*, I hurriedly disconnect from the Internet, shut down my computer, and replace the phone cord back into the jack. Nothing like jumping in with both feet. Geeze, I hope

I don't regret this. With a distracted sigh, I take off my heels, take off the belly chain, and head straight for the shower. Heck, I am already halfway there, might as well shower now rather than later.

The shower is awesome, just what the doctor ordered. Warm enough to relax all the muscles that had been held taut during the past three hours, but cool enough to help reduce some of that internal fire. That was definitely different and way more exciting. Going into the D/S room was definitely a good move. I am actually quite surprised by how much I enjoyed being dominated like that. It was extremely sexual. I'm going to have a long night ahead of me, starting my shift *this* worked up, already.

I step out of the shower and towel off, then go in search of my uniform. I work for an erotic dance club called 'Club Illicit' as a cocktail waitress. It is a high class place with a very wealthy clientele, and the amount I make in tips each night allows me to only work three nights a week. Of course, I don't make nearly as much as the dancers, who are all very beautiful, very sexy, women. Robert, my boss, sure knows how to pick them.

My shifts start at 8:00 PM and go until closing, 2:00 AM. I requested to work the weekend nights because the pay is better. Tonight is only Thursday, my first shift this week. I like to keep my Sunday nights free.

After donning my skimpy outfit that consists of a long white shirt with tails, a red cummerbund, a red bow tie, black fishnet stockings, black flash pants, and black heels, I begin to work on my makeup and hair. Satisfied with the results, I head to the kitchen for a quick bite to eat. Choosing the remains of a leftover salad and a toasted bagel with tuna fish mixed with creamy horseradish, I gobble my dinner down and head for the door. Robert doesn't like it when we're late.

Club Illicit is about a fifteen-minute drive from my apartment, and I usually don't have to worry about any traffic at this time of day. One of the many benefits of working nights is that I'm less likely to encounter a person suffering from the road rage seeming to totally consume motorists these days and spreading like one of the world's most infectious diseases. I start the engine of my reliable little Honda and speed off to work, listening to my favorite tunes and mentally preparing myself for the night ahead.

CHAPTER 2

◾

THE DANCER

As I walk through the door of Club Illicit, the interior is already a bustle of activity. Provocative music is playing through an incredible sound system, dancers are warming up, stretching, practicing, patrons are being shown to their seats, and mouth-watering appetizers are being placed on all the tables.

The club consists primarily of a huge, curved stage, placed directly in the middle of the main room, surrounded by strategically placed tables and chairs. There are poles spread out along the stage for the dancers to grab on to and use as props, if needed. The decor is classy and tasteful, appealing to even the most skeptical guest. The atmosphere is warm and friendly, attracting a wide variety of customers.

I head for the employee lounge, clock in, greet Jeff, the bartender, with a quick hello and a peck on the cheek, and begin taking orders and serving drinks. It's a fairly easy job, the most grueling part being the aching feet destined to plague me after six hours in heels.

9:00 PM . . . the first dancer takes the stage. Each girl dances for fifteen minutes, then takes a forty-five minute break, allowing for four different dancers to take the stage each hour. The first temptress to perform is Shauna, a very dark and exotic dancer. Her greatest assets are her golden eyes, incredibly accented by her creamy-chocolate skin. She creates the illusion of a half-woman, half-feline predator, stalking her prey. I pause to watch a few minutes of her show, envying her ability to shed her inhibitions and dance so freely. Thirsty customers call me from my daydreams back into reality, and I scurry off to fill another drink order.

The next dancer to take the platform is one I haven't met before, and again I find myself drawn to the rhythmic movements coming from center stage. Where does Robert find these ethereal women, and more importantly, how does he keep them? She is an exquisite redhead, one of the most beautiful women I have ever seen. Huge green eyes, long, soft, copper-glazed hair. Statuesque, her curves fall in all the right places.

She must have noticed me watching her, and flashes me a brilliant smile to show her appreciation. Or, at least, that's what I'm assuming the smile is for . . . but once we make eye contact, she doesn't let go. She keeps me hypnotized, drawn to her, watching her every move. I am spellbound. I stay, transfixed by her performance the entire fifteen minutes while she silently and intimately makes love to my soul, never once removing her eyes from mine. Whoa . . . did she affect everyone in the audience the way she had just affected me? I look around at all the slack-jawed, captivated expressions, and have my answer. She is extraordinary. It is in that split second that I realize that I will not be complete until I also experience that feeling, that power. I head off in the direction of Robert's office, impatient to share with him my recent discovery.

* * *

"I want to dance."

"Excuse me?"

"I want to dance."

Robert looks me over, trying to ascertain whether I am serious.

"Do you realize that all my dancers are in their early twenties? You're thirty-something, aren't you?"

Insulted, yet not willing to back down, I reply, "Well, yes, but that is beside the point."

Still eyeing me critically, Robert asks, "Have you kept yourself in shape?"

"I go to the gym every day. I jog. I hike. I Roller-blade. I'm every bit as fit as those girls you have out there dancing right now."

"Really, now? Take off your clothes."

Now it was my turn. "Excuse me?"

"I said, take off your clothes."

I stumble and falter, thinking he can't possibly be serious.

"Look, if you can't take off your clothes, right here, right now, for only one person, how can I possibly expect that you'll be able to disrobe and dance for crowds of fifty or more? Take off your clothes."

Okay . . . okay, this is a test. I've got to make good. This may be my one and only shot, and this is so important to me right now. I need this experience.

"Can you give me a minute? Do you have any music I can undress to?" Courage, Randa, courage. Go slow.

"Sure, there's a whole selection over there by the CD player. Go find yourself a favorite song and play it."

I saunter over to the counter that houses the CD player and discs, making sure I put emphasis on the slow, sultry way my hips sway as I move. I begin to realize that if I want this job, I'm going to have to do more than dance for it. I'm going to have to dance and seduce. Looking over at Robert, I ask myself, *Can I tempt this man? Can I drive him so crazy that he'll promise me anything? If necessary, can I fuck this man?* Oh, yeah. He is very handsome, very sophisticated, and extremely charismatic. I could fuck him. Better yet, I could fuck *with* him. Take him to the brink and then stop. I smile a small, evil smile and choose my selection.

The room is suddenly filled with the melody of a sultry, haunting song. I return to the center of the room, directly in front of Robert, and give him one last look, full of purpose and promise. He grins, slightly amused and expectant, and leans back, waiting for the show to begin. I close my eyes and begin a slight back and forth sway, moving to the music. I let it envelop me, invade me, possess me until I am completely connected with the music, until I've forgotten who I am, where I am.

As the music takes me, I begin to remove my clothing, starting with the red bow tie and cummerbund and tossing them aside. Next, I slowly unbutton my blouse, my fingers pausing for effect, until I have every last one undone. The natural undulation of my body causes my blouse to shift, slide, and float delicately from my shoulders. I continue to dance to the seductive tunes spewing from the CD player, my new lover. I grasp at the imaginary hands caressing me, sliding down my body, following their path. With a will of their own, my hands remove the flash pants, the only barrier remaining between my most hidden and protected secret and his eyes.

I open my eyes, aware that I am standing before Robert in nothing but a lacy bra, fishnet stockings, and heels. I stare directly into his eyes, noticing that the self-assured, semi-cocky demeanor has been cast aside and replaced with an expression of shock and surprise. I continue to stare knowingly at him, certain that I will win this small battle. Now the seduction really begins. My gaze still penetrating his, never wavering, never releasing, I continue to dance for him, edging closer and closer to where he sits in his chair. He shifts uncomfortably, perhaps not quite ready for what he invited.

I come right up against him, knees touching knees, and remove the remainder of my clothing, but, as a second thought, decide to put my heels back on. I make sure that he is within reaching distance, watching him struggle with his self-control, wanting to touch me yet not allowing himself to do so. I straddle his lap, then slowly lower myself down, until I am sure he can feel the center of my blazing inferno consume his ill-prepared crotch. His teeth are bared as he sucks back an unwelcome groan.

"Close your eyes and let me touch you." Not wanting to break the spell, he is very careful not to initiate anything. His arms hold the chair behind his back with a death grip. He can feel my fingers on his face, massaging his forehead, his cheeks, his scalp . . . my breath tickling his nose. I thoroughly scrutinize his features, attempting to memorize every last line on his face. I rake my fingers through his hair, massaging, gripping, exploring, still swaying to the music.

My breathing begins to increase, coming in faster, erratic intervals, and Robert appears to have stopped breathing altogether. I stare intently at his lips, subconsciously licking my own. My fingers lightly move across his eyes, closing his lids, as I bend forward and place a butterfly kiss on each corner of his mouth, then up to the tip of his nose, and to each of his closed eyelids. My hands grip his shoulders as I move to my right, kissing across his face, down around his neck, and over to his left ear. I know he can hear the urgency in my breathing, sensing my need. I attack his ear in earnest, butterfly kisses forgotten. Nibbling, sucking, licking, and probing, I begin fucking his ear. He can hear my small moans. Somehow, this is no longer a game . . . I want this man.

I abandon his poor ravaged ear and start kissing back across his neck, his chin, his jawline, and over to his other ear where I give it the same treatment. I bathe his ear with my warm, wet tongue, sliding it all around, in and out of every conceivable crevice, my breathing getting more and more desperate. I begin to gyrate on his lap, feeling his erection, wanting frantically to feel it inside me. Can I continue with this cold-blooded seduction, or will I need to satisfy myself?

With a whimper, I slowly slide away from his body, pushing my ass to the edge of his lap. The heat emanating from my pussy onto his knees is overwhelming. He can barely contain his lust, his struggle becoming more evident with each bead of sweat that forms on his forehead. I look into his eyes before I resume my assault. My eyes no longer contain a promise, but a raw, animal lust. I part my teeth momentarily, and with a snarl, go back to feasting.

As I continue to kiss further down his neck, I catch a whiff of his cologne, cologne mixed with something else. Him. His musk. His scent. It's rising from his pores, combining with my senses, taking over. I want to absorb it. I want to feel it intermingle with every part of me. Damn, I want him naked. I rip and pull at his shirt, until he offers to help, and together we successfully remove it completely from his body. God, he's got a great chest. Wide, expansive, covered in soft, downy fur. I slide my hands down his chest and savor the feeling of running my fingers through it. I look back up at him, this position no longer effective. With an evil chuckle, I slowly slide down his leg, my pussy lips spread wide, gripping his pants the entire way down.

I spread his knees and legs wide apart, crawling between them. I kneel on the floor, between his legs, at a perfect height to continue. Licking my lips, I lower my head. He gasps as he feels my tongue at the waistband of his trousers. Not knowing exactly what my intentions are at this point, his cock starts getting very jumpy and eager. I slowly glide my wet tongue from side to side, all the way across his waistband, teasing. Will I go down, or will I go up? I return to the middle and slowly start licking my way up, until I have found his navel. He lets out an agonized, "Agrh." His hands finally release their death grip on the chair and swing around to grab my hair. My tongue pushes in and out of his navel, filling it with moisture, creating a squishing sound every time my tongue ventures back in that direction.

My tongue sears him with the heat of a volcano as it leaves his belly button and travels upward, toward his nipples. Again, I feel him brace himself, and his grip gets tighter in my hair. Kissing . . . licking . . . sucking . . . biting . . . all the way up. He feels the warmth from my breath bathing his right nipple, as my lips remain poised above it, waiting. It starts to pucker up, even before I touch it, just from the heat, just from the expectancy. He utters a warning growl, and knowing that I'm treading on shaky ground, I finally lower my mouth to encase his aching nipple. The heat, the wetness, the sensation of my gentle biting and scraping of his nipple, shoots straight to his cock. If I don't finish this soon, he is going to completely lose control. He groans out my name, over and over again . . . Miranda . . . Oh, Miranda . . . please, please . . . Randa . . . Randa . . . as he continues to pull and tug at my hair. After giving his

---

left nipple the same attention, I work my way back to the center of his chest and start to lick and kiss downward. My hands are resting just above his pecs, and I slowly rake my fingernails downward, keeping cadence with my kisses.

"Now it's your turn. Take off your pants." Not needing to be told twice, he quickly removes the offending garment. I grip the waistband of his boxers, and remove them as well. He sits back down again, and I take a minute to admire what I've just uncovered. His cock is beautiful, masculine, powerful. I subconsciously lick my lips as I stare at it. Mmmmmmmmmmmm, and his legs are equally as sexy, strong and muscular. I settle myself back in between his parted legs, running my hands up and down them, from his thighs to his shins and ankles, and then back up again.

I choose a leg and start biting my way up . . . mid-thigh, higher . . . higher. Not too hard, not too gentle, but enough to get a reaction from him, his cock jumping with each nip, until my nose rests in the middle of his balls. Again, I take a deep breath and indulge in his smell. Without being able to hold back any longer, I start to lick and kiss his balls, getting more and more urgent. I try to get them both completely engulfed in my mouth, but they are too big and I have to settle for one at a time. I gently suck, lick and saturate each one in warmth and wetness until I decide to move onward. The moans coming from him are inhuman. . . .

I work my way up the shaft of his cock, licking it . . . bathing it. I pull myself away temporarily and stare directly into his eyes, as I take both of my breasts in my hands and begin an erotic display of groping them. I take them and squeeze them together, letting my thumb and forefingers reach up to pull my nipples straight out, extending them out half an inch . . . three-quarter of an inch . . . one full inch. Quite certain that I have his undivided attention, I lower them until his balls are resting on them, and continue to knead and milk them gently around his balls.

My mouth finally returns to his cock, which is soaked from its own juice and twitching out of control. I teasingly dart at the tip of it, still massaging his balls with my breasts, licking . . . darting . . . teasing . . . I slowly lower my lips, and they part and separate as the head of his cock enters my intensely hot mouth. I slowly work my way down his cock, giving just the head of it attention . . . sucking on it, swirling my tongue around it, surrounding it in heat and wetness. Slowly I work my way further and further down, until he feels the head of his cock at the back of my throat, and my lips around the base. I come back up again . . . and slowly back down . . . up and down . . . up and down . . . staying down this time . . . as I begin to milk him. He feels the back of my throat squeezing against the head of his cock, back and forth, squeezing . . . pulling . . . consuming . . . opening further . . . going down . . . devouring . . . back up again. Now I start to pump faster, one hand reaching up to the base of his cock, softly twisting and turning, as my mouth pumps up and down, rotating on his cock. My other hand lightly grips his balls . . . faster and faster . . . Uhhhhh. . . . He can hear the moans coming from deep within my throat as I suck him for all he is worth. Oh, I want him to cum . . . want to feel his cum splashing . . . squirting . . . deep, deep into my throat . . . pulsing . . . thrusting . . . back and forth, up and down . . . frenzied . . . I feel him start to swell, growing larger, filling my mouth entirely with his massive presence. Knowing he is so close . . . continuing . . . milking . . . squeezing, swirling . . . heat . . . intense heat . . . steaming, surrounded in a pool of lava . . . I feel him

. . . I feel him . . . "AAAAAAAAAAAAAAAAAAAa-ggggggggggggggggghhhhhhhhhhhhhhhhhhhh!!!!!!" With an incredible burst, he explodes, pumping into me, shooting load after load. I pull away just in time to get the last shot sprayed directly on my face . . . on my lips . . . and he watches incredulously as it dribbles away . . . down . . . disappearing under my chin. With his eyes still closed, he utters a feeble, "Okay, okay . . . you've convinced me!"

I relax and lay my head against his thigh until my breathing returns to normal. "There's only one thing that I'm really worried about. I've never had any instructional dance training. I don't know any technical moves. I suppose I can bluff it with just natural instincts, but I would really appreciate it if I could have a crash course in . . . something."

"No problem, Miranda. I'll fix you up with one of the girls. Maybe one or more of them will be willing to teach you a few tricks, but it will have to be on your own time."

"No problem," I reply, gratefully, as I scamper around in search of my articles of clothing.

Robert haphazardly pulls himself together, then reaches for the intercom on his desk, buzzing into the dancers' dressing room. "Angela . . . I need you in my office if you have a moment."

"Sure, I'll be there in just a minute," is the musical reply.

By the time the soft knock indicating Angela's arrival is recognized, both Robert and I have completely pulled ourselves back together. Only the most perceptive of people would have been able to deduce that anything out of the ordinary had just occurred. "Come on in."

I am stunned into immobility as the gorgeous red-headed dancer I had already seen perform enters Robert's office. I can only gape at her, openmouthed. Robert notices my reaction, but shrugs it off. "Angela, have you met Miranda yet? She was one of our cocktail waitress up until a minute ago, but she's expressed her desire to dance to me, and I have decided to give her the opportunity. She is going to need a little help. She has never had any professional training before, and I told her that I would ask you girls for assistance in teaching her a few things. Is this something that you'd care to do, as a favor to me?"

She smiles and winks at Robert and says, "I'd be happy to, Robert." Then she turns to me, extends her hand and says, "Welcome, Miranda. Pleased to meet you."

I also extend my hand to her and we clasp. The instant that contact is made with her skin, a shock so astonishing fires its way through my hand, down my arm and into the pit of my stomach that I'm certain it leaves a scorch mark on my palm. She controls the clasp, gripping my hand just a little longer than necessary, holding my eyes prisoner with her own.

I whisper, "Pleased to meet you as well, Angela . . ." *What's happening to me*, I wonder. "Thanks for offering to help me."

"My pleasure, Miranda. When would you like your first lesson?" she asks, as she finally releases my hand. "Shall I arrange to meet with you at your house during the afternoons, or would you prefer somewhere else?"

"No, the afternoons at my apartment are fine. Want to . . . ah . . . start tomorrow, let's say, around . . . noon, and, uh, go from there?" I manage to stammer out.

"That sounds perfect, Miranda. I'll see you tomorrow." I give her my address and phone number, thank

Robert again, and leave his office, somehow managing to get through the rest of the night with visions of redheads and sultry green eyes haunting me.

The next morning arrives much too quickly, and I find myself anxious about the upcoming dance lessons. *Did I imagine all that sexual tension last night between Angela and I? Was it just me? Was she purposefully flirting with me, testing my reaction, or is that just how she is? Some women just exude sexual energy, regardless of who she's with. Maybe she is just that way, and I misinterpreted the vibes radiating off of her as a "come on." Yeah, that's probably all it was,* I manage to half convince myself.

I quickly shower and select one of my many dance leotards to wear for the upcoming lesson. Even though I've never taken dance lessons before, I have acquired quite a collection of tights and bodysuits that I wear regularly to the gym for my daily aerobics classes. They ought to work out perfectly.

Angela arrives at 12:00 PM sharp, looking all fresh and excited about the upcoming lesson. We exchange pleasantries and small talk, and then Angela takes the initiative by asking me where the tape player is. I point it out to her and wait while she gets it set up just the way she likes it. She looks around my apartment and frowns, obviously not happy with the size of it. Her face does lighten up when she spots my mirrored closet doors. "We'll dance in front of your closet so you can see, as well as feel, the moves." I nod, perfectly content to let her call the shots.

She gets up and walks over to the closet just as the music starts playing. "Come over here and stand in front of me, facing the mirror." I do as told, feeling the warmth from her body disperse and encase my back as if it were an article of clothing. We make eye contact, and immediately the feelings from the night before come rushing back. Oh, my. . . . Oh, my . . . This is going to be tough. She bends down and retrieves a long leather belt from her bag. "We need to stay as close together as possible, so that you can feel my movements flow with the music. This belt will make sure that you can't get away." With that said, she winks and begins draping the belt around both of our midsections, pulling me very tight and close against her. Then she latches it and says, "There, that should do it. Now, I want you to hold my hands and keep your feet as close to mine as possible. The more of our bodies that remain in constant contact, the more you will learn. Ready?" I gulp and nod my assent.

She immediately starts to move, taking my arms with her, taking my body with her. I am overcome with emotions and sensations that are unfamiliar to me, but in some strange way, all too familiar.

"Stop fighting me, Miranda. Just relax against me." I try to let myself go slack against her. Is it my imagination, or did she just inhale sharply? She is taking me, step by step, into her world of erotica.

"Keep your eyes open, Miranda. Look at me while we dance." I obey, getting lost in her beautiful green eyes, as she continues her seduction and steals my essence. I am no longer in control of my body. She has assumed control. I only hope that she is worthy of possessing it.

After a couple of hours of showing me the most enticing ways to remove my clothing, different styles of arching and bending to inflame both male and female spectators, and certain methods of rotating my hips, we decide to call it a day. I breathe a heavy sigh of relief that I got through the ordeal intact. Even though Angela's eyes hinted at a certain desire for me, she never let it go further than that, for which I was grateful. I'm not confident that I have the strength to resist any intimate advances that she might make, and I'm not sure that I would truly want to. Oh, God, wait until I tell my husband of this new discovery. I just shake my head and return my focus back to Angela.

She is in the process of reclaiming her tape and gathering her belongings. "Same time tomorrow?" I ask.

"You bet, hon. See you tonight at the club."

"Angela, thanks a million for doing this for me. I just want you to know how much I appreciate it."

"No problem, Randi, I'm enjoying myself. It's a nice distraction from my otherwise humdrum routine."

Randi? I think to myself. It would seem that I've acquired a new nickname. "Okay, then, see you tonight."

I look at the clock; only 2:00 PM. I can still catch a couple of hours of sun if I hustle. Now that I'm going to be baring my body to the world, I want it to have a nice, golden hue. I hurriedly change into my skimpiest swimsuit, pull out the lounge chair, and settle back to revel in the sun's warmth. Before I know it, I've dozed off and find myself caught up in one hell of a steamy dream.

A man, an unidentified man, takes me to this cottage out in the country, in the middle of nowhere. It is beautiful, picture perfect, with lush green grass and groves of trees. As soon as we get there, he takes me out back and blindfolds me. Next, he removes my shoes, and we start walking. The soft, thick, cool grass feels exquisite across my bare feet, sensual, just as he knew it would. We stop and he slowly backs me up until I am leaning against the trunk of a tree. He tells me not to move, and begins to remove my clothing, slowly unbuttoning my shirt, resisting the urge to cup and squeeze my breasts. All I can feel is the slight breeze caressing my nakedness. When my shirt is off, no longer an obstacle, he removes my pants, and I am left standing before him, completely bare, still blindfolded and feeling very vulnerable. "What are you going to do?" I ask, but there is no response.

The next thing I feel is my right wrist being bound with something soft, then my left wrist. He walks me a few paces away from the tree trunk and raises one arm, attaching it to a limb of the tree, directly above and slightly higher than my head. The second wrist is then brought up and tied to the same tree limb. I am standing there, totally exposed and completely helpless, when I hear his footsteps retreating. "Please don't leave me alone like this! Please!" Again, I receive no response from him.

I utter a cry of despair and hang there, wondering. Did he invite all of his friends over to watch? Were they all standing there, ogling me? Oh God. I stand there for what seems like hours before I hear footsteps again. I pray that they are his. I hear breathing. It's driving me crazy that he won't assure me that it's him, that everything is all right. Say something . . . please, say something. Next thing I know, I am being splattered with something warm and slippery. Oil? Oil is being squirted, poured and dribbled all over my entire body, and I can feel it sliding downward. The slippery liquid begins dripping over my breasts, causing my nipples to pucker, dripping between my ass cheeks, dripping over my pussy, seeping into the folds of my lips, causing me to squirm. Oh, it feels so delicious, so erotic. Somebody help me.

Next, I feel hands, his hands, so strong and masculine, touching me everywhere, rubbing what I can only assume to be baby oil onto my body, making sure he doesn't miss one crevice. He has me moaning now, begging for more. One of his fingers slips inside my pussy, teasing me, then is abruptly withdrawn. "Oh, please, please . . . don't stop . . . I want you. . . . I am dying. . . ." Not only does he *not* continue, but again, I hear his footsteps retreating. I start to whimper pathetically, struggling to cope with the anger I feel toward this man for reducing me to such a primitive level.

I hear him return, but he is no longer alone. I hear a female voice, pleading. I can't quite make out what she is saying. I become terribly still, trying to pick up pieces of their conversation. *What is he up to*, I wonder? He comes closer, she comes closer. I can hear her now: "What are you doing? You are scaring me . . . please . . ."

Oddly, I now have some idea of what is about to happen, knowing she still has none, that she, too, is blindfolded. I haven't uttered a sound. He commences to tie her to the same tree limb as I, exactly in the same spot, face to face. I can feel her confusion, her desperate breathing against my lips as she begins to realize that she and he are not alone. "Is there someone else here?" He doesn't answer her either. After she is secured to the limb, he pushes us together and holds us close, nose to nose, breasts to breasts, navel to navel, hips to hips. We both suck in our breaths, afraid to move. He releases us and our bodies instinctually move farther apart. Lastly, he takes off our blindfolds, allowing us to witness each other's degradation.

It's her. It's Angela. He introduces us . . . "Miranda, meet Angela. Angela, meet Miranda." I open my mouth in shock. I look over at him. He is also naked and stroking his big, thick cock. I am overcome, intensely aroused. I look back at Angela and we begin to assess one another. She is beautiful, exquisite. Soft and incredibly feminine. She also has baby oil rubbed all over her body. I can tell by her perusal of me that she is also not disappointed. We are still not touching one another, except at the wrists where he has us bound together.

Eager for us to get over our shyness, he takes a large, vibrating dildo out from some secret hiding place and positions it between our bellies, so that the tip is just barely grazing our clits. He holds us together again and says, "Don't let this dildo fall. If it falls, you'll both be sorry." He lets us go and we automatically take over, pressing our bodies as close together as possible, keeping the dildo stationary. The vibrations the dildo creates causes us to rock together, first toward her, then toward me, the tip of the dildo vibrating directly on our clits when we do this.

We moan and look at each other, our eyes glazing over. She takes one of her legs off of the ground and wraps it around one of mine, keeping us locked tightly in place. I take my opposite leg and do the same. Our breasts are sliding together, rubbing together, vibrations wracking our entire bodies. We look at one another in helpless abandon until she licks her lips, groans and presses her lips toward mine. My last bit of resistance is worn down, and our lips lock. I can't believe how soft it is, how wonderful it feels to kiss a woman, to kiss *this* woman. I inhale her breath, sucking it deep into my own lungs, tasting her tongue, wanting to fully consume her. We are wild, helplessly mad for each other, completely forgetting his presence, struggling with our restraints, wanting to feel more.

As if reading our thoughts, he releases one of my arms from the tree, and the opposite one of hers, so that we can embrace the other more closely, touch one another. The moans and whimpers are driving him crazy.

He can tell that we are both on the brink of orgasm. He walks up behind Angela and thrusts himself deep into her pussy, throwing her over the brink and into a galactic climax. She pulls her head from mine and screams out in wild ecstasy. Satisfied, he withdraws from her and approaches me from behind and thrusts himself deep into my sex. Angela is still grinding her hips toward me, making sure the vibrator is hitting its mark, rocking back and forth. He is filling me up, pumping into me, arms reaching around to pinch and pull at my nipples. Oh God, I can feel it building . . . building . . . The waves begin crashing over me, and I gasp and shudder as I am also thrown into oblivion by the most magnificent of climaxes. He withdraws from me and stands beside the both of us, finishing himself off with his hand, masturbating furiously, grunting, breathing hard until he, too, releases an animalistic groan and shoots out his cum with an explosive force, directing it all over Angela and me, covering our bodies with his thick, white, hot cum.

I wake up, drenched in sweat. Oh, God. How can I face her? I have sunk to my lowest. God, I'm hot, so very hot. How long was I out? I glance at the clock, 4:30 PM. Shit, I'm probably sunburned. Great way to start out a new career in dancing. I pour myself a large glass of water, topping it off with a handful of ice cubes and head for the bathroom to inspect the damage.

Something's changed. Something in the eyes. Staring back at me is a very sexual, wanton creature. Where did she come from? I am amazed at this transformation. All this from one silly little dream? No, it's more than that. All this from one amazing revelation. I can be sexually attracted to a woman. Does this make me bisexual, or even more frightening, a lesbian?

I remain transfixed by the woman in the mirror. Suddenly separated from the image, I watch as she removes an ice cube from her glass and begins to suck on it in earnest, trying to quench the fires consuming her. It is extremely cold, and she circles it around her lips and mouth. The ice cube begins to melt and forms a trail of droplets from her mouth, down her chin to a puddle on the floor.

The next ice cube she holds to her lips and begins a sucking, in and out motion. It is slick and moist against her lips, and she moans with the delight of its cooling effect. No longer satisfied with just enticing the mouth, she starts to move the cube lower, covering her neck and throat with ice-cold kisses and relishing the sensations of the inevitable meltdown.

The trickles of water weave their way inside her swimsuit top. A sigh of inexplicable delight escapes her numb and frozen mouth. She feels her breasts respond to the invasion, contracting and vibrating with anticipation. Not being one to deny herself, she dips an ice cube into one of the cups of her top and begins to swivel the ice cube back and forth across her nipple, causing shudders of vehement proportions to overtake her and render her helpless, depending solely on instincts and intuition.

Once her breasts have been thoroughly violated and the ice cube completely melted, her hand grabs a fresh cube from the glass and continues it's movement downward. Rivers of water droplets spew forth, manifesting a multitude of shudders from her unsuspecting, quivering abdomen. She is helpless to stop abandoning herself to absolute pleasure.

Her hand pauses at the barrier provided by her swimsuit bottom, breaks through, and continues on its quest for fulfillment. The contrast of the iciness of the cube to the steaming vapor rising from her core spins her

---

into semiconsciousness, where she is ruled by immediate needs, accountable to nothing. Drip after drip drives her onward, seeking culmination. Unable to stop herself, she inserts what's left of the ice cube into her center . . . fucking herself with the cube until it is completely melted and fizzles away.

Not yet satisfied, she resumes her assault with a brand new ice cube, and with a sharp intake of her breath penetrates herself a second time. This ice cube is colder, larger, creating a more intense and instantaneous reaction. She ignores the urge to remove the cube. This time her efforts are circular, directed at her clit, an irresistible and devastating combination. Her body goes into spasms and convulsions, producing the consummation she so desperately required, hurling her forcibly back into reality.

With a heartbreaking sob, I collapse to the floor and weep with the knowledge of what I have become.

Needing immediate answers, I frantically surf the Internet, searching for explanations. I quickly settle on the "Half and Half Club." I need to speak to a woman who has "experienced" another woman. *Beep, beep, beep.* Dolphina responds.

<Dolphina> I Hi, there, lonely?
<Aphrodite> I Hi there, yourself. I'm looking for answers. Can you help?
<Dolphina> I Depends on the questions,. . . . fire away.
<Aphrodite> I Well, I've just recently come to the realization that I could possibly be a lesbian.
<Dolphina> I What are you really saying?
<Aphrodite> I I'm serious. . . . after 34 years of think-

		ing that I'm attracted to men, bam! I find out differently
<Dolphina>	I	Confused, huh? Answer me one question. . . . What do you believe to be the meaning of life?
<Aphrodite>	I	The meaning of life, huh? Well, if I could answer that, I'd be the most popular person on the planet.
<Dolphina>	I	I'm serious. What is the meaning of life?
<Aphrodite>	I	Well, I assume, the pursuit of happiness. . . .
<Dolphina>	I	Exactly! And what makes you happy?
<Aphrodite>	I	Well, I'm not exactly sure. . . . I suppose there are a bunch of things that make me happy . . .
<Dolphina>	I	And how do you know what makes you happy?
<Aphrodite>	I	Trial and error?
<Dolphina>	I	Bingo. . . . Now what was your problem again?
<Aphrodite>	I	I think I'm a lesbian . . .
<Dolphina>	I	And why do you think you're a Lesbian?
<Aphrodite>	I	Well, uh. . . . because I felt "something" while I was with a woman.
<Dolphina>	I	Are you ashamed that you felt "something" while with a woman?
<Aphrodite>	I	Yes. . . .
<Dolphina>	I	Why?
<Aphrodite>	I	Because it's not natural . . .
<Dolphina>	I	Who says?
<Aphrodite>	I	Society . . .
<Dolphina>	I	Are you listening to yourself?
<Aphrodite>	I	Yes, sounds pretty pathetic, huh?
<Dolphina>	I	Not being one to judge, yes. . . . Look, do you like ice cream?

<Aphrodite> | What does that have to do with any-
thing? Yes, I do like ice cream.

<Dolphina> | All flavors?

<Aphrodite> | No, not all flavors. . . .

<Dolphina> | How about men? Are you attracted to
all men?

<Aphrodite> | Of course not . . .

<Dolphina> | Do you feel that it makes you less het-
erosexual by not being attracted to all
men?

<Aphrodite> | Not at all . . .

<Dolphina> | Ok, then, are you attracted to all
women?

<Aphrodite> | No . . . where are you going with all
this?

<Dolphina> | Think of "people" as being different fla-
vors of ice cream. Some you like, some
you don't. Some brands you prefer,
some you'll never eat again.

<Aphrodite> | So, there is nothing wrong with me
wanting another female?

<Dolphina> | Nothing at all. . . . Life is too short. Find
and do the things that make you happy,
as long as it isn't at someone else's ex-
pense. Another thing, don't get hung
up on the labels society has created to
categorize "bisexuals" and "lesbians."
We are all just people in the pursuit of
happiness.

<Aphrodite> | Hmmmm, you've been very helpful. I'll
think about what you've said, thanks.

<Dolphina> | Hey, if you ever want an online experi-
ence with a woman, I'd be happy to
help you out there, as well.

<Aphrodite> | Ok, I'll keep that in mind. Thanks again.

Feeling a little more at ease, I shut down the computer and prepare myself for the night ahead.

Friday night. Club Illicit is always packed on Friday nights. Robert and I decided that I should continue playing the role of cocktail waitress for the remainder of my shifts this weekend, giving me a full week of training with Angela to become more confident and comfortable dancing. He did suggest that I spend as much time as possible watching the different dancers, picking up different techniques and styles which I could incorporate into my own routines, without, of course, neglecting the patrons. The night passes without any significant incidents.

Again Angela proves to be very punctual and comes bounding through my door the next day precisely at high noon. Her excitement is infectious, and I can't help but smile.

"Oh, Randi, guess what? I came up with the greatest idea last night and already got it okayed by Robert. Now I just have to see if it is anything you'd be interested in."

"Come on in, sit down, let me get you a glass of lemonade, and tell me all about it." After pouring two glasses of lemonade, I sit down beside her and eagerly wait for her tale to begin.

"Well, I was thinking, that maybe you were going to be a little nervous your first few times dancing, so I was trying to come up with an idea on how to ease you into it. Then I thought, well, maybe, the first few times, I could dance with you, so you wouldn't be alone. And *then* I thought, well, heck, maybe we could come up with a really erotic routine involving the both of us, and it could become a new attraction to the club! It would be something new, would probably be great for business, and would help ease you into dancing. And if it really took off, it could be a permanent addition to the lineup. What do you think?''

"Wow, Angela. It sounds great. I appreciate that you're looking out for me. You don't usually find that type of personality in the dancing business. Usually, dog eat dog, you know what I mean?''

"Well, it will help my career out as well. I think we'll make a dynamic pair on the stage. I already have a few routines floating around in my head. How about we put in a couple extra hours of practice each day, so we can at least nail one routine down by next Thursday night?''

"You got it. Ready when you are.'' Needing no further encouragement, Angela takes my hand and begins teaching me the steps. There is no room for the sexual foreplay of the day before. We are suddenly two professional women on a mission and can't be distracted by such games. I breathe a heavy sigh of relief as I realize that I've, once again, been miraculously let off the hook.

After four hours of grueling lessons, I decide that I've had enough for one day. "We ought to call it quits. You still need to make sure you have some fire left for tonight, Angela.''

"Oh, no worries, Randi,'' she replies with a wink. "My fire's just beginning.'' God, why does she do that? She confuses me constantly with those sexual innuendoes, knowing that at the very least I can interpret them two different ways, always leaving me guessing. Was that an innocent remark, or was she insinuating that I turn her on, and that spending hours dancing with me lights her fire? I look at her quizzically, but she says nothing more.

"Ok, then, see you tonight.''

Saturday night. My last shift for four days. I can barely concentrate on my job tonight, just wishing it to be over. I'm ready to move on, to start dancing, to start dancing with Angela. I'm not sure what is going to happen between us, but all I know is that I'm looking forward to finding out. Maybe nothing will happen. Maybe it is all totally innocent. I know that I will never initiate anything, so it will definitely have to come from her.

The routine that she has put together for us is going to be sensational. Even though the heat isn't there while we practice, once the steps become second nature, instinct and emotion will take over. The heat will be back, I'm sure of it, and I relish the challenge of facing it.

Another incredible day. The sun is shining. . . . the birds are singing . . . the bees are buzzing with not even the hint of a cloud in the sky. I guess the old saying, "It never rains in Southern California," is proving to be true. It is the perfect weather to rejuvenate my soul. Taz walks by and rubs up against my leg as if to say, "Hey, you've been neglecting me lately."

"Sorry, buddy, come up here and sit in my lap for a minute." Within moments, Taz is purring and satisfied, ready to forgive and forget.

The afternoon is spent entwined with Angela, the routine finally beginning to take shape. We are fast becoming good friends, opening up to one another, taking our relationship to a higher level. I still haven't shared with her the dream she starred in, but that can wait. After all, we've only known each other for four days. Maybe I'll invite her over one evening and introduce her to the world of "chatting." I bet she'd enjoy that.

Finally, an evening all to myself. I lovingly run my fingers down the sides of my monitor, anticipating the night ahead. I love Sunday nights. The most interesting people seem to come out of hiding, and it's never a disappointment. With my glass of wine beside me, I waste no more time in firing up the computer.

CHAPTER 3

■

THE VOICE

I am fairly picky. Anybody with a handle like, "HornyMaleNeedsFemale" or "10InchCock4U" is immediately eliminated. My attraction is the mental stimulation I receive. If I want to masturbate, I don't need a computer to do so. Although I do find that there are a lot of people out there just looking to have sex with their computers. They should just go rent a porno movie or something. I'm looking for *mental* sexual foreplay. I want to discover interesting people with different lifestyles who are willing to share their experiences and widen my own. I'm looking for . . . something unique, something exciting . . . something I can't quite put my finger on. I'm looking for that heart-stopping, opening line. I'm looking for . . . *beep, beep, beep.*

<ArrogantWit> I I know what a woman wants. . . . I know what a woman needs. . . .

<Aphrodite> I Well, then . . . it's settled. You must be a woman yourself

<ArrogantWit> I Sarcasm does not become you, Aphrodite.

<Aphrodite> | And how would you know what be-
              comes me?

I like this guy already. He'll keep me on my toes. I
sense an approaching battle of wits.

<ArrogantWit> | I find it gratifying that even while you
               are acting aloof, your body responds
               to me, your pussy clenches and aches
               with need, your nipples throb. . . . I
               can smell you.

Oh God, it's difficult to breathe. I feel him enter
me . . .

<Aphrodite> | What is it, exactly, that you want from
               me???
<ArrogantWit> | I want your soul. . . . My prick reaches
               inside you, grabs hold and consumes
               you. . . . I am your breath.
<Aphrodite> | Geeze, you demand a lot from a first
               date. . . .
<ArrogantWit> | You and I are going to have many
               dates, I can feel it.
<Aphrodite> | Your name suits you.
<ArrogantWit> | Yes it does, now, the question is . . .
               does your name suit you? Are you
               truly the Goddess of Love, or a pa-
               thetic imposter?

Oooo, he's baiting me. A challenge. He's going to
try to manipulate me by insulting my skills as a . . . as
a . . . woman.

<Aphrodite> | Try me.

———————

51

<ArrogantWit> | I want your phone number.
<Aphrodite> | You can't have my phone number.
<ArrogantWit> | Just as I suspected, an imposter. What are you afraid of?

Damn, he's good.

<Aphrodite> | I don't know you well enough to give you my phone number.
<ArrogantWit> | Okay, what would you like to know?
<Aphrodite> | Well, your name for starters, where you live, what you do, that sort of thing.
<ArrogantWit> | Well, you can call me . . . "Wit." I live in Connecticut and I'm a writer. Now, what's your phone number?
<Aphrodite> | Glad I asked . . . a little on the private side are you, Wit?
<ArrogantWit> | You have all you need to know. You're phone number? We're just wasting time. You are only delaying the inevitable.

God, what a cocky son of a bitch! But, still . . . I'm intrigued. He "affects" me.

<Aphrodite> | You're not going to get my phone number, so quit asking. I'll compromise, though. I'll e-mail you a picture or two of me. That way, you'll at least know what I look like, even if you can't hear me.
<ArrogantWit> | It doesn't matter what you look like. What matters is how you respond. . . . I want to hear your breath catch when

I call you, I want to hear you sigh and gasp when I fuck you with my voice. I want to hear you beg me to continue, but mostly. . . . I want to hear the intense rapture in your voice when you finally yield to me and convulsions consume your entire body. . . .

I am utterly speechless and seriously consider giving him my phone number.

<Aphrodite> | You certainly know how to plead your case . . .

<ArrogantWit> | Give me your phone number, Aphrodite. I promise you, you have nothing to be afraid of. If you decide you don't like it, tell me to go away, and I'll never bother you again.

<Aphrodite> | I tell you what, Wit. Let me give it some thought.

<ArrogantWit> | I own you, Aphrodite. You'll be able to think of nothing else until you yield. Sweet dreams.

Well, I guess I found what I was looking for. I wasn't expecting it to be quite so intense and overpowering. Why didn't I give him my phone number? That's why I'm here, right? Trying and experiencing new things. . . . Maybe I *am* afraid, but of what? I can always hang up if it gets too weird, and he did promise to leave me alone if I didn't like it. What am I afraid of? Maybe I'm afraid that I *will* like it, just another embarrassing discovery about myself. Maybe I'm afraid that he really will steal and control my soul, turning me into a mindless sex toy.

Well, that was enough for one night. With a sigh, I put the computer to rest and attempt to sleep. He is right. I can't think of anything else, my mind replaying the conversation and wondering what would have happened had I given him my number.

The next day flies by, my dancing lessons suddenly becoming less important as my need to find Wit again grows. I have decided that I will find him tonight and give him my phone number. Chalk one up to Wit. He wins the first battle, ah, but who really wins? As soon as Angela leaves for the day, I jump on my computer. I have to wait for hours, but finally he appears. Beep, beep, beep.

\<ArrogantWit\>	I	C'est moi. Tu m'avez oublie!
\<Aphrodite\>	I	C'est moi/It's me . . . Now what's the rest????
\<ArrogantWit\>	I	Your breath!
\<Aphrodite\>	I	. . . oh . . .
\<ArrogantWit\>	I	Do you remember? . . . Perhaps you do . . . necking as a teenager . . . that you could lock mouths and breathe in and out of each other. It was very sexy and dizzying because of the lack of oxygen. . . .
\<Aphrodite\>	I	Auto erotica . . . ?
\<ArrogantWit\>	I	I always thought how sexual that was . . . and that when I was fucking . . . it was a similar situation with my cock and her pussy . . . locked . . . nothing else in or out . . . just the sex heat drawing us together.
\<Aphrodite\>	I	Mmmmmm. . . . Been thinking about this, have you?

<ArrogantWit> | So tell me, precisely what have *you* been thinking about?

<Aphrodite> | You win. . . . You were all I could think about Here is my phone number. (555)111-2222

<ArrogantWit> | Ah, sweet surrender. . . . Get used to it, it's only the beginning.

(Screw you, buddy. Now I'm starting to regret *submitting* to him. . . .)

<Aphrodite> | Remember, you promised. I tell you to "get lost" and you will, right?

<ArrogantWit> | Promise still stands. Now get off of the computer so I can hear your sweet, sexy voice.

Oh God. What have I just done? I disconnect the computer and reconnect the phone and wait. Within seconds, the phone starts ringing. I don't have to answer it. . . . I don't have to answer it. . . .

"Hello."

Silence. My breath catches as I imagine all the demons from hell on the other end of the phone line.

"You're scared, aren't you?" whispers a dark and sexy voice.

"Ah, a little."

"The only one you have to be afraid of is yourself. What's your name?"

"Miranda."

"Miranda . . . beautiful name. Where are you right now, Miranda?"

"Sitting at my kitchen table," I respond breathlessly. Yes, I can tell, this will surpass any and all previous

---

55

mental stimulation. This will be the grand daddy of all mind fucks.

"Is that where you want me to take you? At the kitchen table?" the sinister voice asks.

"Uh . . . no. I don't know. . . . I don't know what to expect. . . ."

"Take off your clothes, Miranda. I want you completely naked."

Do it Miranda . . . do it. Experience it. Nobody has to know but you and him.

"Give me a minute. . . . I need to put the phone down."

What are you doing? What are you doing? Oh, God . . . but I proceed to comply with his demand, stripping off each article of clothing until I am completely nude. Then I sit back down at the table and pick up the phone.

"I'm totally bare now . . ." I whisper to him, as if in pain.

"Mmmm, do you have a cordless phone, Miranda, and a headband that we can use?"

God, does he have to keep saying my name over and over like that? "Yes. . . ."

"Good, go get them. Keep the phone to your mouth the entire time. I want to hear you breathe, Miranda."

Oh, God. . . .

"I have them."

"You're breathing heavily, Miranda. Can you hear how you are struggling?"

"Yes . . ."

"I want you to secure the phone to the side of your head with the headband, so that it stays comfortably in place over your ear, and the mouthpiece by your lips. Can you do that? I want your hands free, Miranda."

"I can do that . . ." *Oh God, we haven't even begun and already he has turned me into a quivering mass of*

56

gelatin. I don't know if my senses can handle this.

"The headband is working. It'll stay put, for a while, anyway."

"Go lie down in the middle of the room. I want you on your back, legs and arms spread wide."

"Why?"

"Just do it! Let me know when you are in that position."

"Ok. . . . I'm there."

"Describe to me what I see, Miranda, what you are doing. . . ."

"Unnhh . . . this is really hard for me . . . I am lying in the middle . . . of . . . my living room floor . . . umm . . . completely naked . . . ohhh . . . with my arms . . . and legs . . . spread out wide to my sides."

"Now, open your mouth as wide as you can, and hold it like that until I tell you otherwise. Is your mouth open?"

"Uh huh. . . ."

"That is the position I always want you to be in. Ready, waiting and open for me. Ready for me to take on a whim, wherever and whenever I choose, and whichever orifice I choose. All three will always be open and available to me. Is your mouth still open?"

"Uh huh. . . ."

"Okay, you can close it. Keep your arms and legs spread wide."

"Why are you doing this to me?"

"I want you to know who owns you, Miranda. I want you to know whose voice controls you."

"Oh, God . . ."

"Someday, I'll have you spread out like this and waiting for me, outside, in the middle of the day, with hundreds of people watching to witness this control I have over you."

57

"No . . . no . . . never. . . ."

"And someday, I'll have you spread out like this, tied to a bed, and will invite my friends over to use your body, over and over . . ."

"Stop it . . . you're starting to scare me now . . . stop it. . . ."

I hear him chuckle.

"I'm sorry, I'm going too fast for you. I apologize."

"Apology accepted, I think. . . ."

"Miranda, I want you to take your hands now and caress your body. Go slowly, get to know it. I want you to touch everywhere, and then describe to me what you're doing."

"No . . . I'm sorry. . . . I just can't do this . . . please. . . ."

"You can't do what, Miranda? You can't touch yourself, or you can't describe it to me?"

"I can't describe it to you. . . ."

"Ok, then, you are going to have to follow my directions. Take your hands and place them on your belly. Can you feel it quivering?"

"Mmmm . . . yes . . . uhhhhh. . . ."

"Press down on it. Knead it, push it, back, back, into the floor. Are you getting aroused, yet?"

"Oh, yes. . . ."

"Move your hands upward to your breasts and stroke them. Let me hear your moans, Miranda."

"Mmmmm, Oh God . . . Oh. . . ."

"Now pull at your nipples. Pinch and pull them as hard as you can. I want to hear you cry out. Do it, Miranda . . . squeeze them. . . ."

I start emitting small whimpering noises until it becomes too much for me to bear.

"Uh . . . unhhh . . . oh . . . mmmm, mmmm, owwww-wwwwwch, Stop, please stop!"

"Ok, you can stop. I want you to take two of your fingers and reach down to the opening of your pussy and touch yourself there. Are you wet, Miranda?"

"Oh yes. . . . I am so wet . . . drenched. . . ."

"Stick those two fingers deep inside, Miranda. Get them covered in your juice. Then take them out and suck on them. I want to hear you taste yourself, Miranda."

Oh, God. . . . Oh God . . . this is too . . . too lewd. . . . I don't know if I can bring myself to do it.

"Go on, Miranda. I'm not hearing anything. Taste yourself for me."

In one helpless, desperate plunge, I coat my fingers with my scent, returning my fingers to my face, and forcing myself to succumb, once again, to his wishes, shamefully inserting my fingers into my mouth and sucking them clean.

"Good, girl. I knew you could do it. Did you like how you tasted?"

Bastard.

"It was okay. . . ."

"I'm going to have to go soon, Miranda. I want to hear you scream out my name before I do. I want you to cum for me, Miranda. Masturbate to my voice. Fuck yourself with one hand, while the other hand works on your clit. Lose yourself in my voice, Miranda."

"Oh, God . . . Wit . . . I'm there . . . talk to me. . . . Oh, God. . . ."

My hands take over on their own volition, knowing exactly where to go and where to touch to achieve the indescribable pleasures of sexual release. My head swims with his words, his voice, as he takes me higher and higher, closer and closer to fulfillment.

"Let yourself go, Miranda. Appease your need. Satisfy your hunger. Feel my breath as it bounces off of your face. Feel my hands as they stroke your fevered body. Feel my cock as it glides into you, pushing deeper and deeper, producing an involuntary arching of your back. Feel me as I take you down that swirling path of pleasure. Release, Miranda, release. Give in to my voice. Surrender to me Miranda, give yourself to me. I need to hear you as you shudder in ecstasy. I need to hear your moans, your sighs, your gasps of delight. Cum for me now, Miranda. Cum for me, now!"

Unable to resist this ultimate torture any longer, I cry out in bliss as my body peaks, then shudders and convulses in a series of rapturous tidal waves, finally pulsating into peaceful oblivion. My God, that was incredible! I'm not sure, but I thought I also heard *him* cry out, satisfying his own needs as well. When my breathing returns to normal, I say to him, "That was incredible. I had no idea."

"I wonder, if, from now on, every time your phone rings, if . . . your pulse will mysteriously accelerate, your breathing will inexplicably become more rapid and your panties will suddenly become so suffused with moisture that you'll have to change them. I wonder if that will happen. Good night, Miranda."

Damn, what a jerk! How could I allow him to use me like that? Then, as I sit and think about it in depth, I come to realize that it was I, not he, who was doing the using. I wanted to experience this different form of sexual play. I wanted him to call and monopolize my body. I wanted to feel total surrender, yet in *my* way, in a safe environment. Mission accomplished, right? So why I am so pissed off? Screw him. I got what I wanted, and I won't dwell on it. It was fun. It was liberating. Time to move on.

* * *

Tuesday morning. Time to focus on Angela and dancing again. Our dance routine is going to knock them dead this weekend, I just know it. It'll be the very boost I need into the exclusive world of solo, erotic dancing. The steps are becoming less practiced, more instinctual and intuitive. Angela has praised me more than once on my natural abilities, skeptical of the fact that I have never danced before. Still doubting my natural talent, I can only hope to become *half* as skilful as she, and prove a credit to her on the stage Thursday night.

Angela appears totally confident in both of our abilities and relentlessly pursues perfection. Her patience astounds me, and I continue to question her motives. Why is she so willing to help me?

After another sweltering afternoon of rehearsing, do I want to spend another evening on the computer? Yeah, I need to exorcise this demon as quickly as possible and return to my "real" life. Activating lights, beeps and buzzes while I collect my basket of goodies to snack on, expedites my entry into my online fantasy world once again. With high expectations, I begin my never-ending search. Within seconds, I begin hearing the "beeps" indicating an invitation. Sure enough, the name demanding my attention is "ArrogantWit." I don't know if I want to talk to him yet, still a bit miffed at his conceit.

<ArrogantWit> I Did you find yourself salivating every time the phone rang today?

<Aphrodite> I For your information, I didn't think of you once. You really are an egomaniac.

<ArrogantWit> I Sure you didn't, keep telling yourself that.

<Aphrodite> I I'm not even sure I want to talk to you

right now. You're not a very nice person.

<ArrogantWit> | You're not looking for a nice person, Miranda. You are looking for something taboo. You crave excitement and unpredictability and . . . me.

<Aphrodite> | It's time for you to go now, shoo fly. . . . I'm not in the mood for you right now.

<ArrogantWit> | As you wish. . . .

Why does he have to be like that, and more importantly, why do I care? No problem, I'll find somebody else. Somebody just as exciting who is a bit more fun and lighthearted, not so dark, deep, and suffocating. *Beep, beep, beep.*

<ArrogantWit> | Miss me, yet?

Against my will, I find myself smiling.

<Aphrodite> | You are something else, do you know that? Trying a different approach, are you?

<ArrogantWit> | I keep hearing your moans in my head. I can't stay away. My prick points at your name and I follow.

<Aphrodite> | Nice to know that you are not altogether immune to my charms . . . You just provided me with a dangerous weapon to use against you. . . .

<ArrogantWit> | Laughing, Oh please be gentle with me. . . .

<Aphrodite> | So, who was thinking about who all day? Hmmmm?

<ArrogantWit> | What have *you* been thinking about? Bring me up to date on your adventures.

<Aphrodite> | Oh, this and that. . . .

<ArrogantWit> | Well . . . too bad we're not talking. . . . It would be nice to awaken your darkest desires through experiences I'd arrange for you.

<Aphrodite> | Yeah, it is a shame, isn't it. . . . So, why aren't we talking? I've forgotten . . . must have been something presumptuous that you did. . . .

<ArrogantWit> | No. It was your childish attempt to show your independence.

<Aphrodite> | Oh yeah. . . . How quickly one forgets. . . . So, what do you suggest?

<ArrogantWit> | I suggest that you fly to Connecticut, and meet me in a fancy hotel room, and that I breathe in and out of you— both with my mouth, and with my cock—the entire week.

<Aphrodite> | You think you could get enough of me in just one bitty, bitty week?

<ArrogantWit> | It would be you, sweet Aphrodite, that would be left crying and begging for more. . . . Tell me, am I like a bad cold . . . ?

<Aphrodite> | Oh no . . . let me think . . . you are, more like a recurring nightmare. . . .

<ArrogantWit> | I appear from behind you
. . . and GRAB you against me . . .
. . . and you feel my arousal . . .
. . . and you can't get away . . .
. . . and my cock finds a way inside

63

	you before you know it . . . and. . . . and . . .
	you fucking LOVE IT.
<Aphrodite>	Oh God.. . . .stop it, please, stop it. . . .
<ArrogantWit>	I am your incredible, dark, dangerous mindfuck . . . the mindfuck that you can't escape from . . . that you don't want to escape from. Tell me, Miranda. . . .
<Aphrodite>	What . . . ?
<ArrogantWit>	Who does your mind think of . . . come back to . . . lie back for? Tell me why we so quickly become entwined cock and pussy . . . clit and tongue . . . finger and ass?
<Aphrodite>	The only thing I can figure is that it must be one of those sick, love/hate relationships. . . .
<ArrogantWit>	But tell me . . . what happens. . . . when I'm in your mind, a demon that invades you, possesses you. . . .
<Aphrodite>	You are worse than a damn drug . . .
<ArrogantWit>	Luscious lover. Your smell is as strong as ever. And commands the same, strong, decisive physical determination in me. How often I've felt like I am your clit-oris As hot and responsive . . . As ready and open to my mind . . . As coy and hidden at first . . . then wanton and fuck-happy.
<Aphrodite>	You respond to my smell. . . .
<ArrogantWit>	Yes. . . . You send it my way, don't you?

<Aphrodite> | I don't purposely send it your way, but it still manages to find you . . .

<ArrogantWit> | It emanates from you. Seeks my cock. You need and you seek and you open and you pulse . . . SO loudly . . . inside your head . . . that you can't help but remember the offering of your open pussy, ass and mouth, and the frantic sighs that you gave me so easily . . . just last night. . . .

<Aphrodite> | You are right . . . I can't help but remember . . . and neither can you. . . . You are my demon, I am your Poison Ivy. . . . We are doomed to continuously seek the other out . . . might as well make the best of it . . . we feed on each other. . . .

<ArrogantWit> | Then periodically spit the other out, but ultimately, we swallow. Long helpless gulps of one another. . . .

<Aphrodite> | God, I really like hating you. . . .

<ArrogantWit> | See how much better it is when you're not an immature, defensive bitch. . . .

<Aphrodite> | Only when provoked. . . .

<ArrogantWit> | But I am someone big enough—and patient enough—to let her swing away—and then I hold her arms behind her back, and put my tongue so far down her throat . . . and up her slit . . . that she never wants to move again.

<Aphrodite> | Oh . . . most people would just spank her. . . .

<ArrogantWit> | You give me . . .

<Aphrodite>	I Give you what?
<ArrogantWit>	I Your fuck soul.
<Aphrodite>	I Do you keep it or chew it up and spit it out?
<ArrogantWit>	I I don't throw it away. You might come for it again . . . and again . . . and again.
<Aphrodite>	I How well you know me. . . . Thanks for keeping it safe. . . .
<ArrogantWit>	I I never said it was safe, I just said that I'm keeping it.
<Aphrodite>	I We'll see about that . . .
<ArrogantWit>	I I have this strong desire to share you with a woman . . . to have us hold you and control your body, to open you and let her take complete pleasure on you . . . and from you . . . and for you . . . while I rub my cock over both your bodies, necks, faces, and asses.

Oh great . . . I really needed that image right now. . . .

<Aphrodite>	I Funny that you should bring that up. . . . There is this woman that I work with that I've been thinking about, lately. . . .
<ArrogantWit>	I In what way?
<Aphrodite>	I You know . . . the sexual way. I think I'm sexually attracted to her. It is a very foreign feeling to me.
<ArrogantWit>	I How so? What do you think about when you picture her?
<Aphrodite>	I Well, I'm not sure I've let myself get

	that far. . . . So far . . . I've only "felt."
<ArrogantWit>	Do you picture yourself touching her, or does she touch you?
<Aphrodite>	I told you . . . I haven't gotten that far. . . . I haven't been able to get past the way she looks at me.
<ArrogantWit>	So she is attracted to you as well . . . this is very rare. You should take advantage of it and explore it.
<Aphrodite>	No . . . I could never initiate anything. It would just have to happen.
<ArrogantWit>	What a shame if you should let it slip between your fingers. I believe you would like to be in control of the situation. . . . It would explain why you behave the way you do when we are together . . .
<Aphrodite>	What do you mean?
<ArrogantWit>	You tell me that you wish to be controlled, consumed . . . yet you fight it tooth and nail. I think you truly wish to dominate.
<Aphrodite>	You are crazy. . . . I just need a man that is strong enough. A weak man, one that I can control, frankly, the thought makes me sick.
<ArrogantWit>	Who said anything about a man . . . ?
<Aphrodite>	Hmmm . . . it would never happen. I wouldn't want to open up that can of worms.
<ArrogantWit>	I don't think you'll ever be satisfied until you do . . .
<Aphrodite>	Who the hell are you? How do you

know . . . or think you know, so much?

<ArrogantWit>	I told you once upon a time . . . I know what a woman wants . . . I know what a woman needs. . . .
<Aphrodite>	But all women are different. . . .
<ArrogantWit>	Not so terribly different. . . . The difference is what they will allow themselves to feel, to explore, to seek. . . . What are you feeling . . . right now?
<Aphrodite>	You know what you do to me. . . .
<ArrogantWit>	Show me your clit, please. Show it to the screen. Show me "my" clit.

Ok, enough is enough. . . . I'm not going to carry out this little command. I think it is time to pretend. . . .

<Aphrodite>	Can you see it? Does it excite you?
<ArrogantWit>	It is a permanent taste on my tongue . . . a hot, sticky, pulsing button.
<Aphrodite>	A wonderful, exotic, addicting aphrodisiac. . . .
<ArrogantWit>	Can you take my whole hand into your pussy, Miranda? Milk me. Grip me. Show me how you stretch for me.
<Aphrodite>	No!. . . . God you say the most horrifying things. . . . Sorry . . . but this time I really do have to go.
<ArrogantWit>	Running scared again? Some day you will stretch for me, Miranda.
<Aphrodite>	You really suck. . . .

Well . . . that was interesting. What time is it, anyway? Midnight, wow . . . time flies when you're having fun. With a single push of a button, the fantasy world is put on hold, and another sleepless night looms before me. With a sigh, I stand up, stretch, and head for bed, curious about where my future lies.

I thought that I would have enjoyed such a long stretch of endless days off, with nothing to worry about, nothing I *had* to do, but the days seem to be dragging. Could it be about tomorrow night, am I secretly dreading it? Maybe I am a little disappointed that Angela has put the sexual foreplay on hold, seemingly more obsessed with perfecting the dance routine than toying with me. Did I truly want her to chase me and chase me until I finally caught her? I smile, in spite of myself.

"Afternoon, Randi! Ready for another fatiguing afternoon of dancing?"

"You know, Angela, this seemed like a lot more fun when it came naturally. I'm getting burned out with all this practicing."

"You know, sweetie, you're right. Let's play hooky this afternoon, and go do something else. How about spending the day at the beach, baking our bods and teasing the boys?"

"Now you're talking. Who's driving?"

Angela and I gather up the necessary elements for a day at the beach and head toward the shore. She elects to drive. I am ready to do a little drinking and partying, and this way, I can do so to my heart's content. Angela is decked out in her string bikini in no time, like she had this planned all along.

The beach is fabulous, and I am able to leave behind the stress of performing, as well as my online saga with Wit. I spend the day in carefree bliss, sunning myself, bodysurfing, drinking and cavorting. With Angela as company, I find myself invited to volleyball games and

an 8:00 PM clambake. It is wonderful, the perfect anti-
dote to a seemingly monotonous week.

"You know, Randi, we are going to have to work
twice as hard tomorrow to make up for today. It'll be
our final practice before the big night."

"I know, but let's worry about that tomorrow. I don't
even want to think about work right now."

"Say no more," Angela says with a smile.

As the sun sets and the crowds start to disperse, Angela and I find ourselves becoming more and more
alone and isolated. We have put on a few more articles
of clothing, the ocean breeze and lack of sunshine re-
quiring us to seek extra warmth. As we lie back in the
sand, our feet still bare and mingling with the damp
ground beneath us, we gaze up at the stars. "So, Angela, do you have a boyfriend?"

"Oh, I have a couple guys that I see kind of regularly, but nothing really special. You?"

"Well, I am married to a wonderful man, just kind
of taking a break. I'm doing some serious soul searching."

"Well, I hope it all works out for you, Miranda. You
seem like a good person. How old are you anyway?"

"Thirty-four, you?"

"I'm just twenty-four. Guess I'm just a baby in your
eyes, huh?"

"No, on the contrary. I find you very mature and sure
of yourself. I admire you for that. To be honest with
you, you are the reason I wanted to start dancing. I envy
the freedom and confidence you portray. I wanted to
feel that."

She looks over at me and smiles. She takes my hand
and holds it as the waves wash up beside us and lap at
our bodies.

* * *

The next day, I wake up very edgy and apprehensive. I can't believe the big day is finally here. I start doubting myself, thinking that I'm not talented enough to go through with tonight's performance. What was I thinking? I must have gotten caught up in the heat of the moment and totally lost my brain. I decide that I have to work off some of this anxiety somehow, or I am going to burst. With three hours to kill before Angela arrives, I head to the gym for a little iron pumping and jacuzzi action.

"What the heck happened to you?" Angela is incredulous.

"Angela, I'm so nervous about tonight, I think I'm going to be sick."

"Well, you look terrible. You've got to get over this, or tonight will be a disaster. What are you worried about?"

"I'm worried that I won't be good enough, Angela. I'm not fit to share the same stage as you."

"Oh, hon, nonsense. You are wonderful. You are a natural. I had to work for years to get as good as you have gotten in just one week. Together, we're unbeatable. Believe me when I tell you this, Randi, *you* are awesome. Together, *we* are spectacular. Let's practice just an hour or two today, and then let me give you a nice, relaxing massage. When you dance tonight, leave your conscious mind behind and let your body's natural instinct take over. If you do that, you can't lose. Trust me, Randi. You're beautiful, your body is beautiful, and the music in your soul is beautiful. Now, come on. We have work to do."

Without any logical rebuttals, I reluctantly allow Angela to take me through the motions of our dance routine once again. I start to feel myself soften and respond as her body surrounds me and the music invades me.

Yes, it will be all right tonight, I can feel it.

True to her word, as soon as the rehearsal is done, she orders me to strip down to nothing but a towel, and leaves the apartment. Within moments, she returns carrying a fold-up table and sets it up in the middle of my living room floor. Aghast, I inquire, "Do you *always* carry around a massage table in your car? First the bikini, now this. This is too weird."

"Hey, I'm a dancer. You can't take any chances with being stiff and sore while you're dancing. I always carry my table around with me for emergencies. The swimsuit was just luck." With a pat of her hand to the table and a wink, she gestures to me to lie down, face up. Hesitantly, I comply.

Her hands are very skilled and strong, and I feel silly for ever doubting her. She is a professional, which I should have known from the hours I had spent dancing with her. She starts on my face, easing all the tension from my scalp, eyes, and jaw. Oh, it feels heavenly. She is a saint, I'm sure of it. Next she works out all the knots in my arms, probably accumulated from the many hours spent at the keyboard. She skips my midsection and starts to work in earnest on my thighs. As she works on them, she explains to me how people tend to keep all their emotions and anxieties locked up in the muscles of their thighs. With the hands of a magician, she continues until they are soft and pliable, as tears silently trickle from the corners of my eyes. She spends a few more minutes on my calves and feet, then urges me to turn over so that I am lying flat on my stomach. Drained, yet knowing that the best is yet to come, I wearily comply.

Her hands continue their magical healing, working up my legs to my ass. Without even a moment's hesitation, she pries deeply into the muscle of my taut glute, startling me initially, then lulling me back into a deep, peaceful relaxation. It is amazing to me how she can find sore muscles that I didn't even know existed! She finishes up my massage by spending a full half hour on my back, neck, and shoulders. Before I know it, I am sound asleep, sleeping more soundly than I have in a long time. Both my abused body and tormented mind are rejuvenated.

A rude buzzer awakens me, and it takes me a few moments to get my bearings. Still on the massage table, I glance over at the clock. 6:00 PM. Wow, a good three-hour nap. I also notice that there is a note from Angela sitting on my kitchen table. Groggily, I sit up and pad, barefooted, across my carpeted floor to the kitchen table and read the note.

You fell sound asleep. I didn't have the heart to wake you. I felt the rest would do you good. I set the alarm for 6:00 so you would still have plenty of time to get ready for tonight. Think sexy, erotic thoughts, and I'll see you at nine.

Love, Angela.

She thinks of everything, I muse, and I smile as I march off in search of a scalding shower.

Totally refreshed and revitalized, I feel as if I can take on the world. I feel sexy and alive, not an unruly curl to my hair, my makeup smoothing on flawlessly, setting the tone of perfection for the remainder of the night.

I arrive at the club at 8:00 PM sharp, amazed at how crowded it is for a Thursday night. Robert must have been advertising "something special" for this weekend, and curious people have come out in droves to glimpse the sensational event. The intensity in the club has risen a notch, with onlookers swarming at the edge of the stage, faces expectant. I scurry off toward Robert's office to get the schedule of events for the evening.

"Heya, kiddo. All ready for tonight?" is Robert's friendly greeting.

"Yeah, I think so. I'm a little nervous, but I think that will go away as soon as I hit the stage and the music takes over. Angela's been great this week, Robert. She has taught me so much. If all goes well tonight, you should give her a raise."

"Listen, Randa. If all goes well, she won't even notice an hourly wage increase. Her fans will take care of her."

"Good point! Well, I'm off to the dancers' dressing room. Want to give me the schedule for tonight?"

"This is what I have in mind. The first hour, I'll have four of the regular girls do their fifteen-minute solo acts. Then, at 10:00 PM sharp, you and Angela will go on. Angela said the performance could last as long as thirty minutes. Take all the time you'd like. I'll have three other dancers standing by and ready if it ends up being shorter than that. The rest of the night, I just want you to watch and learn. Does that work for you?"

"Well, yes . . . I suppose. I kind of feel guilty earning my paycheck by sitting on my behind all night."

Robert smiles, "Angela has told me of your progress. She says that you are fabulous and have great potential. It is far more worth it for me to nurture this talent into fruition, than to force it from you before it's ready. I'll watch you tonight and decide if you're ready. If I feel you are, we will finish out the weekend as is, but you can start practicing and creating your own little dance routines to use for next week. Now, if you and Angela are as hot together as I think you'll be, you'll also dance one dance with her each night, maybe as our grand finale."

"Sounds perfect, Robert. Thanks for the opportunity."

"You're welcome. Now, go out there and knock 'em dead tonight, okay?"

"You got it!"

By 8:30 PM, I'm already comfortably set up in the dressing room, having been shown by another dancer where all the costumes are kept, where the makeup stations are, and the location of my own, private locker. Angela arrives shortly thereafter, coming over to me immediately, making sure that I'm doing okay. "Let me get you something to take the edge off, Randi. How about a glass of wine? What's your flavor?" I tell her that I'd love a glass of white zinfandel, and she retreats back into the bar area of the club to get my courage.

Angela returns with two glasses of wine and assures me that all will go spectacularly tonight. "How about we go sit at one of the private tables up front and watch a couple of the girls dance while we drink our wine? That'll help us get into the spirit of things, wouldn't you say?" Arm in arm, we stroll to a private table, always kept open and available for VIPs and employees, and try to settle ourselves down while waiting for the excitement to begin. The wine tastes exceptional tonight, going down way too smoothly. I'd better be careful. It wouldn't look good appearing on stage in a drunken stupor.

The first dancer takes the stage and I stare in amazement. This is the first opportunity I've had to watch an entire performance without the interruption of serving a cocktail. It is incredibly sensuous, and I feel my body immediately start to respond. All my senses come alive. My hearing is more acute, my vision is clearer, and the sensitivity of every nerve ending on my entire body has been heightened so that I respond to as little as a whisper of breath brushing across my arm. Oh, God, what's happening? Why is my body reacting this way? Am I attracted to more than one woman? I struggle with the uncertainty as my body continues to heat up.

Angela looks over at me concerned. "Are you okay, Randi?"

"Yes . . . yes, I think so. I just feel so. . . . so . . . peculiar. I think the wine has really affected me." She pats my hand reassuringly as we both focus our attention back to center stage.

After the second dancer has finished, Angela suggests that we head backstage to change into our costumes. We still have half an hour before our performance, but Angela wants to make sure that everything is perfect. She doesn't want any last-minute scrambles to frazzle her before show time. In agreement, we both disappear back into the privacy of the dressing room.

The intense heat coursing through my body has continued to rise unbearably, and I am about to go crazy with the need for completion. Oh God, what I'd do to have a man right now, a quickie in the back room. I just need something to assuage the aching, burning desire devouring me. I look up at the clock, seriously considering paying Robert a visit. Damn . . . not enough time. Oh, help me . . . it is so fierce, so intense that it has become painful. I look over at Angela in confusion. My eyes are glazed over, my breathing has become labored, and my lips are parted as if waiting for an anticipated snack. She must think me mad; however, all she does is send me a look of friendly compassion saying, "Soon, Randi, soon." We both finish with our wardrobe and anxiously wait by the curtain entrance.

The costumes are held together with tiny pieces of

velcro, allowing for quick and easy removal of the garments. Angela is dressed as a man, her gorgeous, copper-glazed hair tucked up into a top hat. She has on a man's suit and is carrying a cane. The crowd is going wild, knowing that the "big surprise" is about to take the stage. Hoots and hollers follow Angela as she wanders out first, acting as though she is on a leisurely stroll through the park.

I am dressed rather prudishly, my hair pulled tightly back in a bun, wearing thick-rimmed eyeglasses, a high-collared, long-sleeved blouse, and a long skirt. My outward appearance is all prim and proper, but concealed beneath that facade is a passionate woman just begging to be liberated. Decadent lingerie, beneath the dowdy clothing, moves sinuously against my body, constantly reminding me that I am, indeed, "woman." I close my eyes and let the music fill me, waiting for my cue to finally make my solicitous entrance into this strange, new, unorthodox way of life.

The music summons me, and I float gracefully out to the middle of the stage. Angela immediately swoops upon me, continuously encircling me as she assesses my potential as her mistress. Not fooled by my outward appearance, she continues her seduction. Then she locks eyes with me, and I am suddenly reacquainted with the Angela I was first introduced to. The smoldering fire is back in her eyes, her intent made quite clear. I gasp as I feel her power, her passion. My highly sensitized body can barely handle this assault. I relinquish control and allow this stranger to have "his" way with my body.

The audience has become totally hushed and still, their attention entirely focused on the scenario unfolding before them, not wanting to miss a single movement. Angela and I have become totally engrossed in one another, oblivious to the spectators. The music is our master, and our bodies respond instantaneously and intuitively. She takes me in her arms and dances with me, our bodies touching and swaying together.

She slowly starts to chip away bits and bits of my defenses, starting by removing and carelessly tossing the glasses aside, revealing a pair of beautiful, dark brown eyes. Next, she removes the pins from my hair, allowing it to fall freely and feather delicately around my face. We continue dancing pressed together as she tenaciously strips me of my final shreds of resistance. The shirt and skirt are both quickly cast off until I am left in nothing but my provocative lingerie.

Embarrassed by my behavior with this strange "man," I flee from "him," arching and pulling away. I grasp one of the poles anchored to the stage and clutch it tightly, fighting the temptation to return to the delicious promises of the stranger. Angela designs an imaginary lasso, casting it my way and catching me in it. She pulls on the rope, bit by bit, until I am wrenched free of the pole and am once again under her spell. My body writhes and oscillates as she pulls me closer, the imaginary rope tugging at me, dragging me, as I desperately fight to keep my freedom.

Finally, I am mashed back up against her, and she lowers her head to bestow upon me a powerful and persuasive kiss, rendering me speechless. This wasn't in the script . . . this wasn't supposed to happen. Oh God. I return the kiss savagely, heatedly, lost in the moment. Angela regains control first, separating our lips by pulling my head backward then kissing down my throat. Without warning, she pushes me away, and I have to struggle to regain my balance. Oh, yes . . . back to the routine.

Still moving to the music, she slowly begins to unmask herself, first by removing her jacket, then her hat, allowing her stunning, fiery curls to cascade down her back. Her captive, shocked by the revelation, stands transfixed, helplessly watching her seducer strip down to nothing but a G-string.

She resumes her stalking, only now as a female. She comes up behind me, pressing the warm, soft flesh of her bare breasts against my back, purring into my ear. She tantalizingly removes my lacy bra and the remainder of my lingerie, until I too am clad in nothing more than a G-string. At this point, the tempo of the music picks up and our dancing becomes more wild and frenzied. Standing back to back, hands linked together, we swirl in a circle, pulling as far apart as we can reach, arching, swaying, undulating, then receding, back to the middle, back together, bodies touching once again.

We turn and face each other, looks of pure animal lust on our faces. We mesh our bodies together, trying to become one, each frantically trying to enter the other. We dance and push and clash and squirm, our bodies contorting and twisting as if in agony. We finally end our performance by collapsing in a heap of glistening exhaustion on the stage floor, signifying, at last, our inevitable union.

At first we hear nothing, just stunned silence. Then suddenly, the crowd goes nuts, screaming for an encore, demanding more. They are ecstatic, throwing money at us like it is candy, hundred dollar bills lining the stage floor. Angela and I look at each other in disbelief and begin to laugh. We stand up holding hands and bow to the onlookers, thrilled with our success. When the commotion finally begins to dissipate, Angela and I disappear backstage, leaving it up to one of the stagehands to collect our spoils.

A jubilant Robert beats us backstage. "Ladies, words cannot describe what I just witnessed out there. You two were brilliant! This is going to spread like wildfire. People will come for miles to behold the incredible beauty of your interaction. My God. I'm speechless." Still excited and laughing, the three of us entangle ourselves in the biggest of bear hugs. Wow! What a night.

"You kissed me! Why did you do that?" After all the excitement finally settles down, I find myself asking Angela that question.

"Honestly, I don't know. I just felt like it. It felt right. I figured it would lend more credibility to the act. Was I wrong to do it?"

"Well, no, I guess not. It might have been nice to give me a little warning, though. Geez, I can't believe how turned-on I was during that show. I don't think I've ever been that aroused before."

"Yeah, it was something, wasn't it. I'm glad I got to share it with you, Randi. It was awesome."

"Well, Angela, we get to do it all over again tomorrow night. I just hope it will be as convincing the second time around."

"Have you finished counting, yet, Angela?"

"Jimminy Christmas, Randi. There's over *three thousand* dollars here!"

"No way!" "I can't believe it myself. I've never made that much money in one night before. I'm not sure I've made that much in an entire weekend before. This is unbelievable!"

"Angela, it's only Thursday night. Do you have any idea what a Friday or Saturday night will bring in, especially once the word gets spread? Oh, my, God."

The next two nights are just as expected, completely packed, allowing for standing room only, word of mouth proving to be the best form of advertisement yet. Angela and I manage to keep the high degree of intensity and heat between us tangible, our desire for one another obvious to the hundreds of stunned onlookers. By quitting time Saturday night, Angela and I have hauled in over five thousand dollars each.

Amazed by the profits resulting from nothing more than pursing an uncertain dream, I mentally begin to treat myself to a shopping trip. What should I do with all this extra money? I suppose I should put it in a savings account for a rainy day. After all, who knows how much longer I'll be dancing for a living? Maybe I should treat myself to a little getaway . . . yes, now that sounds like fun. Where could I go on short notice? Mexico is out of the question. . . . How about Las Vegas? I could treat myself to four days in Vegas, lounging in the most luxurious of suites, napping by the pool during the day and gambling at night. I will make my reservations first thing tomorrow morning for the Luxor Hotel, the most unique hotel on the entire strip, and my personal favorite.

Still too wound up to relax, I head straight for my computer when I get home. At 2:30 AM, the likelihood of encountering any of my "friends" is remote, but finding a new playmate is a definite possibility, and one worth pursuing. This is the time of day when nicknames like Dracula, Wolfman, and NightOwl are more popular, hinting at the personalities existing in the wee hours just prior to the sun making its grand entrance. *Beep, beep, beep.*

<Dracula>   I Are you a Witch?
<Aphrodite> I Depends on how much sleep I've had.
<Dracula>   I A Witch with a sense of humor, even better.
<Aphrodite> I What's on your mind, Vlad?
<Dracula>   I Nothing but the intense desire to sink

		my teeth into the tender flesh of your vulnerable throat.
\<Aphrodite\>	I	And what happens next? Is my lifelight snuffed out in that terrible moment, leaving me dead and forgotten, or do I get a chance at immortality, sleeping away the daylight and slinking in shadows for all eternity?
\<Dracula\>	I	Sweet Aphrodite, I would make you my wife, revealing to you the incredible splendor of endless nights of passion and infinite, soul-wrenching love.
\<Aphrodite\>	I	Well, when you put it that way, it doesn't sound so bad.
\<Dracula\>	I	I must go now. I have a previous commitment. I will sit on your window sill nightly, and protect you from harm, until I have convinced you to be mine.
\<Aphrodite\>	I	Do what you must, oh "Warrior of Darkness." Nite.

Well, that was weird. You never know who or what you are going to run into when you join the on-line world of the all-nighters. *Beep, beep, beep.*

\<ArrogantWit\>	I	Up past your bedtime, aren't you?
\<Aphrodite\>	I	I could say the same for you. Naw, I just got home from work.
\<ArrogantWit\>	I	And what, exactly, does the Goddess of Love do to earn her living?
\<Aphrodite\>	I	I'm a dancer. An exotic dancer. I've had an amazing weekend.
\<ArrogantWit\>	I	You get more intriguing every time I chat with you. I think I'll take that picture, after all.

<Aphrodite>	Maybe, if I still feel like sending it.
<ArrogantWit>	Oh, you'll send it, all right. And I'm sure you'll choose one staggering enough to inflict physical pain upon my poor, unsuspecting . . . cock. Tell me about your amazing weekend, Miranda.
<Aphrodite>	Well, you know that woman I told you about . . . the one I . . . uh . . . like . . . ?
<ArrogantWit>	How could I forget?
<Aphrodite>	Well, she and I have been putting together a dance routine, a unique and erotic routine, and we tried it out for the first time this weekend, and it was a HUGE success.
<ArrogantWit>	I can imagine your slick, hot body, dancing heatedly, craving . . . yearning. . . .
<Aphrodite>	Um, well . . . yes . . . anyway. . . . We made so much money that I am going to treat myself to a little getaway in Las Vegas for my birthday.
<ArrogantWit>	When is your birthday, Miranda?
<Aphrodite>	August eighth, why?
<ArrogantWit>	Aries and Leo . . . two fire signs . . . an explosive combination . . . igniting endless reserves of blazing sexual stamina . . . continuously burning and scorching . . . neither willing to admit exhaustion . . . eventually leaving nothing but charred remains.
<Aphrodite>	Sounds fatal.
<ArrogantWit>	Quite . . . but the road to incineration is paved with ecstasy.

<Aphrodite>	Have you considered seeking professional help?
<ArrogantWit>	Let me guess . . . spoiled, pampered . . . you'll probably be staying at the Mirage, right?
<Aphrodite>	Nope. . . .
<ArrogantWit>	Caesar's Palace?
<Aphrodite>	Strike two. . . .
<ArrogantWit>	New York, New York?
<Aphrodite>	Wrong again. . . . and you thought you had me pegged.
<ArrogantWit>	Ok, then, where? Where would the Goddess of Love choose to stay in a city full of temptation and vice?
<Aphrodite>	The "Goddess" has yet to make her reservations, but if all goes well, she'll be spending her birthday in the Egyptian splendor of the Luxor Hotel.
<ArrogantWit>	That was my next guess.
<Aphrodite>	Ok, you have been way too amiable this morning. . . . What are you up to?
<ArrogantWit>	Miranda . . . I'm hurt. I'm not the monster you think I am. I'm actually a very nice guy.
<Aphrodite>	Yeah, right. And I'm a virgin.
<ArrogantWit>	Miranda. . . .
<Aphrodite>	Yes, Wit.
<ArrogantWit>	I am sleepy. I'm off to bed with delicious thoughts of my naked body in total control of yours, arms and legs entangled, the musk from hours of nonstop, hot, sweaty sex . . . permeating the air . . . but before I do, promise me something
<Aphrodite>	. . . anything . . .

<ArrogantWit>	Before you go to sleep . . . e-mail your picture to me. I find myself obsessed . . . wondering . . . what the sexy, wanton creature I have met online . . . what she looks like. Send me a picture, Miranda. Feed me.
<Aphrodite>	Look forward to a feast, my Arrogant Wit, and indulge yourself. Sweet dreams.

4:00 AM. Better get to sleep soon. Angela and I have a whole new routine to create for the upcoming weekend, plus I have to come up with a routine of my own. First, I have to find a few of my most sexy and devastating photos to send to Mr. Wit. Payback time, although I don't feel quite so cutthroat as I did earlier this week. He was actually quite civil. Hmmmm . . . must have been preoccupied seducing another prospective phone-sex partner. After sending off three killer photos, I fall into a deep, undisturbed sleep, until the determined meows and kisses of my Taz get my attention, well after the clock has chimed 11:00 AM.

CHAPTER 4

■

THE SLAVE

Oh my goodness. Amid my excitement with Angela and dancing and Wit, I'd completely forgotten about my date with BigMan until this very second. That's tomorrow night! *Having second thoughts, Miranda*, I ask myself silently? Well, even if I were, it wouldn't make any difference. Nothing like jumping in with both feet. Well, there's always the code word. I'll call both Angela and Robert and tell them that I'm going on a blind date with a man I met over the Internet, and that if they haven't heard from me by 5:00 P.M Tuesday night, to notify the police. Angela and Robert both try to talk me out of going out with this mystery man, but to no avail. I need their friendship and support, not their advice. Grudgingly, they take down the information I give them and wish me luck.

The rest of the afternoon I spend dancing to sultry music, attempting to put together a solo routine that rivals the other dancers. I decide that a hot bath and an early bedtime would be the best medicine to prepare myself to face tomorrow night.

Finally, Monday arrives. I decide that I had better

check my e-mail, just in case there is a last minute cancellation. There is an e-mail waiting for me from <BigMan>. I feel a surge of disappointment at the thought that our date might be called off. I would have thought I would have felt immense relief. With hesitant fingers, I display the letter on the computer screen and begin to read.

Hoping I'd cancel? I think not. I haven't looked forward to an encounter this much in a very long time. Here are your instructions. Follow them exactly. This is a test in subservience. If you vary anything, there will be consequences.

I want you to wear a very sexy, low-cut black dress, above the knee, with garters and stockings, no panties . . . and no bra. Also, so that I can recognize you, wear a red ribbon tied around your right wrist. You will not be afforded the same luxury. You will not know who I am until I decide to make myself known to you. It is my intent to "train" you in the basics of being a slave. If all goes well and the code word is never used, you will be completely under my command until Tuesday at the hotel's checkout time. At that time, you will be free to go.

The limo will pick you up at 5:00 P.M. and take you to the restaurant. You will ask to be seated under the reservation made in the name of Adam Bigg. I will join you shortly thereafter.

Wanting to make a good first impression, I take special pains with my appearance, making sure that I follow his instructions to the letter. My toilette consists of shaving my legs, all the way up, making them incredibly soft and silky smooth. Next, I closely crop my pubic hair and apply scented lotion to my entire body. I finish up by spraying on my favorite cologne, hitting all my secret, erogenous zones. After a final inspection to make sure that my makeup is enhancing but not too heavy and my hair is soft and alluring, I sit back and wait, anxiously tapping my foot to the rhythm of the background music playing on the stereo.

The limo arrives precisely on time. With no turning back now, I settle myself into the luxurious interior and help myself to a glass of champagne. I am cruising down the interstate in a matter of minutes, hastening the inevitable confrontation between my veritable reality and my fantasy.

I arrive at the restaurant and mention the reservation for Adam Bigg. I am informed that Mr. Bigg has not yet arrived, but should be there shortly. The maître'd escorts me to the table. I feel very nervous, walking into this exclusive restaurant all alone. I feel like every pair of eyes is watching me make my way to the table, men and women alike. I wonder if he is out there, somewhere, watching me, watching my discomfort, seeing my reaction. I'm sure it was his intent for me to be a little off balance and vulnerable. He won't be disappointed. I sit down and start looking around the room at all the other people having dinner, looking for a lone, male figure. No one catches my eye, just a bunch of couples and a few larger groups.

As if in answer to a prayer, the waiter arrives and I welcome the distraction. He introduces himself as Mark, and asks if I would like a cocktail to start off the evening. I explain to the waiter that I am waiting for someone to join me, but yes, I would love a glass of champagne. As I look up at him, I am taken aback by my reaction. He is smiling, but his eyes are intense, devouring me with their power. Maybe it is just because I am nervous and I'm only imagining it. Maybe he likes what he sees. I find myself beginning to flush. The air between us is charged with electricity and my breath catches. I avert my eyes to break the connection, making it fade, and he takes the opportunity to go for the champagne. *Shit*, I'm thinking. *Bad timing*.

The waiter returns with a glass of champagne. I thank him without really looking at him. I don't want to encourage him. I want everything to go just right with Adam. He places the glass on the table, his hand inadvertently brushing against mine. The contact sends shock waves throughout my whole nervous system. I close my eyes and will him to disappear. Finally, I am alone again. I start sipping my champagne, watching all the people, wondering where he is, if he's out there, and when he'll decide to show himself.

Mark returns again with a full bottle of champagne and a note. He tells me that the maître'd asked him to give this to me. We make eye contact again. Oh, dear, I can't believe that just a look can have such an affect on me. A rush of warmth starts spreading throughout, centering in my loins. I can feel him caressing me with his mind. He hands me the note and our hands manage to touch again . . . zap! I'm burning up . . . on fire. *Shit, shit, shit, shit, shit!!!!!* I try to keep my breathing under control, hoping that he has no idea of the effect he is having on me. He pours me another glass of champagne while I read the note.

Am running late . . . get started without me.

Adam.

At my crestfallen look, Mark asks me, "What's the matter?"

"Oh, my date is going to be delayed a bit longer, that's all. May I please order an appetizer?" I order my most favorite of all foods, steamed clams. Mark smiles a devastating smile, and leaves to fill my order. In the meantime, I start sucking down the champagne, trying to alleviate some of my nervousness.

Mark brings my clams, and this time I keep my hands clear of his. He refills my glass and away he goes. *Whew.* I begin to devour my clams. Oh, God, they are soooooooooo good. I try to behave like a lady, but with seafood, especially clams, I am swept away. I have to consciously make myself slow down and stop moaning. I glance up just in time to catch Mark watching me from the kitchen area, laughing. I'm so embarrassed now, I vow to kill Adam when he finally arrives. I look back up, and Mark is gone. I finish with the last bite of my clams, and still no Adam. Okay, this is no longer amusing. He had better show up soon.

Mark returns to my table, this time wearing a worried frown as he hands me another note. Oh great.. . . .now what? This time the note reads,

I'll be there in an hour. I am very sorry. I promise to make it up to you.

Adam.

I throw the note on the table in frustration. Mark asks, "Bad news?"

I practically whine, "Yes, my date is going to be another hour!"

He smiles sympathetically, sits down across from me and says, "You know, I get off work in five minutes. Can I keep you company until he arrives?" I look at him, looking so charming and sincere, not wanting to hurt his feelings. Besides, I am a little tipsy and carrying a very big grudge. This will serve Adam right. "Sure, and I'll make sure you get a very big tip for this!" He asks what I would like for dinner, and I proceed to order another dozen clams.

I sit and fume at the table. I just know that he did this on purpose, and is probably watching me from somewhere in the restaurant, enjoying this little game. I rake my eyes across the room, just daring him to make himself known, casting furious glances at all the poor, unsuspecting people quietly eating their dinners. I still can't determine from the patrons who he could possibly be. Maybe he really wasn't there after all. Maybe he really did run into some trouble.

I strive to keep my anger under control. I am tempted to take the red ribbon off of my wrist . . . well, not quite yet. If I receive one more note, though, it is gone! Finally Mark reappears with a fresh bottle of champagne and our dinners, and sits across from me. He fills my glass, then his own. I thank him very much for his act of charity. He smiles a wolfish smile and says, "Oh, this is no act of charity. . . . I am doing this for purely selfish reasons. . . ."

I smile back as my heart begins to race again. *Oh God, Oh God, Oh God . . .*

"So what's your name?" he asks.

"Miranda."

He says my name, then repeats it, then smiles and says, "I like that name. It is beautiful and exotic, just like you." I smile, but look down, directing all of my attention to dissecting and devouring my second batch of clams. *Don't go there, don't go there,* I keep thinking. *I can't let this happen.*

Mark chose a dinner of a steak and baked potato. He digs in, appearing to be quite pleased with himself. During the course of the meal, he finds all kinds of excuses to accidentally brush against my hand, rub his legs up and down my own, and with each touch, the heat intensifies. He grows bolder and bolder, his gaze more passionate and full of promise. I try very hard not to look at him, but God, he is so attractive. I'm dying, Adam, please get here soon!

All too soon, dinner is over, and a different waiter has taken over to remove our dirty dishes. We are still drinking champagne. I have a very nice buzz going, but not too much. I am feeling very warm and tingly. The lights begin to dim as the band fires up, my body automatically begins swaying to the beat of the music. "Would you like to dance?" Mark asks. I cast a quick glance around the room, seeing if I can spot Adam anywhere, and convinced that he has still not arrived, I accept. I know I am walking into a precarious situation right now, but the champagne has made me brave, and I am still irritated, hell bent on revenge. . . .

We approach the center of the dance floor, and Mark wastes no time drawing me into his arms. I can barely keep from swooning. He is so hard and strong, and smells so good. He has me pressed tightly against him, knowing that at any moment he may have to relinquish his claim, and we start to move to the music. I have my eyes closed and just melt against him. Damn, it feels so good. How am I ever going to be able to face Adam, or my husband, after this little fiasco? I start to seriously consider removing the red ribbon and bolting for my life.

As we dance, Mark's hands start to move around my back, slowly going lower, his face meshing with my hair, rubbing against it, whispering sordid things he'd like to do with me. Oh, God! I'm getting seduced right here on the dance floor. His hands are now on my lower back. I can tell he wants to go even lower and is wondering if he should. I can feel his erection pressed against my pelvic bone . . . ohhhhhhh . . . I'm melting.

I moan softly, and Mark takes that as an invitation to continue. He dances me into a darkened corner of the restaurant where there are no other people, and starts to kiss my neck. Another warm gush of liquid rushes through my body. I can barely stand. His hands are roving over my ass now, starting out as light caresses, then becoming more firm, ending with downright groping. He gets me backed into a corner and pushes up against my body while he kisses me hard and passionately, bruising my lips. I am moving my head back and forth, trying to get back some control, knowing that this is so wrong. I finally manage to break free, and gasping, tell him that this cannot continue and start back for the table. He utters one word that stops me cold in my tracks, "Aphrodite."

I turn around. "You son of a bitch! You absolute, *son of a bitch*!" I am beside myself at this point and start to march back toward him. "I can't believe you would do this to me, Adam, if that really is your name!" I start to flail my arms at him, punching at his arms and chest, releasing all of my anger and frustration. He grabs my arms and pins them behind my back and pushes me back up against the corner of the wall. "Have you forgotten what this is all about, slave! You have been very disobedient, and although I am extremely disappointed, I am pleased by your reaction toward me. I like the fact that you were attracted to me without knowing who I was, but your lack of control upsets me. You should *never* have allowed me to eat with you. You will be punished for that, slave."

On that note, he reaches under my dress and shoves a finger up deep inside me, causing me to gasp in surprise and fright. He has a menacing look in his eyes. "Adam, what are you doing? We're in a restaurant." I all but shriek! He starts to fuck me with his finger, moving it up and down inside me, then adding a second finger, causing me to gasp and moan, his hand pumping faster, while his other is kept busy unzipping his fly. "Well, you're just going to have to hope nobody comes around and bothers us, now, aren't you?" With his erection sprung free, he removes his fingers and all but rapes me right there in the corner of the room.

The shame and humiliation that I know I probably should be feeling is absent. My body delights in this public assault. The fear and shock have vanished, and I find myself enjoying the "punishment" he is inflicting upon me. At this point, I could care less who walked in. "Oh, God, Adam. . . . Oh, Oh, Oh, Oh, Oh. . . ." I continue to moan while he fucks me, pumping into me fast and furiously, kissing me desperately, almost biting. Both of his hands are in my hair, twisting and pulling. I am so overwhelmed with sensations so intense, I can't think. I don't know what I am going to do. I feel as though I will explode! Just when I think I can take no more, I hear the roar of a successful mating, as he shudders and collapses against me.

I wail out my frustration, so close to having an orgasm myself, but denied. I start to hungrily kiss Adam again, trying to bring back the erection that I desperately need right now. He looks down at me and smiles, an evil smile, and starts to shake his head. "Oh, no, slave, this is part of your punishment, and this is only the beginning. Before the night is over, you will be begging for mercy and wishing you had never accepted my offer of companionship at dinner." He pulls away from me, adjusts his pants, takes me by the hand and starts to pull me back into the heart of the restaurant. I am afraid to go with him now, trying to resist and wondering if I should use the code word. "No, please, Adam, no, I'm sorry. You don't understand. . . ." "Oh,

I understand perfectly, now let's go! I'll pick you up and carry you out of here on my shoulder if I have to. . . ."

There is a limo waiting for us when we get outside. He practically throws me into it and climbs in beside me. I continue begging and pleading with him to listen, to understand, to forgive me. "Please, Adam, let's just start over, please!"

"Oh, don't worry, slave, I will forgive you, have already forgiven you, but you need to be taught a lesson." He looks at me with a cold, stony face. I am so afraid right now, I quickly sober up.

We pull up beside the hotel and exit the limo, Adam all but dragging me up to the room. Once inside, I am awestruck by the decor. It is the most beautiful, elegant hotel room I have ever been in. I look around, dazed. It is a huge suite with a four-poster, king-size bed, sitting smack dab in the middle of the room. There is a bar off to the left, a jacuzzi to the right, a sofa, a TV, you name it! There is also a huge bathroom situated off to the right, creating easy access to and from the jacuzzi. I hear the door lock behind me, the sound of the chain getting thrown across being the final clue as to the extent of my enslavement.

Adam briefly looks me over as he walks toward the bar. He pours two more glasses of champagne, walks over to the jacuzzi tub, and turns on the bubbles. He hands me a glass and commands me to join him in the jacuzzi. I'm confused now. He doesn't seem as angry any more. I begin wondering if I should join him or run for my life.

He sets his glass down and starts to remove his clothing, never once breaking eye contact with me. As if he can read my thoughts via my facial expressions, he says, "Don't even think about trying to run, slave. I *will* catch you, and it will be just that much worse for you in the long run." With a sigh of despair, I also start to remove my clothing, but he tells me to stop. I look at him with a question in my eyes. Standing still, I watch him finish undressing and step into the bubbling tub. What a magnificent male animal he is! I gulp.

He seats himself in the warm, frothing water, grabbing his champagne and settling down to face me. "Now you may remove your clothing, and do it slowly." I flush, hesitating for just a moment, and then slowly start to unbutton my dress. I am not wearing much, and as soon as the dress falls gracefully from my shoulders, I am left with nothing but garters, stockings, and high heels. I step out of my dress and notice him smiling appreciatively. "I see you have followed the rest of my instructions. Very good. I will take that into consideration when I deal out the rest of your punishment. Now, remove the rest, but keep that red ribbon around your wrist. You will wear it the entire time that we are together."

"As you wish," I humbly reply.

I finish removing my stockings, garters and heels and walk over to the jacuzzi with my glass of champagne.

"Before you join me, I want you to refill my glass." I acknowledge and head for the bar, giving him a great view of my backside. Again, he is delighted by what he sees, telling me so. Blushing, I carry the rest of the bottle over to the tub and refill both of our glasses. Then I leave the bottle where it will be accessible from the tub.

As I climb into the tub, he tells me to sit on his lap, facing away from him. I do as he requests, and I feel him put aside his glass, as his arms reach around my torso to pull me in close. His chest is against my back, his face at my neck and hair, and his hands are lightly caressing my belly. The bubbles are going off all around us, making it all very sensual. He lightly kisses the back of my neck. *Ohhhhhhh, if he only knew what that does to me*. His hands move up and are fondling my breasts very gently, then leave again.

Suddenly, it feels as if he has five pair of hands, and I feel them touching me everywhere, simultaneously. Are they his hands, or are they the bubbles? I can no longer discern. I feel his fingers dipping between my legs, gliding up and down my thighs, grazing the outside of my lips, but never quite touching me "there." I wriggle in agonizing ecstasy, having forgotten that I should still be afraid. I am getting caught up in the most beautiful sensations. His hands come up to my face, tracing the outline, feeling me, memorizing my face, still kissing the back of my neck.

"Adam . . ." I moan, over and over, until he finally flips me around to face him.

I can feel his erection again, and reach out to touch it. He instantaneously scolds me, "Never assume you can touch me without permission, slave. You must always ask first."

"Oh, please Adam, let me touch you."

"I want you to ride me, slave, guide me to your sweet, wet hole and impale yourself upon me."

His erotic speech moves me, and I position myself so that I can feel the head of his cock brushing against my eager pussy, slowly opening, and sighing with relief as I finally sink upon him, grasping the entire length of him until he has completely filled me. Oh my God . . . what a feeling.

I start to move up and down, the buoyancy of the water assisting me, the bubbles making it very erotic.

"Oh, Adam, it feels so good to feel you so deep inside me." I continue, up and down, up and down, proceeding at a very leisurely pace. I really want to kiss him. "Adam, may I please kiss you?"

In reply, he pulls my face toward his and takes my lips captive. He uses very slow, torturous kisses, keeping in rhythm with the up-and-down strokes, his hands now gripping my ass as he starts to pick up the pace. Oh God, it feels so wonderful. I start to tingle all over.

Before I realize what is happening, I feel him convulsing. He is cumming again! Damn it! I start to ride him more furiously, realizing that I don't have much time left to reach my own peak, but he stops me.

"No, No, No, No, No, No!" I yell out in frustration as he gently pushes me off of his legs. I close my eyes, lean my head back against the side of the tub and wallow in misery.

"Look at me, slave." I open my eyes to focus on his evil grin once again. "I told you that you were in for a long night. You are marvelous, slave. This is going to be almost as hard on me as it is on you." I groan, a long, sorrowful groan.

"Please don't do this to me, Adam. I swear I've learned my lesson!"

"Oh, I don't think so, slave."

"I want you to go take a quick shower now. Everything you need is waiting for you in the bathroom. You have fifteen minutes, and Miranda, don't even think about masturbating in the shower. I'll be watching, I'll know." I glare at him and stomp off, out of the hot tub and into the bathroom. I take my shower and brush my teeth and return just under the allotted fifteen minutes, never once even thinking about touching myself. (Okay, well, maybe once.) My fear has subsided somewhat, but as I look at what he has in store for me, the fear quickly returns.

There are four leather shackles, one hanging from

each post of the bed. Beside the bed is a huge suitcase type of contraption, resembling a small closet. It is open wide, sitting on the coffee table. Hanging on the insides of the doors are more sex toys than I have ever seen in one place before. Vibrators of all shapes, sizes and colors, oils, lubricants, it is obscene! I look away in horror, praying that there aren't any whips in there. I look over at him with my eyes huge and my mouth hanging open, as he innocently sits on the edge of the bed wearing nothing but a smile. "Oh, come on, Adam. This has gone far enough."

"Come here, slave."

"But, Adam. . . ."

"I don't want to have to say it again. Come over here now, slave."

Shit, shit, shit, shit, shit. I slowly start toward the bed. "Don't hurt me, please, Adam."

"Slave, I would never hurt you. The worst will be the sting of my hand across your backside. You can always use the code word if it gets too much for you. Now sit down here beside me."

Okay, if a spanking is going to be the worst of it, I know I can handle this.

I skeptically sit beside him on the bed. In his hands are two sets of fur-lined handcuffs. First he cuffs my ankles together, then my wrists. When he is completely satisfied that I am properly trussed up, he reaches for me and tosses me over his lap. My hands are in front of me, dangling down, cuffed together, with my head looking down toward the floor. My belly is resting on his knees and legs, my ass easily within his reach and quite available to him, and my legs are touching the floor, dangling on the opposite side.

I feel his hand lightly graze across my bottom. I wince, surely knowing what will follow, tensing up, but he only continues to keep teasing my ass with feather-light strokes. I feel his fingers dip into the crack of my ass and run all the way up and down its length, pausing just slightly at my opening, teasing it, and then returning back up again. I feel the warmth start to invade my pussy again. Oh, God, I want to cum so badly. He has me so worked up.

Smack! I am startled out of my thoughts of orgasm. *Smack!* "Now, this is for allowing a total stranger to seduce you." *Smack . . . smack . . . smack . . . smack. . . .*

"Ow, Adam. . . . stop it! Ow, Ow! . . . Come on, Adam, please stop it . . . Stop! Please!" I start to make small, whimpering noises.

Smack . . . smack . . . smack . . . smack. . . . "Not until I am quite convinced that you will never allow something like that to happen again."

Smack . . . smack . . . smack. . . . "Please, Adam . . . I . . . *promise* . . . that . . . will . . . *never* . . . happen . . . again!" I am close to sobbing now.

Smack . . . smack . . . smack. . . . "Okay, I'll stop for now, but I can always start up again, just remember that." Oh, thank God, my ass is on fire, and strangely, that's not the only thing on fire. I squirm in absolute discomfort. He starts to gently stroke my bottom . . . pleased at how rosy it looks, soothing it.

Once again he flips me over until I am seated beside him at the edge of the bed. He pushes me backward, pulling my still-handcuffed arms high above my head, falling on top of me, kissing and stroking me, every-where. *Ahhhhhhhhhh, yes, this is more like it.* I sigh in heavenly bliss. After a couple of minutes, he stops, gets out the handcuff keys, and releases my hands. He tells me to scoot up more toward the middle of the bed, and I comply without hesitation. Then he takes the shackle from the top right bedpost and secures it to my wrist. Next, he reaches for the shackle on the left side, and secures it to my other wrist. Once he is certain that I am securely fastened to the top of the bed, he removes the cuffs around my ankles and fastens each ankle separately to the bottom shackles. I am now completely attached to the bed, spreadeagled and wide open for his pleasure, totally at his mercy.

"Please . . . Adam . . . you promised not to hurt me."

He smiles at me as he stands back and admires his handiwork. Starting at the bottom, he touches my legs, very, very, softly, teasingly, working his way up my thighs, touching them, oh so softly . . . first the outsides, then the insides. The closer he gets to my pussy, the more I squirm. He just lightly glides by it, driving me crazy as he crawls on top of the bed. His hands are now gliding up my stomach and sides again, causing fluttering sensations, barely brushing over my breasts, quickly replaced by his mouth. "Ohhhhhhhhhhhhhh, Adam!"

He suckles at them, sometimes gentle and pulling, other times more roughly . . . biting, nipping, sucking, licking, twisting, then moving up to my neck to continue the kissing and biting there. I can barely stand it. "I want you again. I need you again. I am so hot, on fire. . . . please, Adam. . . ."

"Not yet, slave," he replies.

He rolls over to his closet of goodies and returns with a blindfold. "This will heighten your pleasure, slave. You'll have no idea what to expect next. The fear will intensify all of the sensations, but just remember one thing. You can trust me completely. I will not hurt you. Make sure you don't get too loud. If you do, I'll be forced to put a ball gag in your mouth, making it very difficult for you to shout the code word if you have to."

With that threat hanging over my head, I quickly

agree to be as quiet as possible. "I won't make any noise, I promise."

He fastens the blindfold over my eyes and around my head, wrapping it around many times, confident that I cannot see a thing. I can hear him wrestling around in his closet full of goodies. When he next advances towards me, no doubt in possession of a few sinfully erotic toys, he hovers by my face and asks, "Do you know what Ben Wa balls are, slave?" As I start to answer, I can feel a small, cool, round object being placed in my belly button and being rolled around on my stomach. The ball continues rolling lower, across my swollen clit, down between my pussy lips and then hesitating at my opening.

"Oh, yes," I sigh softly, trembling with expectancy. With a push of his finger, the little ball is inserted deep inside me. I moan out in obvious pleasure.

Then I feel another small, cool, round ball being rolled across my breasts, down across my stomach, over my clit, down between my pussy lips and then pushed up way deep inside me as well. The two balls start to move around together inside me as I squirm, clicking against one another, arousing me further. Before I understand what is happening next, I feel a *third* small ball being rolled across my stomach to follow the same path as the previous two. "Three, Adam? Aren't there only supposed to be two?" "I'm experimenting, slave. You deserve more than just the bare minimum. I want to see how far I can take you."

"Oh, God," is all I can utter as the third ball is pushed inside, disappearing into a sea of liquid fire.

He is right. The sensations are even greater with three, and I continue to wriggle against my restraints. Now I feel a fourth small, cool little ball being rolled around. Only he teases me more with this one, rolling it down across my clit, down to my opening, then passing it by. Down one leg, back up, across my clit again, down the other leg, back up, across my clit once more, and then finally inserting it.

"Oh, Adam . . . no more . . . no more. . . ." The sensations are marvelous, those four little balls, rolling around, each going a different direction, then coming back together, bouncing and clicking. Oh, the sweet torture.

A husky voice whispers in my ear, "Ever played with anal beads?"

"No," I reply, "but I've seen them. I know what they're used for."

He kisses my ear, and then I feel a pressure on my ass. It is his finger, and he has it all lubricated up. He gently inserts his finger, just a little, and I gasp, "Ohhhhhhhhhhhhhh." He wriggles his finger around and around, then removes it. Then I feel a different sensation, a small, round, plastic ball, only this time, it is attached to more balls by a string. He inserts the first ball, then the second. Gasping, "How many, Adam?"

"You'll just have to wait and see, slave." A third, followed by a fourth, finally ending when the fifth ball is embedded intimately and tucked away from sight. He wriggles the string a little, pulling on it just enough so that I can feel the pressure of the beads trying to break free.

"Oh, God, Adam. I can't take this. I need to cum."

"No, slave, you will not be allowed to cum, not yet. If you mistakenly do, the penalty will be severe." Disheartened, I wail like a wounded tiger.

Just when I think I can't take any more, I hear him power up what I assume to be a vibrator. He first moves it across my breasts, getting my already erect nipples to extend even further, then running it across my belly, and down between my legs. He places the vibrating tip right at my pussy opening and wriggles it around in circles, not going any deeper.

"Adam, you're killing me, please!" He moves the vibrator along so that it barely glances off of my clit, at the same time, popping out one of the anal beads. "Oh, Adam, please don't. Please don't do that again, or I will definitely cum!"

Realizing that I am very close, he turns off the vibrator and pulls out the second anal bead. "Oh," then the third bead is removed, "Oh, God," followed, at last, by the fourth and fifth beads. *Moan*. He comes back up to me and kisses me. "That was very good, I'm proud of you for telling me to stop. I may go easier on you than I had originally planned."

With that said, he extends a finger up inside me and begins to remove the Ben Wa balls, until they are all accounted for. Abruptly, I am completely without stimulation, allowing my breathing to begin to return to normal, but my clit remains swollen and aching with need. Adam amusedly pronounces, "I'll be right back, don't go away," and chuckles as he heads off in the direction of the bathroom. All I can do is struggle and shake my head back and forth, still helpless and blindfolded.

After what feels like an eternity, I hear him moving about the main room again. Then I hear the TV!

"What are you doing?" I ask, incredulous. "Watching TV. I have to give you time to completely cool down before I get you all worked up again. Part of your punishment, slave."

"Oh, no. How long do you intend for this to go on, all night?"

"If I feel that I have to, it all depends on you, slave."

"Adam, please. I really have learned my lesson. Come back and finish what you started, please!"

"Sorry, Miranda, not yet."

I curse him under my breath, being careful not to let him hear my expletive. I have no intention of adding any extra time to my "sentence." I endure, laying back, wide open, trying to relax, trying to ignore the burning deep inside me still pulsating, still clenching, still begging. . . .

I awaken with a start. He has something very cold in his hands, and he is rubbing it across my breasts. Ice!

"I'm, awake, I'm awake!" I yell. He chuckles and removes the ice. He begins to rub his cold, wet hands across my face, down my neck, all over my entire body, until his hands are sufficiently warmed up. The room is really warm. "Did you turn up the heat?"

"Yes, I did, slave. We wouldn't want you getting too cold now, would we?"

When his hands return to my body, they are covered with leather gloves. I can smell the leather. Oh, God. I love the smell of leather, instantly probing and awakening my darkest desires. Ohhhhhh. Again he rubs his leather-clad hands across my face, down my sides and stomach, and down between my legs. "Ever been fucked by leather before?"

Oh, God, when he talks like that, it makes me crazy, and an instant rush of heat and wetness travels directly to my core. "No, I haven't." As I say it, I feel his gloved finger slowly begin to penetrate me, working its way deeper and deeper. Oh, I am feeling so violated, yet all I can do is respond, bucking my hips at him, causing him to go deeper still.

I am mad with longing, incoherent, wanting him so badly, aware of the things he is capable of making me feel. "Oh, Adam! Ohhhhhhhh, Ohhhhhhh, Ohhhhhhhhhh!" I continue yelling, over and over, as his finger pumps in and out of me. Oh, man, this is incredible. His gloved thumb is stroking my clit the whole while his finger is penetrating me. "Stop, Adam . . . please stop . . . stop now!"

It kills me inside to ask him to stop. "I am amazed by your control, slave. You are learning very quickly." He stops, but keeps the gloves on. He comes back up to kiss me. I am moaning, dying inside, desperately needing release. This is such torture. He leaves momentarily only to return with an object accompanied by a menacing sound. I know what he has. It's the ice bucket, and it is full. I can hear the ice shift, already starting to slowly melt in the increasingly hot room.

He sits back on the bed and places the bucket of ice on the nightstand. He keeps the gloves on, ensuring his hands stay cozy and warm while they inflict exquisite anguish onto my already aching body. I hear him reach for a piece of ice. I tense up, not knowing where he will place it first. He places it directly on my mouth, startling me. He rubs the ice over my lips, getting them very cold and very wet. Then he says, "Suck it!" I part my lips slightly and start to suckle it. I can feel it melting all over my face and running down my throat. I am moaning as I suck the ice cube. He pulls it out, then pushes it back in, out and in, out and in, thoroughly fucking my mouth with the ice cube. Mmmmmmmmm, I love it. He makes me suck it until it has completely melted. My lips are frozen now. He bends down and kisses them until they are warm and supple again.

He reaches for another ice cube. This one touches my chin and he slides it slowly down my throat, between my breasts, circling around my breasts, and finally to the nipple which instantly responds to the cold. Oh, God, "mmmhhhh . . . mmmhhhhh," I'm a mass of sensations. He teases one nipple, then the other as the ice cube slowly melts. I can feel it dripping down between my breasts, down my stomach and sides. This is so erotic. I am cold, shivering, but I don't want it to stop. The ice cube gradually disappears. He reaches for another.

This time the ice cube begins its journey in the middle of my stomach, moving around in circles, going lower. I am unable to control the squirming of my body, the sensations taking charge, making me disoriented and disabled, at the mercy of impulses. He takes the ice cube completely down the length of my leg, across the bottom of my foot, back up, across my pelvis, down the other leg, bottom of the other foot, back up, until it too, is all gone.

He reaches for yet another cube, this one centering on my clit. The first touch is jolting, as he slides it around and around. "Ohhhhhh, ohhhhhhh, ohhhhhhhhh," I repeat, moaning softly. The ice cube melts down across my pussy lips, causing me to arch up. God, I want to feel him inside me. He takes the ice cube lower, pressing it between my lips. It is so cold. I can barely stand it. I feel it at my pussy opening, spreading me, demanding entrance.

He continues to tease the opening for a minute longer, the cube now melting and dripping directly into my ass. My ass flexes, trying to catch a drop. I am mindless now, no longer capable of conscious thought, relying solely on my senses. All I can do is feel. Then, without warning, he nudges the rest of the ice cube inside, my lips involuntarily swallowing the intruder, inducing a gasp of surprised delight. The ice cube is melted instantly. Again he leaves my side, allowing plenty of time for me to consider how I had behaved earlier, and how determined he is to make me pay for it. In anguish, I resign myself to my fate and patiently wait for the next onslaught, surely forthcoming. He returns the temperature to a comfortable setting and sits back down to watch more TV.

About an hour goes by, my best estimate considering the circumstances. I manage to remain awake this time, writhing in agony for the entire duration. Finally I feel his naked warmth return to the bed. This time he greets me with a kiss. It doesn't take me long to begin responding, and I feel my body temperature rising, warming up again. Damn him, damn him! It shouldn't be this easy.

He has something in his hand, making a small, vibrating noise. He holds it up against my face so that I can feel it. It feels cold and hard, like the Ben Wa balls did, only much larger, like an egg. "Can you guess what this is for, Slave?"

"Oh, God. . . . Oh, God. . . . You're going to push that deep into my pussy, aren't you? I can't take anymore, Adam, I can't."

"It's not going in your pussy, slave, and oh, yes, yes you can. You can take this plus a whole lot more"

"No, please, Adam, it won't fit. It will hurt."

"Trust me, slave," is all he says before I feel the shiny edge of the vibrating egg pushing persistently at my asshole, demanding entry.

It is very slick, obviously very well lubricated. Finally I am able to relax enough to allow it to penetrate, to enter me, to be consumed by my ass. "Ohhhhhhhhhhhhhhhh." It feels wonderful, decadent, like it belongs there. I clench and suck it until it completely disappears, is completely engulfed with nothing but the cord showing. He pulls the cord up between my legs, draping it across my clit, and rests the control box on my stomach. Then he turns it on.

"Ahhhhhhhhhhhhhhhh!" I can feel the vibrations deep inside, radiating along the cord and over my clit. It is so intense. Somebody help me.

He at long last removes my blindfold. My eyes are completely glazed over with passion and need. He is standing beside the bed, totally naked, with his huge, stiff, erection staring at me. My whole body is vibrating now. I can't keep still. He watches me squirm as he begins to stroke his enormous cock. I am hypnotized, watching him manipulate his cock, working it up and down, faster and faster. Impossibly, it appears to be growing larger by the second. Within minutes, he has brought himself to the point of no return, the pressure building, the need to explode undeniable. He leans over me, and with one last stroke, he howls and shoots his immense load all over my face, neck, and breasts, until every last drop is spewed and paying homage to my delectable, quivering body. My mouth is open, trying to catch some, trying to taste him, greedily licking at all I can capture.

He again joins me on the bed and begins to rub his cum into my skin, stroking me all over, touching me everywhere, until every last bit of evidence has disappeared, completely absorbed into my skin.

"It's your turn, now, slave." Adam leaves the egg buried deep inside my ass, still vibrating away, but removes the control box from my belly and away from my clit. He slides me as far down to the edge of the bed as my shackles will allow, then kneels on the floor at the bottom of the bed. I can feel his breath just inches from my clit.

I'm begging him now. "Please, Adam, please. Make me cum. I need to cum. Oh, God, Adam, I'm begging you!" I feel his tongue find my clit and dart at it playfully. "No, please, suck it, grab it. I need to feel your whole mouth on it, please, you're killing me!!!'' Thankfully, I feel his mouth come down on it, completely covering it with warmth and silky wetness. His tongue and lips are everywhere, sliding, consuming, eating me, draining me. I feel the tension, starting at the pit of my belly, the vibrator in my ass making his tongue vibrate, too. It is too much for me. Oh, I'm there, I'm there!

"Aaaaaaaaaaaaahhhhhhhhhhhhhhhhhhhhhhhhh!" I scream out his name as I convulse, over and over again, twitching and pulsing, releasing into glorious oblivion, drowning him with the taste that is only me, listening to him gulp down every last drop. Adam releases my bonds and we fall together into a deep, exhausted sleep.

"You're mine until noon. That was the deal."

"I know, but I'm ready to go now. I want to leave."

"Not until I've had you one last time, slave. You shouldn't have been so hasty to get back into your clothes. You're just going to have to get out of them again. Now, go over to the window and open the curtains."

Wondering what he has up his sleeve now, I walk over to the window and pull apart the drapes, revealing a gorgeous view of the ocean. We are a few floors above ground, possibly the sixth or seventh floor, and I notice a few people milling about in the parking lot.

"Now strip, slave. In front of the open window, vulnerable to the inspection of the seagulls and whoever else happens to look this way. Strip, now!" Adam, unaware of my current occupation, has no idea that this is second nature to me. Smiling my own secret smile, I turn to him in feigned horror, begging him to reconsider. Thinking himself still the Master, he does not relinquish his demand, heading toward me with thoughts of persuasive tactics to help get me over my shyness. Responding immediately, before he can reach me, I turn back to the window and offer myself to the world. With wide, exaggerated movements, I remove every bit of my clothing, standing naked with arms and legs spread apart, presenting to Adam this gift of ultimate submission.

"On your hands and knees, slave, still facing the window." I comply and feel him come up behind me. With a minimal attempt at foreplay, he kneels behind me and begins thrusting inside me, doggie style. Luckily, I am moist enough without the foreplay to accept this intrusion without any hint of pain. It is a wild and furious coupling, resembling very closely the mating of two untamed animals. "I want everyone to see the look of pure lust on your face, slave, as you get fucked from behind. Look at them, slave. Search the parking lot. Will them to catch a glimpse of your passion." Glancing at the ground below, I try to concentrate on his request, unable to, getting caught up in the moment of his savage attack. Like ferocious beasts, we both scream out, signifying the final, ultimate fulfillment, marking the conclusion of our physical relationship.

Incredibly sated and satisfied, and happy with all of the previous night's discoveries, I sit back in extraordinary peace, allowing the gentle, rocking movements of the limousine to lull me to sleep. In less than an hour, I find myself back in my cozy little apartment and greeting a very lonely and grateful Taz. Before it slips my mind, I make sure that I call Angela and Robert to put them at ease, assuring them that I had a wonderful time, and I am back, safe and sound.

CHAPTER 5

■

"THE DOMINATOR"

The remainder of the week passed in a flurry of activity. I was lucky enough to procure a suite at the Luxor, just as I had hoped. I will be leaving first thing next Sunday morning and will stay through Wednesday morning, giving myself plenty of time to get back home before my next shift at the club.

Angela and I spent Wednesday and Thursday dancing and practicing for the next set of shifts. As expected, the performance of our new routine on Thursday and Friday nights met with another astounding reception.

One more shift before Las Vegas. I haven't been online all week and figure, "it's now or never." I'd better get my fix now. It's 3:00 P.M, Saturday afternoon. I never did have a chance to ask Wit how he liked my photos, and he never e-mailed a response. I settle myself in front of my computer once again. *Beep, beep, beep.*

<ArrogantWit> | Leaving tomorrow?
<Aphrodite> | Are you *always* online?
<ArrogantWit> | Disappointed? You came here look-
ing for me. . . .

_____

\<Aphrodite\>	Ah, back to your old self, I see.
\<ArrogantWit\>	Well, I can't stay long, I have to pack.
\<Aphrodite\>	Pack? Going somewhere?
\<ArrogantWit\>	Yes. Didn't I tell you? I'm taking a little trip . . . and plan on spending the next 4 days in . . . Las Vegas. . . .
\<Aphrodite\>	. . . you're lying. . . .
\<ArrogantWit\>	Am I? Well, we'll find out soon enough, won't we?
\<Aphrodite\>	Stop trying to scare me. I'm not going to let you ruin my vacation.

Damn. Why did he do that? He's trying to control me even without a computer . . . without a phone. He is trying to ensure that I will constantly think of him the entire time that I'm away. Oh, he's a gem, priceless. I almost let him do it, too. Clever, very clever, Mr. Wit, but not clever enough. Still, I have trouble shaking off the hand of apprehension that has suddenly fallen upon my shoulder.

He has me cornered, my back pushed up against the hard, warm surface of the club's interior wall. "Beg me to fuck you, Miranda. Right here, right now, in front of all these people."

"No . . . Never," I whisper breathlessly, alarmed by his gall.

"You want me to fuck you . . . you crave it. Now beg me. I want all these people to know who you belong to."

"No! Stop it! Go away," more panicky now.

"You leave me no choice, Miranda. I was hoping to avoid this."

He grabs me by the arm and leads me down a darkened hallway, all the way to the end, where the carpet meets the oak of the restroom doors. After confirming the absolute vacancy of the men's room, he whisks me inside and blocks the door closed with a chair.

"What are you doing?"

"Before this night is over, Miranda, you will beg me. I guarantee it."

I am unable to prevent what is happening; he immediately has me bent over the cold, marble counter, resting on the flat surface dividing the two sinks. My right wrist is tied to the "hot" faucet knob of the sink to my right, my left wrist tied to the "cold" faucet knob of the sink to my left. Next, I am gagged. My reflection in the mirror stares back in wide-eyed disbelief.

The counter is high enough that I am pressed firmly across it, unable to move because of my tightly bound wrists. He reaches behind me and hikes up my dress, high enough to lie across the small of my back, revealing a provocatively bare and exposed ass, decorated solely by garters. Lingering a bit longer than intended, distracted by the delectable sight, he reminds himself of his purpose and begins to rifle through my purse until he finds what he is looking for, my red lipstick. Then in big letters written across the mirror he writes, "Fuck me. It's my fantasy." Then, with a wicked grin, he places a box of condoms and some lubricating jelly on the counter next to me. I shake my head, trying to plead with him, my gag only allowing desperate, muffled cries to escape. *Oh my God, this can't be happening. . . .* Then, with slow, deliberate, steps, he withdraws into the shadows, removing the chair from the door to relax upon and wait . . . and watch . . . bearing witness. Struggling furiously, I try to free myself, when I suddenly freeze, stiff and immobile, as the door opens and a stranger enters, catching my horrified expression in the restroom mirror.

I awaken in a panic, sweat dripping down my chest,

my T-shirt completely soaked, my skin cold and clammy. Oh, thank God. It was just a dream, a damn nightmare. It was him. It was Wit, I know it was. Do I really think of him as that evil, or was it just my reaction to his earlier attempt at a threat? Whew. Trying to relax, it takes all of my strength to finally even out my breathing enough to fall back asleep. I don't awaken again until 7:00 AM; when the alarm buzzer reminds me of the fun-packed day I have ahead of me. By 8:00 AM, I am on the road, looking forward to the drive.

I arrive in Las Vegas around 2:00 PM and get checked into my room. The long drive has made me hot and sweaty, and I find myself longing for a nice, refreshing dip in the pool. It's my birthday today, and I am looking forward to celebrating it here, in star-studded Las Vegas. At thirty-four, I'm still peaking and really shouldn't feel old, yet I can't help but glance around the room, just to reassure myself. Yeah, okay, I can still hold my own.

It is gorgeous outside . . . hot, hot, hot, just like I like it. A dry hot, the kind of hot I can lay in for hours. Although the pool looks inviting, I head for the lounge chairs instead. I don't leave anything to chance, especially when Mother Nature is involved, so better get the rays while the getting is good. I spread tanning oil all over my body, periodically pausing to look up and absorb the activity in and around the pool. I notice lots of good looking, proud, tanned bodies eagerly stretched out on display for whoever chooses to notice. There are moms and dads enthusiastically playing games with their children in the water, tossing the smaller ones back and forth, chasing and dunking the older siblings. Squeals of delight surround me as I continue to watch.

I can't help but wonder if *he* is out there. He said he would be here, trying to frighten me with his sinister promises. I seriously doubt that he would put his life on hold just to come out to Las Vegas to play mind games with me. After getting over the initial fear, it has become fun wondering, watching, pretending. With a wicked smile, I settle back in my chair, beckoning to the sun to kiss and toast my body into a golden bronze, while delicious fantasies of mysterious, dark men fill my thoughts.

One hour goes by before I decide to flip over and work on tanning my backside. I am dozing on and off, continuously returning to a vivid state of erotic dreams. As if the sun wasn't hot enough! Finally, after another hour, I decide I've had enough. I jump in the pool as if on fire, trying to extinguish both the internal and external heat consuming my body. I float around playfully, relishing the cool water against my hot body.

The elevator is packed, and I feel uncomfortable squeezed up against all these strangers. The air in the elevator is suffocating, threatening. An eerie feeling washes over me, almost as if being alerted to impending danger. I try to shake off the sensation, praying the twelfth floor arrives quickly. In a panic, I exit the elevator and head for my room. The feeling immediately dissipates. Too much sun, I figure. What I need right now is a nice, relaxing bath and a little pampering. Perhaps even a little, afternoon nap.

I am awakened from my afternoon siesta by the rude ringing of the telephone. Now, who the heck could that be? Nobody knows I'm here. Must be the front desk. Sleepily, I look over at the clock, 6:30 PM. Oops, didn't mean to sleep that long.

"Hello."

Pause . . . my heart sinks to the bottom of my stomach. It's *him*.

"You looked incredibly hot in that black bikini this afternoon."

Oh, God . . . he's bluffing, right?

"How did you get my room number?"

"I watched you all day today. It was easy."

"You're lying. You're just trying to scare me."

"That's twice you doubted me. . . ."

Click . . . dial tone.

Okay, Randa, get ahold of yourself. You told him you were staying at the Luxor. All he had to do was call to find out your room number, and he knows you own a black bikini. After all, you sent him a picture of yourself wearing it. It was just a good guess. Yeah, that's all. Don't let him ruin your fun. Willing my breathing to return to normal, I head for the bathroom and take a quick, refreshing shower.

I am going to take extra pains with my appearance tonight, on the off chance that Wit truly is staying here. I want to give him an eyeful. Randa, Randa, Randa . . . your teasing is going to get you into trouble someday, I silently warn myself. Throwing caution to the wind, I dive through my suitcase until I find the dress I am seeking. It is a very sexy, very short, curve-hugging blue dress. I slip it over my head, and down my otherwise, naked body. Next I slip on a pair of cute, comfortable sandals and take one last look at my reflection. I am extremely pleased by what I see and descend to the casino on a cloud, prepared for a night of gambling and fun.

After about two hours of feeding the hungry little one-armed bandits, I feel quite content and satisfied. No need to push my luck. As it is, I am miraculously managing to stay even, if not slightly ahead, of the game. Feeling just a tad tipsy from all the wine I had consumed while sitting at the slot machines, I head off in the direction of sustenance. Not wanting anything too heavy, but needing some food to help counteract the alcohol, I opt for a turkey sandwich at one of the fast food counters randomly placed throughout the casino. It's not until the final bite that I notice the condition of my hands. I stare in distaste at my blackened fingers and palms, completely having forgotten what those silver coins were capable of. Great! I wonder what kind of despicable germs I've just invited into my body. With a grunt of disgust, I head off into the direction of the nearest restroom.

I find myself in a deserted section of the casino, having gotten completely lost and unsure of which direction to take. Finally I spot a restroom, way back in a corner, and head toward it. It is a small restroom, probably used mostly by employees, tucked away from the hustle and bustle of the main casino. I notice on my way in that there is an elevator right next to the door, making it convenient to take back to my room. I glance at my watch. Only 10:00 PM. Maybe I can catch a good movie on TV before I turn in for the night.

After washing my hands, using the restroom, then washing my hands again, I exit and walk over to the elevator. Ah, this is a different one. Most of the elevators that I had seen earlier only covered certain floors. One elevator covered floors one through five, the next elevator, floors six through ten, and so on. This one, however, went all the way from one to twenty-seven. Neat; I must have found the room service elevator or something. I press the up arrow and wait patiently for the elevator to arrive.

In less than a minute, the elevator dings at me, the arrow indicator light goes out, and the doors open, revealing a totally empty elevator. What a nice change from this afternoon's experience. As I step onto the elevator, I am forcefully pushed inside from behind, and a hand is held tightly against my mouth until the doors close behind. Taken totally by surprise, it takes me a second to register what has just happened. What the . . . ?

After the doors close, my assailant swings me around to face the closed doors, still standing behind me, one arm gripping me around the waist, the other still locked tightly onto my mouth. The hand around my waist reaches out and presses the light indicating floor twenty-seven, then forcibly returns to grab at my crotch through the fabric of my dress. I am paralyzed with fear, thinking that this is it, I'm going to be raped and murdered.

I start to flail and panic, when I hear the Voice, "Don't scream and don't move, my little slut." He removes his hand from my mouth and slides it down to rest across my throat in a warning grasp. Oh, God, it's him. I don't know if I should be thankful or more afraid, but at least I feel as if I have a chance now. His hands are alternating between caressing my throat, squeezing it just to the point where I can't breathe, then releasing it, to grip and squeeze my crotch, now ignited and responding to the adrenaline pumping through my veins.

"What are you going to do with me?" I manage to gasp. No longer frightened for my life, my senses begin responding to the manipulation of his knowing hands, sweeping over me with a swift onslaught of sexual desire.

"You like this, don't you? You've dreamed about this day for years, haven't you? Being taken by a stranger, having no control over what happens to you . . . You are at my mercy, Miranda, and you love it."

Unable to answer him, I just continue my ragged breathing as I slump against him and give in to the overwhelming stimuli he is creating in both my mind and body.

The elevator continues its slow ascent, passing my floor. My heart is pounding, from fright or anticipation? Right now, they are one and the same. "How wet are you right now, Miranda?" His hand releases its hold on my dress and slowly works the dress up to my waist, leaving my thighs, hips, and ass totally bare. He pulls me as close to him as possible, until I feel the rough fabric of his jeans brushing against my exposed ass, his erection quite evident. His hand returns, unhindered now by the fabric of the dress, and slowly teases the bud at the top of my pussy, before sliding a finger downward to rest at my opening. His finger is immediately drenched in wetness, and he moans, "Oh, yes. You do like this. Don't try to deny it. Your body betrays you. I've always told you that I own you, and now I can prove it." His finger then dips a little further, a little deeper, until it is surrounded by the silky wet heat of my pulsating, traitorous pussy. He wiggles his finger around and around, stretching my opening, then pushing back further, going deeper inside. His finger starts to fuck me now, hard and fast. I gasp and moan as I desperately clutch to the sides of his legs, needing something to brace myself against, fearing that I will collapse and fall into a quivering mass of liquid at his feet.

Ding. The elevator has reached the twenty-seventh floor. He quickly removes his finger as the elevator doors open, but intentionally leaves my dress up around my waist. Thankfully nobody is waiting to ride the elevator down. He takes my hands and holds them behind my back as he marches me forward and into the hallway. I hiss at him, "For God's sake, pull my dress back down! Somebody might see me!"

"I want people to see you like this, Miranda, to know that you're my whore."

"I'm not your whore, so stop this! Stop this right

now!'' I launch a full blown attack, kicking, squirming and twisting, trying to break free. He immobilizes me with one, quick, painful crank of my arms up my back, reducing me to a whimpering slave with no choice but to walk down the hall, bared for all to see.

In answer to my prayers, we don't encounter anybody on our excursion to his room. I'm pretty sure that he knew we most likely wouldn't, but wanted me to experience the embarrassment and anxiety regardless. Bastard! He pauses at his door momentarily to remove the key from his pocket, maintaining the excruciating hold on my arms the whole while. The door opens and he thrusts me inside, closing and locking the door behind us.

He forces me further into the room, until I am standing in the main living area, and I gape in horrified fascination at the sight that greets me. There, lying in the middle of the bed, is an incredibly beautiful blonde-haired woman, spread out wide and on display. She is tied to the bed so that her bottom is resting right at the foot of the bed, her legs are draped over the edge and spread wide, each of her legs tied to a different bedpost. Her arms are also each individually tied to the upper-most parts of the bed, stretched as far apart as possible. She is blindfolded, has a short, fat, penis-shaped dildo held securely in her mouth, but the most significant aspect, the attention grabber, is the very large and very black dildo protruding from the center of her open, splayed legs. The contrast between the inky blackness of the dildo and the milky-white creaminess of her soft flesh is utterly erotic and mind-boggling. The view is almost enough to make me faint.

I try to look away, but he keeps my head steady, forcing me to continue to watch, to soak it in, to forever implant this image into my brain. I am too stunned to speak. "Rachel was a very naughty girl today. She's been tied up like this for over an hour. Why don't you go give her some relief by removing her gag, Miranda?" For the first time since our encounter, I am completely free of his touch. I slowly shake out and massage my aching arms as I hesitantly wander over to the bed. The sight continues to mesmerize me. I reach around the back of her head, enjoying the soft, silkiness of her hair brushing against my hands, untie the gag, and remove it from her mouth. She starts to cough, gasp, and sputter as she tries to regain control over her mouth and return it to its normal size and shape. I can't help but notice how soft and enticing her lips are, and am alarmed at my reaction to this exquisite creature.

Finally able to speak again, Rachel utters, "Please . . . please remove . . . remove . . . it." I look over at Wit to see what his reaction to Rachel's request is going to be, when it hits me. This is the first time I've seen his face. Our eyes make contact, and I again am completely taken aback. I thought his words were powerful, I thought his voice was powerful, but nothing prepared me for the compelling power of his physical self. I knew from that moment on, my life would never again be the same. No wonder he was so damned arrogant. God, he just exudes confidence and power, raw . . . masculinity, the type that just plays upon the gullible female psyche. And his eyes, the overwhelming intensity of them is astounding.

He smiles a small, knowing smile and then nods his head toward Rachel. "Well, go ahead, Miranda. Remove it."

Finally finding my voice, I protest, "You can't be serious . . . I can't. . . . No, I can't. . . ."

"I'm only going to say this to you once. If you do not do exactly everything I say, when I say it, you will

---

find yourself in a situation similar to Rachel's right now. Understand?'' Oh, God . . . oh God . . . sorry Rachel. I walk around to the foot of the bed and stare uncertainly at her . . . at it. "You have to be very careful, Miranda, or you'll hurt her. You don't want to hurt her, do you?''

"No, no, of course not. What do I need to do?''

"Rachel, what does she need to do?''

I watch as Rachel writhes on the bed, rocking her head back in forth in an obvious mixture of dread and desire. Her hips start rotating, start to elevate off the bed, causing this thing inside her to move. She starts to grunt and groan, twisting, pushing, trying to expel the massive cock with her movements. "Please,'' she whispers, "please, go slow . . . start pulling, slowly . . . please.'' The urgency in her voice startles me into action, assuming her to be in the most horrible pain. Wit knows better. He knows how aroused Rachel is right at this second, how she loves to be stuffed with the most massive of props, the bigger the better. As soon as that dildo starts coming out, she is going to convulse and explode into a huge orgasm. He can't wait.

"It's okay, Rachel, it's okay. I'll get it out for you.'' Bracing one hand on her mound, I take my other hand and reach around the dildo. It is so big that my fingers can't close around it, and I keep thinking to myself, this poor thing, this poor, poor thing. Close to tears, I start to slowly back it out of her, trying to go in small circles, separating her skin from the latex. She starts screaming and bucking, and Wit has to run over to her and stifle her screams by placing his hand over her mouth.

"You animal,'' I yell over to him. "How could you?'' I desperately work on the dildo, pulling, rocking, rotating . . . coming, coming, almost there. . . . "I've almost got it Rachel, just another second or two.'' With a final, muffled scream, her body convulses and shakes for what seems like an eternity, finally falling limp and lifeless onto the bed. One final tug, and the offending appendage is completely removed and cast aside.

With the fury of a wild beast, I race over to Wit and start beating on him, hitting him, kicking him, screaming the whole while, "Look what you've done to her. You've killed her!"

"I didn't kill her, you silly girl. She just passed out. She does it all the time. You just gave her one of the best orgasms of her life." I stop and look at him confused, as if he has two heads, as it finally sinks in.

In another fit of rage, I resume my assault. "Of all the lowlifes! You're lower than the lowest pond scum. You . . . you . . . you absolute jerk! Do you know how scared I was?"

"Not as scared as you should be. Do you have any idea what you are doing? You're still at my mercy, and to be honest with you, I don't appreciate this juvenile outburst. Stop swinging at me this instant."

I stop immediately, the horror of what I've just done freezing me to the spot. "Oh, God, I'm so sorry. I didn't mean it. I was just so scared for Rachel, thinking that you hurt her. You can't blame me for that."

"I can blame you if I choose to blame you. Now follow me." He yanks me over to a spot in the middle of the room and finishes removing my dress. I had forgotten that it was still resting against my waist, while my ass remained brazenly displayed. "Take off your shoes." I immediately jump to do his bidding, trying very hard not to provoke any more anger, and kick them aside. I am standing completely naked and helpless before him.

He reaches for a pair of handcuffs and slaps them on my wrists. Attached to the center of them is a long chain, and he wastes no time in attaching it to a hook in the ceiling. My hands and arms are pulled upward, stretching way above my head and securely fastened. I am starting to feel that all-too-familiar feeling again. Fear mixed with anticipation . . . pure, depraved lust. Oh God, help me. How can I react this way? Why does my body respond this way? I have truly sunk to a new low.

Next, he reaches for another device, designed for keeping a pair of legs spread wide apart. It is a solid steel bar, about three feet in length, with handcufflike clamps at both ends. He attaches one of the clamps around one of my ankles, kicks my feet wide apart, and then affixes the other clamp to the other ankle. I am as obscenely displayed standing up as poor Rachel is, still a helpless captive on the bed.

My chest is rising and falling in rapid succession, revealing to *him* my hidden fear and burning desire. My lips are parted, my eyes half closed, resigning myself to the exquisite tortures that are certainly headed my way. He leaves momentarily, returning with a bowl of water, a washcloth, a razor and a can of shaving cream. My eyes widen in alarm, realizing his intentions. He sets his utensils aside and kneels before me, his face directly centered at the apex of my legs, and warns, "I'd stay very still if I were you. Wouldn't want any nasty nicks to mar that soft, beautiful flesh of yours." He picks up the can of shaving cream, shakes it, and dispenses the gel onto my pubic region, using his hand to mash and lather it into the delicate hairs that protect it. This intense scrutiny of my most intimate and sacred area is too much for me to bear, and I throw my head back in shame and humiliation, hoping to erase this total degradation. The next thing I feel is the cool, dangerous edge of the razor blade as it proceeds to eliminate any indication that my thirty-four year growth of womanly down ever existed.

With his task complete, he still lingers, touching and probing, admiring his handiwork. Oh, how much more can I endure? I am sure he hasn't even gotten started. He pulls and stretches my lips, amazed at how thick they are. He can't resist the urge to kiss them, and leans his head forward to place a wet, delicate peck at the center of my sex. I moan again, and begin to squirm. Inspired by my response, he settles in, prepared to initiate a full-blown offensive, and increases his intensity as he sucks, licks, and slurps fervently. He is merciless as he heightens my hunger, feeling me reaching, grasping for fulfillment. Just when he feels I am at my wit's end, mindless and writhing in ecstasy, he pulls away. "Oh, please, oh please, don't stop now. I need you to finish."

"If you want release, Miranda, you are going to have to get it from Rachel." No, no, no . . . the denial fading as my body's demand to be satisfied rises.

He releases me from my confines, unlatching the handcuffs and removing the ankle bar. He walks me over to where Rachel is still sprawled out on the bed. He loosens her bonds and rearranges her so that she is more centered on the oversized bed, then fastens her down tightly again. She has finally recovered consciousness, but quietly awaits her fate. Wit must have known her for a long time. He has her very much under control.

"I want you to shave her, Miranda, just like I did you. I want her void of any pubic hair and silky soft to the touch. You can use the same razor I used on you." I hear Rachel suck in her breath, but she says nothing. I go through the same motions that Wit had used on me, rubbing the gel onto her mound, waiting for it to lather, then slowly removing all the unwanted hair. It feels very strange to touch another woman so intimately, and I am embarrassed that I did so without any objections. *Well, it's not like you had any choice, Miranda*, I keep repeating to myself. When I am all done, I rinse and warm up the washcloth, giving her a final wipe, rubbing her clean.

Next he hands me a bottle of baby oil and tells me to pour some on her stomach and then massage it in. While I pour the oil on Rachel, Wit reaches up and removes her blindfold, revealing the most startlingly beautiful blue eyes I have ever seen. I watch her eyes flutter as I continue to rub the oil into her stomach using light, butterfly strokes. I can feel the muscles of her abdomen twitch and spasm with each tickling caress. Soft sighs escape her lips as she abandons herself to the sensations I am creating. Wit reaches out and stops me from continuing, and I glance up at him questioningly. His expression has changed, barely contained desire burning deep within his eyes. What Rachel and I are about to engage in has him worked up to the bursting point.

"Straddle her with your knees, and sit on her stomach. Then massage some oil onto her breasts." His breathing is becoming ragged now, his eyes glazing over. I straddle her as requested, slowly lowering myself until my pussy makes contact with the slick oil on her belly. Ohhhh . . . I rub myself back and forth, delighting in the sensations shooting through my ravaged and swollen clit. Mmmmmm, this is so sinfully delectable.

I slowly drip oil onto her breasts, one drop at a time, finally beginning to understand my role, and evolving into it. I am the dominant one. I am in control of this lovely woman. I have the power to provide her with the sweetest of tormented ecstasy. Wow, what a heady feeling. I've always thought I'd prefer the submissive role, but with a woman, with this woman, I am enjoying being in command. How perceptive of Wit to sense this hidden desire in me and force it to the surface. I look over to him and flash him a grateful smile. He winks and nods his head shrewdly.

I watch her torso jump as each deliberate drop invisibly scorches her aroused body. When satisfied that she is sufficiently covered, I toss the bottle aside and languidly knead the oil until it is absorbed into her skin. She flinches as I lightly graze the sides of her breasts. God, her skin is so soft. Is my skin this soft? I never realized. . . . My ministrations increase, becoming more ardent, more forceful, moving up onto her breasts to pull at her nipples. She arches her back and gasps aloud, panting replacing her earlier ragged breathing. She is in heavenly rapture, moaning and undulating as I continue my relentless torture.

Her lips are slightly parted and glistening with her obvious desire. Her face is so soft, so flawless, so beautiful, that I indulge myself and give in to my impulses, bending over to taste her soft, full lips. The nectar that I lure from her mouth is sweet and plentiful, and I lose myself in the task of completely robbing it from her body and absorbing it into my own. She kisses me in return, anxious for me to continue with my seductive possession of her hot and eager body. Wit, on the sidelines, is hardly able to contain himself. As we kiss, our breasts rub together, sending wave after wave of electrical current deep into the pits of our bellies.

As I leave the tenderness of her thoroughly explored and savored mouth, I lie flat against her body and slide down as I press fiery little kisses down her throat and over to her nipples. I alternately grip the enthusiastic buds between my teeth, gently scraping and pulling them out as far as they will stretch, holding them there until she gasps and begs for me to release them, then returning them back to their original size. Watching the mixture of pain and pleasure cross her ravishing features creates an even deeper level of gratification and arousal. *Oh great, now I discover that I'm a sadist as well. Will this never end?*

I continue my downward slide, pressing hot, sticky kisses down her ribcage, and further down to her freshly shaven sex. My legs drape over the edge of the bed as my knees touch the floor, my torso folded over the bed at my hips, making my ass and pussy quite accessible. I touched her earlier, while I shaved her, but I've never, ever gone down on a woman before. Can I do it now?

"Do it, Miranda." I hear Wit croak from behind me. "Taste her. Make her cum . . . make her cum again, this time with your mouth, with your tongue. Do it." He pushes my head down, back into her womanly sex, urging me to continue.

I tentatively snake my tongue out and glide across and around her outer lips. Mmmmm, not too bad. I think I can do this. My tongue continues its exploration, seeking, inquiring, questioning, pleased with all the discoveries and answers. I become more bold, now diving into creases and crevices, drinking and gulping at the juices flowing freely from her body, threatening to drown me. Rachel is bucking and thrusting, out of control, lost in the throes of wild abandon.

"Please, Miranda . . . please, finish me off. Suck on my clit, please. . . ." Not confident with my ability to satisfy a woman, I take her advice and move upward until I find the tiny, hidden jewel. I completely cover it in wetness, taking it into my mouth, sucking and pulling at it while encircling it with my tongue. She goes wild, madly panting. "Yes . . . yes . . . yes . . . oh yes . . . keep doing that . . . perfect . . . don't stop . . . suck harder . . . yes . . . yes . . . *Oh yes, Miranda!!!*" she screams as her body convulses a second time that day, wave after wave of intense pleasure crashing over her and catapulting her into a different dimension.

Wit is now desperate for a release of his own. So am I, still so hot, yearning, searching for my own, elusive sexual zenith. With a growl, he pushes me aside, releases Rachel's bonds, then reverses her position on the bed, so that her head is now at the foot of the bed, her feet toward the headboard. Again he fastens her tightly to the bed so that she is defenseless once more. "Rachel, I want you to eat Miranda now, lick and suck her into a furious climax while I position myself behind her and fuck her." Then he lowers me back onto her, this time with me sitting on her face, bracing my feet on the floor to keep from crushing her slender neck with my weight.

I feel her tongue and mouth begin to invade me, and my body becomes wracked with delicate little shivers. Just when I think the pleasure cannot get any greater, I feel the tip of a hard cock poised at my opening, seeking entry. In one smooth thrust, he is buried deep within me, sliding along my silken, lubricated sheath. He groans out loud, exhibiting his intense rapture, and begins to pump in and out of me with long, furious strokes. I can barely remain conscious, unable to cope with the double teaming of Rachel's tongue and Wit's cock. Mercifully, I peak quickly, the prolonged buildup throughout the day having kept me poised on the verge of a dam-bursting climax. I scream as an earthquake plows through my body, causing multiple, endless shudders, ripples, and convulsions to explode and erupt into neverending cascades of shooting stars, illuminating brightly, slowly fading, then finally dying out. Wit is right behind me, unable to resist the quivering and pulsing of my pussy as it grips and squeezes his cock, throwing him into his own paroxysm and bringing him to a state of exhausted, elated bliss.

We all fall back onto the bed, thoroughly spent. Wit finally releases Rachel from her prison. She remains on the bed and rubs at her arms in an attempt to regain the circulation. Had I been trussed up for that long, I would surely be making my voice heard. Who knows what kind of a relationship they have. Since Rachel did not appear to be in any obvious distress, maybe Wit knew exactly what he was doing. Maybe he knew her limits and brought her just to the very edge. Is that what his plans were for me? Did he intend to spend the next three days pushing me to my limits? Did I truly want him to accomplish that?

"Now what?" I ask apprehensively, already sickeningly aware of the answer. "Am I free to go now? Have you had your fun?"

"Are you going to lie there and tell me that you did not enjoy these last couple of hours, Miranda? Are you still in such denial?"

"Well, no. I did enjoy this experience, but I don't think I'd like to repeat it. It was too intense. A lifestyle like this would probably kill me. I don't know how you and Rachel can do it."

"Rachel does whatever I ask her to do, without question. Just as you will learn to do. I'm not through with you yet, Miranda. There is still so much of you left unexplored. I want to open you and release your inhibitions. I want you to realize the depth of your sexuality and embrace it. I won't stop until you cum at the sound of my voice, upon command. Watch this."

"Rachel, open yourself to me." Without hesitation, Rachel stretches out on the bed, mouth open wide, legs and arms spread wide apart, just as I had done when I spoke to Wit over the phone. "You're going to cum for me, Rachel, and I'm not even going to touch you, isn't that right?'' Rachel nods, her mouth remaining open as her body starts to respond to Wit's voice. Wit is straddling Rachel, on his hands and knees, towering above her. His hands are positioned by her sides, just under her outstretched arms. His knees are placed on the insides of her widespread thighs, making sure that I still have an unobstructed view. Her eyes are enslaved by his unrelenting gaze.

"Watch closely, Miranda. Watch how I manipulate her mind so that her body reacts as if I were truly touching her. . . . Rachel, my dick's in your mouth. I want you to suck it.'' Rachel shapes her mouth as if it truly did contain the desired appendage, and mimics the sucking motion of a blow job, not neglecting the occasional swirling motion of the tongue. I stare, amazed.

"I've got your nipples between my teeth, Rachel. I'm biting them, scraping my teeth against them as I pull them further and further out.'' She makes a strangled noise, as if in pain, and miraculously, her nipples start to tighten and extend outward. Entranced, I remain rooted to the spot, waiting for the next astounding display of mind over matter.

"Your pussy is getting so wet, Rachel. You want a nice, hard cock to slide inside you, don't you?'' Not losing a stroke on the imaginary cock in her mouth, Rachel nods the affirmative.

"Can you feel the gigantic, thick head of a dildo pressed at your opening, slowly stretching you open, wider and wider, slipping deeper and deeper into your hot, aching pussy?'' Rachel starts to whimper now, her hips rocking back and forth, trying to fuck the mythical cock. Her body is twitching and arching as if one hundred pair of hands were touching her everywhere.

"Fuck the dildo, Rachel. Fuck it hard. Feel it hit

against the inside wall of your pussy, as deep as it can.'' Rachel increases the speed at which her hips are rocking, her pussy lips flexing as if she were gripping tightly to a prized possession, not wanting to face the consequences should she let go.

"That cock in your mouth is getting ready to explode, Rachel. Are you ready, Rachel? Can you take it all? *Swallow! Now!*'' Amidst endless gurgling noises, Rachel's throat starts to contract as she chokes down immeasurable amounts of saliva, believing it to be Wit's cum, gulping and gulping until it has all been completely swallowed, except for one small drop poised at the corner of her mouth.

"That's a girl. You liked that, didn't you? Feel how your clit is just throbbing, Rachel? Feel it grow and swell with need? Oh, it is getting so hard, sticking straight up from between your lips. Can you feel how it yearns for attention, Rachel? Just one stroke of my tongue against it and you'd cum, wouldn't you?''

Rachel, still frothing at the mouth, shakes her head back and forth, softly whispering, "yes . . . yes . . . yes.''

"Can you feel my breath stroking your clit, Rachel, making it even harder? My lips are so close.'' Rachel's breathing has become very erratic, her body contorting, begging for release. "My tongue and lips are on your clit now, Rachel, all slippery and wet. It is all you can take. Cum for me now, Rachel. *Cum! Cum! Cum, Now!*'' Rachel releases a small yelp as her body convulses and spasms in orgasm, her ravaged body now experiencing its third climax in little over two hours.

Wit looks over at me, triumphant. "See what you have to look forward to, Miranda.''

"I don't want that, Wit. I want to leave. Let me go, now, please.''

133

"Nice try, but no can do. You will stay here until I say so."

"This is kidnapping, Wit. You have to let me go. You are holding me against my will."

"You don't even know what your will is, Miranda. You're staying until I'm convinced that you do."

"Rachel, take Miranda into the bathroom and shower. I want everyone cleaned up nice and fresh for round two." Bitterly, I allow Rachel to lead me away, my mind frantically searching for a way out of this mess.

Away from Wit's watchful eyes, Rachel transforms, changing from a mindless puppet into an assertive little Jezebel. "Now it's my turn, Miranda, and you had best yield to my every whim. Wit will be very angry if you displease me, and there's no telling what he's capable of when he's mad." Not foolish enough to dismiss her threat, I continue to play along, waiting patiently for my opportunity to escape. Sensing my acquiescence, Rachel smiles and turns the knobs on the shower, waiting for the optimum water temperature, before ushering me in. She follows, sliding the shower doors closed, the foreboding sound symbolic of the life I was inadvertently leaving behind, quite possibly unable ever to return.

"Stand still while I wash you." I comply as Rachel proceeds to thoroughly bathe my body, leaving no crack or crevice untouched. She creates a thick, soapy lather of bubbles between her palms, then starts to rub it over my shoulders, arms, breasts, toying momentarily with my nipples, taking special care to assure they are totally clean. The next onslaught is directed lower, my abdomen completely covered in soapy lather, while Rachel's fingers find my pussy and attempt to rid it of any evidence of sexual play. Her soapy fingers invade me . . . penetrating . . . washing . . . cleansing.

My eyes close, allowing myself to get lost in the abrupt stimulation. She surprises me by kissing me, sucking the breath from my mouth, suddenly becoming very aroused. She presses her body against mine, the soap working as a lubricant, causing us to slide against one another. She releases me just as unexpectedly as she had taken me, and rinses the finger that had been penetrating me, only to reinsert it, again and again until all indication of soap is removed.

Next, she soaps up her hands and wraps them around me, centering on my behind. She slowly massages my ass, until a thick lather is formed, and then cautiously places a soapy finger on the resistant opening. Her persistent finger prevails, and gains entrance into the forbidden tunnel, soaping and cleaning it with steady, tenacious strokes. I moan and sway on my feet, feeling violated, yet enjoying the intruder immensely. Satisfied that I am completely scrubbed clean, Rachel abandons her task, and reaches for the removable shower head. She looks at me wickedly and says, "Sit back on the ledge, Miranda, and spread 'em."

The shower is very large and spacious, consisting of a built-in bench to assist a woman with shaving her legs. Apprehensive, I sit back and brace myself as I tentatively spread my legs apart. Rachel reduces the water pressure and rotates the adjustable massage shower head to the pulsating action and turns toward me. She directs the intermittent stream of water straight at my clit, causing me to jump. Getting closer, she alters the direction of the spray, pulsating it against the opening of my pussy, finally finishing by teasing the entrance to my ass. By the time the shower has ended, I am squirming in sexual frustration, looking forward to another round of deviant copulation.

We walk back into the main room, the atmosphere

greatly altered. The lights have been lowered and scented candles are burning brightly from several different locations around the room, permeating the air with a heady, seductive aroma. The scent is unfamiliar to me, but probes my subconscious, invoking dark, sexual images. Already at the height of arousal, the candles prove almost too potent, immediately flooding my sex with moisture and heat.

Wit crooks his finger at me and beckons me to him. He is sitting on the bed and invites me to join him. Wanting nothing but to assuage the burning need within, I go to him, ready for whatever he has in store for me. "It's your turn to become hostage to the bed, Miranda. Lie down and try to relax while I fasten your bonds." I lie back, and within moments find myself as helplessly displayed as Rachel had been when I first saw her, unable to move more than an inch in any direction. My bottom is resting at the foot of the bed, my legs are bent over the edge and spread wide, each tied to a different corner. My head is resting in the center of the mattress with my arms spread wide and attached to the headboard by longer restraints. God I hope I can trust these people not to hurt me. I've really gotten myself into a fix now, escape seeming less and less likely as the minutes tick by.

"Rachel dear, would you please hand me a candle? I want to play a little game with Miranda."

"What are you going to do?" I whisper. Rachel hands Wit a long, slender, burning candle. "Don't hurt me, Wit. This isn't supposed to be about pain."

"Let me tell you what's going to happen, Miranda. I am going to slowly drip hot, melted wax all over your body. It may sting at first, but it will immediately subside when the wax makes contact with your skin and hardens. Some areas on your body will be more tender and sensitive, and the hot wax hitting those areas will cause greater discomfort for you. You may even consider it painful, but I assure you, none of it is unbearable."

"Please don't do this. It scares me. I just want to leave."

"Rachel, come kneel here on the floor between Miranda's legs. I'm going to need you for this little game." Rachel does as she is told, her breath inches from my pussy. "You don't get to leave, Miranda. I want to push you to your limits, showing you depths of ecstasy that you never knew existed. Now, continuing with the entertainment I had planned, each time a drop of the hot wax makes contact with your skin, Rachel will simultaneously lick at your clit. Drop . . . lick. Drop . . . lick. Soon, you'll find yourself looking forward to the sensation of the hot wax piercing your skin, knowing that Rachel's tongue is right behind it. You'll become so aroused, you'll be begging me to pour the wax all over your tortured body, and your mind will become confused, not being able to distinguish the difference between the pain and the pleasure. It will all become pleasure, and your body will always respond as such. Do you believe me, Miranda?" Speechless, I shake my head side to side in denial.

"Now, Rachel!" The first drop takes me by surprise, landing in the middle of my abdomen. I gasp at the intense stinging as well as the feel of Rachel's warm, wet tongue lapping at me. My eyes are huge now, watching Wit, carefully observing my reactions to the contradicting sensations being inflicted upon my body. I follow the path of the candle. He is holding it at an angle about a foot above my body, moving it in all directions, causing me to wonder where the next drop will fall, the anticipation even more painful than the hot wax.

"Now!" Another drop scorches me on my hip, while Rachel pulls through on her end, giving me another agonizing lick. "Now!" This time, the drop falling just below my right breast, followed faithfully by another lick by Rachel. "Again!" A hot, agonizing drop descending to land on my inner thigh, the pain causing me to cry out and arch, quickly soothed by the sensation of a wet, slithering tongue. Oh God, the drops are getting more frequent and more intense, and combined with Rachel's teasing, I am being driven mad.

I find myself looking forward to the next drop, wanting it to arrive as quickly as possible, diminishing the time Rachel's tongue is taken away from my throbbing clit. He was so right, so right, making me hate him all the more for it. "One more time, Rachel!" Another scalding drop lands directly on my erect nipple, sheathing it in wax, causing another cry of pain to be torn from my lips.

Wit pulls the candle away and looks at my face, shrouded in tormented uncertainty. "Beg me to continue, Miranda. You want me to, don't you? You love the way it feels when it hits your skin, knowing that Rachel will be right there. Your body is begging me, Miranda, if you could only see how it squirms. Now, beg me."

"Oh, God. Don't make me do this, please."

"Beg me, Miranda. The longer you take, the more begging I'll require from you." Knowing that I have no choice, I again surrender to him.

"Ok, please continue, please."

"Continue what, Miranda? What do you want me to continue?" He is smiling now, quite pleased with himself, knowing how hard it is for me to verbalize, to ask, to beg.

"Please continue dripping hot wax onto my body. Please continue to let Rachel help. Please, I'm begging you."

"How do you want Rachel to help? Say it, Miranda."

"I want her to lick me when the wax hits my body."

"Where do you want her to lick you, Miranda, where?"

"Please stop . . . this. I want . . . I want her to lick me on my clit. Please, Wit, I'm in agony. Please continue. Don't make me beg anymore."

Satisfied, Wit tilts the candle once again and tells Rachel to continue licking and sucking at my clit, and not to stop before he tells her to. I feel Rachel's mouth descend and latch on its target, just as a shower of hot droplets floods my skin, burning everywhere. He is merciless as he keeps the continuous flow of melted wax coming, while Rachel attacks my clit and pussy with renewed vigor and passion. My body, dazed by the mixed signals, doesn't know if it should shrink back in pain, or succumb to the erotic delights, now unsure which is which. Unable to hold back any longer, contractions start to ripple through my body, causing me to buck and arch up on the bed, screaming out as the intensity of the orgasm peaks. I have no control over the spasms possessing my body, and hopelessly ride them out until they have subsided, leaving me gasping for air. The intensity is so overwhelming, that tears unwittingly spring to my eyes and slide down my face.

Wit bends over and kisses away my tears. "I know how hard it can be to let yourself go, Miranda." I resist the urge to spit in his face, and angrily look away. "Ah, I see a little fire back in those eyes. Good. Now we can move on."

"Move on?" I ask, incredulous. "It must be three in the morning! Don't you ever rest? Don't you ever sleep? I can't keep up this pace!"

He laughs and says, "Don't worry. I'll give you a little break. I'm going to go downstairs to the bar, have a couple of drinks and try and make some new friends. If you're very lucky, these new friends will want to come up here and meet you. Won't that be fun? Until then, I'll leave you in the capable hands of Rachel, who'll try to remove the dried wax from your body as painlessly as possible." After whispering a few instructions to a pouting Rachel, Wit leaves the room, closing the door ominously behind him.

Rachel begins to gently remove the hardened wax. I involuntarily suck in my breath each time a piece is removed. The wax has hardened and become entangled with the tiny, delicate hairs lightly covering my torso, making it impossible to remove without pulling out the hairs as well. I take this opportunity to try and convince Rachel to let me go, she being my only chance at freedom.

"You know what he's doing, don't you?"

"What do you mean?" she asks, confused.

"He's trying to replace you . . . with me."

"You're crazy. I mean everything to him." The next piece of wax is removed with a little less finesse. Ouch.

"How long have you two known each other, Rachel?"

"Six years, why?"

"Well, it's obvious that he is growing bored. He is going to spend the next three days trying to create another playmate, his attention focused on you less and less. I can see it in his eyes."

"Nice try, Miranda, but I'm not going to let you go. He'd kill me if I did."

"What do you suppose he is going to do with me

after exerting endless amounts of energy trying to enslave me, let me go?''

"Of course he is going to let you go. He can't take you back with us."

"Why can't he, Rachel?"

"Because you have your own life to get back to and we have ours. He can't just displace you. There's no permanent place for you with us. He's just having a little fun right now."

"What if I don't want to go back to my old life? What if he succeeds, and I become dependent on him, begging him to take me with him when he leaves? He'll take me, Rachel, and do you want to know why?"

"Why?"

"Because he created me. I will be his work of art. Have you ever known of an artist who spent hours painting a portrait, or a sculptor who carved out a masterpiece, only to leave it behind? His ego won't allow him to leave me, Rachel. He'll take me with him, and I'll be a challenge, much more exciting than his six-year-old slave."

"Do you really think so, Miranda? I'd die without him." Feeling a little ashamed for the pathetically frightened look marring Rachel's beautiful features, but knowing I have to continue, I nod in agreement. "Oh yes, yes I do, Rachel. Why do you think he is so determined right now? He has only three days to completely enslave me. He is going to give his every, conscious thought to making me his. He won't have the time or energy for you anymore. It'll be very sad to watch. It is obvious how much you care for him. Either way you're going to lose him."

"Either way?"

"Yes, either way, whether he takes me with him or lets me go, you'll lose him."

141

"Why will I lose him if he lets you go?"

"Because, Rachel, you are both holding me against my will. As soon as I'm free, I'll have you both arrested for kidnapping and numerous sexual assault charges. This is not a game to me. It is not what I want. If you let me go, right now, I promise not to notify the police."

I hold my breath as I watch a mixture of emotions cross her face, ending with her lips pressed stubbornly together, and her chin thrust out. "Okay, Miranda. I can't risk losing him to you, and I certainly don't want either of us ending up in jail. If I let you go, will you promise to never make contact with him again, not even on the computer?"

"Oh, Rachel, I won't, I promise! You're making the right decision, trust me. We'll both be much happier if you let me go. Please hurry. We don't have much time before he gets back!"

"He's going to punish me for this, you know."

"No he won't. Tell him that I threatened you with the police, and that you were very afraid he would end up spending the rest of his life in jail. Cry while you are saying it to make it more convincing. He won't be able to stay angry at you knowing that you did it to protect him."

"That just might work; besides, it's always fun when he gets a *little* upset with me. I like that kind of punishment. Okay, Miranda, you're free to go."

I scramble into my clothes, saying a quick goodbye as I bolt from the room, not leaving any opportunity for second thoughts. It's only been about twenty minutes since Wit went to the bar, so I have some time to run to my room, get my things and get as far from Las Vegas as possible.

The trip to my room is a very unsettling one, with constant glances over my shoulder to assure that I'm not being followed. For all I know, Wit knew I was going to ask Rachel to help me flee, and this is just another one of his games. He probably told her to let me go, and then he and his new "friends" were going to be ready to pounce on me as I opened the door to my room. I can see the gleam in his eyes as he thwarts my attempted escape, and then watches as I am repeatedly punished by his new partners in crime. The penalty for my indiscretion would, most likely, be severe, probably being passed back and forth between a variety of men, and possibly women, to use as they please.

Just the thought of what might happen, is making me quite nauseous, and I find myself hesitating at my hotel door. I try looking in the peephole, but all that greets me is complete blackness. Not willing to allow my imagination to get the best of me, I defiantly place the key in the lock and open the door. The room is as empty as I had left it and, in justified haste, I gather up my belongings and head for the hotel lobby. I make my exit as stealthily as possible. I don't feel totally safe until I am in my car and headed southwest, leaving the lights of "The City that Never Sleeps" far, far behind me.

CHAPTER 6

※

THE ENTITY

Well, that was close; too close, as a matter of fact. Thank goodness I was able to play upon Rachel's insecurities, presumably my only chance to get away from Wit. Granted, I enjoyed everything he had introduced me to, but I suspect that was about to end. The thought of being gang-banged didn't appeal to me at all, not even to the darkest side of me. Actually, right now, nothing could be more inviting than a soft, comfy, safe place to sleep. I am so tired, so very, very tired, and the prospect of that cozy, warm bed seemed further and further away, with nothing but miles of endless desert stretching before me.

The adrenaline that has kept me going is finally beginning to dissipate. Trying to keep my eyes open is proving very difficult. Continuing on in spite of the countless times my head has bobbed toward the wheel, I fight the urge to stop. I should just pull over and catch a few hours of sleep before I continue on home, but what if *he* decided to pursue me on this desolate, desert road? I can't risk him catching up with me and becoming his love slave once again, I just can't. I have to keep going.

Well, if nothing else, I sure did learn a valuable lesson from all of this. I had best be very careful if I am going to arrange meetings with any more of my online friends. I was pretty lucky that BigMan turned out to be such a trustworthy guy, even though I had taken steps to protect myself with that liaison. I hadn't actually planned the meeting with Wit, but I did open myself up for trouble when I told him of my plans. I never expected him to try and find me. Never again, I vow, as my head makes another sleepy nod toward the dash.

Popping my head back up, my eyes focus on what appears to be . . . no, it can't be . . . a bear, standing in the middle of the road, hypnotized by my headlights. I slam on my brakes and swerve. The car veers to the right, miraculously missing the animal, plowing through the shoulder of the roadway, into the thistly, rocky ground of the desert. The car somehow manages to come to a stop, my forehead thrust into the steering wheel by the momentum. With one last conscious glance, I see the bear . . . no, it's a man, approaching then, mercifully, complete blackness.

The last thing I remember is being carried from my car by a pair of strong arms. I struggle, my confused mind believing that I had, once again, been discovered by Wit. The voice that soothes me, however, is not his, but a more comforting one, enveloping me in a sense of total safety and protection. Unable to remain awake any longer, I yield and collapse against this blessed stranger, convinced that I'll be unharmed in his mystical presence.

When I wake, the sun is shining brightly through the window of a strange cabin. Even in my groggy state, I can tell that it must be well past noon. I look around. The unusual room is primarily Indian in nature. There are animal hides adorning the walls and floors, not to mention the ones keeping me warm on the rustic bed that I've been sleeping in. Many different animal skulls, all decoratively painted, are placed throughout the room. All in all, it is quite masculine, yet very tranquil and calming.

The sound of someone entering the room directs my attention to the impressive presence completely filling the doorframe. His features are stony and chiseled, not unkind, very much Indian. Long, shining dark hair flows freely down the middle of his back. He wears a vest made of some type of animal hide, leaving his bulging arms bare and visible. His tight blue jeans flatter his long, muscular legs.

He's carrying a cup of steaming liquid and holds it up toward me. "Welcome back," he smiles, revealing a beautiful set of teeth, "I trust you slept well." Uncertain, I slink lower into the bed, seeking the cover and protection offered by the animal skins.

"I think so. Who are you, and where am I?"

"My name is Garen, and this is my little home away from home. You hit your head when you drove off the road, and since we are miles away from any hospital, I thought you could recover here. Would you like something to drink?"

"Ah, yes, thank you. By the way, my name is Miranda. Thanks for helping me."

"You're welcome, you had quite the late night last night."

At the mention of last night, all my previous anxieties come flooding back to suffocate me. As I start to hyperventilate, Garen sits on the bed besides me, sets the cup of tea aside on the end table, and strokes my hair and face, whispering soothing words of comfort. "It's okay. You're safe. Nobody is going to hurt you.

Shhhhhh, It's okay." He cradles me in his arms rocking me back and forth.

"What are you running from, Miranda?"

"Running from? I'm . . . I'm not running. What makes you think I'm running from anything?"

"Miranda, I ask again, what are you running from? I can't help you if you won't let me." As he speaks, his one hand starts to lower its path, moving down my face to rest on my neck. His fingers are light and teasing, resting on my throat, feeling my pulse, feeling it quicken. Oh, God. . . . "You have a haphazardly packed suitcase with you, a small travel bag, and you were driving to nowhere in the middle of the night. You are running from something, Miranda.

"Besides," his hand slips lower now, to my chest, caressing just above my bare breasts. *Oh, God . . . how long have I been sitting like this? When did the covers slip away to rest in a heap at my waist?* "How many women travel . . ." his hand going even lower now, slicing between my breasts, "covered in . . . wax?" As he says the word, he rips a dried piece of wax off of my torso and holds it up in front of my face, daring me to dispute it. The spell he was weaving is suddenly broken and I push him away.

"Just go away, will you? Leave me alone. I'm running from myself, okay? I'm running from myself. . . ." With that admission, I begin to cry, deep, heartfelt sobs, all the uncertainty and anxiety I've been burdened with over the previous months rising to the surface. Long, sorrowful, cleansing tears of hopelessness and despair flow freely. I recover from my embarrassing display with the knowledge that any obstacles clouding my judgement have also been washed away, leaving me more alive and receptive.

"I'm sorry. I don't know why I did that."

147

"Hey, don't worry about it. I bet you feel better now, though, don't you?" He looks over at me with a boyish, expectant grin, and I can't help but to be taken in by his charm.

"Yes, I do feel better, but what I really need is a shower. Do you happen to have one handy?"

"Right through that door. Your suitcase and travel bag are already in there. You should have everything you need."

"Okay, thank you." As Garen leaves the room, I shake my head, wondering what new adventure I've gotten myself tangled up with.

I spend an extraordinary amount of time in the shower trying to rid myself of memories and caked-on wax. The wax is removed with a little effort; the memories remain to haunt me. Putting it all in perspective, I decide that last night wasn't so terribly bad. Everything that happened was enjoyable. Never once did Wit or Rachel hurt me. Why was I now trying to erase the entire experience? Do I feel shame for enjoying it? No, I think it is all based on what might have happened had I not gotten away. Even then, I can't be certain that I wouldn't have enjoyed it. So, now that I have experimented with all these taboo curiosities, why don't I feel any more satisfied and at peace? Why is the restlessness still lurking? What have I still left to uncover? Those questions went unanswered as I step from the shower and reach for a large, fluffy towel.

With only comfort in mind, I select a loose fitting pair of sweat shorts and a baggy crop top made from the same material to lounge around in. I spend a little more time on my face and hair, trying to make myself look a little better than I feel, and then wander off in search of Garen. I try to ignore the insistent rumbling noises in my stomach. How long has it been since I've eaten? I find him in the kitchen, apparently in tune with my hunger, pulling sandwich fixings from the refriger-ator. "You look all nice and refreshed. How about a sandwich to top it off with? You must be starving."

"Thank you. I'm famished!" I pile my bread high with generous helpings of sliced turkey, ham, Swiss cheese, lettuce, and tomatoes, and sit back at the kitchen table to wait for Garen to join me. We eat our respective sandwiches in silence, each lost in our own thoughts.

After lunch, Garen announces that he has something he'd like to show me. I follow him to his living room, a nice, open area with lots of windows and happy, healthy plants blooming everywhere. In the middle of the open area are a couple of propped open easels, with paintings and sketches strewn casually about. "I want you to see my paintings, Miranda. I feel that you will appreciate them."

His paintings portray nature and animals coexisting and mingling with humans, seeming to capture both the human and animal spirit in each and every one of them. "Garen, these are spectacular, breathtaking. Do you sell your art?"

"No, I paint for myself, purely to feed my soul. It is a creative outlet for me, a way to express myself and my beliefs. Maybe someday I'll share them with the world, but for now, I paint only for myself."

"Wow. I feel emotions when I look at them, like I'm a part of the painting myself. I feel what the birds feel, I feel what the wind feels, I feel what the humans feel. It's spooky, Garen. How am I able to feel those things?"

"Miranda, you have an open mind, an open heart. You can feel the passion I felt as I painted them. They are as alive to you as they are to me. It's not as strange as you'd think. Nature is all around us. Everything is alive. Everything has a spirit. We just have to stop and listen to recognize it.''

Why is my body suddenly trembling? Why is my skin instantly alive with sensation?

"I have one more to show you, Miranda.''

"Please, Garen, I'd love to see it.''

He unveils what must certainly be his masterpiece. I gasp and am held spellbound as I gaze at the obscure, mystical mating ritual displayed on the canvas before me. I study it, understand it, become part of it. It is a painting of a bear . . . or is it a man, or is it of a bear with a man's face? It appears to keep shifting, never staying the same, bear, man, bear, man . . . bear and man. In his grasp is his mate, a feline . . . no a woman, again the image appearing to shift and change. One moment I am seeing a powerful lynx, baring her teeth in displeasure, while the next, I am seeing a beautiful woman, head thrown back in absolute ecstasy. Lynx, woman, lynx, woman . . . lynx and woman. The bear/ man is behind the lynx/woman, having mounted her from behind, animal upon animal, and the longer I stare, the more I feel. The shapes continue to shift and move, making every animal thrust tangible. I can feel it. *I* have become the lynx, Garen, the bear.

I look over at Garen, unable to move. He is shaking, having broken out into a sweat watching the effect his painting is having on me. Breaking the final shred of resistance, he growls and charges at me, knocking me to the floor, knocking the wind out of me. He rips at my clothing, shredding it all to pieces, as if he had claws, and I try to fight back, kicking and scratching only to realize that my own hands have taken the shape of feline paws, claws extended. Oh God . . . oh God, I start to flail in my panic, only to be subdued by Garen's warning bite to my neck. I feel his teeth, poised and ready for the kill should I move as much as an inch. I feel his breath, coming in ferocious ragged gasps. Sensing my surrender, he releases his hold on my neck, and I catch a quick glimpse of his face as he flips me over, forcing me to lie on my stomach. The face that greets me is not that of Garen's, but that of a bear's, and I screech out in terror as he mounts me from behind. In one swift thrust, I am impaled, the shock of the aggressive mating paralyzing me, as the bear lets out an enormous growl, drowning out the snarls and hisses of the overpowered lynx.

Instinctually, I raise up to my hands and knees, allowing him easier access and deeper penetration. Garen has awakened my primitive need, meeting and matching frenzied thrust for frenzied thrust. Over and over we lunge, back and forth, like the wild animals we appear to be. Unable to take the raw, sexual combat any longer, Garen parries one final thrust and then allows himself to be consumed by the fire, yelling out his rapture for all to hear, as he convulses and collapses behind me.

He falls down beside me and pulls me to lay on top of him. He is Garen again, thank goodness. He begins to kiss me deeply, drawing from me my secrets, my soul. "Now, sweet Miranda, it is your time to soar." With that, he picks up my hips and sets me down on his still-rigid staff, inserting it deeply, as he allows my own weight to carry me.

This time, he is unhurried. He bends me so that I am laying flat against him, feeling him buried deep inside, as he starts to slowly move and grind against me, creating a friction against my clit to coincide with his slow, torturous plunges. He continues to kiss me, never letting my lips free, keeping them captive the entire time he sways with my body. The longer he kisses me, the more of me he seems to enter, meshing completely with both my body and soul. The effect is toe-curling, as shards of electricity run up and down my legs, to the pit of my belly, to pierce my nipples and to finally weave their way deep into my spiritual being. The sensations overwhelm, bringing tears to my eyes. I try to pull away. He holds me fast, not allowing me to break the current, the voltage continuing to flow through me, picking up speed with each passing cycle. "Let yourself go, Miranda." I hear his voice echo inside my head. "Don't fight it. Let yourself go and soar." Releasing a final sob into his mouth, I relax against him, allowing the current to take me, no longer resisting. The dam breaks, releasing a flood of emotions and feelings joining with a shuddering, convulsing body swirling its way to ecstasy. All at once, the body is satiated and releases, while the mind and soul soar, reaching for, and attaining, the ultimate contentment. I drift off into slumber, now aware of which path my future must take.

"Ma'am, ma'am. Are you all right?" The urgency in the voice and the persistent knocking finally penetrate my subconscious, startling me into reality and into the face of the law. Shaking myself awake, I roll down the car window to speak with the concerned state trooper.

"I'm fine, officer, I must have fallen asleep. I'll be on my way shortly."

"Okay, just checking to make sure you were all right. Drive safely, now."

"Okay, thanks."

Whew, what the heck just happened? Why am I back in my car? Where is Garen? Oh, God, was there ever a Garen? Oh, please don't tell me that it was all a dream! It was too real... and too... too exquisite to be a dream. Damn. I look down and notice that I am still wearing the dress I had on the previous night, and sure enough, my torso is still decorated with colorful wax pieces. I drive off in dismay, wondering if those could possibly be animal scratches on my backside?

CHAPTER 7

∎

THE FRIEND

The trip home is, blessedly, an uneventful one. Taz, as always, is very happy to see me, reacting as if I'd been gone a month rather than a day. After feeding him a special treat, and suffocating him with hugs and kisses, I look around my tiny apartment, again restless. Even though I am comforted being back in the safety of my own little home, I really don't want to be alone right now. Realizing that the solace of the computer will not be enough tonight, I risk calling Angela, understanding of course, that she'll be curious about my abrupt return.

After a quick shower, this time making sure all signs of the wax are removed, I change into a breezy, summer dress and drive off in the direction of companionship and security. The drive to Angela's home is a peaceful one, winding down isolated roads in the middle of nowhere, yet only minutes from the hustle and bustle of the city. I didn't even know this area of town existed, secretly tucked away and hidden amongst lush vegetation. The homes out here each have a generous yard and plenty of privacy. Now I know where Angela spends all the money she makes. Living out here must cost her a fortune.

Her domicile is backed up against the end of a cul de sac, and completely surrounded by palm trees. It is a gorgeous house, and I find myself anxious to get a peek inside. I can't believe she was keeping this little secret from me.

Angela greets me with an enthusiastic, "Hi," and a nice, warm hug, and ushers me inside. She is dressed in a colorful silk kimono, flawlessly accenting her stunning red hair and creamy complexion.

"A 'humble abode,' huh?"

She blushes and says, "Well, I don't like to brag. . . . Would you like the grand tour before we eat?"

"Would I? Just try and stop me!" After removing my shoes in the foyer, I follow after Angela, marveling at everything from the plush cream-colored carpeting to the beige leather sofas and chairs, to the marble and black bathrooms, ending finally with exquisitely provocative paintings and statues. Her three-bedroom, fairy tale home has me green with envy, being everything I have always wanted and more.

I jibe, "What . . . no weight room?" She laughs, "Well, actually, the weight room is accessed off the back porch, next to the steam room." Flabbergasted, I follow her again, as she leads me outside onto a screened-in porch and down to the weight and steam rooms. The weight room is awesome, filled with one of everything from a treadmill to free-standing weights. She even has a VCR and a large-screen TV for her workout video tapes. Two of the four walls are covered in mirrors, a ballet barre running the entire length of one of the mirrored walls.

"No wonder you stay in such awesome shape," is all I can manage to mumble after this last discovery.

The steam room is located adjacent to the weight room and is fairly small, seating a maximum of six people. The therapeutic aroma of eucalyptus is still lingering about, penetrating my senses. "Any more surprises, Angela? Perhaps a jacuzzi tucked away somewhere?" With a mischievous twinkle, she saunters over to a panel of switches on the porch and begins to flip them on, one at a time.

I watch in amazement as her backyard begins to light up, one section at a time, all visible from the back porch. The first sight to appear is, indeed, a cozy little jacuzzi situated on the concrete deck just beyond the porch. Next appears a spectacular built-in swimming pool, complete with a diving board and a small slide. There are also lights which illuminate the interiors of both the jacuzzi and the swimming pool, leaving the deck itself shrouded in darkness. The rest of the lights beyond the concrete deck reveal lush, green grass and an assortment of exotic flowers encircling a dozen palm trees strategically planted along the interior of an eight-foot-tall privacy fence.

"My God, Angela! How do you maintain all of this? Do you do it all yourself?"

"Oh, my, no! Are you kidding? I have a landscaper who comes over once a week to attend to the yard and pool. He's awesome and maintains it all effortlessly. He's even shown me a few things I can do myself to keep things in tiptop shape between visits. It doesn't take any time at all, especially since I'm usually the only one that ever uses it. I don't have people over very often. I enjoy my privacy and time to myself."

"Don't you ever get lonely, Angela, living in this big house all by yourself?"

"Not really. If I start to feel a little lonesome, I just go out and find a good time, but usually I am fine."

"I didn't intrude, tonight, did I?"

"No, *I* invited *you* over, remember? It'll be fun. Let me go get dinner. We can eat it out here on the porch and enjoy the warm breeze as we talk. Sound good?"

"Sounds heavenly. Do you need any help?"

"Nope, I'll be right back."

Making myself comfortable, I select a chair at the patio table and face it so that it looks out over her yard. Angela had turned most of the lights back off again, leaving only the jacuzzi and pool interior lights on, giving her backyard a warm, seductive glow. Boy, I'd love to live here. What an awesome place to be able to call your own. Angela's first trip back out to the porch consisted of carrying an ice bucket with a bottle of wine protruding from it, and two wine glasses. After filling both glasses and returning the bottle to its bed of ice, Angela disappears again. Sneaking a sip, I savor the taste as I wait.

Finally Angela returns, carrying a tray laden with an array of mouth-watering delicacies. "Hope you like chicken Caesar salad," she says, as she sets an incredible-looking salad in front of me.

"I love chicken Caesar salad, Angela, but this is almost too pretty to eat. You've outdone yourself. Thank you."

"Anything for a friend, Randi." She also places a large fruit platter in the center of the table, complemented by a delicious yogurt/cream cheese, vanilla flavored fruit dip.

As we begin to eat, Angela blurts out, "Ok, Randi. Let's have it. What happened in Vegas that made you cut your trip short?"

For the next hour, I proceed to tell her everything, starting with my obsession with the computer and separating from my husband, to ending with my mystical encounter with Garen. She is pretty quiet throughout my entire confession, interjecting a compassionate response when she thinks it appropriate, but mostly remaining very thoughtful as she digests both her salad and my story. The wine disappears very quickly, and we are already halfway through our second bottle by the time dinner is over.

"Well . . . that's some revelation, Randi. You should keep a journal! Things like that don't happen every day, you know, let alone all in the same month."

"Pretty amazing, isn't it?"

"I'd say, most people don't get that kind of excitement in an entire lifetime. I'm really glad that you're okay, though. Something really horrible could have happened to you."

"Yeah, I know, but at least now, I think it's over. I felt something open inside me, an awakening, if you will, while I slept on the side of the road just outside of Vegas. When I dreamed of my encounter with Garen, and he entered me as a bear, I felt an awareness, as if he were unlocking my subconscious. It was all very weird, but I know now that I've been going about this all the wrong way. The answers are in my computer, not in my encounters, and I'm determined to find them as soon as possible so that I can get my life back."

"Don't worry, Randi. You'll find them. I'll miss you when you do, though."

"Thanks, Angela, but I don't intend to lose touch, regardless of the outcome, promise."

"Want to go for a dip?" she asks, nodding in the direction of the intimately lit swimming pool.

"Wish I could, but I didn't bring a suit with me. You didn't tell me you had a pool."

Grinning devilishly, Angela stands up from the table and unties her kimono, dropping it to the floor. "Who needs a suit?'' She makes her way out the porch door, across the concrete patio and to the diving board, bare-assed naked. She calls for me to join her, then dives gracefully into the pool. ''When in Rome. . . .'' I whisper to myself, as I hurriedly shed my clothing and dive in after her.

''I haven't been skinny dipping for years, Angela. This is great!'' Slicing through the water, feeling it caress my bare skin, gives me a sense of freedom. I am secure; nobody could possibly witness our naked play. We alternate between sliding down the slide, diving off the board and jumping in from the sides, pounding each other with the spray from a dozen cannonballs. It feels marvelous to leave the stress and responsibilities of adulthood behind as we cavort around the pool, acting like carefree little children.

Afterward, we float peacefully on our backs, gazing up at the moon, exchanging mundane chitchat. I float myself over to a corner in the deep end of the pool, next to the diving board, and prop my elbows up along the edge. Angela swims over to me, trapping me in the corner and faces me, her hands placed on either sides of my elbows, trying to keep herself from sinking as well. Her green eyes bore into mine and she suddenly becomes very serious. ''So, Randi, I'm curious, curious about Rachel. Tell me more about what happened between the two of you.''

Oh, oh. The heat in Angela's gaze mixed with the wine is overpowering, the sexual tension between the two of us flooding back with a vengeance.

''Well, I pretty much told you everything, Angela,'' I gasp. ''What else did you want to know?''

Positioning herself even closer to me, our bodies almost touching, she looks me directly in the eyes and says, ''I want to know if you liked it, Randi. Did you enjoy touching another woman? Did you like having another woman touch you?''

Defenseless against my attraction to Angela, and powerless to stop her determined seduction, I utter a pleading, "Angela. . . ." unsure if I truly want to cross this line with her.

"Yes, Randi?" she whispers seductively, her breath close enough to caress my face, the sweet smell of strawberries and wine still lingering on her lips. Panicking, feeling the passion and desire building inside, I try to move away, sliding along the side of the pool, but Angela stops me by pressing the full weight of her bare body against mine, until I'm completely flattened back up against the corner of the pool. The silkiness of her body combined with the velvety caresses of the lapping water prove too exquisite to deny, and I relax against Angela as she continues to wreak havoc upon my senses.

"Randi, you never answered me. Did you like it?"

"Yes, Angela, I liked it," I whisper breathlessly.

"Have you ever thought about touching me, Randi?" Captivated by her eyes, I can only nod in response, my eyes beginning to mist and cloud over with emotion. Smiling, she whispers, "I've wanted you since the first time I saw you, Randi, watching me dance as you stood still with your tray of cocktails, oblivious to everything around you but my dancing."

"You're the reason I wanted to dance, Angela. You were so free, so alive . . . so beautiful."

"Were Rachel's lips as soft as mine?" she asks, as she leans her head toward mine and bestows a delicately erotic kiss.

"Oh, God, no, Angela. Not even close." Still gazing directly into my eyes, she takes one of my hands and places it on her breast. "Was Rachel's skin as smooth as mine?"

"Angela," I whimper. "Please. . . ."

Taking her hand and running it alongside my breast to come back around and cup it fully, flicking her thumb back and forth across my nipple, she asks, "Was Rachel's touch as enflaming as mine, Randi?"

"No, no, no . . . for God's sake, Angela. . . ."

Taking my arms one by one, she detaches me from my perch against the pool's edge and carries me across until our feet can finally touch bottom. Then she guides me over to the steps where we sit and begin to kiss in earnest. Our hands touch one another everywhere, exploring, teasing, enticing. Wanting to be in control, Angela takes my hands and holds them up to grasp at the pool entry railing. "Keep your hands on the railing, Randi."

I arch up as Angela's fingers find my swollen clit. Her fingers rub around in circles, not letting up for a moment. Her arm cradles me, keeping my back from rubbing against the concrete steps of the pool. She is positioned slightly to my side, one leg thrown across my legs while her soft pussy is pressed into the edge of my thigh. Her hips are rocking back and forth, causing friction on her own clit as her pussy rubs up and down against my leg. We are both moaning into each other's mouths, extremely close to fruition. The budding stimulation and continuous swirling spreading from deep within, hastens my arrival, and Angela's patient and practiced fingers are flooded with my juices as they take me over the edge and into a whirlwind of sensation and ecstasy. Angela is right behind me, as the final graze across my leg sets off her own series of shudders and spasms, her muscles contracting as they squeeze and pull against my ravaged thigh.

"You're spending the night, Randi. This may never happen again, and I'm not letting you go until I've completely enjoyed you. Let's go." If she was expecting an argument, she got none. I was in total agreement, not wanting to leave before thoroughly experiencing Angela as well. She pulls me from the pool and escorts me back to the screened-in porch. Down near the weight room is a sliding glass door, and we enter her house through this opening. It leads directly into her spacious bedroom. Complete with walk-in closets, it connects to a huge master bathroom. "Time to shower off so we can get all dirty again," Angela proclaims wickedly.

After washing the chlorine from our bodies, Angela and I are eager to move on to other exciting adventures. As I finish toweling off, Angela gathers up sleeping bags and comforters and takes them out onto the porch. After a few minutes with her still not returning, I wander out to the porch to see what she is up to. She had spent the time making us a cozy little bed in the middle of the porch, and was currently spread upon it nibbling at what was left of the fruit platter. Patting the spot beside her, she encourages me to join her.

I lie on my side facing her, with the fruit platter dividing us. She dips a strawberry into the cream cheese dip, and presses it against my lips until I open them and devour the intrusive fruit. She repeats the gesture with each of the different pieces of fruit, getting more demanding and messy with each one. Pretty soon, I have fruit juice dripping down my chin and cream cheese dip smeared all across my lips. As I raise my hand with the intent of wiping my mouth and chin clean, Angela holds up her own to stop me. Confused, I watch as she moves the platter out of the way and pushes me back into the softness of the pile of comforters. Next, she straddles me, sitting gently on my abdomen, as she holds my hands above my head. Leaning over, she begins to lick and suck at my chin and lips until all signs of fruit and dip have disappeared. The familiar warmth starts to spread through my body once again, as I begin another journey into insatiable lust.

Still sitting on my stomach, Angela reaches for another strawberry and immerses it, once again, into the cream cheese dip. This time she takes the strawberry, starting at my throat, and slowly moves it downward, leaving a trail of pink cream behind it. She slowly encircles one breast, then moves upward to completely cover my nipple in cream. When all the cream is removed from the strawberry, she sucks on the end, holds it in her mouth, and leans over for me to take it from her with my own mouth. Our lips and teeth make contact, the strawberry bitten in half during the provocative kiss.

After Angela swallows her portion of the strawberry, she again commences to lick my body clean, following the trail of dip to my taut and erect nipple. Next she selects a juicy, round grape, completely covering it with the white, sticky cream. She continues where she left off, encircling my other breast, bathing my other nipple and trailing down to bury the grape in the crook of my navel. Again, her lips and tongue set me on fire as she assaults my second nipple and pillages the grape from its resting place, leaving no trace of its existence.

Angela selects another strawberry, a big, fat, juicy strawberry, and my body begins to squirm in anticipation of its creative journey. No longer sitting on my stomach, Angela starts at my belly button and begins to spread the cream downward, causing my stomach to contract and flutter, until the strawberry is resting directly on my clit. Agonizingly, Angela slowly spreads the cream in circles, unmercifully teasing, even stooping so low as to obtain a second helping of the dip to ensure a thick and complete coverage, entombing my clit until she is ready to set if free.

Dipping the fat end of the strawberry into more of the cream, Angela centers it against my moist and eager opening. Pushing it in, spreading my pussy wide open, Angela poises the strawberry right on the edge, keeping it from becoming sucked inside as well as being pushed out. It is positioned just perfectly to keep me open and wanting, each flex of my pussy causing a drop of strawberry juice to trickle enticingly down across my lips to stop in a pool at my anal opening. The sensations are almost too much for me to bear.

"Don't let anything happen to the strawberry, Randi. It had better be there when I'm ready for it." The excitement of her playful threat in itself is almost enough to send the strawberry spurting from my body as another wave of wetness descends without warning. I suck in my breath as I feel Angela's tongue begin to move downward from my navel, slowly licking across my mound and centering, finally, on my buried clit. It only takes her seconds to uncover it, to reveal it, as her warm, wet mouth and tongue completely engulf it. Within minutes, I am again hurled into the throes of a phenomenal orgasm, the poor strawberry becoming mush as violent contractions sweep through my body. Angela wastes no time in gobbling down what's left of the strawberry, marveling at the exotic flavor achieved by the mingling juices. Her tongue dives deep inside, making sure every last drop of strawberry and cream have been accounted for. With a satisfied grin, she hands me what's left of the fruit platter and states, "Your turn."

The next hour is spent mimicking her actions to the best of my recollection. The thrill of watching her body respond to my touch is more intoxicating than the wine was, giving me another idea of how to drive her wild. Once the final strawberry has been devoured, the taste of Angela's own powerful climax still fresh upon my lips, I reach for what is left in the wine bottle. "Open up, Angela," I threaten, as the wine bottle is ominously poised six inches above her face. Before she has time to react, a stream of wine flows from the bottle, hitting her on her closed mouth and spraying outward. "Shall we try that again? Open up." This time, Angela's reaction is much quicker, and she is able to swallow most of the wine.

I continue to slowly torture her body, methodically pouring out small amounts of the ice cold wine over the most sensitive areas of her body, watching it jump and squirm uncontrollably. With only a small amount of wine left, I concentrate the remainder on her clit and slowly pour the contents from the bottle, completely saturating the blankets beneath her. Making sure that the top of the wine bottle is safe and free from any glass chips or shavings, I slowly insert the bottle into her and begin to fuck her with it. She is beside herself, urging me on, bucking against the bottle, wanting it deeper, begging for me to thrust it into her harder. Afraid that the bottle could hurt her, I refrain, causing her more anguish, until she reaches down and guides my hands in the desperate rhythm and force required to carry her into euphoria. The frenzy continues until, at last, she reaches her pinnacle, collapsing into a shuddering mass of vibrations, as tremors consume and rule her body, finally subsiding to leave her totally sated and appeased.

Not wanting to spend the remainder of the night sleeping in wine-soaked blankets, Angela suggests that we drag our exhausted bodies back into her bedroom for a much deserved sleep. Groggily, I comply and, as I sink into the downy comfort of her feather mattress, expel a satisfied sigh, content with the world and all I've discovered.

CHAPTER 8

■

THE AUTHOR

The next morning, I am awakened by the aroma of
bacon and eggs and coffee. Angela is nowhere in
sight, but the clatter of pots and pans and running water
provides me with enough of a clue to deduce her current
location. Even fighting a hangover, I'm still sharp as a
marble. Chuckling at my own silly humor, I sit up and
look around in search of something to wear. I have no
idea where I left my dress—probably still outside on
the porch—but suddenly, in the light of day, I don't
feel comfortable strolling around Angela's house butt-
naked.

There is a fluffy gold robe tossed across the arm of
a chair easily accessed from my position on the bed. It
still never ceases to amaze me how thoughtful Angela
is, always thinking ahead, working out every obstacle
before it ever becomes one. Gratefully, I reach for the
robe and swaddle myself in its softness. It smells of
Angela, her favorite perfume mixed with her own feminine scent, bringing back the memories of the previous
night. This is going to be an interesting morning. Are
we going to act as if nothing ever happened and go on

as before? Is Angela going to expect, somehow, that we are now lovers, a full-time couple? What exactly is it, that I expect? Hmmmm, with these thoughts mulling through my pounding head, I crawl out of bed and head into the kitchen.

"Good morning, Angela. How can anybody sleep with all the racket you're making out here?" I ask her playfully. "Got anything for a hangover?"

Angela looks up at me and smiles, looking just as beautiful, fresh out of bed, as she does when she's all dolled up. "Good morning, Randi. How did you sleep?"

She hands me a glass of ice cold tomato juice as I answer, "Marvelously. Your bed is so comfortable. Thanks for all the hospitality."

"You're welcome. Now, plant it. Breakfast is served."

Breakfast, of course, is awesome, consisting of low-fat omelets, turkey bacon, and breakfast potatoes. The coffee is hearty, giving me the extra edge I need to fully return to awareness. Deciding that it is necessary to broach the subject, I venture, "Now, what, Angela? Where do we go from here?" It's obvious from her demeanor, that she too has been trying to make sense of the encounter.

"Well, Randi, I've been thinking about this all morning. I don't think we should blow it out of proportion. I'm glad it happened, I really enjoyed myself, but I do realize that we each have other commitments. You have a husband to go home to, and I've got my own little relationships to consider. I don't regret it, but I don't think we should pursue it, either. I think we should chalk it up to a wonderful experience, and if it happens again, great, but we shouldn't expect it to. I want us to remain the best of friends, and I'm warning you, I'm going to continue to tease you unmercifully and mess with your head. Now, how about you? How do you feel?''

"I knew it! I knew it! You *were* flirting with me all those times. Man, you're good. You left just enough doubt to mix me all up. Watch your back, girlfriend, revenge is sweet! By the way, I couldn't have said it better myself. This is exactly the way I'd like to continue our friendship, just as it was before.''

Reluctantly, I head in the direction of the shower and gather up my clothes, knowing that I'll soon be leaving this miniature spot of paradise. If it weren't for Taz, I would have begged Angela to let me rent a room from her, promising to be the most thoughtful and respectful of roommates. There is no way that her cream-colored carpeting and furniture would survive my fluffy black cat.

Within the hour, I've said goodbye to Angela and am on my way back home. I have some serious consulting to do with my computer when I get there, determined, at all costs, to figure out the *pull* and appease it. I need to feed my soul, isn't that what he said? The computer is my tool, but I have to decide how to use it. With a zillion thoughts floating in my head, I pull into my driveway and enter my apartment.

I look at my computer as if seeing it for the first time, analyzing it from every angle, observing it in a different light. Closing my eyes, I rub my hands along the cold, hard surface of the monitor, trying to recollect everything Garen had said to me and recapture the feeling of total freedom and liberation I had felt in his presence. "The computer will set you free. . . ." are the only words I can hear. Of course the answers are in the computer, or I wouldn't be so drawn to it. What I need to know is how, or why. Realizing I was going to have to answer those questions on my own, I sit down and prepare myself for a mental marathon.

I enter the chat rooms. What if this is my problem? What if this is what I'm doing wrong? Maybe the answers aren't in the chat rooms at all but contained in some other leg of the web? How will I ever find the answers? Sticking to what I know, I remain in the chat rooms, searching for a name with significance. Before I can settle on a particular title, one comes looking for me. *Beep, beep, beep.*

<Abductor> | I enjoy abduction fantasies . . . you?

<Aphrodite> | Only if I get to be the "abductee" . . . and I'm released, unharmed.

<Abductor> | Imagining you walking through a dark parking lot . . . fresh from the shopping mall . . . in a skirt, heels, and pantyhose looking very professional. . . . I'm watching you from my van.

<Aphrodite> | I'm burdened with packages, obstructing my view, my walk becoming very unsteady . . .

<Abductor> | You pass the van . . . a door slides open. You are off your feet in an instant, packages tossed in behind you. It's dark and you fall back . . . landing on a mattress on the floor of the van.

<Aphrodite> | Oh, my God. . . . I start to scream . . . flailing, trying to fight you off . . .

<Abductor> | Delighting in your struggle . . . your skirt already hiked high as you try to escape. A hand is placed on your thigh, another on your mouth.
"Do as I say and you don't get hurt." Squeezing your leg in warning.

<Aphrodite> | I nod my head in compliance, sensing the seriousness of your threat. . . .

<Abductor> | Removing my hand from your mouth . . . and raising your skirt. "I want to see these lovely legs I have been following all evening."

<Aphrodite> | Horror seeping over me, I begin to beg you: "Please, let me go. . . . Don't hurt me."

<Abductor> | "I will put you in control, my dear. It's up to you whether you are hurt or allowed to leave with everything intact but your dignity."
I kneel as I watch you on the mattress. "Lift your skirt for me. Do as I say, and you have nothing to fear."

<Aphrodite> | "Promise me . . . I'll do everything you say . . . just promise not to hurt me before it's all over, please . . ." Lifting my skirt . . . higher and higher . . .

<Abductor> | Watching you closely . . . you see the bulge in my pants. I unzip as I watch, "Very pretty, my dear . . . lovely pantyhose . . . all the way up now. That's right, up to the waistband. Let me see it all." Taking out my cock as I watch. . . .

<Aphrodite> | My skirt is around my waist, my pubic mound barely visible through the pantyhose . . . watching as you release your cock. . . .

<Abductor> | Moving around to your side . . . my cock now exposed. Opening the jacket of your business suit . . . I can see your

bra through your blouse. Reaching to touch. . . .

<Aphrodite> I I Squirm . . . breathless . . . not knowing if I'll live to see tomorrow . . . petrified that I'll respond to you, even more petrified that I might not. . . .

<Abductor> I One hand reaching down to your legs . . . finding your pussy through your silken hose. The other begins to unbutton your blouse. . . . "Touch my cock."

<Aphrodite> I My legs involuntarily twitch, wanting to close yet not daring to . . . breasts heaving toward your hand, arching, pressing outward, trying to keep from hyperventilating. One hand hesitantly reaches for your cock as I continue to stare at it, torn between watching it and acknowledging the thrill of power burning in your eyes.
Touching your cock now, gripping its velvety hardness. . . .

<Abductor> I I Push your blouse open . . . lovely, lacey bra . . . caressing . . . squeezing. My other hand finds the clasp on your skirt, unzips and pulls it off. "Get up on your knees . . . Take off your blouse. I want you posing for me, doggie style in just your bra and pantyhose . . . NOW!"

<Aphrodite> I Releasing your cock as if it burned me, casting my shirt aside, still unable to control my breathing or fear. . . . Rolling over and getting up to my knees, displayed before you on all fours, in

171

nothing but a bra, pantyhose and heels. . . .

<Abductor> | Positioning my cock by your mouth. . . . "Tell me . . . who are you wearing those pantyhose for?" Touching my cock to your lips . . . "After you answer me, suck it . . . my captive . . . if you ever want to get out of here alive.". . . . Cock is raging hard . . . already oozing precum.

<Aphrodite> | "Oh, God . . . I'm wearing these pantyhose for you . . . only for you, for your pleasure. . . ." Licking my lips as they glide across the head of your cock to fully engulf it in incredible heat and wetness, striving to please you, hoping it will keep me alive . . . moaning deep into my throat as you begin to fuck my mouth . . . slippery and sliding, hitting the back of my throat to pull back out to the tender softness of my lips, then thrusting back in again. . . .

<Abductor> | "Yesssss . . . yessssssss" . . . holding your head . . . guiding you . . . reaching down . . . feeling your lovely face as your cheeks stretch to take my cock. Pushing your bra straps off of your shoulders . . . pumping my cock into your eagerly cooperative mouth . . . pumping. . . .

<Aphrodite> | I can taste you. . . . I take my mind elsewhere, creating a scenario that allows myself to enjoy what is happening. I'm not being forced, I'm with my partner. Blocking everything else out . . . feel-

172

ing you brace yourself against my hair, unwittingly tugging at it . . . pumping . . . in and out, in and out . . . faster, slower. . . . feeling my tongue swirling around your head and down your shaft . . . taking me . . . fucking me. . . .

\<Abductor\> | Suddenly pulling you off of my cock . . . pushing you back . . . shoving your bra off of your tits . . . exposing them . . . hurling you back to reality . . .

Feel my hard, wet cock between your legs . . . poking at your pantyhose . . . my lips on your nipples, biting them . . . sucking . . . licking . . .

THE DOOR TO THE VAN SUDDENLY OPENS AND TWO MORE MEN ENTER . . .

"I've been waiting for you two," I tell them. "I've got her all warmed up."

\<Aphrodite\> | Oh, God, NO!! Please!!!

\<Abductor\> | In an instant they are on you . . . a fresh cock at your mouth . . . a hand pulling your head toward it. You forget about my cock so close to your pussy, until you suddenly hear your lovely pantyhose tearing.

\<Aphrodite\> | Help me, help me, help me. . . . I silently scream as I feel myself about to be violated . . . the rush of cool air swarming against my recently exposed pussy, as another strange cock starts sliding down my throat, bending my head way backward . . .

\<Abductor\> | A touch . . . then a finger . . . then two . . . then my hard cock at the lips of your pussy, pushing in . . . deeper . . . as the second cock begins to pump down your throat. You feel a third . . . moving across your breasts . . . jerking off onto your hard nipples. You feel him pounding his cock as he watches you suck and be fucked.

\<Aphrodite\> I Twisting in agony as my body is used so degradingly. . . .

\<Abductor\> I Pushing in . . . beginning to pound . . . in . . . out . . . fucking you . . . ripping your hose . . . hard as a rock . . . relentlessly pounding into you. At your mouth, his cock becomes harder still, his balls contract and spray his load into your throat . . . pulling out and spraying his cum onto your pretty face. . . .

\<Aphrodite\> I Oh God, Oh God, Oh God . . . trying to scream only to choke and gurgle on the cock stuffed deep into my throat . . . sputtering . . . covered now in his cum . . . feeling how your cock ravages me. . . .

\<Abductor\> I Pushing you to the floor . . . forcing my cock so deep. You are released from his cock only to feel mine about to explode inside you, while, on your tits, you suddenly feel the white hot spattering heat of yet a third cock. The pungent aroma of his semen invades your nostrils. I stiffen and EXPLODE inside you . . . again and again and again.

\<Aphrodite\> I Being used like this, covered in semen, feeling your cock thicken and swell as it shoots load after load deep inside me, I can't bear it . . . your cum meshing with what's left of my pantyhose, dripping from me. . . .

<Abductor> | As the cock from your tits is placed on your mouth for you to clean, I pull out of you, cleaning my cock on your torn hose . . . spreading the semen. . . .

"Let's take her back to the house," you hear one of the other men suggesting. "She's way too much fun to let go right away."

<Aphrodite> | Obediently cleaning the offered cock and panicking at the suggestion of taking me back to the house, I begin pleading, "Please, no. You promised to let me go if I behaved. I've cooperated. You've had your fun, now please let me leave."

<Abductor> | "I promised to let you leave, but I didn't say when. Keep her occupied boys, while I drive." The two men fondle and grope you the entire way home, not allowing you a moment's peace.

<Aphrodite> | Suffering silently, wondering if I'll ever be allowed to leave.

<Abductor> | We arrive at the house and carry you up the stairs. Throwing a few props over to my friends, I suggest, "How about if we attach her to the ceiling using these. That way we can have at her from all sides."

<Aphrodite> | Horrified, I struggle as my arms are lifted high above my head and at-

		tached to a device, suspending me from the ceiling. Thankfully, you've allowed my feet to remain flat on the floor.
<Abductor>	I	You remain clad only in your shredded hose, your bra still attached but pushed up above your tits, and your heels. "Why don't you boys strip down while I go off in search of the whip."
<Aphrodite>	I	"Oh, God. You promised not to hurt me."
<Abductor>	I	I return in a few minutes, totally naked and carrying a very menacing looking whip. It has a thick, sturdy handle made of leather, and twelve leather tentacles slithering from the center. Also in my hands are a pair of nipple clamps. I tell one of the guys to attach them to you. "I want her nipples hard and erect the entire time we have her. These will make her nipples super sensitive, intensifying the bite of the whip lashes."
<Aphrodite>	I	Crying out as the nipple clamps are clasped to my breasts, causing them to stiffen and harden and remain in that state. Squirming as your two cronies tweak and pull at my breasts, making sure the clamps are securely fastened. Watching you with fear and apprehension as you approach me with the whip.
<Abductor>	I	Upon you now, the leather whip gliding across your skin. Pressing it into your face . . . forcing you to smell it . . .

pushing the handle between your lips. "Suck it."

<Aphrodite> | Opening my mouth, stretching it wide to accommodate the thickness of the handle . . . swooning at the intoxicating scent of the leather straps as they tickle my nose . . . bracing myself. Watching as the two men stand by, stroking their cocks back to life.

<Abductor> | Pulling the handle from your mouth . . . teasing your body with tickling strokes from the whip, sliding it up and down and around to your back where you can no longer see me. You feel the threat of the whip as it lingers on your ass. . . . I raise my arm to deliver the first stinging swat. . . .

<Aphrodite> | My body tenses with expectancy, praying you'll be merciful. . . .

<Abductor> | The first lash lands on your ass . . . your body recoiling in surprise and shock. Enough to get your undivided attention, but not enough to cause you any real pain.

<Aphrodite> | "Uhhhh . . . please stop . . . no more, no more. . . ."

<Abductor> | "Beg me to *whip* you instead, and I'll keep it on the gentle side." The whip raises a second time, this time landing with a little more force on the back of your thighs.

<Aphrodite> | "Okay, Okay! . . . Whip me again, please."

<Abductor> | "Where?"

<Aphrodite> | "On my back. Whip me across my

---

back . . . then my ass again, the back of my legs and then come around front. I want you to whip my tits."

<Abductor> | "Delighted that you're enjoying my little game, captive." True to my word, I keep the lashes mild, keeping you jumpy, but not hurting you. A nice rosy glow is beginning to cover your entire body. With my attention directed to your front side now, I call one of the boys over to stand behind you. "Fuck her up the ass while I whip her pussy."

<Aphrodite> | "Oh God, no. Please, I can't take this. Let me go."

<Abductor> | You feel the head of a cock pressing insistently against your anal opening, pushing against it, slowly working its way in. At the same time, you are distracted by tiny, little flicks of the whip aimed directly at your clit.

<Aphrodite> | I strain against the man as I feel him enter my forbidden passage, trying to separate the sensations being simultaneously inflicted upon me . . . the bite of the whip as it lashes across my clit, my taut and bursting nipples, my ass completely filled and violated . . . panting . . . groaning. . . .

<Abductor> | "Boys . . . do you think we can make our little captive cum?"
"How about if I turn this whip around and fuck you with it? Would you like that, little captive?"

<Aphrodite> | "No . . . no. . . . It's too big . . . too thick. . . ." I manage to stammer out

between the powerful thrusts being inflicted in my backside.

<Abductor> | "I think forcing our little prize into orgasm will be the ultimate humiliation, wouldn't it? Get the lubricant . . . we're going to have to grease her up good for this one."

<Aphrodite> | "Oh, God . . . not this . . . don't make me. . . ."

<Abductor> | The second man approaches with the lubricant just as the first one has reached orgasm in your precious ass. Not wanting to be left out, he positions himself behind you, ready to take over as the first man steps aside. In one instant your ass is relieved, only to become refilled by another massive cock. Deciding to relieve myself again, before taking you over the edge, I use the jelly to grease my own cock up, and hold it up to your pussy. "Let's see if she can take us both at once."

<Aphrodite> | Feeling as if I'm being ripped apart, stretched wide open at both entrances . . . as you slip further and further into my pussy . . . standing up and facing me with your arms wrapped tightly around my back, pumping into me with the same steady strokes as your friend is using in my ass. The friction caused by your cocks, separated by only a thin membrane, proves to be too much, and you both find yourselves concurrently exploding into your own, separate passages.

<Abductor> | I slip from you in exhausted ecstasy whispering, "It's your turn, hon." You squirm and carry on as if it is the worst sentence I could have possibly imposed, making me all the more eager to accomplish it. "Look at her boys. She doesn't want to cum. Who wants to fuck her with the whip while I nibble on her clit for a while?"

<Aphrodite> | Kicking out at you, trying to keep you away. "Stop it, you son of a bitch! Leave me alone."

<Abductor> | "One of you grab the whip, the other grab her hair. If she starts to kick again, pull on it. That should keep her still." One of the men has a tight grip in your hair while the other one begins to smear lubricant all over the immense handle of the whip. You feel it balanced against your lips as I kneel down and face your clit. On cue, the handle is deliberately inserted into you as I seek out and drown your clit with my saliva. The attack on your clit is ruthless. . . .

<Aphrodite> | Against my will, I feel sensations begin to swirl and take over. Unable to stop the assault on my clit, united with the incessant thrusting of the whip's handle, I have no choice but to resign myself to the traitorous pleasure building . . . and building . . . and building . . . until only the small gasp that is torn from my lips and the vibrations contorting my body indicate to you that you have succeeded in your quest.

\<Abductor\>	"Let's take her back home boys. I think we're finally through with her."
\<Aphrodite\>	Well, that was an interesting little fantasy. Act it out much?
\<Abductor\>	Not nearly as much as I'd like to. I do have to say, you were much more fun to play with online than most of the others. Usually my fantasy fizzles out while I'm still in the van. You've got a gift, lovely Aphrodite.
\<Aphrodite\>	Oh, do I, now? And what would that be?
\<Abductor\>	The gift of imagination . . . the stories you could conjure up. . . . And with that incredible sexuality . . . there'd be no stopping you. You should write a book.

You should write a book. . . . You should write a book. . . . You should write a book. . . .

You should write a book! The words appear to raise themselves from the screen, reaching out to me, bobbing in front of my eyes, hitting me over the head with the force of a sledgehammer. I should write a book! My God, is that what the pull was all about? It wasn't about having sex with strangers . . . but rather, *writing* about having sex with strangers! I'm stunned at the simplicity of it all. Just the thought of writing a book has the adrenaline surging through my veins, my nerve endings all fired up. Thanking my *\<Abductor\>* profusely for the wonderful chat, I end the session and begin to formulate a story. This should be pretty easy, most of it being based upon true experiences. Without another moment's hesitation, I jump over into my word processing software and begin to type. As the words begin to flow across the screen, I feel months of pent-up restlessness flow away with them, my soul finally finding true fulfillment.

CHAPTER 9

∎

THE WIFE

Turning the last page, my husband exclaims, "I'm sorry, honey, but Miranda is a slut . . . A shameless, self-absorbed hussy! I can't believe her husband would take her back after all of that."

"Well, he loves her. He wanted her to go out and experience those things."

"Yeah, right . . . so he said in chapter one. It was a damn good book, though. I really enjoyed reading it. So, promise me one thing."

"Anything, my darling husband, anything."

"If you ever really do meet an Angela, introduce her to me, will ya?"

Giggling, I chase him up the stairs, playfully swatting at him for his tasteless remark. "Well, I don't know about that, but how about we start at chapter one and see what happens when we get to the Angela chapters?" Laughing outrageously, we fall back onto the bed, becoming entangled with one another, paving the road to our own little novel.

SWEET REVENGE

CHAPTER 1

∎

BURDENS

Writing a book based on sexual exploitations can be pretty tricky, I'm slowly but surely discovering. After all, there are only so many ways to describe an orgasm, and after about the seventh one, all possibilities are exhausted. Regardless, I continue writing, determined to capture all the emotions and passions that ruled my waking moments over the past couple of months, and even those that managed to slither into my subconscious, revealing themselves in the most erotic of dreams.

So much has happened to me recently, and as I relive those weeks through my writing, I experience the same breathless thrill that I encountered initially. Reflecting upon my actions now, I find that I am very lucky that no harm had befallen me. I had taken far too many risks all in the name of "soul searching," yet wouldn't reverse any of it had I the opportunity to do so. During each encounter, I learned something new about myself, and for that, I am very grateful. I experienced hidden desires and was pushed to my limits, therefore realizing exactly what those limits were. I found that I was unbiased when it came to choosing a partner, and that I could enjoy sex with both men and women alike, as long as there was some initial attraction. Also discovered was how heightened my arousal became when I was just a little bit frightened and uncertain of what would happen next. I realized that I loved to be sexually dominated by men, yet received equal gratification from either dominating or being dominated by, another woman. So many discoveries, so many experiments yet none as powerful as the final disclosure, my desire to write erotica.

It wasn't that I needed to experience all those sexual unknowns to achieve the ultimate satisfaction and contentedness that I'm feeling now, but who knew that then? I just hope that during my quest, I did not cause any irreparable damage that would keep me from returning to my previous life, and most importantly, to my husband. Nick, the foundation of my existence, always there for me, willing to set aside anything to place my needs above his own. Nick, the most unselfish human being on the planet, his patience rivaling that of any saint. Nick, my endless love, helplessly caught up in my scrambled emotions, his only options being either to allow me the freedom to find myself, or to leave.

Three months ago, he chose to let me go, giving me the time and space I needed to discover who I was and what I wanted. Three months ago, he was okay with that decision. Now, I wonder, will he still feel the same way? What if, during his own soul searching, he had a change of heart? He's had an enormous burden to bear, has had repeated blows to his pride as well as many months of existing in hopeless confusion. What if he has discovered that it's not worth it, that *I'm* no longer worth the pain and struggles he's had to endure? It's a possibility, a possibility I shudder to acknowledge. Now that I have everything all worked out in my own head, now that I understand that it is he, and only he, who I truly love and desire, will he decide differently? It would be a pain I would not want to live with, yet a pain I wholeheartedly deserve.

I hadn't contacted Nick once during our three-month separation, and hesitate doing so now. I needed to make the break clean so that I could chase my demons without constant reminders and never-ending guilt. Yet, I needed to call him now. With my book almost complete and my inner turmoil finally stabilized and at peace, I am ready to return home. Now, my only concern, did I have a home to go back to? As I pick up the phone, my hand trembles with trepidation, holding back the tears that threaten to spill over as I dial the 11 key numbers to my uncertain future.

"Hello."

"Hi, Nick."

"Miranda? Thank goodness, I've been worried sick about you! Are you okay?"

"Yeah, honey, I'm fine. I'm sorry I didn't call you sooner, but I just couldn't."

"Well, when you left, I did kind of think we would

3

keep in touch, you know? I didn't expect you to just fall from the face of the Earth.''

"Well, I've had quite the adventure, most of which I am quite ashamed of. I don't think I can ever come home.''

"Don't talk like that, Miranda. Of course you can come home. I really miss you. It would kill me if you never came back.''

"Honey, you don't know the things I've done. I've been unfaithful . . . more than once. I'm a horrible person.''

Silence.

"Honestly, I was expecting that, Miranda. I could tell you were restless. It would have surprised me more if you had told me that you *hadn't* slept with anyone else. The bottom line is, do you still love me?''

"Of course I still love you, from the bottom of my heart, which is why I hate myself so much. How could I love you that much, yet still be able to cheat on you?''

"Look, quit beating yourself up, sweetheart. I snagged you up right out of high school. Most people get to experiment and sow their wild oats during college, getting it out of their systems before they get married. Neither one of us had that opportunity. It would be unrealistic to think those urges could just be buried. I don't blame you, Miranda. I'm not thrilled, but I don't blame you.''

"So, have you had the urge to sow your wild oats as well?''

Chuckling, Nick says "Nah, not yet. I think we have another ten years or so before we have to worry about that.''

4

"God, it's so nice to hear your voice again. You always were my best friend. So, now, the big question . . . Do you want me to tell you what's been happening these last few months, or would you prefer to remain blissfully ignorant?"

"Well, as much as I'd like to remain oblivious, I'm afraid it will be much easier for me to deal with if everything is laid out on the table. I think the more we communicate and talk about it, the more quickly we can both heal and move forward."

"Are you sure it wouldn't just torture you to know everything?"

"An overactive imagination can sometimes prove more detrimental than the actual reality. I'd rather know, and I promise you that I can deal with whatever it is you have to tell me. I just want you back. I love you, Miranda. I'll love you till my dying breath, and then, if possible, beyond that."

"I don't deserve you. Now I feel even worse than before. I think I would have preferred for you to yell and scream and cast me into eternal damnation."

"Ok, ok . . . Let's not overreact. You haven't killed anybody, have you?"

Laughing, I say, "No, nothing that serious."

"Ok, so tell me, darling, what exactly have you been up to for the last three months?"

"Well, for starters, I got a job as an erotic dancer at a very upscale nightclub."

"You've always wanted to do that, haven't you? I remember, when we first got married, the offhanded comments you would make about the female strippers, how much you admired their confidence and abilities to shed their inhibitions. So, you finally did it, huh?"

"Yup."

"Damn."

"Why damn?" Oh God, if this bothers him, the rest is going to *kill* him.

"I only wish I could have been there. I would have loved to see you live out that dream, Miranda. I wish *we* could have shared that."

"Honey, it was something I had to do on my own. I'm not sure I could have let myself go, knowing you were watching. I was safe in my anonymity, free to be who I was without fear of being judged or rejected. If I failed in front of an unknown audience, I could slink away without anyone being the wiser. If I had failed in front of you, I would have died."

"Miranda, sometimes you are such a child. Do you think that the man who loves you would judge you? I would have admired you for your courage to pursue your dream. Even if you were the *worst* dancer I had ever seen, I would still think you were the most wonderful."

Smiling, I say, "Thanks, Nick."

"Promise me you'll dance for me someday, Miranda."

"I promise. Now . . . time for confession number one."

Smirking, Nick remarks, "You mean, number two, but go on."

"I gave my boss a blow job to get the dancing position. When I first started working at the club, I was only a cocktail waitress."

"Oh, I see. So your boss wouldn't let you dance unless you blew him? What a jerk."

"Well, not exactly. I kind of, um, panicked. I approached him with the idea, and because of my age, he was not convinced that I could live up to the standards of the 20-year-olds. So, to prove that I could, I auditioned, danced and stripped for him. Knowing that I only had one shot at the job, I panicked and got carried away. Besides, I got so turned on while I was dancing . . . Well, regardless, it was totally my idea."

"Oh, I can hardly wait for confession number three."

"We don't have to do this, you know."

"Call me a pervert, but so far I've only felt amusement and arousal by your confessions. The thought of my lovely wife, naked and on her knees, giving head to another man . . . well, um, is very stimulating."

"Ok . . . here goes. I have been exploring the domination/submission practices on the Internet chat rooms. . . ."

"And . . ."

"Was talked into meeting with one of the men I met on-line."

"Hmmmm . . . So you beat the poor boy into submission, huh?"

"Not exactly," I giggle. "I discovered that I like the submissive role."

"Yeah, right! Who are you and what have you done with my wife?"

"He actually played quite the nasty trick on me. We were supposed to meet in a restaurant, and if we were attracted to one another, would move forward with lessons on how to become a good slave. Well, I got there first and my 'date' never showed up, but the waiter catered to me nicely. To make a long story short, it turned out that the man I had met over the computer was posing as my waiter. He then felt the need to teach me a lesson in self-control."

"Oh, man, do I really want to hear this? He didn't hurt you, did he?"

"Oh, goodness no. In a nutshell, he took me to a hotel, tied me naked to the bed, and spent the remainder of the night teasing me close to orgasm, then denying me. It was very frustrating."

To my surprise, my husband bursts out laughing.

"What, exactly, is it that you find so funny, mister?"

"Oh, oh, what a precious vision you've just placed in my head, Miranda. I would have killed to be a fly on that wall."

As his laughter starts to die down, I venture, "You're not upset?"

"Nope."

"You're lying. You *have* to be upset."

"No, really, I'm not. I'm finding that if I separate my pride from the entire scenario and just focus on the mechanics, it's kind of like watching a movie, with my lovely wife being cast in the starring role. The thought of you tied up and helpless, squirming in wanton frustration is giving me a raging hard-on, Miranda."

"Oh, really now? It would seem that my husband has his own secret desires as well."

8

"Go on, Miranda. I can hardly wait for confession number. . . . What number are we on, anyway?"

"Ok, wise ass, I met this other guy in the chat rooms who was obsessed with getting my phone number. I finally broke down and gave it to him."

"Did he call you?"

"Oh, yes . . ."

"Well??? What did he say?"

"He made me attach the phone to my ear with a headband so that my hands would be free, made me strip naked and then lie in the middle of my floor with my arms, legs and mouth spread wide open."

"Why did he do that?"

"I think it was his attempt at making me feel vulnerable. He also said that he always wanted me to wait for him that way, open and available, ready for him to take on a whim, all orifices continuously offered for his pleasure."

"So, *that's* how you've been spending your days . . ."

Laughing, I say, "No. But I'm sure *he'd* like to think that."

"So, what else did he *make* you do?"

"Well, then he *made* me masturbate. At first he wanted me to touch myself and describe to him what I was doing, but I couldn't verbalize it. I was too embarrassed. So, he opted for second-best by telling me how and where to touch, listening to my breathing increase with each command, my moans getting louder and louder until he brought me to the brink. I swear to you, it must have turned him on more to hear me cum than it did me. The whole experience was absolutely thrilling."

9

"You'd better be careful. I heard you can go blind if you do that too often!"

"Ah, always the comedian. Still want to hear more?"

"Of course . . ."

"Well, you know how I told you that I started dancing, right?"

"Uh huh."

"Angela is the name of the girl who taught me to dance. I found myself immediately attracted to her. She is a lovely redhead with creamy, golden skin, bright green eyes, long, long legs, and a great pair of hooters."

"Hey, girls aren't supposed to describe other girls using the term, 'hooters.' That's a guy's term."

"Oh, quit pouting and keep up with the times, will ya? So, Angela and I created a very erotic routine where we danced together, touched one another, slid up and down each others' bodies, you name it. It was just shy of us having sex on stage. The crowd loved it, and we made a ton of money. So, after a very successful weekend, I decided to treat myself to four days in Vegas. I made the mistake of telling my phone sex companion my plans, and he had a little surprise waiting for me when I got there."

"Oh?"

"Yes, oh. He watched me the entire day until I was alone in a very remote part of the hotel, abducted me in an elevator and took me to his room. He had his girlfriend tied to the bed with a huge dildo sticking out from between her legs and made me remove it. Then I was forced to perform and submit to the most degrading acts."

"Well, don't keep me in suspense. . . . What did he make you do?"

"Well, he tied my hands above my head and hooked them to the ceiling, then forced and kept my legs apart with a three-foot, steel bar strapped to and between my ankles. Then, he lathered me up and . . . shaved me."

"Shaved you?"

"Yeah, shaved me. It was humiliating, but he never hurt me. Next, he freed me and had me pour baby oil over his girlfriend, Rachel, and rub it into her. He made me sit on her stomach and rub and slide all over her. I had to kiss her, and pinch her, and penetrate her . . . and . . ."

"AND?!?"

"Calm down there, cowboy. AND . . . 'go down' on her. I had to make her cum, and vice versa."

"Did you like it?"

"Honestly? Yeah, I liked it. Actually, the whole encounter really turned me on. The only drawback was that I was so scared. I had no idea what was coming next, and never knew for sure that I was safe. I'm sure that's why it was so intense, so exciting."

Coughing, Nick said, "Well, it's working for me. So, what happened next? He just let you go?"

"Oh, no. He wasn't through with me yet. He had Rachel take me into the shower to get me good and clean for round two."

"Round two?"

"Yup. When we got out of the shower, I got introduced to the hot wax treatment."

"I'm sure you're not talking about hair removal, are you?"

11

"Oh, no. What he did was actually quite diabolical. He tied me to the bed, took a lighted candle and let it drip onto various places on my body. He had Rachel kneeling between my open legs, and every time the melted wax scorched my skin, Rachel was ordered to lick my clit. Let me tell you, after a while, that little game messes with your head. By the end, I was begging to be bathed in the hot wax, just to keep her mouth on me until I came."

"Ah, the old 'there is no pleasure without pain' adage."

"He's a master at it. It was at that point that I got really frightened. I knew I had to get out of there as soon as possible. His next words really freaked me out."

"What did he say?"

"He ordered Rachel to clean the dried wax off of my body while he went and made some 'new friends' in the casino bar. He said that if I was lucky, he would bring them back to meet me."

"Oh, God, Miranda. What did you do? How did you get away?"

"When he left, I begged and pleaded with Rachel to let me go. I threatened to have them both arrested. I put the idea into her head that if she didn't release me, I would replace her in *his* affections. I played upon her insecurities until she finally untied me and let me leave. I raced to my room, gathered my things and drove away from there as fast as my speedometer would take me, that is, until I almost hit a bear."

"You almost hit a bear, in the middle of the desert? Did that asshole drug you?"

"No, he did not drug me, but it was like I was

drugged. The whole next episode is very fuzzy to me. I think I had sex with it . . . um, I mean . . . him . . . Um . . . I really don't know what happened. I swear, at one point he was a man. He even told me his name.''

"Ok, this is too bizarre even for me. That couldn't possibly have happened.''

"Well, you may be right. I hit my head when I slammed on my brakes. When I finally regained consciousness, I was still in my car, on the side of the road, trying to explain to 'Officer Bob' what I was doing there.''

"I hope you didn't tell him that you had just had sex with a werewolf.''

"No, of course not, and he wasn't a werewolf. He was a bear.''

"He wasn't anything. It never happened, Miranda. You knocked yourself out. Probably hallucinated the whole thing.''

"Maybe. Do you want me to continue?''

"I'm not sure. Are the rest of your sexual encounters with humans?''

"Yes.''

"Ok, I'm listening.''

"Well, I was very upset when I got home, so I called Angela and basically invited myself over to her house. We talked for a while, had a little dinner, went skinny dipping in her pool and then she kissed me.''

"Hmmmmm . . .''

"You've gotten awfully quiet, Nick. Are you still okay?''

"Just absorbing everything. You gave me a pretty big pill to swallow.''

13

"Yeah, I know. I actually wrote a book all about it. One of the guys I chatted with suggested that I channel my talent and energy into creating the ultimate erotic novel."

"Jesus Christ, Miranda. Just how many lives have you lived in the few months that you've been away? You wrote a damn book? Like a finished, complete book or a short story kind of thing?"

"No, it's a regular novel-size book. I'd love for you to read it when I get back home."

"Just try and stop me. So, when do you think you'll be coming home?"

"I'm pretty much ready to go now. I just have to give my notice at work. If I can get out of here in a week, I'll leave then, but I may have to wait two weeks. I don't want to leave Robert and the club in a bind."

"I understand, but I really do miss you. It's going to be the longest two weeks of my life."

"I miss you, too, Nick. I love you."

"Love you too, Miranda. See you soon, ok?"

"Ok, bye-bye."

"Bye."

Well, that went surprisingly well. I had expected Nick to blow a gasket or at the very least, start ranting and raving. Amusement and desire were two emotions I never thought would surface after confiding to Nick my darkest transgressions. The lack of an outburst is even harder to take than a full-blown temper tantrum, making me very edgy and suspicious of his motives. What is he up to? Well, enough effort spent on trying

14

to analyze that particular conversation, I have a notice to give. Picking up the phone, I automatically start to dial Robert's phone number, offhandedly wondering if he will even be at the club this early in the day.

CHAPTER 2

FAREWELLS

"Club Illicit, Jeff speaking."

"Hey, Jeff, this is Miranda. Is Robert in?"

"Yeah, I think he's back there in his office. Hang on a minute and I'll check."

"Hey, kiddo. How's it going?"

"Hi, Robert. I'm afraid I have some bad news for you."

"Why do I have the feeling that you're going to be leaving us? Please don't tell me that you're going to be leaving us, Miranda."

"I'm so sorry, Robert. It's time for me to go home now. I've worked things out within myself, and I've worked things out with my husband. I need to go back."

"Damn, I knew it was too good to last. Well, it sure was great having you around. You sure helped business pick up here at the club."

"I feel really guilty after all the time and energy

you and Angela invested into making me a dancer. I feel that I let you down."

"No, you didn't let us down. You've paid for our efforts a hundred times over. So, when's your last day?"

"I can give you two weeks' notice if you really need it. Otherwise, I'd like to get out of here as soon as possible. I feel desperate to get back home."

"Well, there's no sense forcing you to work any more shifts. You'll be too distracted by thoughts of going home to be convincing on stage. I can cover your shifts with the other girls, but it'll be tough finding another partner for Angela and the 'Dynamic Duo.' I'll work that out with Angela. Maybe she has some chemistry working with one of the other dancers that I'm not aware of."

"Oh, God, Robert. You are too wonderful. Sure there will be no hard feelings?"

"None at all, sweetie. I'm happy for you that your life is back on track. You have to promise to stick around long enough for us to whip you up a killer going-away party, though."

Smiling, I say, "Ok, I think I can accommodate *that* request. When were you thinking of holding the party?"

"Well, with this short notice, I'm kind of in a tough spot. Sunday nights are pretty slow anyway. How about I close the club for that night and we'll have us a private party? I'll leave Angela in charge of the guest list."

"It sounds wonderful. I'll need a couple of days to pack, so that will be perfect. Thanks, Robert, for being so thoughtful and kind."

17

"Don't mention it, kiddo. Hey, Miranda?"

"Yes, Robert?"

"I just want you to know something."

"Ok, I'm listening. . . ."

"Miranda, I just want you to know . . . that you were the best damn blow job I ever had."

Mortified, I respond, "I was hoping you had forgotten that. Um, well, thank you, I guess. . . ."

"Bye, Randa. See you Sunday evening, six o'clock sharp."

"See ya, Robert."

Thank God that hurdle is crossed. Besides phoning Nick, that was definitely the most difficult obstacle I had to face. What a weird thing for Robert to say. I wonder if there was a point to it? Maybe it was his way of saying goodbye. Maybe it was his way of telling me that I had made an impact and would always be remembered. Maybe it was a hint that he wanted an encore performance Sunday night. Yeah, that was probably more like it. Men!

Of course, telling Angela I'm leaving isn't going to be any picnic either. She has become such a great and special friend in such a short period of time. Of course, she will understand and wish me well. If only I could wrap her up and take her home with me. Realizing that I need to contact her before Robert does, I hurriedly dial her phone number. Within moments, her sweet, melodious voice fills the receiver.

"Hey, Angela. It's Randi."

"Hi, yourself, girlfriend. What's up?"

"I was wondering if you had any plans for this evening?"

"Not a one, why?"

"Well, I need a girl's night. Feel like coming over for dinner and wine and hours and hours of chitchat?"

"Can't think of anything else I'd rather do. Should I bring my P J's? I don't want to be driving home too late or too intoxicated."

"Yeah, let's make it a sleepover."

"Do you want me to bring anything else?"

"Nope, just your P J's."

"Ok, then, I'll see you around five?"

"No, come over now . . . I mean as soon as possible, and don't answer your phone if it rings in the meantime."

"What's going on, Randi?"

"Nothing, it's just that Robert may try to call you and I need to speak with you before he does."

"Oooo, I don't like the sound of that. Ok, I promise not to answer my phone, and I'll be at your place in a half hour tops."

"Thanks, Angela. See you in a bit."

"Bye-bye, Randi."

Ok, now that everything is all in place, what am I going to fix for dinner? Brilliant move, Sherlock, invite her over for dinner when there's nothing in the house to eat. Well, we could always order Chinese and have it delivered. Yeah, that's perfect, that way we don't have to waste any time in the kitchen. Checking my alcohol reserves, I decide that there is plenty of wine to keep us happily buzzing all night long if we so choose. With all of my pressing matters reasonably addressed, I finally sit back down at my computer and commence to make the finishing touches to my novel.

Angela is at my door within twenty-five minutes, just as I complete the final round of editing and start the document to printing. Realizing that it is going to take probably close to another half hour to get my entire book printed, I leave it be while I focus my attention on playing the perfect hostess for Angela. Greeting her at the door with two glasses of wine in my hands, I invite her in and offer her a glass. "I propose a toast," Angela announces, "to good friends."

"I'll second that," I say as I raise my glass high in the air to make contact with hers, the clinking noise sealing the toast. Greedily, we both gobble down the entire glass of wine, setting the pace for the wild night sure to follow.

"Here, take this for a refill while I go find a place to put my overnight bag."

"Oh, you can just go set it in the bedroom for now. We'll figure out the rest as the night goes on."

Once again, the wineglasses are full, and I wander back out into the living-room area carrying them. Angela returns and decides to take advantage of my occupied hands by taking my face between her palms and planting a huge kiss directly on my startled lips.

"Well, I've missed you, too," I laugh out, dismissing the incident as a joke, finding it a bit difficult to disguise the rosy glow slowly spreading across my face, as well as the sudden increase of my heartbeat.

"Ok, Randi. I want to know what's going on right

now. No beating around the bush, no dragging it out for hours. What's happened?''

"Well, at least have a seat on the couch, for goodness' sake, and take your wineglass back.''

Smiling, she relieves me of one of the glasses and plops her derrière down, sinking into the generously stuffed cushions. Joining her, I sit back and close my eyes, enjoying the relaxing effect of the wine, the sofa and the company.

"I'm glad you came over, Angela. I just wanted to tell you, in person, that I'm moving back home to be with Nick again. It's time.''

"Oh, Randi, that's great! I'm happy that things have worked out between the two of you.''

"Well, more like, I've finally worked things out with myself.''

"So, when are you leaving?''

"Monday, and you're in charge of my going-away party on Sunday. I've already talked to Robert and he insisted that the club be shut down for the night so he could throw me one humdinger of a party. That's why I didn't want you answering your phone. He was going to call you to ask to help him with the arrangements.''

"Ah, I see. Well, no problem, I'll be happy to help, but I sure will miss you.''

"Yeah, since it is such short notice, I want to spend as much time with you as I can before I leave. I'm really glad you didn't have plans for tonight.''

"Well, even if I had, I would have changed them the minute I found out what was going on.''

"Angela, guess what else?''

"What?''

"You know how you jokingly mentioned that I should write a book about all my recent wild sexual escapades?"

"Yesssss . . ."

"Well, I did. It's all done, just finished it today. It's printing as we speak."

"No kidding?! That's wonderful. Can I read it?"

"Sure! Besides, you're one of the main characters. You *have* to read it."

"This is so neat, Randi. I can't believe you actually did it. Is it hot?"

Winking at her, I said, "You tell me. Let me go get it and you can start reading it. It's probably going to take a few hours, but we have plenty of time. While you are doing that, I'll order out for Chinese food, ok?"

"Sounds awesome, bring it on."

Collecting the pages that have already been printed, I present them to Angela. The glee on her face is contagious, and I laugh at her eager expression, resembling a child at Christmas. Leaving Angela once again to refill our glasses and place our dinner order, I finally settle back down beside her. She is already thoroughly engrossed, oblivious to the fact that I've returned.

"I ordered sesame chicken and chicken lo mein. It should be here in about thirty minutes."

She nods but is clueless to what I just said, and continues reading.

Dinner arrives just as Angela is finishing up chapter 1. "Time to take a break and eat, sweetie."

"Geeze, Randi. I felt like I was right there. It's awesome."

22

"Glad you're enjoying it."

Angela eats her dinner in record time, eager to get back to the novel. Time passes fairly quickly, with her taking a moment here and there to comment on a certain event or to ask a question. I spend my time watching her as a delightful pink glow slowly spreads becomingly over her features.

By 10 P.M., Angela has read my book from cover to cover and is squirming quite uncomfortably on the couch. "Randi, I loved it, especially the parts about me, and now I am seriously horny."

"Sorry, I should have warned you about the possible side effects before I let you read it. Shame on me."

"Hey, will you show me how to chat in the computer chat rooms? It sounds like it is a lot of fun. Maybe a little cyber sex will help cure what ails me."

"Sure, grab a chair and come on over."

Sitting side by side, I show Angela all the steps involved with connecting to the adult chat rooms. I show her all the different rooms she has to choose from, some of the symbols and lingo used in the chats, and then spend the first few minutes just eavesdropping in certain, specific rooms. "Ok, Angela, what do you want your nickname to be?"

"Oh, I don't know, what do you think I should use?"

"Let's see ... you could be 'ExoticDancer,' or 'Angel,' or 'SunGoddess,' or 'SeaNymph,' or ..."
" 'SeaNymph'? I like that one. Let's go with Sea-Nymph."

"SeaNymph it is."

As soon as we assign Angela a nickname to identify

23

herself, the invitations to chat privately begin to pour in. Angela playfully answers as many as she can, not being able to keep track of any of them. Finally, one catches her eye, and the remainder of her suitors are left unceremoniously behind

<Poseidon> | Have you ever been seduced by the Ruler of the Seas?

<SeaNymph> | Can't say that I have. Is he any good?

<Poseidon> | Sit back and relax, and you tell me. . . .

<SeaNymph> | An invitation full of promise . . . how can I refuse?

<Poseidon> | You are roused from a deep slumber by an intangible force, beckoning you from your ocean-side condo to the sandy beach surrounding it. It is well past midnight, yet you inexplicably leave, clad only in your sheer, white, lacy nightgown to walk along the deserted surf. The full moon illuminates your chosen path, guiding you to your predetermined destiny. A cloaked figure follows your ghostly apparition at a discreet distance, inspired by the delicate footsteps left behind in the moist sand. There is a slight breeze. It captures your flowing, long hair in its caress, simultaneously molding your nightgown to your feminine curves. The figure is held momentarily immobile, transfixed by your ethereal beauty and purity. He watches you throw your arms open to embrace the unpredictable power of Mother Nature. Carefree, you smile and continue on your journey, letting your senses guide you. The stranger continues to follow, never letting his presence be known. Eventually, you come upon an abandoned lifeguard tower, and are drawn to examine it more closely. At your feet, you discover four stakes anchored solidly into the sand, seemingly unaffected by the driving, churning waters of high tide. The stakes are situated in a perfect square, approximately five feet apart in each direction. Attached to each stake is a round, metal eyelet, designed obviously with the intent of securing some type of object to it. You are curious about the contraption, but dismiss it as perhaps an anchoring station for cages used in trapping shrimp or clams. Focusing your attention once again on the lifeguard tower, you notice four cuff-like accessories hanging from hooks on the side of the tower. Involuntarily, you lift one of the cuffs from its resting place, inspect it closely and realize that it was made to perfectly fit your wrist. Slowly, you take the soft, wide cuff and wrap it around your wrist, marveling at the snug fit. Raising your arm to the moonlight, you admire the primitive bracelet as if it were a cherished piece of jewelry. Until . . . your attention is drawn to the curious little clamp protruding from the outer side. As the realization dawns on you that these clamps were made to attach to the eyelets on the stakes below, you bend down to validate your theory. Surely enough, within seconds, your wrist is tightly secured to the stake, with little room for movement. Shuddering, you unclasp your wrist and stand to face the tower once again. Disconcerted to discover that the innocent docking station for sea cages is, indeed, a cleverly disguised trap used instead for human bondage, a sense of panic overtakes you, urging you to leave immediately.

"Oh, God, Randi, this guy is good. I don't know if I'll be able to handle the effects of both your book, and his chat."

"Yeah, he's making it pretty easy for you to just sit back and enjoy. Usually, they want you to tell the story so their hands can be free for . . . uh . . . other uses."

Subconsciously, Angela's own hands find their way up to her breasts, lightly caressing them through the fabric of her thin shirt, unobstructed by a constricting bra. Watching her get lost in her chat, I remain very still and quiet so as not to break the spell. Her nipples respond immediately, standing proud and erect while she heatedly twists them.

<Poseidon> I Pausing just long enough to remove the imprisoning bracelet from your wrist, you are thwarted when an unexpected gust of wind forces you flat up against the lifeguard tower. Suddenly, it is no longer the wind that keeps you pressed tightly against the weather-beaten structure, but a hand, a strong male hand pushing commandingly against your lower back. You gasp in fright as you hear a seductive male voice attempt to reassure you, "You have nothing to fear. Trust me. Give yourself to me and you shall know true bliss." The voice is hypnotic and thoroughly calming, and you find yourself relaxing against the pressure directed on your back. The voice continues to murmur encouraging words, lulling you into a peaceful sense of security. You remain flattened against the tower, although the hand has long since been removed. You feel two hands now, caressing you, sliding up and down your sides trying to memorize every inch of your womanly secrets.

Angela's involuntary moan redirects my attention back from the computer screen to her face, her beautiful features twisted in the throes of unfulfilled passion. Her hands have slid down from her breasts to slide against her stomach and sides, itching to go further, yet hesitating. Her short skirt has naughtily ridden up, exposing most of her soft, creamy thighs, which have also begun to spread farther and farther apart in an attempt to ease her discomfort.

Watching Angela's passion intensify has done nothing but inflame my own sexual desires. Right now, all I can think about is how much I want to touch her, to help ease her torment, to soar with her. Carefully arising from my chair, I move to position myself resting on my knees directly behind her. As I continue to read the words over her shoulder, I succumb to my urge to touch her.

<Poseidon> | Your hair is lifted from your neck, only to be replaced by warm, wet lips pressing tantalizing kisses to the newly exposed flesh. You arch your back and moan against the sensations fluttering in your belly.

Lifting her hair, I help her to feel the corresponding sensations as she is reading, kissing and licking the back of her neck, gently biting and sucking, inciting gasps from her perfect lips.

<Poseidon> | Another strong gust of wind appears out of nowhere, and with it, the tearing of your nightgown, completely rip-

ping it in two. You are pulled away
from the barrier of the tower, only to
have the wind abscond with the remains of your nightgown, carrying it
off into the distance to be swallowed
up by the sea.

I reach around, not at all hindered by the armless
chair. My hands slowly begin to unbutton her sheer
blouse, as my lips continue to kiss her neck and
shoulders. Once the buttons are undone, I pull it open
wide and reach for her bare breasts. My grip is firm
as I squeeze and rub them together, causing her legs
to spread even further apart in desperate need.
''Randi . . .'' she breathlessly whispers, then continues only with her soft moans.

<Poseidon> | Shivering, you attempt to look behind
you at your secret lover, but his hands
come up to hold your face immobile.

"Don't look at me. I shall remain
faceless, an everlasting fantasy. Now,
take another cuff and place it on your
other wrist."

As you move to obey, you feel his
hands come around front to cup your
breasts, squeezing and caressing them
into two wanton mounds, yearning to
be devoured. With your brain barely
able to comprehend, you are finally
able to secure the second cuff tightly to
your wrist. You see a strange, masculine hand reach beyond your shoulder

as the voice commands, "Stay as you are. I will fit these last two cuffs to your ankles myself."

Afraid to disobey, you remain frozen as the hand lifts away the two remaining cuffs from the tower and secures them to your ankles. With your desire mounting, and fate uncertain, your breathing becomes irregular, almost panting. The hands work slowly back up your silken legs, caressing simultaneously the inner and outer side of each leg, grazing carelessly at your swollen sex. Your lips are thick and glistening, hungry with need. Your hips are rocking slowly back and forth, anticipating the promise of indescribable ecstasy. Your nipples are taut and extended, greedy for unlimited stimulation.

Taking her aroused buds between my thumbs and forefingers, I begin to roll them back and forth quickly, causing an aching friction and immediate response. Gripping the edges of the chair, Angela begins to cry out, her bottom scooting back and forth across the chair, her hips rotating wildly. "Randi . . . I need . . . I need . . ." she tries to gasp out what would ease her torment, but is unsuccessful.

Lowering my hands to her knees, I begin to slide them slowly back up, marveling at the incredible softness of her legs. My thumbs reach the apex of her thighs, pushing the skirt up the final few inches to reveal her freshly shaven pussy. My thumbs toy with her outer lips and clit, while my fingers move down to seek out her moisture. Finding it, my fingers become possessed, all moving at once. My thumbs remain teasing her clit, while my fingers take turns pulling at, spreading, kneading and entering her pussy.

"Keep reading, Angela," I warn, making her refocus her attention on the computer screen, while I continue her subtle torture.

<Poseidon> | "Give yourself to me," the voice commands and asks you to lie, face up positioned between the four stakes anchored in the ground. Warily, you protest, "But the tide is coming in. Soon this whole section will be under water . . ."

"Trust me," is all you get in response.

Unable to resist, you lie down, centering yourself in the cool sand between the four stakes, hoping the voice can be trusted. "Close your eyes." Once your eyes are tightly shut, the stranger bends down to latch all four clasps to the corresponding eyelets. You are tethered completely, rendered helplessly immobile. Finished with his task, he retreats from your view, absorbing the erotic scene displayed before him. The complete trust the sea nymph has placed in him is intoxicating, filling him with an even greater sense of power. He has chosen his subject well and reclines against the tower to wait. You are confused by his sudden absence, unable to locate him through your limited scope of vision. "Where did you go? Why have you left me?"

Again, "Trust me," followed by, "Just relax, enjoy and FEEL. . . . Close your eyes and feel, you have nothing to fear."

The voice once again inspires trust, and you relax as much as possible in your spread-eagled state. You feel the waves lapping at your feet, feeling like one hundred tongues paying homage to your beauty. The water level inches its way up higher and higher as the tide continues to rise. The waves are gentle, rocking, caressing their way up your defenseless body, first your feet, your calves, your thighs. You squirm at this newly discovered foreplay, each lapping wave resembling a blanket of hands and tongues. You have a multitude of lovers, simultaneously bathing you in their passion, each touching you in a different way, invoking new and varied pleasures. Keeping your eyes closed, you find it easy to give yourself completely, basking in the abundance of sensations. The waves are splashing against your inner thighs now, probing at your most secret places, requesting entry but getting none. Ripples of pleasure radiate throughout your body. Your body cries out for fulfillment, begging to be taken completely. The stranger watches your arousal and slowly disrobes until he is as gloriously naked as the writhing sea nymph lying on the ground before him.

The water level continues to rise, completely covering your abdomen in warm, salty wetness. Your body is sucked further and further down as the tide swirls and pulls the sand out from under your backside. The wet sand slithers its way down the crack of your ass, teasing and tormenting you further.

"Please," you whisper, but get no response. The water level continues to rise further and further, completely covering your belly with each wave and reaching upward to lick at your breasts. The waves feel like hands now, grasping and pulling at your breasts only to leave and then return. Over and over your breasts are massaged, molded, folded, twisted, and suckled at. You are oblivious to the impending danger of the rising water, still focusing solely on your pleasure. It's not until you feel the water at your chin that you open your eyes and begin to panic. "Please, the water is getting too high. I'll drown if you don't release me."

"Trust me."

The sexual awareness of your body is only heightened by your fright, enhancing every sensation tenfold. The next series of waves causes you to hold your breath with your eyes clamped tightly shut. Inevitably, the waves completely cover you, from head to foot. No longer able to reopen your eyes, you finally feel the weight of your mysterious lover lowered upon your ravaged and aching body. Still having to hold your breath with each passing wave, you gasp as your lover enters you.

He holds himself tightly inside you, waiting for the water to recede, slowly withdrawing from you at just the same moment. Again and again this ritual is repeated, swiftly entering you as the water covers you, then withdrawing as it pulls away. You find yourself gasping for air, your breaks in between waves becoming shorter and shorter, your time under water increasing. As the fury of the ocean increases, so do the speed and frequency of his thrusts, hurling you into another dimension. Your mysterious lover peaks with you,

joining you on your journey into a
heavenly abyss.

"Randiiiiiiiiiiiiiiiiiiiii!!!!" Angela screams, as the
dual assault from Poseidon's words and my fingers
throw her over the edge into a much-sought-after and
needed release, sending several breathtaking shudders
and spasms rocketing through her entire body. When
she recovers enough, she warns me, "We're not finished, not by a long shot. Let me say goodbye to my
new friend, and then . . ."

<Poseidon>　|　As soon as he is able, he releases you
from your watery prison and disap-
pears, leaving you coughing and
gasping for air. The entire ordeal was
more exciting and fulfilling than any
you had ever encountered, and you
find yourself returning, night after
night to the same location. The deserted lifeguard tower is still as you
remembered, yet there is no sign of
the puzzling wooden stakes. Still,
you offer yourself to the ocean, reveling in the sensations the pulsing
water incites as it begins to lap at
your hot and eager sex.

<SeaNymph>　|　I'm going to marry you someday.

<Poseidon>　|　Is that a promise or a threat?

<SeaNymph>　|　It's a promise. I've never wanted
someone as badly as I want you right
now. I have to go, but I'll e-mail you
later with details about myself.

		Maybe we can arrange to meet some day?
<Poseidon>	I	My name is Antonio. I will look forward to your e-mail. Include a phone number, please.
<SeaNymph>	I	Antonio, I'm Angela. Nobody has ever gotten to me the way you just did. You'll get my number and then some.
<Poseidon>	I	Good night, then, lovely Angela. Till next time.
<SeaNymph>	I	Till next time, Antonio.

As I turn from the kitchen counter to carry the glasses of wine back to the living room, I am startled to see Angela standing there, blocking my exit, and looking angry. Surprised by her sudden appearance and the look on her face, I warily place the glasses back down on the counter and ask, ''What? You're not mad at me, are you? I just wanted to help you out. You looked like you were in mortal pain.''

''And how about you, Randi? Did any of that turn you on?''

As Angela asks me these questions, she advances towards me, forcing me to back away uncomfortably.

''What's under that dress, Randi? Are your panties soaked, or aren't you wearing any? Do you want me, Randi? Answer me!''

Angela continues towards me as we make a complete round through the kitchen with me backing up now into the living room, heading for the sofa.

Aware that I am totally aroused by what just hap-

36

pened and that I do want her desperately, I begin to nod, "Yes, Angela, I do want you."

Stopping when the backs of my legs run into the arm of the couch, I wait breathlessly for Angela to reach me. I've never seen her in this state: angry, passionate, agitated. I don't know what to expect. Although her skirt is back in place, her shirt is still unbuttoned and hanging open, giving her a disheveled, sultry appearance.

"Did that turn you on . . . taking advantage of me, helpless in my lust? Did it?!"

Grabbing my hair, Angela pulls my face to hers and begins to kiss me, hard and punishing. With her other arm wrapped around my back and her left leg braced against the side of the couch, she brings up her right knee and pushes it up into my crotch, grinding it hard against my bare pussy and clit. Even though the act was meant to hurt, to punish, it felt good, and I push back into it, sucking up between my lips as much of her knee as I can get.

Irritated that I am enjoying the attack more than fighting it, Angela pushes me from her, causing me to topple over backwards onto the couch.

"Stay put. I'll be right back."

Squirming against my discomfort, my back resting flat on the cushions, the small of my back draped across the arm, and my legs dangling over the side with my feet barely touching the floor, I wait as Angela disappears into my bedroom. When she returns, she is carrying a small cat-o'-nine-tails whip and a wooden paddle.

"Angela, what are you doing?"

"Teaching you a lesson. I don't like being taken advantage of like that."

"Well, it seems to me, you already had this planned, regardless of what happened tonight, am I right?"

With a wicked grin, Angela states, "Perhaps. I like to be prepared for anything. Now, spread those legs wide and hike that dress up to your waist. I want to see that hungry little pussy."

Not wanting to spread her ire any deeper, I comply quickly, praying silently that she'll go easy on me.

"That's a girl," she remarks, quite pleased.

Kneeling down between my legs, Angela settles herself so that she is directly eye level with my pussy. Setting the paddle aside, but keeping the whip firmly in her grasp, she begins to kiss the inside of my right thigh, softly at first, then gently biting. Once she has succeeded in aptly moistening the entire length of my inner thigh, she moves slightly aside to create more room, then slaps my inner thigh with the whip. Slowly, she works her way up, whipping with varying intensities ranging from warmly arousing to bitingly painful.

Soon I am squirming and crying out, begging her to stop. When she is satisfied with the rosy color of one thigh, she turns her attention to the other, kissing and biting it, covering it in wetness. I suck in my breath as I wait for the first, stinging slap. I don't have long to wait, and soon find the sensations of the first whipping being repeated on my other thigh. I endure as much of the prickling and burning sensations as possible, and again beg her for mercy. She stops just when I think I can bear no more, then centers her attention on my pussy. I cringe as I realize she has the same fate in store for it as she did my thighs.

"Are you scared, Randi? Is your pussy quivering? It should be. Have you ever had your pussy spanked before, Randi?"

Shaking my head to indicate no, Angela assures me, "Well, I'll make sure you like it."

Still positioned between my thighs, I tense as she moves her face closer to my swollen lower lips. Immediately, I feel the softness of her mouth make contact, slowly licking and sucking them into her mouth, teasing them with her tongue. She releases them only to seek them out again, toying and toying with them, splitting them apart with her tongue, then pressing them back together. Purposefully avoiding both my clit and my opening, she continues to kiss and caress, until I can take no more.

Gasping, begging her for release, I am rewarded by a stinging lash of the whip directed squarely on my clit.

"No, Angela, no . . ."

Another, then another, then another, all in rapid succession, all making contact with different sections of my ravaged pussy. With my hips bucking wildly to avoid further contact with the whip, I beg Angela to stop.

"Please, Angela, no more, no more. I'm sorry I took advantage of you. Please, stop."

Realizing that she has reached my breaking point, she stops the whipping, and concentrates on soothing me once again with kisses. This time, she allows her lips and tongue to graze over and tease my clit, as well as dive deeply inside.

"Oh, Angela, Angela, I'm going to cum."

As soon as the words are uttered, I regret it, because she immediately removes all stimulation to my aching sex.

"No, I'm afraid not yet, Randi. First, you're going to let me spank you."

"But you just did, Angela."

"I want your ass, too. Get up."

Reaching her hand out to assist, she helps to pull me up from my awkward position on the couch. Then, directing me to stand behind the couch, she pushes me forward so that the top of the couch is pressing firmly into my belly. My torso, head and arms are all bent over and pressed into the cushions on the other side, my hands curling around the edges for support.

"You keep your hands on that side of the couch, Randi. If you try to block any of your spankings with your hands, I'll give you five more swats each time you do."

"Ok, ok . . . just hurry, please. I can't take much more."

Picking up the wooden paddle, Angela stands behind me and lifts my dress up over my ass to reveal her newest target. Sliding the paddle in circles across each cheek, Angela takes her time, taking pleasure in my misery. I receive three swats right off the bat, one squarely centered in the middle, the other two singling out each cheek. Then I feel nothing but the smooth wooden surface of the paddle gliding across my cheeks again.

"Angela, please hurry. Don't torture me like this."

"Randi, I'm going to drag this out as long as I can."

Three swats, middle, right, left, then soothing smoothness. Just as the stinging begins to subside, Angela smacks me again, bringing with them, three sharp "Ow's." Her torture is slow and methodical, allowing me enough time to recover so that the slaps are never unbearable. After a short while, Angela decides to add a little spice to the spanking, just to liven things up a bit. Leaving me alone for a moment, she disappears back into the bedroom. My ass is sore and on fire right now, and I involuntarily wiggle it trying to get some relief.

Angela returns in time to catch my display, only to say, "I like it. Keep wiggling. I want you to wiggle like that until I'm done with you."

"Oh, God, Angela . . ." is all I can say as my wiggling inadvertently rubs my engorged clit back and forth along the top back of the couch.

Watching as she picks up the whip again, I sigh in resignation as I realize she is going to whip my behind with it as well. However, I am soon to learn my mistake as I feel her probing my ass with some lubricant and pressing the handle of the whip into my anus.

"Just relax, Randi, it's not very big."

Slowly she works the entire handle deep into my ass until nothing but the nine leather straps remain dangling down.

"Now, this should make things interesting, just make sure you keep wriggling. I think I'll get serious about spanking you now."

Groaning from the pleasant pressure now filling my

ass, I continue wriggling my ass in circles as Angela begins to swat in earnest. Without any breaks at all, she goes from center, to right, to left, then right back to center again. Each swat sends the whip handle thrusting inward, making me feel as if I'm being fucked in the ass and spanked all at the same time. Combined with my clit getting friction from the couch, I am mindless, squirming between the pleasure and pain. Swat after swat continues to fall, until I am screaming out Angela's name and convulsing into a shuddering heap on top of the couch. Once Angela realizes that I'm in the throes of an orgasm, she throws down the paddle and inserts two fingers deep inside my pussy, thrusting in time with my contractions.

When my spasms have subsided, she pulls my totally spent and limp body up from the couch, rips my dress from my body, pushes me to the floor, then removes her own clothing. Falling on top of me, she grinds her pelvis into mine and begins to kiss me. Her breasts rub against my breasts, her clit against my clit, and in a matter of moments, her overstimulated body is reaching its second climax of the night. She screams out her fulfillment into our tightly locked mouths, the muffled and strangled sound dissipating rapidly as I swallow them down.

The next morning finds us both complaining of headaches and hangovers. Somehow we had managed to crawl to the bed before falling asleep, but I'll be damned if I can remember doing so.

Despite her haggard appearance, Angela still manages to look beautiful as she smiles at me and asks,

"Last night was fun, wasn't it? I had a really, really great time! Thanks for having me over. I'll think I'll get out of here so I can get going on planning your party. I only have a few days to prepare. See you Sunday, Miranda! Call me if you need anything before then."

"Ok, Angela. Thanks for keeping me company last night. I'm glad we had a chance to say our goodbyes."

Angela turns to me and wickedly says, "Oh, is that what you call it? Hmmmmm . . ." Laughing, I throw one of my slippers at her retreating back. "See you Sunday, Angela." "Bye-bye, hon."

The remainder of the week is spent packing and getting everything ready to move. Most of my things have been mailed to my home directly, wanting to take as little with me as possible. It is sad taking my computer apart and stuffing it back into its protective crates, rendering it lifeless, but I smile as I recall all the memories it holds for me. Ah, the tangled webs we weave, indeed.

Sunday morning arrives, and with it a phone call from Angela.

"Party's all set, Randi. See you at the club at six o'clock sharp."

"Okay, dokey. I'll be there."

"Oh, and Randi?"

"Yes?"

"Bring a swimsuit."

"A swimsuit? What on earth for?"

"Surprise . . . Just bring one, preferably a one-piece."

"What did Robert do, have a hot tub installed? Just for little ole me?"

"You'll see."

"Well, uh, should I dress a certain way? You've got me worried now."

"Wear whatever you like, love."

"Ok. See you tonight."

I find myself approaching the doors to the club warily, unsure of what I'll find on the other side. I opted to wear a comfortable pair of jeans and a T-shirt, figuring that whatever Angela has planned isn't too fancy. After all, she asked me to bring my bathing suit.

I open the door to complete mayhem, the party appearing to have started quite a bit earlier. All my friends are there, the dancers, Jeff, Robert, and even some of my most favorite clients. The party was in full swing, a tapped keg surrounded by hoards of thirsty people. Angela greets me at the door.

"Come on in, sweetie. Don't be shy. What's your pleasure tonight? I'll have Jeff whip you up the drink of your choice."

"I think I'll nurse on margaritas tonight. Thanks, Angela, everything looks beautiful."

"You're welcome, Randi. Nothing is too grand for my bestest friend ever!"

Cornering Jeff, Angela asks him to blend up a pitcher of margaritas, and then comes to join me at one of the tables surrounding the stage. We sit there and talk for about an hour, socializing with everyone who stops by to say they'll miss me and wish me well. Suddenly, I get this eerie feeling, looking about the room trying to figure out what's amiss.

"Is something wrong, Randi? You look like you've seen a ghost."

"I'm not sure . . . I . . ."

Scanning the room, I desperately seek out the cause of my unease.

"Oh, goodness, now I know . . . All the men are gone. How weird! Are they all out back smoking cigars or something?"

Just as I finish my question, the lights dim and the music comes on full power, blaring the Y.M.C.A. song out over the speakers. I look at Angela for an explanation, only to see her grin from ear to ear, her focus directed to center stage.

Targeting my gaze there as well, I am shocked to see all of the guys dressed up in costumes, ranging from construction worker to police officer, strutting about on the stage. They have begun to dance to the music, whimsically stripping down to nothing but G-strings.

Robert walks to the microphone and announces, "This is for you, Miranda! In appreciation for all you've done for us! Woooo!"

All the men leave except for Robert, Jeff and two of the best-looking bouncers, opting to finish out the performance as a foursome. They are comically trying to portray four sexy gay men, exaggerating every pelvic thrust ridiculously. Angela and I can't stop laughing, and tears well up in our eyes as we watch. The fearsome foursome's finale is a close-up view of their behinds as they proudly carry themselves backstage.

***

"Oh, God, Angela. That was soooo great. I haven't laughed that hard in a long time. How did you get those guys to agree to do it?"

"I had to promise them a week's worth of tips!"

"No!"

"Nah, they were happy to do it. They figured it would be the perfect sendoff."

"Oh it is . . . it is . . . it's priceless. I wish I had my video camera!"

"Don't worry, taken care of. I'll mail you the tape."

"You're awesome, Angela."

"Yeah, I know. Hey, here they come again."

Again I focus my attention to center stage. The music has changed to a melody that is very near and dear to my own heart.

"Angela, that's our song. The one we dance to. Why are they playing that one?"

"Just wait and see."

Immediately I see what she means, as Jeff comes strutting out on stage wearing Angela's costume, complete with top hat, tux with tails and the cane. He mimics Angela's dance routine admirably, appearing very dramatic and serious about his role. Next, we see Robert standing at the entrance, dressed in my prim and proper costume, waiting for his cue to come on stage. He looks ridiculous, the dress barely fitting him, wobbling in a pair of high heels. The drama unfolds as Jeff attempts the seduction of the prudish maiden, stripping her clothes from her with the use of his cane. I start another round of giggles as Robert is left standing in a bra, G-string, and garter and hose.

Next it is Jeff's turn to reveal his true identity, that of a woman. Oh, this is going to be good.

Jeff whips off his top hat, to reveal a lush and beautiful mass of shimmering red hair.

"Is that your wig?" I ask Angela in surprise.

"Uh, huh."

"So cool."

Jeff continues undressing until he, too, is clad only in a bra, G-string, and garter and hose.

"Oh, my God, Angela. I never knew Jeff was so well hung!"

"Me neither," Angela replies, with obvious interest.

The boys prance around on their heels, their total lack of grace adding to the humor of the whole scenario. Jeff reaches out for Robert and ensnares "her" in an imaginary lasso, pulling Robert closer and closer. Finally, Jeff has "her" in her clutches and begins a mock seduction, rubbing her body against that of her captive. The boys are hilarious as they rub their bras against each other, feigning desire and passion, fighting against their unnatural attraction. After several pulls and pushes, twists and gyrations, Jeff and Robert fall into a heap on the stage floor.

Thunderous applause follows their performance, the two male dancers blushing proudly. Taking their bows, they exit the stage and get dressed to join the rest of the party animals, the party still in full swing.

I take a moment to go thank Robert for the wonderful show. He is still somewhat embarrassed, but pleased that I had enjoyed it so much. I spy Angela on the other side of the room talking to Jeff, looking very cozy and chummy, wooing him with her charms.

I know where she's going to end up tonight, the shameless hussy!

Angela then runs over to me excitedly. "Now it's our turn. Where's your suit?"

"It's on the table, why?"

"Go get it and meet me backstage."

"You're the boss."

By the time I arrive backstage, Angela is already in her suit and whispering conspiratorially to Jeff. There are a bunch of men gathered in back, all strangers to me, attempting to push a large, square sandbox onto the stage.

After changing into my suit, I once again join Angela.

"Ready for some mud wrestling?"

"Excuse me, Angela. You never said anything about mud wrestling."

"Nope, I didn't, did I? All the same, you and I are going out there and wrestle."

"Ah, come on."

"It'll be fun, you'll see."

Angela leads my reluctant body on stage. The lights are all out except for a spotlight directed on the huge mud box taking up most of the stage. Angela places me in one corner, while she goes to stand at the opposite corner. Jeff picks up the microphone and begins to announce the match.

"Attention, attention. Ladies and gentleman. For your pleasure tonight, we have the battle of the babes, live from Club Illicit. In this corner, standing at an impressive five foot, ten inches in height, weighing in at 145 pounds, the Amazing Amazon Angela!"

Hoots and hollers follow Angela's introduction.

Then Jeff walks over to me, raising my arm as he announces, "And in this corner, we have the one and only, the Mesmerizing Miranda, standing at a measly five foot, six inches in height, and weighing only 120 pounds. But don't let her timid looks fool you. She's a tough cookie. May the best babe win!!!!"

Another round of thunderous applause follows Jeff's speech. At the sound of the bell, Angela starts advancing towards me. Having no other option, I leave my corner to face her, only to be immediately tripped to plunge face first into the mud. Not willing to let her get away with that, I grab for her ankle and pull her down to join me. Soon we are scrapping away, mud flinging everywhere. For the most part, Angela has the upper hand, dominating most of the match, but I still manage to get a few good licks in. By the time the match is over, neither one of us is recognizable. Ever the diplomat, Jeff decides to declare the match a tie.

CHAPTER 3

∎

TEMPTATIONS

I replay the events of the party over and over again in my head as I drive, each mile taking me further and further away from my life as a dancer, and all the new friends I had made. Lost in my thoughts, I fail to take the proper exit off the freeway, taking one that, instead, leads me to desolation. Finally aware that I haven't seen anything for miles, I am relieved when I spot a run-down motel. Keeping focused on the little building so as not to pass it, I pull into the parking lot with apprehension.

The motel is situated just on the outskirts of a small town with a seedy little diner settled off to its right. My last thought as I trudge up to the second floor carrying my overnight bag in one hand and Taz in the other is, please, just let it be clean. I look around with a sense of unease. Gloomy storm clouds have begun to build, getting darker and more ominous with each passing moment, adding more to the overall dreary outlook of my overnight haven.

Relief floods through me as I open the door to a pine-scented interior, giving, at least, the illusion of cleanliness. The room is very quaint and comfortable, and for the first time since I've entered this backward town, I feel that I can take a full breath and relax. I unpack Taz from his crate, giving him free roam to explore his new surroundings. After I see to his needs, I concentrate on taking care of my own. Spending just a few minutes in the tiny bathroom to freshen up, I optimistically venture out into the unknown for directions and entertainment.

The motel clerk is kind enough to give me directions so that I can be on my way home again first thing in the morning without any more problems. He also tells me that the only happening place in the entire town is the restaurant-bar down the road a mile or two where everyone gathers to watch sports on the big screen TV, as well as shoot the shit. In conclusion, he also warns me that there are very few women in town, and even fewer that frequent the bar, so I should be prepared to be the only female. Thanking him for his time, I hurriedly walk to my car, hoping to avoid the storm assembling determinedly above my head. I soon find myself pulling into the parking lot of the very bar I was warned about. Miranda, what are you doing? Try as I might, I just can't keep myself from seeking out trouble and finding it.

The bar, an obvious source of pride, appears immaculate and in excellent repair. Shiny hardwood floors welcome me as I enter, my eyes quickly zooming in on an empty bar stool. Heading in that direction, I admire the masculine décor, sturdy and rustic, yet curiously modernized with state-of-the-art technology in the electronics department. There is a large-screen TV in one corner, supplemented by several smaller TV monitors hanging at various locations throughout the bar. It seems that no matter where you end up sitting, you have a bird's-eye view. The stereo system is also state of the art, using many speakers for the ultimate surround sound.

I decide to take a seat at the bar, hoping to engage the bartender in some polite banter to help quell the unease of being alone in a strange town. All around me booths and tables are filled with loud, rowdy men, shouting excitedly at the TV monitors.

Apparently, a highly wagered football game is on, with lots and lots of money on the line. And . . . there isn't another female to be spotted anywhere. Where did I end up, the Twilight Zone?

Choosing a stool that offers the best view, I settle myself in comfortably, taking pains to keep my short dress from riding up and revealing more of my thighs than necessary. I should have changed into a more conservative outfit before leaving the motel, but I was anxious to get out and explore. Suddenly regretting my hasty decision, I hail the bartender, desperate for a false sense of courage.

The bartender saunters lazily over toward my stool, his smile becoming broader as he closes in.

"Good evening, ma'am. What can I get for you?"

"I'd love a glass of your house wine."

"Coming right up."

I watch as he digs out a clean glass, making sure that it is good and cold, ice crystals clinging precariously to the edges, then sets it down on a napkin placed directly in front of me. As he fills the glass with wine, he asks, "So, what brings you to our little town? We don't get many strangers passing through. We're not exactly located 'on the way' to anywhere."

Smiling, I reply, "Well, I kind of took a wrong turn, got lost and ended up here. I was tired and figured I'd better call it a day before I was forced to spend the night in my car."

"Sounds like you made a wise choice. So, I'm Jack. What's your name?"

Reaching my hand across the counter, I respond, "Miranda. Nice to meet you, Jack. So tell me, are there any other women in this town, or am I in big trouble?"

Laughing, he shakes my hand, stating bluntly, "The few women that we do have in this town are all married to the biggest and meanest sons of bitches. They are all off-limits. So, I'd imagine that you might be the center of attention once these lugs open their eyes and realize that you're here."

"Oh, charming. Maybe I can scoot on out of here before anyone notices?"

"Well, if you must, but there's not a whole heck of a lot to do around here. You'll be okay. For the most part, these guys are well-behaved. Besides, that wedding ring on your finger will probably dissuade any unwanted advances."

"True, true," I whisper as I pick up my glass and drain it in one swallow, focusing on my ring and realizing how anxious I am to get back home.

"Can I buy you another?" Startled, I look over to my left where a man has somehow managed to seat himself without me even noticing. Before I have a chance to answer him, he says, "Hey, Jack, how about a club soda and lime for me, and another glass of wine for this lovely lady?"

"Sure thing, Tim."

So, his name is Tim, and mighty presumptuous as well. I have half a mind to refuse his unwanted act of chivalry. This guy is trouble with a capital "T," I can feel it. Looking him over closely as Jack gets the drink order together, I have to admit that he is a mighty fine-looking bundle of trouble. Very rugged and clean, his good looks consist of soft, dark brown hair with boyish floppy bangs and round, wire-rimmed glasses, giving him a "Clark Kent"-ish appearance. Innocently disguised behind those glasses, his compelling brown eyes miss nothing, and he turns casually in my direction to catch me blatantly staring at him. Embarrassed, I quickly look away, but remain unable to keep my gaze from continuously wandering back to his.

"Thanks for the drink, but you really should have let me answer. I wasn't going to accept it."

Tim retaliates by staring back at me, until I begin to feel quite uncomfortable and squirm under his intense scrutiny. Still, he continues looking deeply into my eyes, looking for clues, wondering how to proceed.

With our gazes still locked, he utters, "Not very friendly, are you?"

Angered by his reaction, I am finally able to pull my eyes away.

"Look, I just don't want you to get any wrong ideas, ok? I don't want to mislead you by being too friendly."

"Fair enough," is his cocky reply.

Without warning, Tim slides off his stool and moves around to stand directly behind me. I can't see him, but I can feel him, hovering, causing the little hairs on the nape of my neck to stand erect, waiting. I can feel his breath on my hair, and I remain immobile as I wait for him to make his exit. Instead of leaving, however, he places his hands on my shoulders and starts to slowly slide them down my arms. The instant I feel his touch, I melt, turning to butter, and am unable to ask him to stop. Encouraged by my silence, he bends to whisper into my right ear, his hands now working their way back up my arms.

"Where is your husband?"

Shakily, I answer, "at home," and close my eyes as I allow myself to become molded by his hands. Oh, God, no, please, not again, not again. I am on my way home, to my husband. I can't give in to my lustful impulses anymore. What the hell is the matter with me?

"Your body is responding to my touch. You are attracted to me, admit it. Let me take you back to your room. Your husband doesn't ever have to know."

Panicking, I blurt out, "No! Now get away from me. Go on, leave, please!"

I feel him stiffen behind me, and I pray that he'll finally leave me alone.

Once again, I feel his breath on my ear as he whispers, "How much?"

Initially confused by his question, I repeat, "How much? What do you mean, how much?"

His voice becomes more menacing as he explains,

"How much . . . money . . . will it cost me to take you home with me for the night?"

Furious, as the implication of his question slices through my gut, I turn around and slap his smug face as hard as I can, followed quickly by a shower of sticky wine.

"You stupid jerk," I hiss at him, finally gaining the attention of all of the bar patrons, as well as a flabbergasted Jack.

"What the hell is going on over here?" he asks incredulously.

"It's okay, Jack," Tim calmly replies. "I'm leaving. I have to go back home now and change before I go on duty tonight."

Tim walks over to Jack and whispers something in his ear. Jack nods a couple of times, then finally says, "You got it."

As Tim leaves, he turns once again to face me. Pointing his finger in my direction, he whispers dangerously, "You are going to regret that you did that, little lady."

Undaunted, I watch his retreating figure walk out the glass doors and across the parking lot, never once glancing back in my direction.

When I turn back to Jack, he is shaking his head. "Boy, I wish you hadn't done that."

"You should have heard what he said to me, Jack. He flat out called me a whore!"

"Just behave yourself for the rest of the night, ok?"

"Me?! Me behave?! I was doing just fine until he showed up. Who is he anyway? Is he your relief bartender or something like that? I'm not going to run into him again am I?"

"Let's just put it this way, if he wants to run into you again, he will."

"Oh, great. Let's hope I discouraged him enough to stay away. Can I have another glass of wine, please? My other one has mysteriously gone astray."

After my fifth glass of wine, I am feeling delightfully buzzed and at ease again. Even though I keep catching surreptitious glances by various men, not a move by one of them is made in my direction. The football game is long over, replaced by some sort of ridiculous wrestling match. I end up asking Jack for a deck of cards, alternating between games of solitaire and an occasional game of blackjack when he has a moment to spare.

Yawning, I realize that I will have to walk back to my room, being a bit too intoxicated to drive, and I try to recollect exactly how far away the motel is from the bar. It seemed like just a minute or two drive, so it can't be that far. Besides, it is a very small town. Nothing is far away from anything, I manage to convince myself. Toying with the idea of sticking around until the bar closes and asking Jack for a ride, I decide against it after recalling our previous conversation about the lack of available women in this town. It is best that I don't tempt anybody.

After rummaging through my purse to find enough cash to pay off my tab as well as leave a generous tip, I decide to sneak away from the bar while Jack is distracted at the other end. Nobody else seems to notice my exit, and I can't help but breathe a deep sigh of relief as I slither out the doors undetected. My relief is short-lived, however. A bolt of lightening lights up the sky, followed immediately by a loud clap of thunder. Within seconds, a huge downpour causes me to change my plans. Digging into my purse for my keys, I bolt across the parking lot to my car.

"Damn."

I realize that my skimpy dress offers me little in the way of protection, modesty and warmth. I can see clear through it, leaving absolutely nothing to the imagination. Looks like I'm going to be spending the night in my car after all.

Shivering uncontrollably, I decide to turn the engine on and pump some heat into the car. I don't have anything else in the car that I can use to cover up with, not even a sweater. Maybe I *will* end up having to take my chances with Jack after all.

I turn on the ignition and search for a decent radio station. Immediately, my car becomes bathed in flashing lights. It takes a few moments for my alcohol-hazed brain to deduce that it is not an incredible display of lightening, or even that the bar has suddenly blown up, but rather the flashing red and blue lights of a police car. "Crap, this is all I need."

The large, charcoal outline of a uniformed presence makes its way toward my driver's side window. I am temporarily blinded as an intense beam from his flashlight is shone directly at my eyes. As soon as I have my window completely rolled down, he removes the light.

"What's the problem, officer?" I ask, as I struggle to regain my sight.

"Well, well, well, if it isn't my old friend. Drinking

and driving is against the law, little lady, even in our backward little town."

That voice, I recognize that voice. I become sickeningly aware that the police officer that I am currently at the complete mercy of, is none other than Tim. Oh, I am in so much trouble.

"I swear I wasn't going to drive. I was actually going to walk back to my motel, but then it started raining. I was only trying to keep warm and wait until the rain stopped, honest."

"Sorry, honey, that story might work on some cops, but not on me. It's a crime to even sit behind the wheel of a car in your condition. Now, please step out of the car."

"Oh, come on, you can't be serious."

"Do it now, or I will add an additional charge of resisting arrest. Get out of the car."

Unsteadily, I roll the window back up and managed to wrench myself free from the driver's seat and out of the car, unintentionally slamming the door behind me.

"Would you like to voluntarily perform some roadside maneuvers for me? Who knows, maybe you are still sober enough to drive, and this whole mess can be cleared up very quickly."

"It's pouring rain, Tim. Can't we find some shelter first?"

"Hmmmm, is that a refusal?"

"No, asshole," I mutter under my breath. "No, I'll do your stupid roadsides, but I can tell you now, I'm going to fail them. I am way too drunk to drive."

"Darling, you are making my job incredibly easy," he replies with a solicitous smile.

Finally able to focus once again, I look directly at him. Oh, man, does he look good in a uniform, with his hair all wet and clinging to his head and face. I watch as the rain continues to pelt him, dripping down across his nose, face and mouth. How is it that I didn't notice before how sexy his mouth is, with those full, soft lips? If only it were a different time, a different place under different circumstances.

"Well?" he asks.

"Well, what?"

"I asked you to recite the alphabet, are you going to do it?"

"Yes, sir!" Suddenly, my situation has become hilariously funny to me, and I burst out laughing. Here I am, standing in the pouring rain, soaked to the skin . . . my dress totally transparent . . . Oh, shit, I can see my nipples . . . getting ready to say my ABC's . . . for what? It is obvious that he is holding a grudge from earlier, and, probably, no matter what I did, I was going to end up in jail. Hey, if I'm headed to the slammer anyway, I'm going to have some fun screwing with this guy. Giggling, I say, "Ok, ok, ok . . . I'm ready now." Against his directions, I begin to sing, "A . . . B . . . C . . . D . . . E . . . F . . . G . . . U, R, A . . . P . . . I . . . G."

I am rewarded when his features change from amusement to irritation.

Smiling innocently, I ask, "How did I do?"

"You failed. Now, close your eyes, stand with your arms out wide to your sides, and when I tell you, touch the tip of your right index finger to your nose. Do you understand?"

"Perfectly, but you just want me to close my eyes

so I won't catch you looking at my nipples, don't you?''

Shaking his head, he starts to say, "That has nothing . . ." then stops in mid-sentence as he glances down at my chest and realizes, for the first time, just how truly exposed I am.

"Damn, we're going to have to finish this up at the station. You have the right to remain silent.''

He continues reading me my rights, and I begin to laugh anew as I connect my name with the rights. He is reading me my "Miranda" Rights. With my laughing out of control, he curses, turns me around and presses my chest flat up against the car to handcuff me. Retrieving my keys and purse, he leads me off in the direction of his patrol car, where I am unceremoniously dumped into the back seat. During the ride to the police station, I get my laughter under control and focus again on insulting and irritating him.

"Some officer of the law you are. You practically begged me to have sex with you in that bar.''

"I was protecting you. I wanted to make it perfectly clear to all those men in there that you were off-limits. By my acting as if I were interested in you, I kept you safe from their overactive hormones. I wasn't going to take you home with me. You have no idea how much danger you could have been in tonight. Some of those men haven't had a woman in years.''

"Yeah, well, what was the big idea of offering me money?''

"I wanted to make sure that you weren't a hooker.

I would have arrested you right then and there had you accepted."

"Why? It sounds like the men in this town could use one. How about you, Ossifer? When was the last time *you* had sex . . . with a woman, that is?"

"You are a piece of work, you know that? It's none of your business, now shut up before I'm forced to gag you."

I hold my tongue for the remainder of the trip. The police station is at the opposite end of town from the bar, but still only minutes away. It looks dark and cold and lonely, and I begin to have misgivings about the way I've been treating Officer Tim. I didn't want to spend the night in jail. Damn, what had come over me? Duh, alcohol, Miranda. I shouldn't have drunk so much, although I was already beginning to rapidly sober up. Maybe by the time we got to the Breathalyzer test, I'd be at a legal B.A.C. Well, with my luck, something else would happen.

Officer Tim walks me into the building, flipping on lights as he pushes me forward and down the hall to the booking area. It is actually a pretty nice building, with a few old-fashioned, barred cells lined up against the rear wall. The booking desk, located in the middle of the room, is packed with all types of equipment ranging from a mug shot camera to a computer. He orders me to sit on a bench directly across from the desk and not to move. He then seats himself behind the computer and begins to tip tap away.

"Hey, I thought we were going to finish roadside maneuvers in here," I pout, not happy with the sudden lack of attention.

"You weren't taking them seriously. I'm putting you down as a refusal."

"Well, don't I get to blow into some machine or something like that?"

Stopping what he is doing, he looks over the top of the computer screen at me and scowls. "Ok, I'll give you one more chance to cooperate, but you had better not fuck with me again."

The Breathalyzer machine is also located on the booking desk, making it very convenient for him to activate and set up while I remain sitting right where I am. After testing it to make sure it is working properly, he walks over in my direction to get me. "No, games, understand?"

"Yes," I mutter, belligerently.

"Okay, put your lips around the edge of this tube as tightly as you can, and blow into it with all your might. Keep blowing until I tell you to stop."

"Like this?" I ask, and turn towards him, licking my lips provocatively while shaping them into a delicate little "O."

His eyes narrow in warning, and I quickly affix my mouth to the tube and blow before he has a chance to change his mind.

"That's it, keep going, keep going . . . great. Ok, that's enough. You can stop now. It looks like you are a .118, which means you get to be my guest tonight." He announces it way too gleefully, clearly pleased that he will finally be able to exact his revenge.

"Ok, let's inventory your things before we lock them up. Any drugs or weapons you want to tell me about that I might find in your purse?"

"No. Can't we forget all about this and just take me back to my motel? I'm sorry I gave you so much trouble."

"Too late for apologies now, toots. You should have thought about that earlier. I'm enjoying myself far too much to end it all so quickly."

"My name is Miranda. I'd appreciate it if you'd use it in the future."

"Ok . . . Miranda. Watch me go through your things so that you don't accuse me of taking anything. Let's see . . . a brush, lipstick, a compact, perfume . . . What's this?" He shows me a wrapped package, one I don't recognize.

"I don't know. What does it say on the tag?"

"*To Miranda, Love, Angela. I'll miss you.* I'm going to have to unwrap it."

"Be my guest."

However, when I see what he is holding in his hands, I turn several shades of crimson.

"Well, what do we have here? Soap on a rope, it would appear."

I look at him mortified, as I watch him dangle from his finger, a huge bar of soap sculpted in the shape of a very well-endowed penis. Great timing, Angela.

"I think I'll keep this out for a while. If you give me any more lip, I just may have to wash your mouth out with soap."

Oh, what I'd give to be able to wipe the smirk off his all-too-handsome face.

"You're really going to love this next procedure, Miranda."

"Oh, yeah, and what procedure would that be?"

He walks slowly towards me as I back away from him, suddenly scared by the tone in his voice.

He states matter-of-factly, "Well, first, I have to frisk you to make sure you're not concealing any weapons."

"I'm not," I promise, as I bump into the wall behind me.

Pressing his full weight into me as he takes my chin and directs my gaze directly into his, he says, "And then I have to perform a cavity search, to make sure you're not concealing any drugs."

"A cavity search?" I repeat, suddenly very frightened.

He nods, quite happy with this turn of events. Now who was fucking with whom? "And nobody gets to stay in my jail until I'm convinced they are scrubbed clean and wearing orange pajamas."

"I have to take a shower? I can assure you that my hygiene is impeccable."

"No, you don't get to take a shower, I have to give you one. I can't trust you without handcuffs on until you are safely behind bars."

"You can't do this! There are rules against this. You have to go get a female officer."

"Sorry, hon, not only are there no female officers, there are no other officers period. What you see is what you get. I am the undisputed law in this town. Now, stand still while I frisk you."

I suck in my breath as his hand leaves my chin to join the other on a thorough search of my body. Starting at my shoulders, they slide slowly, too slowly . . . down, over my dress and across my breasts, then under my arms while his thumbs remain to tease my nipples. My breasts react instantly, tightening and growing to stand fully erect, and I am unable to stifle an unwelcome moan. His hands move around behind me, pulling me away from the wall and up against him again, as they move tantalizingly across my back to return to my sides. Slowly down my sides and over my hips they travel, then one hand slips across my belly, causing it to quiver, while the other hand explores the small of my back.

Gasping, I sputter, "I'm sure this isn't the proper procedure for frisking a female prisoner."

"Well, there's no reason why we can't make it interesting, is there?"

"I can think of at least one hundred of them," I stammer.

His hands inch their way lower, the rear one lightly grazing across my ass, while the front hand presses into my abdomen, precariously close to my mound. Oh, God, I think, as my knees threaten to give out. He crouches, getting down onto one knee, as he finishes his inspection, assuring himself that I have no weapons attached to my bare thighs.

Standing erect, he presses me flat and holds me tightly against the wall. He whispers, "No weapons. How about drugs?"

"No, I promise I don't have any," I whimper as I feel his right hand inching its way up under my dress and along the inside of my thigh. "Please."

"Please, what?"

"Please stop. I don't have any drugs."

"As much as I'd like to believe you, I can't trust anybody, no matter how pretty they may be."

His fingers toy with the lips to my pussy, tickling

them, pulling at them, twisting them and separating them. Now it was his turn to moan. Taking two of his fingers, he begins to slide them up my silken passage, amazed by how much moisture he finds.

"Oh, God. You're so wet. You're not supposed to be this wet. You are going to make this twice as hard on me."

He chokes on the words, closing his eyes as his breath becomes more ragged, blowing softly against my nose. Once his fingers are fully inserted, I feel him wiggle them around, searching. My hips begin to undulate and squirm, wanting him to continue, to go deeper, but instead his fingers began to slowly withdraw, leaving me mindless with wanting.

"No drugs there," he manages to croak out.

With his fingers still covered in my juices, he reaches around me once again and pulls me even more tightly against him. I feel his erection immediately and want more than anything to have him throw me to the ground and fuck me right there. But instead, his hand reaches under my dress until one of his fingers finds my anal opening and begins to slowly trespass. I collapse against him, dependent on him to keep me from falling, my arms still cuffed behind my back. The sensations that his intrusive finger is causing are mind altering, and I begin to involuntarily move and buck against him.

"Stop, stop it."

"Almost done," he whispers, as his finger reaches its limit, and satisfied that I have nothing smuggled in there as well, begins a slow retreat. "Maybe I made that a little *too* interesting," he utters, as he pushes me away to lean back up against the wall.

We continue to stare at one another while attempting to get our breathing back under control. Damn, I wish he'd kiss me. I wonder what he's thinking right now. He's probably wishing he wasn't a cop, I'd bet. I'm certainly impressed by his control, although I think his game went a little further than he intended. Serves the bastard right. I hope his damn erection never goes away.

"Well, it looks like I'm going to have to take a shower myself, a cold shower. After you."

Pulling me away from the wall, he pushes me ahead of him.

We pause before a locked door, and Tim has to temporarily unhand me while he searches for the key to open it. Once unlocked, he opens the door and ushers me inside ahead of him, flipping the lights on as we enter. The room is completely tiled from ceiling to floor with a big drain in the middle. Placed along the walls and ceilings are showerheads, situated at different heights. Against the wall directly in front of me, the tiles are covered with metal bars similar to the ones used in the jail cells out in the main room. Several bars, horizontal as well as vertical, crisscross one another, giving the appearance of a gigantic, continuous tictactoe game.

Officer Tim leads me over to the bar-encompassed wall, placing me directly under one of the showerheads. He turns me around, and releases one of my wrists from the cuffs, finally allowing some movement back into my arms. My relief is short-lived, however, and soon I find my still-cuffed wrist being pulled toward the wall and attached to the bars.

"Why do you have to do that? I'm not going anywhere."

"Just making sure of that, Miranda. Now stay put while I go get the rest."

"Like I have a choice," I utter in disgust.

He returns in a matter of minutes carrying three more pairs of handcuffs, and embarrassingly enough, my soap on a rope.

"What the heck, since you brought your own, I figured, why waste the taxpayers' money?"

I start to struggle, not at all liking the direction this shower is taking.

"Settle down, Miranda, and relax. You may actually enjoy this if you give yourself half a chance."

"I'm not enjoying anything, you egotistical bastard. Let me shower on my own."

"Nope," he says, and once again heads in my direction, the handcuffs clanking ominously.

I fight him with my free hand and kick at him. Somewhere along my journey, I seemed to have misplaced my shoes, making my bare feet an ineffective weapon against him. Within moments, he has me subdued and completely cuffed to the wall. Each arm is stretched out to my sides at shoulder level, while my legs are similarly separated and cuffed to the wall at the ankles, feet still touching the floor. With my legs spread so indecently, my dress has ridden up my thighs, revealing an unobstructed view of my unprotected pussy. God help me.

Tim walks to the far corner of the room and begins to fumble with his clothing.

"What are you doing?" I ask in a panic.

"Chances are good that I'm going to get very wet

during your little scrub down. I'm just making sure that my uniform stays dry."

I watch him continue to strip down until he is wearing nothing but a tank-top T, a conservative pair of boxers and a massive erection. Even his socks are removed, and hung up next to his uniform, safe from the spray of the shower.

Placing his wrist through the loop at the end of my penis-shaped soap, he walks back over to me and, without warning, turns on the cold shower. I scream as I am taken by surprise by the spray, then continue screaming as I realize the water is freezing cold. He drenches me for nearly a solid minute, then turns the water off, standing back to admire the view. My dress, once again transparent, clings provocatively to my body, leaving nothing to the imagination. My nipples, startled by the cold, stand out proud and erect.

"Miranda, if you weren't a married lady, I'd fuck you right now."

With nothing but angry snarls escaping my lips, I say nothing, and continue to glare hatefully at him.

Once his need to stare at my body subsides, he turns the water back on, this time a tepid warm. He leaves the water running, making it difficult for me to see as my hair is pummeled downward, water dripping into my eyes. I begin to panic as he starts to lather the large, soapy phallus and brings it menacingly close to my lips. He touches the tip to my chin, then begins to trail it down my neck, working it into a lather then massaging the soapy suds into my skin with his hands. Gripping the soap once again, he rubs it with increasing strength into my dress, working it into a bubbly lather. He stops to tease my nipples with the tip for a moment, before continuing downward.

Before I know it, my dress is a wet, soapy mess and his hands are working furiously to keep it that way. He is touching me everywhere, squeezing my breasts, rubbing my stomach and roaming his hands around to my back. He begins to moan as he gets caught up, once again, in his sexual game, rubbing his torso up against mine and grinding his hips between my legs until he is as completely soaked and soapy as I am. I am also swept up in his passion, mewling aloud.

"Kiss me, Tim. For God's sake, kiss me! Please. . . ."

I feel his hand grip my hair as his lips descend upon mine, taking them in a deep, punishing kiss. In the same instant, I feel the head of the soap pushing at the entrance to my pussy, prying it wide open, then penetrating swiftly. I gasp into his mouth, the sound being sucked in and swallowed by his hungry tongue. Urgently, he thrusts the soap deeply into me, then back out again, giving me little opportunity to catch my breath. His lips and teeth suck and bite at me while his hand continues to thrust the massive dick in and out. On the verge of collapse, he finally removes the soap, bending down to bite at my nipples.

The overwhelming ferocity of his lust leaves me no choice but to cry out. His attack is rough, his passion all-consuming. He chews on my nipples like a starved animal. Finally, unable to contain himself any longer, he hastily removes his boxers. In one swift motion, he is buried deep inside me, surprisingly stretching and filling me even deeper than the huge soap had.

71

The sound that comes from him as he enters me is primal, exciting me all the more. With his arms wrapped completely around me, trapping my body against his, he returns to kissing me, while stroke after wild stroke continues to spiral me upward into the inevitable arms of ecstasy.

With one final thrust, we simultaneously cry out, both swept away in the unrelenting tide of our orgasms. Their power is torrential, leaving us gasping and panting, exhausted. We stay plastered to the wall, his arms wrapped tightly around me for several moments while the water continues to splash upon our spent bodies.

Finally, Tim reaches up to turn off the shower.

"Damn, I'm sorry. I can't believe I lost control like that. If you'd like to file charges, I deserve it."

Still gasping for breath, I respond, "No need to apologize. I . . . uh . . . well . . . kind of enjoyed that. But . . . if you're feeling guilty. . . . how about you let me go and we call it even?"

"Deal, but are you sure you want to go right away? I've got a nice, cozy bed tucked away in the back that I'd love to see you lying naked in."

"Hmmm, unhook me from this wall, and I'll think about it while I'm drying off.

Grinning, he releases me from all four sets of handcuffs and tosses me a warm, fluffy towel.

Deciding to put the whole experience behind me, I politely decline his offer.

Disappointed, he offers to give me a ride back to the motel. The trip is made in complete silence, each of us counting our blessings, grateful for the happy ending.

Dropping me off in front of my door, he teasingly warns, "Now please try to stay out of trouble."

Laughing, I reply, "Don't worry. I have no intentions of leaving this room again until tomorrow morning. By the way, that'll be 500 bucks. . . ."

I watch in amusement as his face turns several shades of green, worried that he might suddenly become quite ill.

"What??!!" He sputters.

"Gotcha!" Giggling, I scramble into my room before he has a chance to react to my nasty little trick.

The next morning finds me back on the correct road again, heading for home. Pleading with fate, I beg not to run into another obstacle, quite sure I would be unable to survive another night like the last. Humming to the music on the radio, I turn my thoughts to the drive, the miles passing quickly and without a glitch.

CHAPTER 4

■

GUILT

The excitement coursing through my veins as I take in all the familiar and beloved landmarks of my home is immeasurable. The majestic mountain, standing alone, serves as the backdrop for the sleepy little town, a startling contrast to the vibrant, raging river running along the side of its wide-bottomed base. My whole body comes alive and begins to tingle as each well-known turn is precisely executed. Faces that I had formerly seen on a daily basis are miraculously reappearing, making me feel as if I had never been gone. The air smells sweeter, the grass looks greener. Mother Nature on her best behavior to welcome me home with open arms. I receive one last surge of adrenaline as I make the final turn into my parking space, my heart skipping a beat as I watch Nick race out of the house to greet me.

Unable to hold back the tears, I blindly race towards him as well, leaving the car door sprung wide open, at which a confused Taz gingerly exits.

———

"Oh, my God, honey. I'm so happy to be home. I missed you so much."

"Oh, Miranda, Miranda, Miranda. Now that you're back, I'll never let you go again."

Crying and laughing simultaneously, I grab hold of his face and begin placing kisses all over it, savoring the look and feel as if I had just found a lost, precious treasure, which in fact, is exactly what I had found.

"Oh, God, Nick, how could I have been so foolish? How could I have left you like that?"

"Miranda, it was something you needed to do, maybe, ultimately, to make you realize exactly what you already did have. It's okay, honey, it's okay."

A litany of "I'm sorry's" follow Nick all the way to our front door, which he has managed to whisk me away to without my feet ever once touching the ground.

In an old-fashioned, romantic gesture, Nick picks me up, cradle-like, and carries me through the threshold of our front door, keeping my lips imprisoned with his own. Once inside, I am unceremoniously dumped onto the living room couch as Nick frantically works at removing his clothing. Unable to keep his passion at bay, he falls on top of me, impatiently tugging at my sundress until the bottom is gathered up around my waist and plunges deeply into my unobstructed opening. The coupling is wild and fierce, passionate and needy, trying desperately to cram three months of lovemaking into one incredible session. Amazed by his stamina after so many months of celibacy, I surrender myself to the most powerful explosion of masculine dominance ever known to me, and continue to ride out the storm, screaming, as I am swept away by turbulent shock waves of inde-scribable ecstasy.

Kissing me back to consciousness, Nick grins deeply as he searches my eyes, obviously very proud of him-self. He cockily offers me his hand in assistance, si-lently labeling every man I had slept with during the last few months as amateurs not worthy of the *attempt* at pleasuring his wife. Pulling me up until I am stand-ing shakily beside him, he smiles wolfishly at my dis-array and whispers conspiratorially that he has a surprise waiting for me up in the bedroom. Unsure if I am physically capable of handling anything at the moment, I hesitantly allow him to guide me up the stairs and into the bedroom.

At first glance, nothing appears amiss or out of the ordinary, and I look at him with a question in my eyes, wondering if I might have overlooked some-thing. Still grinning ear to ear, Nick asks me to close my eyes, and then gently takes my hands into his own. "No fair peeking." He playfully kisses the tip of my nose and raises my arms up above my head.

I feel my wrists being enclosed and automatically lift my gaze. My wrists are now tethered to the ceil-ing. Gasping in profound disbelief, my eyes travel the entire length of the ceiling, noticing for the first time, the deep, recessed track running from the top of the bed all the way into the bathroom.

I look back to my wrists, noting how each has been individually encased in its own moccasin-soft, leather bracelet, coming together in a single chain attached deep into the track. The track is similar to what you would find in a track-lighting configuration, only indented into the ceiling, rather than exposed. The chain or pulley that I am attached by is also pulled tight, stretching me so that I am just able to remain flat footed on the floor. I look over towards Nick for an explanation.

Nick has made himself comfortable, propped up against several down pillows resting against the headboard of the bed. I find myself centered on the floor at the foot of the bed facing him, watching the lazy, satisfied smile that spreads knowingly across his face, his arms crossed and folded behind his head.

"Miranda, life as you know it is about to change."

Struggling against the cable, testing its strength and durability, I mumble a feeble, "What do you mean?"

"I mean, my sweet wife, that you have just become my obedient sex slave. From now on, you will do what I tell you, where I tell you and how I tell you. You want to dally in the dominant/submissive lifestyle, now you shall, for real, for good."

"Come on, Nick, you've got to be kidding?" But even as I protest this absurd turn of events, I feel my face flush, my pulse quicken and a surge of fluid square in the middle of my sex. Watching my features change as I digest the implications of his words, Nick stands up, still stark naked and strolls casually over to the dresser. He picks up a pair of scissors and heads my way.

Sucking in my breath, I stand motionless as he places the flat, cold edge of the scissors against my throat and slowly starts to slide them down my chest. I can feel his closeness, his breath mingling with mine, and I close my eyes, trying to block out the menacing atmosphere suddenly threatening to suffocate me.

"You are my plaything, Miranda," he whispers. I feel the scissors snip away one of the shoulder straps of my skimpy sundress, causing it to slide and hang limply.

"You are at my mercy, totally at my beck and call," he utters in my ear, finalizing the meaning with a second snip to the other shoulder strap, watching as my dress falls in a pile at my feet. Shuddering in my nakedness, I open my eyes, focusing on the threatening pair of scissors still caressing my skin.

"Do you want to know why you will become my most loyal and dedicated sex object, Miranda?" he asks as the scissors continue upward until they stop at my lips.

"No, why?" I ask, frightened, wondering, quite frankly, if he has totally lost his mind. "Because of your guilt, my dear, sweet wife. You will pay any price to have that washed away, and the price I require is your total submission. Whether you realize it now or not, it is also what you crave, what you require, what turns your insides into mush and satisfies you body and soul. You wouldn't escape it if you could, and now it is all yours, Miranda."

"No, Nick. I can't live like that. I experienced the tip of the iceberg in Vegas and it was horrible. I couldn't handle it. You can't do this to me."

"You couldn't handle it because he meant nothing to you, he didn't own your heart. I do. You love me and will do this for me, because I am willing to do this for you. It's the only way we can continue, Miranda. You have changed, and if I want to keep you,

I also have to change. There is no turning back. For me to carry this out, I have to commit to it, beginning to end, no second thoughts, no periods of doubt. You will be my sex slave and exist in eternal bliss. I have already decided. You no longer have a choice or a voice in this matter. Now, suck on the tip of these scissors and pay homage to your new Lord."

Oh, God, what have I done, I wonder, as I spread my lips in supple surrender, taking the tip of the piercing blades into my mouth to suck on them, trusting in my love that I have nothing to fear.

Satisfied, he removes the scissors from my mouth and again begins the terrifying journey down my soft, tender skin, stopping only to torture my erect and inquisitive nipples. I gasp as I feel the coolness tease them slowly, lightly grazing and scraping and terrorizing.

"Please," I whimper, but nothing follows.

Looking deeply into my eyes, locking onto and holding them hostage, Nick finally decides to leave my nipples. He continues downward, taking the scissors at a sharper angle, pressing more deeply and dangerously into my abdomen, causing my stomach to quiver with fright and anticipation. Holding perfectly still, I wait, dreading his next move. I feel the scissors mischievously toy with my clit and then move downward, moving around in a circle just brushing against my fat and swollen lips. Even in my fear, my desire cannot be disguised, and I shamefully part my legs, waiting for the imminent penetration.

With a chuckle, Nick warns, "Now hold very still. I don't want to hurt you . . . too much."

To my surprise and relief, he only places the tips

just inside my lips and continues a circular motion asking, "Ok, now where is it? Where is this book you wrote?"

"It's in the car, in my briefcase on the back seat. Everything's still in the car," I manage to gasp out brokenly.

"Ok, my lovely, don't go away." Withdrawing the scissors and placing them at a safe distance, he quickly throws on a pair of sweat pants and heads off down the stairs.

Frustrated, I kick at my ruined dress, grumpily wondering what the remainder of the day has in store for me.

After what seems like at least four trips back and forth to the car, Nick shuts the door with a certain finality. Energetically, he pounces his way back up the stairs, my manuscript possessively clutched to his side.

"I'm going to have to keep you inspired while I read your book, now let's see . . . what can I do to distract you?" Setting the book on the bed, Nick goes on to explain, "I purchased a few new toys for us to experiment with when you got back. Now seems like as good a time as any to try a few of them out."

Accessing our secret treasure trove filled with exotic pleasure devices, Nick carefully takes his time sorting through everything that is available to him. Finally selecting a few items, he heads toward me, his eyes full of promise.

Without warning, he latches onto one of my nipples, capturing it between his teeth and pulling it outward. It immediately responds to the stimulation, tightening up and standing out proud and erect. When it reaches the desired length, Nick loops a tiny noose around it, adjusting the tension so that it is just right to keep the blood trapped in the nipple, keeping it firm, rigid and perky. Attached to the shiny, silver loop is a string of baby-blue pearls, ending with another tiny noose. He attaches the second loop around my other nipple, securing it tightly, then tests their sensitivity by licking and sucking on them, mentally registering the intensity of my moans. The string of pearls drapes provocatively down and across my breasts. Satisfied with his artwork, he moves downward to my clit.

Nick next begins to vigorously suck and draw at my clit, encouraging it to bloom from hiding and greet the world. Just as it reaches its peak of curiosity, another device is introduced, a kind of large, gold bobby pin with two imitation diamonds hanging from the bottom ends. Nick slides the clamp down behind my clit, pushing the little bud out and forward, tight enough to keep it from receding back and disappearing. The effect it has on me is devastating, and I begin to squirm in earnest. Nick, not quite through with his subtle torture, moves around to my backside and starts to caress my ass. When I feel him carefully spread my ass cheeks apart and start to probe my anus, I moan, surrendering myself to him.

"Relax," I hear Nick command as he prepares my ass with generous amounts of lubrication.

"What are you going to do?" I demand, not really wanting to know the answer.

"Patience, darling, you'll see."

The next sensation is that of a slick, cool, smooth object being pressed forward, coaxing my ass to slowly open and receive it. Suddenly, it is pushed passed the barrier and is greedily sucked deep into my ass, causing me to shudder and swoon.

"It's just a vibrating egg, don't worry," my husband assures me, as he flips on the remote control and starts the egg buzzing. The antenna of the egg dangles insultingly down my thigh, uncannily resembling a long mouse tail. Overwhelmed, I groan with each sensation, wiggling my hips and squirming uncontrollably.

"You'd better settle down, Miranda. You're going to stay exactly as you are until I'm done reading your book, and I don't want any interruptions either. If you get too carried away, I'll gag you."

"Please, Nick, this is torture. You can't leave me like this. It'll take you hours to read that book."

"I'm counting on it," is his heartless reply.

It took Nick exactly six hours to finish reading my novel, six of the most excruciating hours that I've ever had to live through. It wasn't enough that I had to remain standing and endure his subtle torture, but to make things worse, he constantly adjusted the speed of the vibrating egg to remind me that it was still there. There was no hope of being lulled into a hazy state of consciousness, blocking out the routine vibrations coursing through my body. No, I was made to feel every single fluctuation. By the time that Nick was through reading my book, I was in dire need of attention and, from the look of his erection, so was he.

Easing himself off the bed, he removes his sweat pants and pads barefooted in my direction. His eyes are glassy, and it is obvious that my story had quite an effect.

Crushing my body against his, he kisses me furiously.

"Quite the hot story, Miranda. Thanks for the insight."

He drops down in front of me on his knees, concentrating his efforts on my needy little clit. The first touch of his tongue is jolting, sending millions of tiny shivers along my spine. My hips undulate and thrust forward, greedy for more, craving fulfillment.

Only devoting a few more seconds to pleasuring my clit, he pulls away. "If you behave and do exactly as you're told for the rest of the day, I'll make sure you go to sleep purring contentedly. If not, you'll find yourself back in the same position as you are in now, tossing and turning in frustration all night at the foot of the bed. Understand?"

"Yes, anything. I'll do anything you say."

"Of course you will," he mutters as he moves around behind me.

Within seconds, I feel the head of his erect cock pressing against my salivating pussy, slipping easily inside to become immediately bathed in liquid satin. Nick takes his time, savoring each exquisite stroke as he leisurely pulls at my rock-hard nipples. From this angle, his thrusts penetrate deeply, rocking me to my very core, pushing my body upwards so that I balance solely on my tiptoes. Lost in feelings of intense pleasure, I am reluctantly brought back to reality by the feeling of Nick's body starting to convulse. As his body becomes rigid, his grip tightens on my breasts and I hear him whisper distractedly, "Fuck slave.

You are my fuck slave." Savoring the closeness of my quivering body, Nick holds me until the final spasms pass, his lips leaving a trail of wet kisses across my back and shoulders. Satisfied once again, he pulls himself away.

"I'm going to untie you now. You are not allowed to touch yourself, not in any way. I have a special little outfit that I want you to wear for the remainder of the evening. It's 6 o'clock now, which gives you three hours to fix us a quick dinner and clean the house. I want the bathrooms to be thoroughly cleaned and the house vacuumed. There is no need to worry about the laundry today, that chore will be on your list for tomorrow. Are you quite certain of your obligations for the rest of the night?" "Yes, please, I'm ready." "Ok, you will perform your chores, continuously stimulated as you have been for the last six hours. The egg will remain vibrating, and your nipples and clit will remain clamped. Here, put this on."

I take from him the skimpy assortment of clothing that I am required to wear. Included is a black, lacy bra with the cups totally removed, leaving my breasts exposed, yet supported. Next is a short, white apron, which, while covering my legs to mid-thigh, completely leaves my backside bare, my ass accessible. The outfit is made complete by two white cuffs to be worn around my wrists and a matching choker to wear around my neck. Without hesitation, I don my newly acquired uniform, and undergo a perfunctory inspection. Nick nods his approval, and I take my cue and scurry away, wondering what on earth I am going to fix for dinner. Thankfully, there are plenty of pasta possibilities lounging around in the pantry, and I whip up a very satisfying meal in a matter of minutes.

Nick watches me closely as I go about my duties, analyzing the effect his changed behavior is having on me. Admittedly, I am enjoying myself immensely, loving the little games he has created in an attempt to join "my world." I only pray that they are just games, and that he isn't seriously considering a permanent deviation from our previous relationship. His words threatened a permanent change, yet I can't imagine either one of us maintaining this charade. Besides, this isn't Nick. It is not a natural way for him to act, and he will most likely tire of it quickly. Not really having a choice, I decide to play along for the duration, intent on extracting the utmost pleasure from it, bonding us even closer together.

After dinner, I focus on the three bathrooms, which is obviously what Nick was anticipating. As soon as I bend over the edge of the tub to scrub it clean, he is there behind me, giving explicit instructions.

"Don't turn around, and no matter what happens, you are to continue scrubbing, no hesitating, no pausing, no stopping. Understand?"

"Yes," I whisper, the air suddenly feeling as if it had taken on an identity, swirling around my ass until it feels huge and solitary, a big, bright bull's-eye.

"There will be serious consequences if you do not obey."

"I understand."

Not knowing his exact intentions, but knowing his attention *had* to be centered on my very open and exposed ass, I hold my breath, waiting for the unknown.

As I struggle to keep my concentration on the task at hand, a small yelp is torn from me when the hard, wooden surface of a paddle smacks sharply against one cheek.

"Keep going," he warns.

Even though the paddling is not very severe, the area affected is large, causing a nice, slow, warming sensation. With the element of surprise no longer a factor, only a slight gasp escapes as the paddle is brought down, once again, squarely on my other cheek. With both cheeks toasty, I am unable to keep from wriggling as I continue cleaning the bathtub.

"You have been a very naughty girl, Miranda. I truly hope you didn't expect to get off easily," Nick threatens, as another stinging swat connects perfectly with my already rosy-colored ass. Slowly, with plenty of time to recover from each paddle, Nick continues to spank me throughout the duration of the tub cleaning, making sure that the intensity of the fully immersed egg continues to rise as well. By the time I am finished, my ass is on fire, and I reach my hands around to soothe it. Nick is ready, and grabs them at the wrist to stop them.

"Uh, uh, uh. No touching. Continue with your chores, just as you are."

"But they hurt," I protest.

"Good, now unless you want more, you'd better finish up. You are running out of time."

I manage to breeze through the rest of my chores, no longer distracted by Nick. Even though he remains hovering and ever watchful, he keeps his hands to himself. I finish up thirty minutes under the deadline, pleasing Nick immensely. Tethering me back to my station at the foot of the bed once again, he slowly caresses my body as he showers me with praise.

"You were awesome, Miranda. What a charge I got from your total obedience. Your ass was so sexy, squirming and red, reaching for every swat of the paddle. It begged me to spank it."

My uniform, held together only by Velcro strips, is slowly removed until I am standing totally naked.

"As a reward, we are going to take a bubble bath together, and then you'll be on your own for the rest of the night. You can be and do as you please until we wake up in the morning, and then, you're mine again.

"Oh, Nick, I've always been yours," I whisper as I reach my lips towards his in a sizzling kiss.

After removing all of my jewelry and the egg nestled deep within my ass, Nick releases me, heading for the huge Jacuzzi tub positioned in the corner of the master bathroom. Relaxing in the hot, soothing water, we begin to chat about everything that's been going on in our lives since we have been separated. He asks me all kinds of questions ranging from the simple, "Did you miss me?" to authenticating the tiniest details mentioned in my book. "Is everything true?" "Did you really . . . ?" "How much did you enjoy having sex with a woman?"

We talk and laugh for hours, reminding me of how it used to be . . . before . . .

"So, guess who I got back in contact with, while you were off tramping around?" Nick asks with an amused smile.

"Don't have the foggiest, who?"

"JD and Vicki Mason, you know, from college."

"No, way! How did you manage to hook back up with them?"

"Well, I had a little time on my hands . . ."

"Yeah, yeah, yeah, enough with the guilt trip already. So, what have they been up to these last years?"

"Some interesting things, although they're both still entrapped in corporate America."

"Did you tell them that I had temporarily lost my brain and we were currently separated?"

"Well, I didn't phrase it quite that way, but yeah, they know we were having some problems. Actually, JD was just a little too excited about that. He mentioned that he has wanted to get into your pants for years, and wondered if you were available. He said that he and Vicki have a very open marriage and can, um, experiment with other people, as long as they tell one another. He wants you bad, Miranda."

"So what did you tell him?"

"I told him that it was up to you, but I think I've changed my mind now."

"Oh? How so?"

"My little secret, but you'll know when the time comes."

Now what did he have up his sleeve?

"Yeah, they are planning to visit this winter and go skiing. We've got a hut trip all planned out."

"Great, that sounds like a blast! I can't wait to see them again."

We continue chitchatting, about this, about that, enjoying the peaceful ease of one another's company. Every so often, Nick's big toe floats my way to nestle between my thighs, teasing the swollen lips of my pussy. Still very agitated and unfulfilled from Nick's earlier treatment, I welcome the intruder and squeeze my thighs tightly together, hoping to trap it there.

With the water temperature rapidly cooling, and our skin close to prune status, Nick and I decide to call it quits, hurriedly exiting the tub to wrap our bodies in plush, matching terrycloth robes. Leisurely, we walk hand in hand back to the bedroom and sit on the edge of the bed, sleepy smiles plastered on both our faces. We shed our robes and snuggle deep into the covers, becoming sandwiched in layers of comforting heat. The warmth rising from the heated waterbed caresses our backs as the covers work on toasting our tummies. Sighing in contentment, I turn on my side to face Nick, who is already gazing at me attentively.

"It's so great to be back home, Nick. I can't believe how much I've missed everything, and how much I missed you. I love you."

"I love you, too, Miranda. Come here."

Scooping me up in his powerful arms, he pulls me over to lie on top of him.

We spend hours feasting on and adoring one another's bodies, slowly taking our time to explore and remember. The lovemaking doesn't end with just our physical beings, but goes beyond, deeper, to our hearts, to our souls. With the beauty of each kiss, each touch, each thrust, another wound is mended, another lie untold, both knowing that there will never be anyone who could replace the other. Purring contentedly, I fall into a blissful and peaceful sleep.

CHAPTER 5

◼

CONSEQUENCES

Rise and shine, my little lovely," Nick croons into my ear as his hand gently swats at my bottom.

"Can't I sleep just a little bit longer?" I whine pathetically.

"I'm afraid not. I've got interesting plans for you today, and I'd like to get an early start."

"Oh, man, I was hoping things were back to normal after last night. Last night was wonderful, Nick. I miss that."

"Sorry, darling. You can't have your cake and eat it, too. If you behave and do as you are told during the day, the nights can be similar to last night. If not, well . . . you get the picture."

"What if I don't want this anymore?"

"Honey, not only do you want this, you *need* this. Your mind and body crave it. I won't lose you a second time, Miranda, when you get that restlessness again. Now, get up and hit the shower. I'm hungry."

Groggily rolling out of my nice, comfy bed, I begrudgingly enter the shower, wanting it to last forever. I know that as soon as I exit, my brief moments of freedom will be over, and I'll be once again at Nick's mercy. As I absentmindedly stroke my body with the soapy bath sponge, I wonder what Nick has in store for me today. I have to admit, yesterday was extremely exciting. Nick sure had arranged for an unforgettable homecoming. Oh, well, I was just going to have to go with whatever he had planned. He is my husband, after all, and I have to trust him. He would never do anything to hurt me, would he? No, no, no, he just wants to teach me a lesson, I am sure of it.

As I depart the shower and reach for the towel, Nick hollers out to me, "No, stop, Miranda. Leave the towel be. Walk to the foot of the bed and just stand there, just as you are."

"But I'm soaking wet."

"I know, now come here."

Leaving tiny puddles of water in my wake, I wander to the foot of the bed.

"Now what?"

"Just stand there. I want to watch the water roll down that gorgeous body of yours. I want to see droplets making suicidal leaps as they fall from your nipples. I want you to feel every drip caress your body as if they were my fingers. Just stand there and feel, Miranda."

It is amazing what the mind can do. I don't think I have ever considered the feel of water droplets trickling down my body as anything other than annoying, let alone erotic. But here I stand, feeling each individual drop magically touching me as fingers, winding their way down across my neck and back to slither secretly between the cheeks of my ass. Their curious cohorts, meanwhile, wiggle across my chest and down my belly, some being content to gather in my navel, while others seek out a different treat. It seems, however, that all the water beads ultimately end up where Nick has anticipated, cradled in the folds of my nether lips, to slip and drop tantalizingly down to the carpeted floor. My eyes close in an effort to feel each drop, shutting out any distractions that would remove any bits of sensations.

Just when it appears that my body is mostly dry, Nick gets up and decides to position me directly under the ceiling fan in our bedroom. With a flip of a switch, the blades swirl into motion, starting out slowly and caressingly, building into a cool blast. Almost immediately, my body responds. Goose bumps rise up over every inch of my skin, while my nipples pucker up and squeeze together tightly. More water droplets are coaxed from my hair to tumble down across my body, and Nick decides to feast upon one that has managed to land right on the tip of my nipple. Intentionally grazing his teeth across it as he licks at the tiny drop, Nick looks up at me to observe my reaction. He is not disappointed as my eyes close once again, reveling in the delights of the flesh.

When there are no longer any droplets escaping my dampened mane of hair, Nick decides that it is time to move on, and turns off the ceiling fan. Slightly aroused now, I stand there, waiting for whatever Nick has in store for me next. Rifling through one of the drawers of our massive headboard, Nick returns with the jewelry I'll be required to wear for the morning.

In his hands are five pieces of soft leather. Two bracelets, two anklets, and one throat collar, all different from what I was wearing yesterday, but still very similar. Each piece is about two inches wide and baby soft, and each piece has a very menacing little gold ring permanently attached. The collar actually has three gold rings, one on each side of my neck, directly below my ears, and the other directly in front.

Once Nick has succeeded in securing all five pieces in place, he reaches for a black leather bag and starts to look through it. Finding what appears to be a leash, he takes it out and attaches it to my collar. Zipping up the offending bag and tucking it under his arm, he takes the end of the leash and gives it a tug, saying, "Follow me, my little pet." Trembling, I follow, the anticipation of what the future holds almost too much to bear.

Nick doesn't lead me very far, just over to our dining room table. It is rectangular, made of a light-colored, solid oak with rounded corners, and is far too large for just the two of us. But it works great for our numerous get-togethers with family and friends, and complements the dining area beautifully, justifying the extravagant purchase. The sturdy base of the table doesn't consist of actual "legs," but rather three thick, large slats resembling an upside-down "T." Two are located at each end, and the third, directly in the middle of the table. What strikes me as curious this morning is that Nick has the table covered with a white mattress pad.

"Up on the table, Miranda," Nick commands, as he effortlessly lifts me up at the waist, setting me down at one of the ends. "Now, lie back."

"What are you going to do, Nick?" I ask, confused by this bizarre request.

"I'm going to eat breakfast. Now lie back."

"Ok, ok . . . just curious, is all."

I recline against the padded softness of the mattress pad as Nick proceeds to manipulate my position.

"Scoot down . . . more . . . more. That's right, I want that sweet ass right at the edge of the table. Perfect."

Then I watch as he digs into the black leather bag that housed my lovely golden leash, and he begins to pull from it several different lengths of chain, each with a clasp at both ends. Oh, great, I think sarcastically.

Spreading my legs obscenely wide, so that my knees are pulled back behind the rounded corners of the bottom edge of the table, Nick works quickly to secure a chain attaching my ankles to the bottom "T" of the table. Selecting the perfect length, he is able to keep my legs totally immobile. I make a mental note to take a better look at all of our furniture from now on, hoping to discover the different locations throughout the house that I can possibly become "attached" to in the future. Next, Nick pulls my arms out perpendicular to my sides so that my wrists lie curled under just at the edges of the table. Longer pieces of chain are needed to attach my bracelet cuffs to the middle "T" of the table. Finally, I am completely fastened to the table, not able to move my arms or legs more than a fraction of an inch. Nick finishes up with a hot, wet kiss to my mouth, promising to return soon.

I listen for what seems like twenty minutes as he

rattles pots and pans and bowls in the kitchen. It obviously is not going to be a cereal morning. Waiting patiently, relaxing against my bonds, my stomach begins to grumble as the first aroma of pancakes reaches my nose. Oh, God, I hope he is planning on sharing that breakfast. I'm starving. As the pancakes continue cooking, Nick begins bringing utensils and accessories to the table. Soon, I am surrounded by butter, syrup, milk, coffee, napkins, etc. By the time Nick seats himself, I am salivating.

Always the gentleman, Nick feeds me first, selecting the seat closest to my face and hand feeds me bites of sticky, steaming pancakes. I gobble down all that is offered, thankful that I am not neglected. Wondering how I am going to be able to drink anything to wash down the pancakes, I am put at ease when Nick puts a straw to my lips and says, "Open up." I do, and he lets go of the top, releasing a small surge of milk onto my tongue. Slowly and methodically, Nick continues sticking the straw back and forth into the glass of milk, then releasing the cool liquid into my mouth, soon completely quenching my thirst.

"Aren't you going to eat, Nick? I thought you were starving."

"I am, but I wanted to take care of you first so I could totally enjoy my breakfast without having to worry about you."

"I'm perfect, Nick, go on and eat."

"Ok, I won't be long."

Quickly cooking up another batch of pancakes, Nick returns in less than ten minutes with another steaming pile, only this time he seats himself at the foot of the table, directly between my widespread legs. He pulls himself up so close that I can feel the skin on his arms and chest as they accidentally brush against the insides of my thighs. How on earth is he going to eat there? There is no room for his plate.

My question is answered immediately as I feel one warm pancake deposited squarely on my lower abdomen. That sensation is quickly followed by that of warm, sticky syrup being poured over the pancake to run over and down my sides. Not wanting to deny my pussy any pleasure, Nick makes sure a steady stream is directed that way, and I squirm as it slowly slides down and disappears into the crack of my ass. I hear Nick whisper a satisfied, "Oh yeah," as he bends his head down and begins to lap at the syrup teasing my wriggling pussy. His tongue masterfully finds all the residue, stopping to say a quick hello to my clit as well as probing the inner folds of my lips, then delving deep inside my opening, retrieving every last drop. My body protests frustratingly when his attention is diverted back to consuming the forgotten pancake, still resting quietly on my belly.

I hold my breath as I feel his fork push in on the pancake, pushing my stomach in as well. Using the flat side to cut the pancake, I am soon introduced to the cold, hard edge of the fork as it cuts through, then the tiny, scraping bite of the prongs as they gently press in to gather up the bite. These sensations are repeated over and over, with Nick lingering longer in between bites to lightly drag the fork across and down my belly. My stomach begins to quiver and spasm as each tickling path is created.

When Nick is finally finished, I am on fire, wanting nothing more than to be fucked right there, as is.

"Fuck me, Nick, please. I want you to fuck me just like this, syrup and all."

"Funny, Miranda, I was thinking the same exact thing."

Standing up, the table at a perfect height, Nick guides his already swollen and erect cock toward the eager and hungry opening winking at him from the table. Gripping the insides of my thighs for support, Nick begins a steady stream of long, hard thrusts, rocking the table with their intensity. My hips try desperately to reach up to meet his thrusts, but are unable to move because of the solid chains. Oooo's and Ahhhh's are jarred from my mouth, as I lose myself in the glorious feelings of this alien lovemaking experience. The jolting increases as Nick picks up speed, his orgasm approaching rapidly. Soon, his grip on my thighs tightens, his hips making one final, deep thrust forward, his head thrown back in rapture as his teeth become bared and an elated groan is spewed forth. Sweat has accumulated all over his face and torso as I watch his body spasm and shake in the throes of orgasm. Finally, the shuddering subsides, and he collapses against me, for now, totally satisfied.

I know better now than to assume that I will also be allowed an orgasm as well. The game is to keep me in complete and total sexual frustration all day long, so that I will agree to any perverse act, knowing that the promise of relief at the end of the day is dangling before me like a carrot. If I behave, if I do as I'm told, sweet assuagement will greet me at nightfall. Panting in my yearning, I try to ease some of my torment by flexing my inner muscles, only to find that this merely increases my desire.

Once Nick has regained his strength and is able to lift himself from my syrup-laden body, he begins to unfasten my bonds. Finally free from the table, I take a minute to stroke my aching muscles, unused to being held in that position for any length of time. Nick cleans off the table, then gets a dampened washcloth to run across my body, removing any evidence that I had been used as a human table this morning. Fresh and clean once again, Nick refastens my leash and leads me back up to the master bathroom, ordering me to douche while he takes his shower. At a lost to what else to do, I complete the task and wait.

"I have to mow the lawn today," he mentions off-handedly while toweling dry. "I'd like for you to keep me company."

"Of course, I'd be happy to," I reply, surprised, not quite sure if it was directed as a request or a command. "It's a gorgeous day outside, warm and sunny. I'm at your disposal."

Grinning wickedly, he simply replies, "I know."

Standing by docilely, I watch as Nick dresses in a pair of loose-fitting, casual shorts and a matching muscle shirt. I find myself physically drawn to his toned, powerful body, his physique absolutely flawless, pleased that I can consider it all mine.

Grasping me by the leash once again, he leads me back downstairs and towards the sliding glass doors which open into our fenced-in backyard. As he tries to guide me through them, I stop suddenly, causing him to yank painfully on the collar.

"Nick, I can't go outside like this. Somebody might see."

Turning to face me with an amused expression on

his face, he replies, "Nobody is going to see you, Miranda. The fence is too tall. Besides, it's nobody else's business what goes on in our backyard."

"Yeah, but, there are second-story homes all around us. Somebody looking through a second-story window can easily see into the yard. I won't do it."

Angrily, Nick pulls on my leash until I am taken off balance and stumble outside. "Yes, you will. When are you going to get it through that thick skull of yours that you'll do what I want, whenever I want? The choice is no longer yours."

"Damn you, Nick," is all I can utter before I am propelled across the lawn to be placed up against a warm, sunny section of fence. Once there, I am introduced to more eyelets recently imbedded into the smooth, wooden slats, with clasps hanging suggestively down. Positioning me so that I am facing the yard, Nick takes one arm and attaches the bracelet to one of the clasps. Then, stretching my other arm out in the opposite direction, that bracelet, too, is attached to an innocent-looking clasp. Finally, my ankles are hooked to their respective clasps, leaving me plastered flat up against the fence, spread-eagled.

Satisfied that I am going nowhere, Nick busies himself with preparing the lawn mower, while I cast surreptitious glances towards the neighbors' windows. The glare from the sun shining against the windows makes it impossible for me to see in any of them, causing a slight panic as my imagination starts to run amok.

Nick mows the section of grass directly in front of me first. When he is through, he turns off the mower momentarily to set up the water sprinkler.

"What are you doing?" I ask suspiciously.

"What does it look like I'm doing? Watering the lawn, of course."

"But I'm in the way. You're going to have to move me so I don't get all wet."

Shaking his head, Nick smiles, but says nothing, as he reaches over to turn on the water. The sprinkler is the old-fashioned type, with a wide, sweeping back-and-forth motion. I watch as the wall of water starts to rise and head my way. Nick has already managed to get himself out of the danger zone, and watches lazily as the first sweep of the water covers my body. The shock of the ice-cold droplets hitting my sizzling skin causes me to scream out and curse at Nick.

"Nick, it's freezing! Please, turn it off!"

"No, I think I like it this way just fine, but I think I'd be careful about how loud you scream. You might get nosey neighbors peeking out their windows to see what the ruckus is all about."

"Damn you, Nick!" I screech as another wave passes by, stabbing me with hundreds of tiny, icy needles.

I remain strapped to the fence for another half hour, alternating between sweating in the scorching heat of the sun and shivering from the icy water each time it passes by. My body is exhausted from continuously being thrown from a warm, relaxed state to one of total tension as I brace myself for each brutal wave.

Finally Nick is done mowing the lawn and moves the sprinkler head to another section of the lawn. Then he comes and stands to admire my wet-puppy appearance. Looking very thoughtful, he begins to unclasp my ankles, then my left wrist, still leaving me tethered to the fence by my right wrist.

"I want you to face the fence now, so that I can gaze upon your luscious backside."

"Oh, please, Nick, no more water. I feel like I've gone through shock treatment or something."

"If you behave and do as you're told, there won't be any more water. I'm going to unclasp your other wrist now. Don't do anything silly, just turn around and face the fence."

I find myself plastered, once again, flat against the fence. I turn my head so that my right cheek is lying flat against the smooth wood, my scope of vision suddenly limited. Nick disappears inside the house, but I am thrilled to find that he has not set the water upon my naked skin again to torture me. Resting comfortably, I wait, wondering what is going to happen next.

Nick comes back out and stands beside me so that I can see him clearly. Looking rather menacing, he shows me a nice smooth spanking paddle, and taps it teasingly against his palm.

"Are you wondering what this is for, Miranda? Getting a little excited?"

"Nervous is more like it. Why are you going to spank me? I've been behaving myself."

"You've had little choice. But you were very naughty while you were away, weren't you?"

"Nick, I apologized for that. I am extremely sorry for what I did. I thought you forgave me."

"Oh, I forgive you, but you're not going to get away with it scot-free. So . . . Miranda, how many men did you fuck while you were away?"

"Uh . . . two . . . I think."

"And what are their names?"

"Adam . . . and Wit."

My response is immediately rewarded with two deafening blows of the paddle against my ass, Nick repeating each name before striking. I scream out in pain and humiliation, begging him to stop.

"And how many women did you fuck while you were away, my little slut?"

"No, no . . . please don't," I start to cry. "I'm sorry. I won't do it again."

"Oh, you'll do it again. You can't help yourself. But just know, that every time you do, you'll be punished. Now, how many women did you fuck?!"

"Two . . ." I wail piteously.

"And what are their names?"

"Rachel and Angela."

"Rachel and Angela," Nick repeats, as my backside is powerfully swatted two more times.

"Is that all? Think carefully . . . if you forget one, you'll get spanked twice as hard."

"Does . . . Robert . . . count?" I manage to ask in between sniffles.

"Ah, yes, the blow-job boss . . . Yeah, I think he counts too." CRACK!!!!

Again I yelp as the paddle swats my already stinging behind.

"Anybody else?"

"No . . . no, I don't think so . . . unless you want to count Garen."

"No, hallucinations don't count. Are you sure there's nobody else? You've behaved yourself since you left California?"

Oh, my goodness . . . Tim! I had completely forgotten about my encounter with the law. Should I tell Nick about it now, or keep it a secret and hope he never finds out? Shit, I had to come clean. I didn't want any more secrets between us.

"Um . . . there was one more. . . ."

Amused, Nick moves back around to my side so that he can look at my face.

"You've got to be kidding?! What could have possibly have happened on your way home?!"

"To make a long story short, I got lost, found a place to stay for the night, got bored, visited the local bar and pissed off a cop. He waited for me to leave the bar and arrested me for DUI. I swear, I wasn't going to drive, I was just trying to keep warm until the rain stopped. I was soaked."

"So, you fucked him to get out of being arrested?!" Nick asks incredulously.

"Not on purpose!" I exclaim in my defense. "I made him angry, so he started screwing with me. He made me submit to a cavity search as well as a scrub down. I was handcuffed, so I had no choice. He ended up getting carried away and fucked me."

"You were raped by a cop. . . . What the hell is this world coming to?" Sighing, he looks me in the eye and asks, "Ok, the important thing is . . . Did you like it? Did you respond? Did you fuck him back?"

"Yes . . . yes . . . and yes . . ."

"I thought so. So, what is his name?"

"Tim . . ."

Exasperated, Nick repeats the name Tim and then dishes out one final swat. SMACK!!!!

"Ok, my sweet little whore wife every day we are going to come out here and tie you to the fence like this. And every day, I am going to spank you at least six times in memory of the six people that you've cheated on me with. And with each swat, you are going to yell out the name of the person that you are being spanked for. And if it is too cold to do it outside, I'll find some place to punish you indoors. And if you should happen to have sex with another person, with or without my knowledge, you will confess it to me, and I will forgive you, and you will have an additional swat attached to your punishment. Every day you will be reminded of your infidelities until I'm either too old to swing the paddle, or too old to care.''

Releasing me, Nick ushers me inside. Never before have I felt such shame and misery. If I could just take it all back, I would. Racing up the stairs to our room, I throw myself on the bed and cry. Nick decides to leave me alone for the time being, rinsing away his own demons with the hot spray of the shower.

''I've got some errands to run today,'' Nick announces as he gets himself dressed. Take the afternoon to do whatever you'd like. I'll be home around five with dinner, ok?''

''Ok,'' I answer remorsefully. I had finally regained control over my crying, but was still suffering from a bad case of the ''guilties.''

''I guess you don't want me to go with you?''

''No, I just wanted to give you a little time to yourself. You're not going to be getting much of it for a while, so you'd better take it while you can.''

''Don't do me any favors.''

Smiling, Nick looks at me and says, ''That's my girl. I like it much better when you're angry.''

''Screw you.''

Laughing, Nick comes over to gently swat my behind as he kisses me goodbye.

"Go on and do something fun. Don't waste the afternoon pouting, ok?"

"Ok. See you around five."

Sitting up, I watch as Nick leaves the room and then the house, wondering silently if I really have only been home for two days. It feels like forever since I actually made a decision for myself, was my own person again. Was I really going to be able to live like this? Realizing I had to give Nick some time to work through his own scrambled emotions, I decide that I will play it by ear and take it day to day. Once it was out of his system, he would get tired of the game and things would go back to normal. They just had to!

Well, with a free afternoon, there was no question as to what I was going to do. Zipping down the stairs to the basement, I switch on the computer to see what's happening in the cyber world.

<StudMuffin>	I	Miranda, is that you?
<Aphrodite>	I	Who wants to know?
<StudMuffin>	I	It's me, JD.
<Aphrodite>	I	JD Mason?
<StudMuffin>	I	In the flesh! Well, sort of . . . So, how have you been?
<Aphrodite>	I	Wow! Nick told me that he got back in touch with you guys. Small world, huh?
<StudMuffin>	I	Yes, it is. So, what else did Nick tell you?

<Aphrodite>	l	Oh just that you were hot for my bod. Other than that, not much.
<StudMuffin>	l	He gave me away, the dirty rat. Did he also tell you that Vicki and I were coming out there to visit you guys?
<Aphrodite>	l	Yeah, sometime after the snow starts flying, right? He says we're all going to go on a cross-country ski/hut trip together. Sounds like a lot of fun.
<StudMuffin>	l	So, can I steal you away for a while and have my way with your body?

Shifting uncomfortably on my still sore ass, I reply . . .

<Aphrodite>	l	Oh, I don't think that would be such a good idea.
<StudMuffin>	l	Why not? Don't you find me devastatingly irresistible?
<Aphrodite>	l	LOL . . . I haven't seen you in over fifteen years. I can't quite remember the power of your charm!
<StudMuffin>	l	Quite potent actually. There will be no way that you'll be able to keep your hands off me!
<Aphrodite>	l	Well, then . . . you have the answer to your question.
<StudMuffin>	l	So, do you and Nick have, um, an open marriage now?
<Aphrodite>	l	Now?
<StudMuffin>	l	Yeah, he told me what's been happening. It works great for Vicki and me.

\<Aphrodite\>	And you have no problems with it? No jealousies? No insecurities?
\<StudMuffin\>	Not a one. Just one rule. We have to tell one another, preferably *before* we have sex with someone else.
\<Aphrodite\>	So your pursuit of me is going to be relentless, isn't it?
\<StudMuffin\>	I don't give up very easily.
\<Aphrodite\>	Well, then, may the Force be with you.
\<StudMuffin\>	Still playing hard to get?
\<Aphrodite\>	I won't say yes, I won't say no. It'll just depend on circumstances and . . . Nick.
\<StudMuffin\>	Nick? What's Nick got to do with it? He said it's all up to you.
\<Aphrodite\>	Nothing is up to me these days . . . He is exacting his revenge.
\<StudMuffin\>	Sounds serious.
\<Aphrodite\>	It is, but hopefully it is just a passing fancy, otherwise, you and Vicki may have a surprise house guest!
\<StudMuffin\>	Come on over, babe. I've got room for ya!
\<Aphrodite\>	I'm sure you do, Mr. Stud, but I'm not quite ready to bail, yet.
\<StudMuffin\>	You know I'm always here for you!!!
\<Aphrodite\>	So, Mr. Open Marriage . . . how many women have you had sex with since you've been married?
\<StudMuffin\>	The truth? Hmmmm . . . about ten why?

<Aphrodite> | Does Vicki know about all ten of them?

<StudMuffin> | Well . . . she knows about half of them.

<Aphrodite> | You're not quite sticking to the rules, then, are you?

<StudMuffin> | Ok, you've embarrassed me. The first five were before we had the open marriage. I got caught on my sixth one, so I had to fess up. That's when we decided that the open marriage was the way to go.

<Aphrodite> | You're lucky she didn't dump you.

<StudMuffin> | Aren't we the pot calling the kettle black? Anyway, she realized that I truly loved her, just couldn't keep my hands off beautiful women. And . . . she decided that she had her own desires she wanted to explore, so it ended up working out. It took some time though.

<Aphrodite> | Want to know a secret?

<StudMuffin> | Sure. I'm all ears.

<Aphrodite> | Nick spanked the crap out of me this morning . . . one swat for each person I was unfaithful to him with.

<StudMuffin> | Oooooo . . . and how many swats did we end up with????

<Aphrodite> | Six . . . God, they hurt, too.

<StudMuffin> | Tsk, tsk, tsk . . . naughty little girl. Did it turn you on?

<Aphrodite> | Getting spanked?! Not at the time, but thinking back on it now . . .

<StudMuffin> | So, you'll get spanked again if I'm successful in seducing you?

<Aphrodite> | That pretty much sums it up, yep.

<StudMuffin> | Can I watch?

<Aphrodite> | You're evil! I'll make sure that if I get spanked for it, Vicki spanks you as well!

<StudMuffin> | I'm bigger than Vicki.

<Aphrodite> | You're not bigger than Vicki, Nick and I put together, so don't go getting cocky on me now.

<StudMuffin> | Ok, truce, you win . . . for now. I'd make your head spin . . .

<Aphrodite> | Excuse me?

<StudMuffin> | I'd make your head spin. I'd hold you down and eat you. For hours and hours I'd lick and suck you to orgasm until you couldn't see straight. It's my most favorite thing to do.

<Aphrodite> | Ohhhhhhh . . .

<StudMuffin> | What's the matter? Cat got your tongue?

<Aphrodite> | More like . . . tongue's got the . . . cat.

<StudMuffin> | You just think about it. I'll see you in December if I don't see you in the chat rooms before then. Gotta run.

<Aphrodite> | Alright then . . . see you in December.

The remainder of the afternoon is spent joining several different chatting sessions, none developing into anything interesting. I am quite relieved when Nick walks back through the front door toting with him a large Hawaiian pizza and a bottle of champagne. "My love, dinner is served!" he announces extravagantly.

Nick asks how my afternoon went, and I tell him how I was able to hook up with JD and chat for a while. He is quite pleased that we were able to talk, realizing that it won't be quite so awkward when the Masons first arrive in December, now that some communication has transpired. Otherwise, it would have been like meeting a couple of strangers and would have taken quite some effort to get to know them all over again.

"I want you to do me a favor tonight, Miranda," Nick declares between bites of pizza.

"What's that?" I ask with a sinking feeling washing over me.

"I want you to get back on the computer and try to find Wit."

"What in God's name for?! I don't ever want to talk to that man again!"

"You won't be doing it for yourself. You'll do it for me."

"But why, Nick?"

"I want you to get him to talk to you, apologize for running out on him, then beg him to call you again."

"Why do you want him to call me?"

"I want to videotape you having phone sex with him. The picture in my mind of you surrendering completely to a voice on the other end of the phone is so erotic to me. Your book described it beautifully, but I want to see it for myself."

"Nick, I don't want to. It's not going to work anyway. I'll never get him to talk to me."

"He'll talk to you. I don't care what you have to say, make him talk to you. Get him to call you tomorrow morning . . . around ten should be good."

"Do I have to?"

"Yes, you have to. Now, let's finish up with dinner. I want to go fishing!"

Fishing . . . hmmm . . . funny word for it. I find myself in front of the computer for the second time today, hoping and praying that <ArrogantWit;mt will not be available tonight. My hopes are immediately dashed as the all too familiar nickname looms frighteningly before me. What is it about him that sets my nerves on edge at the very sight of his name? Nick, undaunted, sits comfortably in a chair beside me, eager to catch a glimpse of the sparring match sure to ensue. I am relieved of the burden of trying to come up with a catchy phrase to get him to talk to me, as he is impatient and pounces upon me first.

<ArrogantWit>	I	Well, if it isn't the little birdie that flew the coop . . .
<Aphrodite>	I	Well, if it isn't the puppet master . . .
<ArrogantWit>	I	Puppet master? I like it. Symbolic of how I control you.
<Aphrodite>	I	I was referring to Rachel . . . *I'll* never be your puppet.

"Come on, Miranda. You're not supposed to fight with him. You have to get him to call you. Don't screw this up."

"Okay, sorry. He just brings out the worst in me."

\<ArrogantWit\> | Why are you here?

\<Aphrodite\> | I'm not sure. I'm restless. You don't suppose . . . I might, perhaps miss you? Egadsssss!

\<ArrogantWit\> | Flattery will get you nowhere.

\<Aphrodite\> | Actually, I came to apologize. . . . and to make sure Rachel is ok.

\<ArrogantWit\> | She'll recover. Don't worry about her.

\<Aphrodite\> | What did you do to her?

\<ArrogantWit\> | I sent her away to a place where her talents will be put to good . . . and constant use. A place where you belong.

\<Aphrodite\> | I'm afraid to ask. What type of place?

\<ArrogantWit\> | A place that caters to the wealthy. A place where untrustworthy slaves are sent to reflect upon their behavior while servicing hundreds of different masters. A place where they will be retrained on the proper etiquette befitting an honorable slave.

\<Aphrodite\> | How long does she have to stay there?

\<ArrogantWit\> | Until I go and retrieve her. Several weeks at least.

\<Aphrodite\> | You're horrible.

<ArrogantWit>	Don't be so quick to judge. She'll thank me for it, for restoring her status back to that of a good slave.
<Aphrodite>	And you think that I belong in such a place?
<ArrogantWit>	Without a doubt. I don't expect you'd be ready to return for at least six months, maybe even up to a year.
<Aphrodite>	But I have no desire to be a slave . . . not even a bad one.
<ArrogantWit>	Did you get wet as I told you about Rachel's fate? Did you not visualize yourself in her place? Did it not excite you, the thought of being at the mercy of hundreds of different men . . . and women? You already are a slave, Aphrodite. That's why you are here, why you'll always come back. You are my puppet.

"Nick!!!!!"

"It's ok, it's ok. Play his game. We'll get what we want in the end."

"Don't you mean, *you'll* get what *you* want?"

<Aphrodite>	I hate you.
<ArrogantWit>	You hate yourself.
<Aphrodite>	Suppose you are right. Suppose I am your puppet. Where do we go from here? I'm married, remember?
<ArrogantWit>	I've tried to call you . . . your number has been disconnected.

\<Aphrodite\>	I moved.
\<ArrogantWit\>	Give me your new number.
\<Aphrodite\>	Why?
\<ArrogantWit\>	So that I can call you and have my voice enter you to grab hold of your pussy and turn it inside out.
\<Aphrodite\>	And that is supposed to persuade me?
\<ArrogantWit\>	So I can shove my cock down your throat and gag you till you turn blue.
\<Aphrodite\>	Strike two.
\<ArrogantWit\>	So I can fuck you up the ass so fucking hard that I'll split you in two.
\<Aphrodite\>	You don't get many second dates, do you?
\<ArrogantWit\>	I want your new number, cunt. Give it to me.
\<Aphrodite\>	Say please.
\<ArrogantWit\>	Now!

"Miranda, give it to him. We'll have the number changed right after he calls."

\<Aphrodite\>	Ok, I'll give it to you. When do you plan on calling me?
\<ArrogantWit\>	Now.
\<Aphrodite\>	No . . . now is not good. I have to leave in a minute and won't be back until very late. How about tomorrow morning, let's say around ten or so?
\<ArrogantWit\>	The number, Aphrodite . . .

Reluctantly, I type away the ten-digit phone number that will inevitably allow Wit back into my life, whatever the consequences may be.

<ArrogantWit>	I	You will suffer tomorrow. I will not go easy on you.
<Aphrodite>	I	I'll look forward to it. Give it your best shot.
<ArrogantWit>	I	Such a brave and rebellious little birdie. Prepare to have your wings clipped.

"Well, Nick, I hope you're happy. Not only is he going to call, but he has a score to settle."

"Yeah, and I get to catch it all on film. It's going to be my lucky day!"

"You're a freaking sadist!"

"Let's go to bed, Miranda. I find that I am quite impatient for tomorrow to get here."

Shaking my head, I allow Nick to lead me upstairs and into a tormented sleep, images of helpless female slaves being passed around from one man to another, their sole purpose in life being to provide them with pleasure.

CHAPTER 6

■

REPENTANCE

Nick awakens at 8 A.M., eager to get the day started and his video equipment set up. Not at all enthusiastic about the events that will be taking place shortly, I remain in bed watching his progress.

"Where will you be when he calls?" Nick asks, excitedly.

"Probably right here on the bed."

"Ok, I'll set the tripod up right here. Oh, I'm so excited. I can't wait. We should have told him 9 A.M."

"Ten o'clock is soon enough for me."

"I'm going to go and get the other phone extension. I want to be able to hear what he says."

"Whatever. I think I'll take a shower and get fixed up. If I'm going to be starring in a porno movie, I want to look good."

"That's my girl."

*   *   *

The phone rings at precisely 10 A.M. I jump, startled, altering my position on the bed slightly. I decided to wait stark naked, lying comfortably in the warm softness of my down blanket. Nick has already started videotaping, eager to capture the look of anxiety that crossed my features when the phone rang. Giving me the thumbs up, I take it as my cue that all is ready at his end and I am free to answer.

"Hello." Gulp . . .
   "How are you waiting for me?"
   "Open."
   "You know I'm not going to be easy on you."
   "I don't expect you to."
   "Are your hands free?"
   "Yes, just like you taught me."
   "Get a pen and some paper."
   "A pen and paper, why?"
   "Just do it!"
Looking over at Nick, I shrug as I get out of bed in search of pen and paper. Wit is extremely silent as I scurry to gather the items he requested until I have settled myself comfortably back onto bed.
   "Ok, I have them."
   "I want you to repeat what I say, then write it down."
   "Ok, I'm ready."
   "I am Wit's whore."
Shit . . . "I am Wit's whore," I repeat as I scribble the words down and gaze guiltily towards my husband. He shakes his head as if to say, "Don't worry, just do as he says. I want this to be authentic."

"I crave his prick."

"I crave his prick."

"I exist only to please him."

"I exist only to please him."

"Louder!"

Blushing furiously, I repeat louder, "I EXIST ONLY TO PLEASE HIM."

"That's better, now . . . I will always be open and available to him."

"I will always be open and available to him."

"I will wait with my mouth held wide to taste his prick."

"I will wait with my mouth held wide to taste his prick."

"I yearn."

"I yearn."

"I provide."

"I provide."

"I have no choice."

"I have no choice."

"I am Wit's whore."

"I am Wit's whore."

"Did you write it all down, whore?"

"Yes," I stammer, mortified to know that my embarrassment is being captured on videotape.

"Read it back to me, in full. The whole time I want you squeezing and pulling at your right nipple as hard as you can. I want to hear the pain in your voice as you say the words."

I look up at Nick pleadingly, but he shakes his head in stubborn refusal. The rule is that I am to do everything Wit tells me to do, and that is precisely what Nick wants. Squeezing and pulling my right nipple as hard as I can, I gasp out the paragraph written before me.

"I . . . am . . . Wit's . . . whore. Uh, I crave . . . his . . . prick. I . . . exist . . . only . . . to please him. I will . . . always . . . be . . . open and . . . and . . . available to him. I, ohhh . . . will wait . . . with my, with my. . . . my. . . . mouth held wide . . . to . . . taste . . . his . . . prick. I yearn. I provide. Uhhh . . . oh, I . . . have no . . . no . . . choice. I am . . . Wit's . . . whore."

"Oh, that was beautiful, you sexy fuck. Let go of your nipple. How does it feel?"

Breathless, I manage to say, "It hurts, it's throbbing."

"Those were my teeth that you felt, pulling on you, twisting and scraping, biting you."

"Ohhhhhhh."

"We're going to do that again, my sexy whore, this time on your hands and knees. Get on them now!"

Whimpering, I say, "Ok, ok."

Getting up onto my hands and knees, I position myself so that I am facing the camera, knowing that Nick has a perverse desire to watch the tormented expressions play across my face. He smiles his approval and adjusts the camera slightly to accommodate the new position.

"I want you to read it again, this time faster," Wit commands. "While you are reading it, I want you to spank your ass, hard. I want to hear it. If I can't hear every single smack across that sweet ass of yours, we'll keep doing it over and over again until I do, understand?"

"Please . . . why?" I ask. Oh God, please don't make me have to do this.

"Do you want me to hang up?"

"No, no don't hang up," I say, panicking.

"Then do as I say. Now, Miranda. Quickly."

Alternating quick, loud smacks to each cheek of my ass, I recite again, "I am Wit's whore. I crave his prick. I exist only to please him. I will always be open and available to him. I will wait with my mouth held wide to taste his prick. I yearn. I provide. I have no choice. I am Wit's whore."

"Not fast enough, again!"

Spanking myself at a fast and furious pace, I begin again, forgetting the camera, forgetting my husband, solely focused on Wit's presence, his breathing and the sensations rippling across my raw bottom. By the time I have finished reading the paragraph a second time, I am panting and gasping for air.

"Please, not again, not again."

"That's enough for now. Now, get up and go to a mirror. Do you have a full-length one?"

"Yes."

"Go stand in front of it."

I get up off the bed as if in a trance, unaware that Nick is following me with the camera, angling it so that he has a full view of my backside, as well as being able to capture my reflection in the mirror.

"What do you see?"

The vision that greets me is that of a disheveled beauty trapped in the throes of erotica. Flushed skin, glassy eyes, full, rosy lips, erect nipples all combine to paint a picture of a perfect "wanton."

"What do you see?"

Startled out of my reverie, I reply, "Myself. I see myself."

"And who are you?"

"I am your whore."

"You are my cunt."

"I am your cunt."

"Touch your lips. Whose lips are those?"

"Yours?"

"Yes, mine. Say it, they are your lips, Wit."

"They are your lips, Wit."

"Touch your tits. Whose tits are they?"

"They are your tits, Wit."

"Turn around and look at your ass. To whom does that ass belong?"

I turn, attempting to get the best view of my ass as possible, noticing how the deep, red welts still glow brightly from my frenzied attack earlier.

"It belongs to you, Wit."

"Is your ass red, Miranda?"

"Very much so."

"Whose hands were really spanking you this morning, Miranda?"

"Yours were."

"You like what my hands are capable of doing, don't you? They can bring you such great pleasure, the likes of which you've never known before."

"Yesssssss . . ."

"Face the mirror again, Miranda. Touch your clit. Who does that clit belong to? Who has the power to make it swell, to want, to crave?"

"It's yours . . . you do."

"Ok, my sweet slut. Sit on the floor in front of the mirror with your legs spread wide. Touch your pussy. Pull your lips apart and spread them as wide as you can. Open yourself to me. Stretch yourself. I want to see that needy cunt, gasping and begging to be fucked. Can I see it, Miranda?''

''Yessss, yessss . . . Oh God.''

''Lean back a little, I want to see more. Oh God, what, Miranda?''

''Oh, God, I can't stand this anymore. I want you to fuck me.''

''Is your pussy wet, Miranda?''

''Mmmmm, yes, it's wet.''

''Put a finger inside and taste yourself. Tell me what you taste like.''

Slipping a finger inside, I work to get it completely covered with my wetness, finally pulling it away and raising it to my lips. Sucking on it, I strive to find the right words to describe the flavor.

''I taste like woman, Wit. Clean and sexy and wanton.''

''Spread your legs wider, cunt. Now, put two fingers inside.''

''Mmmmmm . . .''

''Now fuck yourself with your fingers.''

''Ohhhhhh . . .''

''What are you doing, cunt?''

''I'm . . . I'm fucking myself with two fingers.''

''Who's fucking you?''

''You are . . . you are.''

''Three fingers. I want three fingers inside that juicy box now. Fuck yourself with three fingers.''

With a little effort, I manage to get three fingers thrust deep inside, fucking myself as instructed. Finding it very difficult to remain seated, I begin rocking backwards with each thrust of my hand.

''Four . . . four now. I want to hear you.''

"Fou . . . four . . . four won't . . . fit . . . Uhhhhhh, ohhhhhhh, ohhhhhhhh, God"

"Yes they will. Do it."

"Eeeeeee . . . Ohhhhhhh. Four . . . I'm fucking . . . myself . . . with four . . . fingers now."

"How does it feel, hmmmm?"

"Good . . . good . . . awesome . . . Oh yes . . ."

"Ok, slut, now it's time for the whole fucking fist. I want you to get that fist up there and fuck yourself raw. Shove it up there, bitch."

"Nooooooooooooo . . . no, I can't. I won't."

"Afraid I'll rip your insides out if I get that close? Huh, Miranda?"

"Stop it . . . stop it . . ."

"Hmmmm, I guess we'll have to resort to Plan B. What kinds of toys do you have? Any dildos? Vibrators?

"A few," I manage to gasp out, glad for the reprieve.

"Get the two largest ones you have. Do you have any clothespins?"

"Clothespins, what for?"

"Do you?"

"Yes."

"Get two of them. While you are getting everything together, I want you to keep repeating, 'I am Wit's cunt. Wit owns me. I am Wit's cunt. Wit owns me.' "

"I am Wit's cunt. Wit owns me. I am Wit's cunt. Wit owns me." The phrase is repeated several times over as I hustle around trying to locate my new instruments of sexual pleasure.

"Ok, I have everything."

"Describe the smaller dildo to me."

Picking up the *smaller* dildo, I look at it carefully as I explain, "Well, it's not so small. It is a clear, white color that glows in the dark, about eight inches in length, one and a half inches thick near the head, two inches thick around the base, and it vibrates."

"Get on your hands and knees, facing the mirror."

Oh, God . . . "Ok."

"Turn it on and stick it in your pussy from behind. I want you to watch the expression on your face while you do it."

Quivering, I do as I am told, slowly sliding it in and watching my face change as each inch is taken deeper and the thickness increases. I can feel the vibrations shooting through my body, deep into the pit of my belly and along my bones. I shudder as the final inch is consumed, releasing a deep, aching moan.

"You have fifteen seconds to get it soaking wet, because after that, it's going in your ass."

"No, no . . . it's too big. It's too big."

"Ten seconds . . . nine . . . eight. . . ."

Bucking my hips backwards to meet the thrusts of the vibrator, I work quickly, wanting it to be as well lubricated as possible before it has to enter my ass. Oh God, how am I ever going to be able to take it that way?

"Time's up. Take it out now."

"Don't make me do this. It will split me in two."

"You'll be surprised at how much you can take when you are this aroused, Miranda. Stay on your hands and knees, keep looking at yourself, put the tip of that vibrator on your asshole and slowly start to work it in."

Whimpering, I say, "Please . . ."

Knowing that the vibrator is well lubricated, I suck in my breath as I carefully poise the head of the imitation cock against my anal opening. As I gently push, I beg my body to relax, knowing it will be much easier on me if it does. Slowly, my ass yields and accepts the invader, as my back arches and nipples tighten against the sensations. I watch my reflection to see my eyes half close and my mouth dangle open, allowing for a string of soft "oooo's" and "ahhhhh's" to escape, while my body dances and hips sway in an attempt to coax in the entire eight inches. Just an inch or two short of my goal, I relay my success story to Wit.

"Ok, it's in. It's all the way in."

"How does it feel?"

"Full, I feel full."

"Do you like the way you feel?"

"Yes."

"Whose cock is in your ass right now, Miranda?"

"Your cock, your cock is."

"And what do you suppose my cock wants to do to your ass?"

"It wants to fuck it."

"Yes, it wants to fuck it. Fuck your ass with my cock, Miranda. Fuck it hard. And Miranda . . ."

"Yes . . ."

"I want you to say, 'I am Wit's cunt. Wit owns my ass. . . .' while you are fucking that sweet ass of yours. Do it now."

A sob escapes as I begin to thrust the huge tormentor

in deeper, then pull it almost completely back out, only to have it repeat the terrifying journey, plunging back in the entire eight inches. My ass widens and relaxes out of necessity, not knowing exactly how long it will have to endure this humiliation. The more I am able to relax, the more I am able to accept the sensations, ultimately growing to like them.

"I am Wit's cunt. Wit owns my ass."

" 'I am Wit's cunt. Wit owns my ass. . . .' "

Sobbing and gasping, ashamed of my reaction, ashamed of my acquiescence, I continue as directed, rhythmically driving the vibrator in and out, watching my reflection in the mirror as I do so. With tears silently sliding down my cheeks, I continue, urged on by the sexy whispers coming from the phone and the intense look of desire clouding my own husband's features.

"I am Wit's cunt. Wit owns my ass. Please, I want to stop now."

"It's almost time, my sexy whore, keep going."

Sobbing, I say, "No . . . No . . . no . . . I am Wit's . . . cunt. Wit owns my ass . . . please . . ."

"I told you I wasn't going to be easy on you. I meant it. Now, stop fucking yourself with that vibrator, but leave it in, deep in your ass. Hold it there with those tight, fucking ass muscles. Is it staying?"

Relieved to not have to thrust it in any longer, I push it all the way in, my ass now thoroughly able to accept the full eight inches without hesitation, and grip it in place.

"Yes, it is all the way in, and staying put."

"Great. Still on your hands and knees, turn sideways. Can you see the end of it sticking out of your sweet ass, Miranda? Can you see how my prick violates you? Can you see how eager you are to please me? I own you, Miranda. I own you.''

"Yes, yes, you do. . . .''

"I want to hear you scream, Miranda.''

"What do you mean, that you want to hurt me?''

"No, I want to hear you scream out in mindless ecstasy, Miranda, ecstasy that I create for you. So far, I've heard you gasp, whimper, sigh, moan, and yes . . . even sob. But I've never heard you scream. I won't be satisfied until you scream, Miranda. If you had stuck around in Vegas, I would have had you screaming.''

"Stop it . . . stop it . . . I can't take . . . this . . . Stop it. . . .''

"Get on your back, now. Keep that vibrator deep in your ass. . . . NOW!!!''

Petrified now, not knowing what is coming next, but assuming the worst, I scurry onto my back, knees bent, legs spread wide, my exposed sex directly in the line of the camera. I can see the absolute look of glee on Nick's face, this encounter obviously surpassing anything his imagination had conjured up.

"Is that vibrator still buried, Miranda?''

"Yes, yes. It's not going anywhere.''

"Pick up the other vibrator, the larger one, and describe it to me.''

"It's huge, soft, flesh-colored. It is a good two and a half inches thick around from top to bottom and ten inches long. It even has balls.''

"Does it vibrate?''

"Oh, yes . . . vibrates and rotates.''

"Now we're talking. Give it head, Miranda. Give my cock a blow job."

"But . . ."

"Now, cunt. I want to feel your lips wrapped around my prick. While you're sucking on it, fuck yourself some more with that vibrator still up your ass."

How did I ever get myself into this mess? Licking my lips, I hesitantly place the enormous tip to my mouth, slowly pushing it in, stretching my mouth extremely wide, almost hurting. I reach down with my left hand next to my left side and around, under my bent leg to grasp the vibrator, still humming expectantly. More slowly this time, I ease the vibrator out and in, and out and in as I lick and suck at the cock stuffed into my mouth. My eyes close as my hips start to buck and rotate, my pussy wanting desperately to be filled.

"How does my cock taste, Miranda?"

"Mhhhhhhhh."

"I thought so. How does your ass feel, Miranda?"

"Mhhhhhhh, mhhhhhhh."

"How does your pussy feel?"

"Mhhhhhhhhhhhhhhhh . . ."

"Do you want to feel my prick in your pussy? Do you?"

"Mhhhhh! Mhhhhh! Mhhhhhh!"

"Take it out of your mouth now. Lick my balls."

Gasping, I remove the massive phallus from my mouth and lick at the latex balls.

"Now is not the time to be a lady, Miranda. I want to hear slurping. I want to hear you lick my balls. Slurp . . . slurp . . . slurp . . ."

Geeze . . . "Ok." I resume the licking frenzy, only this time salivating and slurping as loudly as possible. I can hear Wit's moans increase and deepen, sending another surge of wetness to the center of my pussy.

"Oh God . . . oh God, you're a sexy fuck, Miranda. It's time to fuck you. Stop licking."

Panting heavily now, I remove all oral stimulation, still slowly working the vibrator back and forth in my ass.

"Spread you legs wide, knees bent. Shove that vibrator back deep in your ass and hold it there. I want both of your hands directing my cock to your pussy."

"Ok, ok . . ." Impatient, now, my hips are bucking and rocking uncontrollably, my pussy overflowing with eager moisture, poised . . . wanting . . . craving . . .

"Ok . . . now, with both hands, hold that cock against the entrance to your hot pussy, but don't go in. Just hold it there."

Whimpering, wanting to completely engulf it, yet being denied, I begin to beg, "Please."

"Please, what?"

"Please fuck me."

"Beg me."

"I am. I'm begging you. Please let me feel your cock inside me."

"How badly do you want it, Miranda? Let me hear your need. Let me *feel* your need."

"Oh, God, please. I need it. I want it. I crave it. I need your prick. I need to feel it deep inside me."

"Badly enough to . . . scream . . . for it?"

"Yes, yes, I'll scream for it. I will . . ."

"Damn right you will. Ok, slowly push it in. Try

to take it all, down to the balls. Then, just hold it there."

"Do you want me to turn it on?"

"No, leave it off for now."

Sighing deeply as the delicious feelings of sliding that mammoth penis inside consume me, I push on and push on, wiggling, rotating, until I've managed to completely swallow the entire length. The contrast in pressure between the vibrating shaft in my ass as it meets with the colossal appendage currently housed in my pussy is astounding, and my moans increase with rapid intensity.

"Oh, God . . . oh, God . . . oh, God. . . . It's in. It's all the way in. I'm dying. . . ."

"Now . . . turn it on, vibrator and rotator, and then let go. Arms way out to the side."

Mindless, I flip both controls to the "on" position, and practically get catapulted off the floor from the initial jolt I receive.

"AHHHHHHHHH," is torn from my throat, not quite a scream, but the closest thing yet.

"Close, but not quite, my sweet little whore. How does that feel?"

"Oh, God," gasping, I continue, "I feel like I'm being electrocuted. Every muscle in my body is twitching, my ears are tingling, my scalp is tingling. I'm so full. I want to cum. Wit, let me cum."

"This is going to be an orgasm you'll never forget, Miranda. Do you believe me?"

"Yes, yes . . . I believe you."

"Are you touching yourself?"

"No, my arms are out to my sides. I want to touch myself."

"Where do you want to touch, Miranda?"

"My clit . . . I want to touch my clit."

"It's throbbing, isn't it?"

"Yes."

"It's hard, isn't it?"

"Yes, yes . . ."

"You would just love for my tongue to slide against it, wouldn't you?"

"Oh, God, yes . . . please."

"Ok, whore. This is what you're going to do. You're going to fuck yourself with my huge cock with one hand, you're going to rub your clit with your other hand, and right before you get ready to cum, you're going to stop, grab the clothes pins, and clamp them on your nipples. Then you're going to scream, as you resume fucking your pussy and rubbing your clit while you explode. You're going to do that for me, aren't you?"

"Yes, yes, yes!" I practically scream now.

"Do it, Miranda. Scream for me."

Frantically, needing immediate release, I begin as instructed. Lowering my legs flat to the floor to get the best sensations, I thrust the incredible rotating cock in and out, while rubbing my clit in circular motions. Unintelligible moans . . . urgent moans are being sporadically emitted from my mouth, increasing in volume. Within seconds, I feel the first familiar sensations of an approaching orgasm, the tingling starting at my toes and moving upwards. Knowing that I am extremely close, I stop and grab the clothespins, recklessly clamping them to my sensitive and erect nipples. The scream that is ripped from my body is inhuman, as I am inflicted with conflicting sensations. Quickly I return to rubbing my clit as my legs clamp tightly closed around the cock deeply implanted in my pussy and my body is thrown into wave after wave of never-ending convulsions. My scream lasts for the entire duration, intensifying with every new spasm that washes over me. Finally collapsing in exhaustion, I am further rewarded by the sound of Wit groaning out his own orgasm, simultaneously achieved. Without another word, the phone is disconnected and I am left lying with nothing more than a dial tone.

"That was fan-fucking-tastic!" Nick exclaims joyously. "Take those dildos out. It's my turn now."

For the remainder of the morning and into the afternoon, Nick continues to ravage my body tirelessly. Over and over again, in every imaginable position, my body is taken beyond the brink of ecstasy and back again, each time more intense than the time before. Sighing, I know I will never leave him again, regardless of what his plans have in store for me.

"Don't get too comfortable there, baby, I've still got a punishment to dole out."

Without resistance, I follow him back outside to be tethered to the fence, my round ass a delightful target. Again I scream out the six names that will plague me forever, as Nick places a stinging swat to my cheeks with each one, paying proper penitence for my indiscretions.

CHAPTER 7

∎

RETRIBUTION

The next day proves no less bizarre than the previous three, with Nick's insatiable desire for revenge beginning to scare me. Smiling, he takes the time to enlighten me as to this coming evening's schedule of events.

"I'm having a few of the guys over for a poker game tonight, Miranda."

"Great, does this mean I get a night all to myself?"

"No, even better. You get to be the entertainment."

With a sinking feeling, I ask, "What do you mean, entertainment? I thought *poker* was the entertainment."

"Well, I need your help is all. I need for you to keep the beer and appetizers flowing."

"Nick, you distinctly said *entertainment*. What you are describing now sounds more like *hostess*."

"Ok, Miranda. I'll tell you exactly what's going to happen tonight. That way, you can think about it all day, and imagine, and worry, and fret . . . and become completely turned on. You'll be so scared, yet your pussy will be drenched with anticipation."

"Nick, whatever it is, I don't want it."

"Yes you do, Miranda. Do you realize that you are your own worse enemy? You fight and deny all the things that bring you to your pinnacle of pleasure, and your pleasure is my pleasure, Miranda. I have committed myself to not allowing you to close any doors. You will submit to everything I have in store for you tonight. It's just your choice whether you want to do it the easy way or the hard way."

Not yet resigned, but wanting to be mentally prepared for the upcoming evening, I try to sound more amiable as I ask Nick once again, "Ok, what is it, exactly, that will be happening tonight?"

"Well, sweets, you know that outfit that you wore your first night home to clean in?"

"Yes."

"You'll be wearing that as you serve the refreshments."

"Nick, I'll be practically naked! These are your friends coming over, right? Do you really want them to see me that way?"

"Oh, yes. Now don't tell me that you've suddenly become shy about your body? This should appeal to the exhibitionist side of you."

"But these are your friends, people I know."

"Yeah, they are. They are also men that have desired you from the first day they met you."

"And you're going to let them see me naked? Nick, I'm convinced you've lost your mind."

"Oh, Miranda, this is only the beginning. You

don't think I'm just going to tease them all night long now, do you?''

Panicking, I say, ''Oh come on now. You're beginning to sound like Wit.''

''Maybe Wit knows what he's talking about.''

''No, no . . . he scared me. I ran from him and whatever it was that he had planned. I couldn't handle it.''

''You'll have no choice but to handle it tonight, Miranda. I won't let you run. You love to tease men. You love to get them all worked up. You love a wild, passionate romp with somebody new. You'll get all that and more . . . tonight.''

''Please, Nick, please reconsider. I don't want this. I only want you. I know that now.''

Ignoring my pleas, Nick continues, ''So, Miranda, there will be five men here this evening, all of whom you know. The poker chips will not be symbolic of money, but rather, of your delicious body. The winner of each hand gets one minute with you, to do whatever he wants, short of actually fucking you or harming you. The winner of the entire game gets to fuck you, right there in front of everyone else. I can't wait to see you fuck another man, Miranda. It's been driving me crazy trying to picture it from your stories.''

I collapse to the floor as the implications of what my husband has told me begin to sink into my befuddled brain. How could he do this to me? This man is supposed to love me, cherish me, want me for himself. How could he humiliate me this way? And, of course, the answer is right in front of me. How could I have done that to him? It's his way of evening the score. If I want a life of happily ever after, I need to pay the piper.

"What if one of the guys does something that will hurt me. It may be too late to stop him."

"Don't worry, the six of us have discussed it at length. I've preapproved certain things, and the rest are off-limits. They already know what they can and can't do."

"Who are they?"

"I'll tell you a little later. There may even be one or two in the group that *you've* had fantasies about."

"Nick, I'm going to hate you for this, I swear it."

"Possibly, but I doubt it. It's a risk I'm willing to take to elevate you to a higher level of pleasure. All of the emotions that will be coursing through you the entire night . . . fright, uncertainty, embarrassment . . . will ultimately lead up to the most absolute, extreme fulfillment. You'll be kissing my feet when the night is over. Now, let's go play on-line and get you all warmed up. Then we'll tie you up to wallow in your sexual agony until it's time to get ready. I want you *hot* and worked up for tonight."

As time draws closer for the guests to begin arriving, my anxieties increase and race out of control. Almost to the point of hyperventilation, I beg Nick for something to calm my nerves. A glass of wine, a sedative, anything that he has that would help me make it though the night, but he refuses. He wants me perfectly sober and coherent, fully aware of everything going on around me, so that I can feel . . . everything. I am not going to be allowed to escape into the security of a drug-induced mind.

Again I feel the utmost vulnerability, dressed in my skimpy outfit, waiting as if I were a prisoner sentenced to death row. I can feel my bare breasts as they jut forth from the cupless bra, my nipples puckering in the cool room, curious as to what the future holds. The short apron skirt barely hides the lips of my pussy from the front, allowing all to be seen from the rear view. My ass, round and naked, waits as expectantly as my nipples, flexing in their worried anticipation. The only other accessory to my scanty attire are the five-inch heels that Nick demanded I wear. He wants all my movements to be slow and unsteady, making a quick escape impossible. Teetering nervously, I wait by the front door, ready to answer it when the deafening bell sounds.

I realize now that I have two choices. One, I can fight this all the way, crying out my humiliation to all, therefore compounding it, or meeting it head on with simplified dignity. Although the latter is going to be much harder to accomplish, I begin to feel as if it is truly my sole option. I don't want Nick believing that just because he has the upper hand, I will cower and crumble, nor do I wish to portray to his friends my extreme embarrassment. Fine, if Nick wants a show, then a show he shall have. I will not plead and beg for mercy, but rather shed even more of my inhibitions and enjoy Nick's little game. After all, it's all about sex, right? And I really can't say there's anything I like more, sometimes the more deviant and socially unaccepted sex, the better. Nick promised me that there is nothing for me to fear tonight, that he will not let anyone get carried away and hurt me. Even though this game was staged as Nick's form of revenge, it was also planned with my pleasure in mind.

While we wait for the guests to begin arriving, Nick decides to go over the guest list with me. "Ok, Miranda, I want to let you know who your tormentors will be tonight. I've invited Jake, Kevin, Jerome, Bill and Russ. How's that for a guest list?"

Somehow, hearing the names actually made it seem more real, more inevitable. Previously, I had lulled myself into thinking that Nick was making it all up, just trying to teach me a lesson, that it wasn't really going to take place. With the mention of the five ominous names, all those with whom I am acquainted, my stomach begins to lurch, suddenly sick from the certain reality. I'm not going to get out of this, am I?

Silently, I run all five names through my head, making a mental picture of each guest. First, Russ. Well, it is easy enough to figure out why Russ agreed to participate. Of the five, he is the most sexually active, always bragging about his exploits and perversions. The man has a bigger collection of pornographic movies than the local video store. He also is the best looking of the bunch with black hair and sky-blue eyes. Russ has the physique of a body builder, standing just shy of six feet with a respectable amount of muscles covering his entire body. Unfortunately, the attraction ends there. His shallow personality compounded by a self-centered ego makes it difficult to tolerate his presence for any length of time. Although it's easy to see why so many women fall for him, it's also easy to see why none stick around very long.

Next is Bill, who, I have to admit, is my favorite of Nick's friends. In his mid-thirties, it is hard to figure out why he hasn't settled down with one woman yet. He is very good-natured, always teasing me over the phone when I call Nick at work.

"Hey, Miranda, when are you going to dump that husband of yours and come run away with me?" Or "God, you look good in black." Or "I'm still single, Miranda. I'm saving myself for you."

Even though he has joked for years about "wanting" me, he has never once made a pass or spoken to me in a lewd way. His comments have always been light and teasing. Bill is also very nice-looking with his sandy hair and hazel eyes, taller and leaner than Russ but not quite as eye-catching.

And then there is Jerome, beautiful and proud in all his black glory. Standing taller than the rest, he presents a formidable warrior-like appearance; strong, sleek, commanding. His skin is flawless, enhanced by an incredible pair of golden-hued eyes. Contrary to his intimidating presence, he is one of the most kind and thoughtful people I have ever met, always polite and very soft-spoken. It is hard for me to comprehend why he would agree to participate in such an outrageous poker game. Do I really know him at all? Do I really know anybody? Do I really know myself?

Finally, there are Jake and Kevin, and I group these two together because that's how you'll find them, always together. Two peas in a pod, they are known as the intellectual ones, and you will usually find them immersed in some sort of a computer crisis. If not hardware, then software or training. Although I've always enjoyed the mental stimulation of their company,

I've never thought of them in a sexual way. Now that I am being forced to separate them and see them as men, rather than extensions of their computers, I can see the possibilities. They are both cute in boyish ways, but have always appeared a little shy unless talking about their beloved computers. It's going to be interesting to see these guys in action. Oh, God . . . what am I thinking????

Nick must have been watching my facial expressions as I reviewed and analyzed the names of the players, for when I look back at him, he is grinning ear to ear.

"See, I told you you'd like it. Believe it or not, I'm doing this for you. Do you have any idea how you'll react to being touched by five pair of hands, hands that have itched to touch you since they've met you, hands that your body has never known? Look at how your body responds just thinking about it? You're flushed, your nipples are hard, your lips are parted, your breathing is labored, and, I bet if I touched you right now, you'd be extremely wet. Are you wet, Miranda?"

"Stop it, Nick, this is hard enough," I manage to squeak out as my throat begins to constrict and my eyes to mist.

Coming over to me, Nick pulls me into a gentle embrace, kissing my hair, my eyes, my nose and finally my mouth, softly and tenderly.

"I love you, Miranda."

"I love you, too, Nick."

I jump, startled from my reverie as the doorbell begins to chime, signifying the arrival of the first anxious guest. Not surprisingly, Russ is the first one to arrive, and lets out a long whistle as I open the door, clad provocatively in my scanty attire. "My prayers have been answered. I can't believe this is happening."

Raising my arms, I reach over to give him a welcoming hug. He crushes me flat against him and reaches behind me to clasp my ass tightly.

Whispering into my ear, he states, "That ass is mine tonight, baby."

Closing my eyes tightly, I bravely reply, "Only if you win it, hot shot. Only if you win it."

Next to arrive is Bill, and rather than scoop me up into a hug, he steps back and stares then closes his eyes.

"I'm burning this into my memory forever. You're even more lovely in black than I ever imagined."

With a wink, he joins Nick and Russ in the living room.

"Miranda, can we get three beers in here, sweetie?"

"Sure, be right there."

The sight of me carrying the desired beverages to the living room brings a couple of groans from both Russ and Bill, almost as if it is painful for them to look at me.

"Come on, guys. You act as if you've never seen a half-naked woman before."

"Not one that we've fantasized about for years," they reply in unison.

Smiling, I walk slowly back to the front door, being careful not to topple over on the high shoes.

Jake and Kevin arrive together as expected, and

ogle me in surprise as I open the door to welcome them in. Not being able to meet my eyes, they walk in with their heads bowed down, afraid to take another look.

"Hey, guys, it's ok," I reassure them as I put a finger under each chin and direct their gazes back towards mine. "Look all you like. It turns me on to know that you like what you see."

Turning around slowly, I give them plenty of time to absorb all I have to offer. When I am facing them once again, they are able to meet my eyes and smile.

"Shit, Miranda. This kind of thing just doesn't happen to guys like us," Jake states, matter-of-factly.

"Yeah, I always thought all those stories you read in those adult magazines were all made up. Now I know better," Kevin mutters unbelievingly, shaking his head.

"Hey, there's nothing wrong with guys like you. You are both very nice-looking. You just have to get out more, that's all. Now, what can I get you boys to drink?"

After fixing Jake and Kevin up with a beer each, they head off in the direction of the living room to group up with the rest of the guys. Taking a deep breath, I congratulate myself on how well I've managed to keep my composure so far. Now, as soon as Jerome shows up, we'll be all ready to move on. The more quickly it begins, the more quickly it will be over.

No sooner had I thought it than the doorbell rang once again. Ok, one more time, Miranda, you can do it. As expected, Jerome stands there, tall and powerful, his form filling the entire entrance.

"Come on in, big guy."

Smiling, he enters, looking me over appreciatively. "Are you sure you want to go through with this, Miranda? If not, I'll leave right now."

Trying to put him at ease, I say, "Are you kidding? And give up a chance to spend a minute, or maybe even longer, with a stud like you? Not on your life, my friend."

"Ok, but don't say I didn't warn you," he says grinning as he gropes at his crotch. "I've got a monster under here."

I'm sure the blood drained from my face as the vision flashed through my head. Oh, God. And I find myself even more dismayed as a wave of moisture is carried instantaneously to the center of my sex as I breathlessly think about trying to sheath that monster.

After getting Jerome a beer, we wander back into the dining room, where everyone else is already gathered and settled around the dining room table. Poker chips are divided up into five equal groups and placed in front of everyone sitting at the table. There is one empty seat, which Jerome takes without hesitation. After many "hello's" and some small talk, Nick claps his hands together to get everyone's attention.

"Ok, guys. I think it's about time we get started. Let me go briefly over the ground rules one more time."

The doorbell unexpectedly chimes for the fifth time this evening, and Nick and I exchange confused glances.

"Are we expecting anyone else?" I ask curiously.

"Not that I'm aware of," Nick replies. "Why don't you go answer the door and see who it is."

143

"Dressed like this?"

Grinning evilly, Nick says, "Yeah, dressed just like that. This should be interesting."

Feeling six pair of eyes burning into my ass as I leave to answer the door, I struggle to keep my composure, teetering precariously on the offensive heels. Why did Nick have to insist that I wear these? Opening the door just a crack, I take a peek to see who the intruder is.

A sassy female voice greets me, "So, I hear there's a special poker game going on over here. I'd like to join in."

Damn, how did Celeste find out about this? Pushing her way in, she pauses to take in my appearance.

"Nice outfit, Miranda," she says with a smirk.

Nick's old girlfriend. She still hangs out in our same circle of friends, but we usually don't run into her much. Even though she and Nick have remained friends after the breakup, they try not to stay long in one another's company. I haven't quite figured out my feelings for her yet. There is absolutely no reason for me to dislike her, yet it's almost as if we have a constant friendly rivalry going on, over what, I'm uncertain. After all, I ended up with Nick, but maybe she doesn't see it that way. Maybe with this rift in our marriage, she sees a way for herself to become the victor. Whatever her reasons for being here, I'm not happy about it, not one bit.

"Miranda, who's at the door?" Nick yells from the other room.

"It's Celeste, hon. She wants to join the poker game."

"Great, send her on back."

Celeste, a sexual magnet. With her long legs and a build similar to my own, she is tough to ignore, not like you'd actually want to. Short, dark hair framing a lovely face accented with huge brown eyes, she is a walking wet dream. Strutting over to stand directly in front of me, she grasps my chin between her fingers and looks me straight in the eye, saying, "So, I hear you're the prize. I can't wait to finally get a piece of you." Taking her tongue, she swipes it the entire length of my mouth, from corner to corner, then licks her lips with cat-like satisfaction. "Yummy," she whispers as she heads off to join the men. Oh, goodness, not her too. . . .

Returning to the dining room with a glass of wine for Celeste and a little less aplomb, I warily stand beside Nick wondering at this new turn of events. An extra chair has already been added to the table, and Celeste is purring contentedly sandwiched between two adoring men. Nick hands Celeste a handful of poker chips, equal in amount to those already distributed to the guys. As Celeste's hand reaches out for them, it makes contact with Nick's, curling around his in a display of affection. My immediate response is jealousy, and as I start to feel my temper rising, I realize that the emotion is absurd. For crying out loud, Miranda, here you are ready to service six of Nick's closest friends, and you're getting upset over a little hand holding? Get a grip. Even if she still wants him, even if he still has the hots for her, it's ok. As long as it stays purely physical . . . As long as he doesn't fall back in love with her.

"As I was saying," Nick begins again, "Here are the basic ground rules. As you know, Miranda and I have come to a crossroads in our marriage and have decided to branch out, exploring and fulfilling certain fantasies. As much as I'd like to think differently, I, alone, am not capable of fulfilling them all. Tonight, I want her to experience the thrill of being touched by hands that have never touched her before, knowing full well that it is being witnessed by others. As far as you guys are concerned, I want you to live out some of your own fantasies as well. Maybe there are things you'd like to do with a partner, but have never gathered the courage to ask or try. Maybe you asked, but were told no. Miranda likes a variety of sexual pleasures, sometimes the more bizarre of them being her favorites. Don't be afraid to let your passions run wild. She is here tonight as your plaything, to service you at your whim. We've already discussed the do's and don'ts, with the main focus being that Miranda is not harmed. This game was designed with everyone's pleasure in mind, not as a form of cruelty.

"Adjacent to this dining room table where we will be playing poker, is this other, shorter, more sturdy table. On the table you will find a basket filled with miscellaneous sex toys which you are free to use on Miranda. Anything else you want, you were told to bring on your own. Miranda will stand on this other table while we are playing, unless you need her to get you more refreshments. When you win a hand, you will have one minute to do what you'd like with her. The only other rule is that there will be no penal penetration, and nobody is allowed to bring her to orgasm. Satisfy yourselves, but only I am allowed to satisfy my wife, which I will do much later once everyone else has gone. "There is plastic surrounding the table, as well as a tub and hose out back, so don't hesitate to get messy. The winner of the night will get to fuck her, any way he or she wants to, in front of the rest of us. She will be at the winner's service for an entire hour. Are there any questions?''

Everybody, eager to proceed, shakes his or her head ''no.''

''Ok, Miranda, get everyone another round of drinks then take your place on the table.''

Walking as if in a daze, I obey, bringing back with me five beers and another glass of wine. Once delivered, I go stand in the middle of the shorter table, facing the game. Nick deals out five-card-stud to the six players, opting not to play the game himself. The round goes quickly, and as I wait with a dry mouth, the first winner is announced as Jerome. Crooking a finger at me to join him at the other table, I slowly descend and walk on over. A wide variety of emotions assault me as I make my way, starting with intense fright, lessening to mild panic as I recognize the kindness of his smile, then increasing back up to uncertainty, anticipation and arousal as I witness the promise in his eyes.

Beckoning for me to sit facing him on his lap, I settle myself on him, feeling the hardness of his denim shorts pressing into my bare pussy. My legs wrap around behind and grip the rear legs of the chair for balance.

Closing my eyes, I hear Nick say, ''You have one minute, starting now, Jerome.''

Jerome doesn't waste another second, and descends his warm, wet lips to my own, gathering them up in a toe-curling kiss. His lips coax my own open, as his tongue dives in to explore the deep, dark secrets of my sensual mouth. Groaning, his big, warm hands slide softly up my belly and stop as they reach my breasts, cupping and squeezing them together, then reaching for the nipples. It is my turn to groan as my breasts readily respond and my nipples tighten and swell into two large buds. There is a strong stirring in his shorts, validating completely his reference to a monster, sending another creamy wave of intoxicating juice into my pussy.

Breaking the kiss, Jerome leans me back, until my head rests against the table, my back supported by one arm. Then he greedily goes after my nipples, sucking one after the other into his mouth, bathing them with his tongue, then scraping them with his teeth. At the same time, his other hand slips between my legs, searching for and finding my hot, little sheath. Sending one meaty finger inside to explore the hidden delights sets my hips to rocking, and more moans spew forth from my throat and lips. Deciding that there is enough room for a couple more fingers to join in, Jerome squeezes in two more just as Nick calls out, "Sorry, man, time's up."

"Oh, man, you're cruel," is all Jerome manages to gasp out as he removes his fingers and relinquishes his claim. As I slide off of his lap, he whispers into my ear, "You're wet enough to handle my monster, Miranda. I'm going to win you tonight, that's a promise." Basking in the flush of desire that sweeps through me at his words, I glance down to steal another look at his massive instrument of pleasure, only to be sidetracked by the small puddle left behind.

Surely that isn't from me, is it? I couldn't possibly have done all that.

Round one leaves me squirming and aching to be filled. All I can think of is being stuffed full with Jerome, and I want it now. My body has become consumed by greedy little flames, igniting into a raging inferno just begging to be quenched, and this is just the beginning of my sexual torment. I have hours of endless frustration looming before me, but at least Nick was right. I *am* going to look forward to every hand.

The next winner is Celeste, and she also wants to start out slow. Again, I am asked to sit on a lap, but this time, Celeste stands up first and raises her own skirt up to her waist, showing off a tiny pair of black thong panties. Sitting back down, she has me sit so that my bare crotch rests right up against her panties, with her skirt billowing over both legs.

"Rub against me, Miranda. Rock back and forth. Make my clit hard, as hard as these two nipples are."

Grabbing my nipples in both of her hands, she begins to roll them back and forth between her thumb and forefinger, just as I had done with Angela, only Celeste concentrates on the amount of friction she can provide with speed. Faster and faster she rolls them back and forth, shooting shards of electricity directly to my engorged clit, which is currently rocking back and forth across the silky satin of her panties.

"Now kiss me, my little pet. Kiss me like you want to fuck me."

Leaning into her, I lower my mouth to hers and suck her breath into my own. Her mouth tastes delicious, fresh and sweet, and I do not need to pretend my desire to consume her. I ravage her mouth, kissing it fiercely, passionately, wanting to own every inch of it. Small whimpering noises come from both of us as our arousal escalates. The men are all shifting uncomfortably, even Nick, as they watch us, each getting more and more stimulated.

At one point Russ asks, "Hey, can we jack off while we watch the others go at it?"

"Go for it," Nick replies, stroking his own straining erection through the fabric of his shorts.

When Nick calls "time," Celeste and I are both panting out of control, actually surrounded by a thin veil of steam, while the guys are busy nursing their own throbbing erections. Most have decided that it will be far more comfortable to proceed without the restriction of clothing and have stripped down to their boxers. Both Nick and Celeste have opted to keep their clothing on, for now at least. After providing another round of refreshments, I dutifully return to my pedestal.

Russ looks over at Nick and asks, "Hey, can we have Miranda turn around and bend over for the next round? Nothing against her tits, but she sure has a great ass. I'd like to look at *it* for a while."

Motioning for me to spin around with his finger, Nick replies, "Sure. Now bend over so everyone can get a good look at that luscious ass and pussy."

The first waves of humiliation begin to wash over me as I lean over, bending my knees slightly so that I can rest my palms flat against the table. Because of the size of the heels, I am also forced to spread my legs wider than I would have liked to, just so that I am able to reach and keep my balance. Lots of hoots and appreciative whistles follow my new position, and I have the dreaded feeling that this will now become my permanent one.

The next winner is Kevin, and he is beside himself with what he wants to do with me. Torn between thinking he should just kiss and fondle me as the others had done, and wondering if he'll ever win another hand, he jumps right in and asks for a blow job.

"I'm sorry, Miranda. This may be my only chance at you. I want you to suck me off, and as excited as I am, you won't have any problem finishing me off in a minute. And I want you to swallow. None of my previous girlfriends have ever swallowed. I want to know how that feels."

Walking over to Kevin's chair, he stands to remove his boxers, revealing a very nice erection, then sits back down again, perched at the edge of his seat. I kneel in front of him, between his legs, and without hesitation, completely engulf him in the warm wetness of my mouth. Knowing that I only have one minute to succeed, I get into it immediately, going for broke. I begin by sliding up and down with my mouth, squeezing with my lips and throat, gliding and teasing with my tongue and squeezing his balls with my hand.

After several deep-throated thrusts, I engage my other hand at the bottom of his shaft and work it in unison with the up and down pumping of my head. Twisting my hand lightly as I slide it up and down, making it an extension of my mouth, I continue to suck at him, pumping up and down, up and down, faster and faster, adding a little more pressure every few seconds.

Finally I feel his balls begin to contract in my hand as he lets out a strangled little yelp, followed by, "Yes! Yes! Yes! Miranda, yes, I'm cumming now! Swallow it!"

Capturing the head of his cock at the base of my throat, I give one final squeeze as I feel him begin to shoot down my throat.

Gulping down every last drop, I pull away, just as Nick declares, "Good job, Miranda. Time!"

Satiated, Kevin collapses back into his chair, perfectly content in the knowledge that he may not win another hand. Requesting a drink for myself, Nick allows me to quench my thirst with some nice cold ice water, then immediately returns to my table with my torso folded over and my ass held high in the air.

Winner of round four is Russ and he orders me to stay as I am. Walking over to where I stand on the table, he runs his hands along my ass cheeks, fondling and squeezing them firmly. The table is at just the right height to elevate my ass anywhere from chest to eye level of anyone standing flat on the floor. Russ dives in, greedily eating away at my pussy from behind, leaving it momentarily to kiss and lick at my asshole, then to return. He continues to squeeze my ass tighter and tighter the more his excitement builds. Finally, he removes his mouth and inserts his index finger deep into my pussy, thrusting it in and out while his teeth bite at my ass cheeks.

Trying hard to keep still, I find myself groaning and swaying, loving the feelings he is creating inside. My muscles contract, trying to grip and imprison his finger, as my pussy becomes drenched. After a few more strokes, he removes his finger to toy with my asshole. Pressing the same, well-lubricated finger to my anus, he begins to slowly penetrate it, pushing it further and further in until it disappears. My body arches as it becomes overcome with millions of tiny shudders, and I exhale a small cry of pleasure.

Stroking his own cock with the other hand, he urges, "Push that sweet ass towards me and fuck my finger, Miranda. Go on, fuck it. Faster. Faster."

Just as the tempo becomes frenzied, Nick calls out to quit, and Russ is forced to stop. I remain as is, whimpering slightly as I feel Russ extract his finger from deep within my ass.

"Next time, baby," he whispers before he departs, taking with him a raging hard-on for torment. "Nick, I'm sorry, but I want to see her completely naked," Russ pipes up one more time. "Even though those clothes are sexy, they get in the way. Make her take them off."

Looking over at the table, Nick asks, "Does everyone agree? If it's unanimous, I'll have her do a little strip tease for us."

One by one, everyone agrees that they'd rather see me totally naked, except for the shoes. The shoes have to stay. Straightening up once again, I turn towards the expectant faces of my captive audience and decide to give them their money's worth. Considering that I am only wearing two articles of clothing, I realize my miniature performance is going to be short and sweet, but I wanted to make sure it is also as sinfully decadent as possible.

Sending out a look that says, "Come hither and fuck me," I begin to move my body in slow, sinuous movements. To delay the inevitable, I place two fingers into my mouth and begin to suck on them, closing my eyes and arching my back as my other hand reaches for my pussy. Rubbing at my clit through the fabric of the tiny apron, I slide my wet fingers out of my mouth, down my chin, down my throat to stop at my left breast. The other hand continues to stimulate my clit while my hips gyrate hypnotically. Not wanting my right breast to be lonely, I finally remove my hand from my pussy to caress and pinch at my nipples. With both hands milking my breasts now, I make a show out of how far I can pull and extend my responsive nipples. Finally my hands join together, fingers working to undo the clasp at my cleavage, separating and removing the unwanted garment.

I turn around again, presenting a view of my backside during the removal of the apron. With my hips still swaying provocatively, I untie the apron pulling it away in front of me. Before I toss the apron into space, I reach around behind me to grasp at the string dangling in front, between my legs. Still holding the other string with the hand in front, I take the dangling string and pull it back, seesawing the apron between the lips of my pussy, dampening the cloth with my excited juices. Satisfied with my performance, I stop and do a final pirouette as I whip the apron out into the room. I am rewarded with thunderous applause as well as a look of intense, appreciative arousal from Nick. I turn back around and bend over, signifying the end of the show and the beginning of another round of poker.

Lady luck is playing no favorites tonight, I deduce, as Bill is declared the fifth winner. Needing desperately to assuage his painful erection, Bill also requests a blow job. Instead of meeting him at his place at the table, he comes to me, asking me to sit at the edge of my shorter table while he stands. The angle is perfect, his cock directly level with my mouth. Forcing it in, he asks me not to use any hands and to keep them clasped tightly behind my back. Then, grabbing a fistful of hair in each hand, he pulls my head towards him and commences to fuck my face.

I am not in control of this blow job, the speed and force determined solely by Bill. His pace is fast and furious, making sure to hit the back of my throat with each thrust, causing an occasional gasping gag or gurgle. Thankfully, his desire is also so great that he cannot hold back very long, and removes his cock from my mouth, finishing himself off with this hand. Within seconds he is moaning out his release, as he shoots load after load of thick white cum directly onto my face.

Catching me momentarily off guard, the first shot hits me close to an eye, and the second on my nose, before I can recover and attempt to catch the rest with my wide-open mouth. The remaining spurts are, for the most part, caught by my lips and tongue, with just an occasional drop escaping to dribble stealthily down my chin. Bending down to press a thankful kiss to my lips, he wipes the rest of his mess from my face.

"Hot damn, I've always wanted to do that. That was spectacular."

"You're welcome," I whisper, as I tenderly flex my aching jaw.

As expected, Jake wins the next hand, and I silently wonder if Nick has rigged the deck so that everybody gets at least one chance to win. If not, it is sure a weird coincidence, and I'm sure that I'm not alone in my thinking. Jake decides that he wants to fuck my breasts, but wants me placed very specifically on my little table. Since the table is long and rectangular, he has me lie face up, placing my head at the very top of the table, furthest away yet facing the rest of the players. Then, spreading my legs wide, he has me bend my knees and straddle the sides of the table until my heels are resting on the floor on either side. My pussy is wide-open and facing everyone.

Next, he pulls from the bucket of goodies some baby oil, and begins to spread it generously over and between my breasts. Removing his boxers, he leans over me, placing his hard and throbbing cock to rest in the valley of my breasts. Asking me to take my hands and press my tits tightly together, holding his cock sandwiched in the middle, he braces himself with his forearms resting on the edges of the table, his face inches from my pussy. He begins a back and forth movement, his cock gliding easily between the soft mounds of my breasts. Soon he has his rhythm going and is quickly approaching orgasm. I can feel his irregular breath blow forcefully across my clit, wishing profusely that he would snake his tongue out and touch it. With a few more thrusts, he is grunting loudly, convulsing as his seed spurts powerfully down and across my belly. When he is able, he finally finds the strength to lift himself from me to stand, quickly donning the previously discarded boxers. After blowing me a kiss, he walks back towards the table displaying a thumbs-up gesture directed specifically at Kevin, obviously quite proud of his conquest.

Smiling at me, Nick addresses our guests. "Well, it looks like Miranda has gotten a little sticky. How about we take a break and replenish our beverages while Miranda rinses off in our makeshift tub out back?"

Several murmurs of agreement are uttered as bodies separate themselves from the table, stretching their stiffening muscles, and part in different directions to take care of a variety of different needs.

Nick wanders over to my table and offers me his hand to assist me in rising from my awkwardly proned-out position. Silently thanking him for his thoughtful gesture, I allow him to lead me outside onto the back porch. There, in the middle of the deck, is a large metal tub filled with water, expectantly waiting for me. Without warning, Nick picks me up, cradling me like a brand-new bride, and holds me over it. Before I have a chance to scream in protest, I am unceremoniously dumped into the tub of ice-cold water. Unbelievably, I become completely submerged, standing to find myself resembling a bedraggled puppy.

"Why did you do that?" I scream at a laughing Nick, suddenly realizing that everybody has regrouped to witness this newest fiasco.

Everyone is laughing, although some have the sense to at least try to conceal their mirth. Celeste seems to be enjoying it the most. It was probably her idea in the first place, the evil little bitch.

Outraged and freezing, I attempt to climb out of the tub, but Nick stops me, handing me instead, a bar of soap. "Can't come out until you're all washed up, sweetie."

"For crying out loud, Nick, I'm freezing cold. Let me out."

"I can tell that," he states, as his gaze lowers to stare at my shuddering and puckered nipples. "The quicker you wash up, the quicker you'll be able to get out."

Realizing I have no other option, I dunk back under the water, washing myself as quickly as possible, then attempt another exit from the tub. This time, Nick allows me to get out and hands me a towel. Thank goodness for the warmth of the towel, allowing myself to quickly regain control over my spasmodically shivering body.

"Sorry, Miranda," Nick offers as an excuse. "You were way too excited. It's going to be much more fun watching you go from zero to one hundred all over again. I just feel sorry for whoever wins the next hand. You're not looking too amiable right now."

Casting a murderous glance at him, I stomp back over to my table, my fluffy white towel accompanying me all the way.

"Lose the towel, Miranda."

"I'm still cold, Nick," I whine, pleadingly, at the thought of this little comfort suddenly being taken from me.

"You'll warm back up soon enough. We still have a few more rounds of poker to play."

Walking over to me, Nick yanks the towel from my grasp and whispers threateningly,

"Don't start acting difficult, Miranda, or this poker game will have a completely different ending."

Not wanting to discover what ending Number 2 is, I whisper back, "Ok, ok, I won't." Pouting, I return to my pedestal, trying to quake the remaining shivers still plaguing me.

Another round of poker is dealt out, and as that thought passes through my titillated brain, I chuckle solemnly at the double meaning. They are playing "poke her." The thought is so funny, that I almost begin to cry.

Jerome is declared the next winner, and I feel a sense of relief knowing that it will be his hands touching me next. I hear him softly command me to stand up straight and face him. As I do, he also stands, and looking me straight in the eye, begins to remove his boxers. Once they are down, he kicks them aside and slowly walks towards me, allowing me time to digest the naked, physical specimen proudly on display before me. He is gorgeous, if a man can legally be described as such. His ebony skin is shiny and smooth. His muscles are long and sinewy, flexing with power as each stride is taken. And, he is huge! Unable to keep my gaze from wandering to his groin area, I fixate on his monster, noting that it is nothing short of a replica of my own forearm. Oh my God.

He reaches for me and effortlessly lifts me from the table to hold against his naked chest. My legs wrap around his waist for support as he carries me over to the sofa and lays me down on the soft cushions. Curious, I watch him, wondering what on earth he is planning. He lowers himself on top of me, being careful not to suffocate me with his crushing weight. Immediately, I am surrounded in warmth as Jerome smiles at me and slowly begins to kiss me. Our mouths remain connected for the duration of the allotted time, while his hands slowly begin to rub over my exposed arms, brushing the warmth back into them.

Magically, I get drawn into the kiss, wanting it to last forever, forgetting the cold, releasing my earlier anger. Again, Jerome manages to work me up into a glorious bubble of sexual readiness with little to no effort. When Nick indicates that time is up, Jerome chivalrously removes his body from on top of mine and steps aside, content that he has successfully warmed my chilled body once again.

"Geeze, man, what are you stupid?" Russ asks, incredulously. "Is that all you're going to do with her?"

Smiling confidently, Jerome responds, "I'm a man, not an eager little boy. I can take my time. Besides, the night is not yet over."

Dazed, I return to my table, shivering from something altogether different than the earlier cold. Looking up at Nick, I try to decipher the thoughtful expression suddenly crossing his features. Perhaps the game is not turning out as he intended. Perhaps he is beginning to regret his actions. Whatever the case, it is too late now, as another hand of poker begins and I return to my disgraceful stance on the table.

Celeste wins the next hand and gleefully claps her hands together. "Thank goodness. I was afraid I wasn't going to be able to get another chance at you, Miranda. It's just a shame that Jerome got you all nice and warm again, only to . . . well, you'll see. Jake, Kevin and Russ I'm going to need your help for what I have in mind. Miranda, I want you to lie down flat on the table just like you did when Jake fucked your breasts earlier. Russ, I want you to hold her arms above her head so that she can't move them. Jake and Kevin, I need each of you to hold one foot down to the floor, keeping her legs spread nice and wide for me.''

As the guys move to take their positions, Celeste wanders off in the vicinity of the kitchen. Apprehensively, I lie down with my legs straddling the table, my pussy open wide to wink at the guests still remaining at the table. I feel Russ grab my hands, forcefully holding them together and down tightly to the table. God, I silently wish, please don't let Russ be the big winner of the evening. I start to panic as I feel both Jake and Kevin secure an ankle, keeping each foot tethered to the floor.

"Nick, you promised . . ."

"Don't worry, Miranda. You may not like this, but it's not going to hurt you. Relax."

"Easy for you to say."

Celeste comes sauntering back from the kitchen sucking on a popsicle. Relieved, I begin to relax against the arms holding me down, no longer afraid. Celeste kneels at the foot of the table, now blocking the view from Nick, Bill and Jerome. Not wanting to miss a thing, the three immediately get up and find a spot beside my little table where their view is no longer obstructed.

My ass and pussy are right at the edge of the table, lightly being brushed by the soft fabric of Celeste's skirt. She leans over me, taking the popsicle from her mouth and asks me to suck on it. I open my mouth to accept her offering, grateful as the cool, sweet liquid melts into my mouth and down my throat. I hadn't realized how thirsty I had gotten over the course of the game. After a few seconds, she removes the popsicle, now slightly melted and dripping, to toy with my nipples. She touches the cold treat to one nipple and watches as it immediately responds to the cold stimuli. Then she continues to rub the cold tip around and around, creating a sticky mess. I moan and try to move, reminded that I am held down by three sets of steely arms.

Celeste takes the popsicle and does the same with my other nipple. When she is through, she asks Jake and Kevin to lick me clean, as she continues her torturously cold trail down my abdomen, past my bellybutton to rest on my clit. Each still holding an ankle, Kevin and Jake greedily suck at my frozen nipples while I squirm in the confusion of the conflicting sensations. Cold . . . hot. . . . cold. . . . hot. . . . cold. . . .

"No, Celeste," I manage to gasp out. "It's too cold, please, it's too cold."

Laughing wickedly, Celeste removes the popsicle from my clit to slowly slither it further down, spreading my pussy lips apart with the frozen probe. Knowing that she is short on time, she penetrates me without hesitation, the shock of the cold, piercing sword almost sending me into convulsions.

Jake and Kevin begin to realize that they have their work cut out for them as my body begins to arch and buck against the table. Celeste takes a few more stabs at me with the popsicle, then removes it, lowering her face to my pussy to suck at the melted mess. Reluctantly, Nick is forced to call time and put an end to an otherwise totally erotic encounter. Russ, Jake and Kevin all simultaneously release their hold on me, while Celeste stands and attempts to compose herself.

She looks down at me one last time before retreating to her chair at the table, her Cheshire cat attitude replaced by a look clouded with desire and longing.

Not completely sure if I can handle any more foreplay, I am somewhat relieved when Nick announces that there will only be two more rounds of poker, the second being where the final winner will be declared. Thankfully, I gather the strength to once again stand alone at my little table, provocatively displayed for all to enjoy.

I involuntarily shudder as Russ is named the next winner, wondering what form of perversion he will elect to submit me to. He asks me to get onto my hands and knees, remaining on top of my own table while facing the others. Coming up behind me, he gives my ass a little slap as he goes searching through the basket for the baby oil. Finding it, he begins to dribble it down and across my ass, completely covering me with the oily, slick substance.

Removing his boxers, he places his cock in the crack of my ass, sliding it up and down my crevice. His hands grip my hips and ass, adding to his pleasure as he squeezes my cheeks together to add more friction to his throbbing cock. Several times he slices through me, intent on a fast and furious orgasm. Finally, he is groaning out his release as his cum is shot high into the air only to fall with a splat, square in the middle of my back.

Relief floods through me when I realize he is finished, the ordeal not nearly as sinister as my imagination had envisioned. With another quick slap to my ass, Russ bends over to retrieve his boxers and goes back to the table to join the others, a smug smile plastered arrogantly on his face.

"Nick," I plead coyly. "I'd like to take a nice, warm shower and freshen up before the last hand. Do you have a problem with that?"

"No, sweetie, that's a good idea. Don't take too long."

Wondering sheepishly if there is a window I can escape from without breaking my leg, I slowly work my way up the stairs. Finally being able to remove the sopping, torturous shoes, I throw them aside in disgust and hesitantly enter the shower. The water is warm and invigorating, coaxing me back to a feeling of bliss. I imagine that the water skirting over my sticky skin is Jerome's fingers as they delicately caress and soothe me. I hadn't expected to want him like I do. None of Nick's other friends had quite the same effect on me. But I wanted Jerome. If he doesn't turn out to be the big winner of tonight's game, I won't be able to stop thinking about him. I'll have to beg Nick for another opportunity to fuck him, or arrange my own secret tryst. Either way, I know that I can get through this last hour pretending that it is he who is touching me.

When I am finally ready to return downstairs, I am once again totally in control of my emotions. Without Nick's permission, I decide to dress in some sexy lingerie, using the feel of the satiny fabric against my naked skin to heighten my state of arousal. The white, virginal negligee gives me the appearance of youthful innocence as I make my way silently back into the crowded room.

"My God, Miranda. How is it that you can even

look more beautiful than you did earlier?" utters Russ in amazement. "Damn it, Nick. I want to fuck your wife. I don't care if I don't win. I want her so badly that it hurts."

"Sorry, buddy. Only the winner gets her tonight. Maybe we can work something else out down the road if it doesn't go your way, ok?

"Russ," I add sweetly, "You're already acting as though you've lost. Why don't we wait and see the outcome before you get yourself all worked up?"

"Alright, alright. You're just so damn sexy. I can't help but want you."

"Thanks, Russ. That's one of the nicest things anyone has ever said to me." Sitting down seductively at the edge of my little table, I face the players to watch the final hand of poker being dealt out. My breathing quickens as I watch in excited fascination, wondering who will be declared the victor. The fact that I will soon be taken in front of all these people is both horrifying and exhilarating, sending mixed messages to my overstimulated brain. I squirm uncomfortably as the thought causes my clit to throb and my pussy lips to thicken and swell with desire. I don't think I can wait any longer . . . I don't think I can do it.

Just as I'm about to get caught up in the waves of another panic attack, a huge ruckus focuses my attention back to the table, scowls on everybody's face except for Jerome's. He turns to me with a wide grin, his white teeth a sharp contrast to his dark skin. Just like I'll be. The thought sends another juicy wave to join the puddle already forming at the apex of my thighs.

"I told you I'd win. I hope you're ready to be fucked like you've never been fucked before, Miranda."

The blood is immediately drained from my face, only to be quickly replaced by a surge of heated embarrassment, turning me bright red from head to toe. He just watches me for a moment, taking in the sexiness of my semi-parted thighs, my taut nipples, my clouded eyes. I notice sudden, subtle changes in his demeanor as the implications of his win begin to sink in. His eyes have gone from soft and kind to . . . animal. His nostrils are flaring out with each breath, sucking air in through his tightly clenched teeth. And . . . I can smell him . . . his heated masculinity rising up to reach out and surround me, envelope me. I swallow deeply and continue to stare back at him. The room has quieted down dramatically, as everyone unconsciously holds his or her breath, waiting.

"Come over here to me, Miranda," Jerome commands.

I need no second invitation for I am immediately drawn to respond, ironically feeling like a puppet on strings. Placing his hands on my hips, he closes his eyes and lets his head fall back slightly.

"Undress me."

I reach out my hands to begin unbuttoning his shirt, when he stops me.

"With your teeth. Use only your teeth."

Oh, God. He's so sexy. I pull my hands away and step between his parted thighs. I bend over so that I can reach the first button and capture it in my mouth. It takes a while, but eventually I am able to coordinate my lips, teeth and tongue enough to pop it free. For the remaining buttons, I am forced to kneel up between his legs, my breasts pressed tightly against his twitching cock. His eyes remain closed the entire time I work on the buttons, the loud intake of each breath my only clue to his painful predicament.

When the buttons are all unfastened, I stand back up again and begin to tug at one of the sleeves of his shirt with my teeth. He opens his eyes and sits straight up, attempting to help me with the difficult task. Finally his shirt is removed and I am left with the dilemma of his boxers. Thank goodness he had already taken care of those denim shorts he had on earlier. There would have been no way.

"I'm going to need you to stand up if you want these boxers to come off."

Needing no further encouragement, Jerome obliges me and stands. Again, I find myself kneeling before him, my attention directed now to the sole object of my current desires. In a matter of moments his monster would be revealed, and I would be called upon to feed it.

Gently, I press my face into his belly, my nose burrowing into the circle of his navel, my teeth grasping at the waistband of his shorts. His smell this close is intoxicating, and I pause just a minute to breathe in his scent deeply. I feel his hands gripping my hair, the thought of my mouth so close to his organ quite torturous for him. I begin to tug and pull, being careful not to let go of the snapping elastic too soon, and slowly work the band to rest beneath his balls. I can't keep myself from snaking out my tongue and touching him, the solid mass of muscle before me proving to be too tempting a treat.

Quickly, I work my way behind him, the elastic band hung up on the athletic roundness of his ass. In one smooth jerk, the boxers are pulled to his feet and he steps out of them. Raising back up, I grab onto his hips and press my face into his ass, kissing it gently.

"Lick it. Lick it, Miranda. All of it. Don't stop until every inch is soaking wet from that luscious tongue."

Moaning, I begin to place wet, sloppy kisses all over his cheeks, followed by a thorough bathing with my tongue. His ass becomes soaked, as does my face, as I continue to burrow and press against it. Satisfied that his cheeks are well attended to, I gently pull them apart and lick the entire length of his crack, stopping at his asshole. This is something I've never done before, yet I wanted to do it now more than anything. Bathing his anus in moisture, I press my rigid tongue against the opening and push inside. I am rewarded by his unhindered moans followed by a "Fuck it, baby. Fuck my ass with your tongue."

I comply, getting increasingly more aroused. Any hotter and I'm in danger of self-combustion. I continue probing my tongue in as deeply as it will go and then sliding it back out again until he begs me to stop.

"My cock, Miranda. Suck my monster now."

I pull my tongue from his ass as he turns to face me, his powerful lance glistening shamelessly with need. Knowing that this will be quite the challenge, I start at the bottom, surrounding his balls in wetness, sucking each one up individually into my hot mouth. Then I lick up the shaft, the entire length of him now shiny and wet, and hesitate when I get to the top.

"You can do it baby. Swallow me whole."

Spreading my lips as wide as possible, I begin to work the head of his weapon into my mouth. Before long, I am stretched to my limits, choking and gasping. Willing myself to accept the massive intruder, I settle down and allow myself to become accustomed to his size. With great relief, I find that I am able to breathe again, and begin to manipulate him. Slowly, I work my tongue around as far as I can reach, slickening him up with my saliva. Then I begin to move my head up and down, forcing him deeper and deeper into the back of my throat.

Convinced that I'll be able to see this through, I relax and move one hand down to cup his balls, while the other I reach around to grab at this tight ass. Still feeling it covered in dampness, I venture a finger down to his asshole and slip it in, burying it to the hilt. His hips jerk and his cock is forced even further down my throat, again causing me to gag.

Once I recover, I set upon the mission of the most impressive blow job I've ever given. Bobbing my head up and down, I feel his cock open and widen my throat with each thrust, still squeezing his balls and fucking his ass with my finger. Over and over again he thrusts, I thrust. It seems like an eternity.

He is howling like a madman, "Fuck me, baby, take it, baby. All the way. Squeeze me with your throat. So good . . . that's so good . . . ah yes, ah yes . . . faster baby, faster . . . Ahhh, I'm going to cum Miranda. . . . . . I'm. . . . . . going. . . . .to. . . . .cum. . . . Ahhhhhhhhhhhh!"

Jerome is halfway down my throat by the time he cums, and I can do nothing but take it and accept it.

I gulp furiously, trying to swallow it down, trying to keep from choking, trying to keep from inhaling it and having it drip offensively from my nose. Finally, he is finished, and I feel his monster somewhat slacken, although not nearly enough to account for what I had just swallowed. Pulling his cock from the confines of my mouth, he aggressively pulls me up and off the floor. He continues to effortlessly lift me until my pussy is resting against his belly. He kisses my bruised and stretched mouth with a wild ferocity, as I feel the head of his cock pressing up against my juicy, wet opening. Whimpering into his mouth, I realize that he is going to fuck me right there, standing up with nothing to help brace me from the full impact of his monstrous cock.

His hands move to cup my ass as he lowers me slowly onto his cock, stretching me once again beyond my limits. Little gasps and moans of protest are spilled from my lips, yet my hips continue to wiggle myself further and further down. The sensation is like one I've never felt before, completely stretched and filled. I am quite sure that I now know what it feels like to be fisted.

Allowing me a little time to adjust to his size, he holds me still while he kisses me. Then he lifts me back up and drops me back down repeatedly, fucking me brutally. His hands are merciless on my ass, gripping the lobes of my cheeks harshly, using them to push and pull at me, slamming me down with each ramrod thrust. Over and over I am impaled by him, on him . . . hating it, loving it.

"Talk to me, baby. Tell me what you're feeling. Tell me what you want."

"Jerome," I breathlessly whisper, "I can't."

"Do you like it?"

"Ohhh yes, yes, I like it."

"Tell me how much you like it, baby."

"Oh, God, Jerome, I like it. I love it."

"You want more, baby? You want it harder? You want it faster? Tell me you want it."

"Yes, Jerome, yes. I want it harder," I begin to scream, "I want it faster. Fuck me! Fuck me faster."

"Yeah, baby, that's the way. Talk dirty to me. Make me cum again. Think you can make me cum again?"

"Yes, yes . . . I'll make you cum again. I want to feel you swell inside me. I want to feel your cum shoot all the way through me. Fuck me harder, Jerome! I want you to fuck me so hard that I feel you at the back of my throat!"

"Oh, you sweet, sexy bitch."

Never before would I have thought myself capable of such uninhibited lewdness. If I could see the expressions on the faces of the onlookers, I'm sure I would see a mix of horror, shock, and yes, even envy. But I couldn't see, couldn't focus. Jerome is surely on his way to fucking me unconscious, and I don't even care. It is the most exquisite sexual torture I've ever allowed myself to experience. Just when I think I can take no more of his vigorous pounding, he wails in agony as his second orgasm goes ripping through his body. Collapsing on the couch, with me still skewered to his slackening cock, Jerome remains unmoving, clutching me possessively to his chest.

After several minutes, Jerome untangles me from his body and lifts me away to sit beside him. He has quite the satisfied expression on his face as he asks Nick, "How much time do I have left?"

"You've still got 20 minutes, buddy. Think you have any more left in you?"

"I promised her a good, thorough fucking, man. I'm not done until I've had her ass."

"Jesus Christ, Jerome. She's not going to be able to walk for a week after you're through with her," Russ complains.

"Ah, she'll get over it, good as new in no time."

Already the thought of taking that huge, black monster up my tiny ass is making me flush. You would have thought I had had enough. It was like a drug. He was like a drug. I wanted more. I wanted it all. I wanted Jerome in my ass, God help me.

I look over towards the rest of the boys and Celeste. Most have taken care of themselves, masturbating as they watched Jerome fuck my brains out. Celeste is still obviously very agitated, as well as Nick, both controlling themselves during our entire performance. Celeste was beginning to get desperate, pressing her body up against Nick's, begging him to ease her ache and fuck her. Nick, ready for release himself, rips at her clothing, tearing it from her body. She, in turn, claws her way through Nick's clothing, until the two are standing together, stark naked.

"Jerome? How are you doing in the way of inspiration? Is that horse cock ready to go again?"

"It won't take much, Nick. What do you have in mind?"

"How about if we watch Celeste and Miranda go at it for a while, think that will help?" Nick asks with a wink.

"Oh, yeah. I'll be hard as iron again in no time."

Jerome eagerly leads me from the couch to the center of the room where Nick has lead Celeste. Leaving us to stand face to face, it doesn't take long for her to make the first move. She presses her bare body into mine, still shielded by the negligee, and begins to kiss me, squirming and rubbing her body all over mine. Both Nick and Jerome have brought chairs out and placed them directly behind each of us. Sitting themselves down, they each have a lovely view of our respective backsides. Nick commences to bite and chew at Celeste's ass, while Jerome begins to spread my cheeks, intent on properly lubricating my asshole. I feel his fingers smearing my ass with a gooey substance, poking and prodding, penetrating me deeply with his finger. I desperately hold onto Celeste for support as the invasion continues, until he begins to pull me back and down to sit on his cock.

Nick does the same with Celeste, pulling her down, only his target is her sweet, juicy pussy. She sighs and her eyes flutter closed as she sinks her entire weight down onto Nick's beautiful cock. Then she begins to ride him.

It takes a while longer for me to be able to settle my ass down on Jerome. Despite the lubricant, it is still very tight, the progress slow, and he has to pause between each excruciating inch. Instinctively, my hand reaches for my clit, rubbing it, the friction distracting me momentarily from the punishment of my ass.

"Jerome, pull her hands away from her clit. I don't want her to cum." Nick urgently demands.

"Nooooo," I scream out, but find my arms pulled

aside as I'm ungraciously forced down the several remaining inches of Jerome's huge cock.

Nick and Jerome scoot the chairs together until Celeste and I are touching knees. Reaching out for her, I grab her shoulders for support as Jerome begins to move me up and down on his cock. I swoon at the feeling, my body shivering, going rigid. It's too much for me, the pleasure is too overwhelming, I feel like my body is going to explode. Oh God, oh God.

Jerome startles me with his next request. "Ride me, Miranda. Ride me like Celeste is riding Nick. Stand up and push back. That's the way, baby. Go on . . . faster . . . I know you can fuck me faster. Come on, stretch that sweet ass for me. Suck me in. Feel me in your throat yet, baby? Huh? I want to hear you talk to me."

"Oh, God, Jerome. I can feel you. I can feel you in my stomach. I can feel you in my throat. Oh, God, you're killing me. Mmmmm, fuck my ass, Jerome."

"Fuck my cock, baby. Keep it up, keep going. You're doing great. Ride it, now."

"Oh yes . . . Oh yes. . . ."

"Miranda," Celeste begs. "Kiss me while I cum, honey. Hold me."

Unable to deny her that, we wrap our arms around one another and lock our lips together, still both pumping up and down on our men. Finally, Celeste shrieks out, screaming into my mouth as her body is overcome by spasms, convulsing endlessly in my arms. Nick too groans out his orgasm as Celeste's tight pussy milks him dry.

Jerome is relentless, obviously in no hurry to cum. After Nick and Celeste collapse exhaustedly against each other in the chair, Jerome removes my negligee and picks me up once again, still speared by his massive organ. He carries me over to a spot on the floor, in front of a wall-length mirror, and sets me down on all fours with him directly behind me, also on his knees.

"Watch us in the mirror, baby. Watch my dick fuck you. Watch how wide you stretch for me. Somebody get me the goddammed baby oil!"

Russ jumps to do Jerome's bidding, and is back with the baby oil in record time. I watch as he opens it and starts to drizzle the liquid down the crack of my ass, some being absorbed into my anus, the rest running down to tease my pussy and clit. His eyes hold mine prisoner as he begins to fuck me again with renewed vigor. If I thought I had been fucked before, I was so wrong. I beg him to stop. I beg him to continue. Tears well up in my eyes from the intense pain and pleasure he is creating. I'll never be the same, never, ever. Jerome grabs a fistful of my hair, forcing me to watch the ultimate and complete taking of my ass. He begins to slap my ass on each inward stroke, getting more and more aggressive the closer he gets to his own orgasm. One last thrust and Jerome is once again hurled into climax, throwing his head back and howling his release. The hour is over.

CHAPTER 8

∎

FRIENDSHIPS

The months fly by in a flurry of activity, most resembling some sense of normality. After the poker game, Nick cooled a bit, and was no longer hell-bent on subjecting me to various forms of subtle torture. He must have exorcised most of his demons within those first four days of my arrival back home, although he still does spank me soundly on a daily basis. The amount of swats have doubled, having to account for my time spent with Jerome, Russ, Bill, Kevin, Jake and Celeste. Little did I know that his insisting on my submission to the sexual perversions of his unorthodox poker game would cause me to be penalized for it afterward.

The Masons arrive as expected, the snow creating little delay for their flight. JD and Vicki are ecstatic to finally get here, unable to contain the excitement of seeing us once again and catching up on old times. After spending the afternoon getting reacquainted, it becomes obvious that we are all still quite compatible regardless of the many years and many miles separating our daily lives. Even though we were all just "kids" when we first became friends, we had all grown up with similar points of view and incredibly open minds. Picking up exactly where we had left off was easy, and we are soon chatting away as if it were only yesterday.

JD hadn't changed much in the fifteen years since I had last seen him other than developing a respectable amount of maturity, changing his demeanor from that of a reckless youth to an adult full of cool confidence. Physically, too, he remained similar, holding fast at a solid 6 feet in height, his dark hair dusted with just a few strands of silver. His face was exactly the same: kind brown eyes and an easy smile framed by a nicely trimmed moustache. Only his smile is somewhat different, still polite but brimming with newfound knowledge, no longer shy about concealing his desire to possess me.

Vicki, on the other hand, appears to have changed dramatically, blossoming beautifully into womanhood. Poise and grace have replaced shyness and awkwardness, allowing her physical beauty to shine. She no longer wore her rich, brown hair cut short in a cute, practical style, but rather long and sexy, hanging loose and carefree. Her best features, by far, are her large and expressive brown eyes, always sparkling with curiosity and intelligence. She has also been working out regularly, giving her shape a sleek, muscular appearance, one she is obviously quite comfortable with and very proud of.

Nick suggests that we call it an early night since

177

we had vigorous exercise planned for the following day. Nick had reserved us a gorgeous little cabin, high on the mountain in the middle of nowhere for us to spend the weekend just hanging out and catching up without the inevitable distractions caused by modern conveniences. It promised to be a blast, and I couldn't wait to get started.

The weather couldn't have been more spectacular for our trek to the ski hut. All around us was a sea of glittering white diamonds, a dazzling display as the sunshine kissed the freshly fallen snow. Nobody was complaining, so caught up were we in the total beauty surrounding us, and it didn't hurt that we had minimal supplies to carry. JD and Nick had borrowed two snowmobiles and sleds and carted up most of our provisions the day before, including a couple cases of beer. We had been skiing for hours now, and Nick promised that we would be able to see the hut once we skirted round the next bend. True to his word, the little cabin was in sight before we knew it, and we all quickened our pace, excited to finally reach our destination.

"My goodness!" Vicki exclaims. "It's absolutely beautiful, just like a little house on the *frozen* prairie. I don't think I've ever felt such peace," and then adding after a thoughtful pause, ". . . or isolation. We must be miles from everything and everybody."

"We are *that*," Nick offers. "But that's the whole point of these hut trips, to get away from the hustle and bustle of everyday life and relax. It's going to be a great weekend!"

*　　*　　*

I approach the door cautiously, unable to shake off the reality of civilization, and begin to knock. At Nick's laughter, I turn around to see three faces grinning at me in amusement.

"What?" I ask, somewhat annoyed.

"You don't need to knock, Miranda. Nobody lives here. It's reserved solely for us."

"Well, just in case. Somebody could have gotten lost and stumbled upon it," I suggest in my defense.

"Do you see any tracks in the snow?"

"Well, no . . ."

In a flurry of skis and poles, we all manage to shed our cumbersome equipment, placing them recklessly against the outside wall of the cabin. I step aside as Nick, Vicki and JD brazenly enter the cabin without so much as a thought to etiquette. Following closely behind, I enter hesitantly, still concerned that we may be intruding upon strangers. My three companions excitedly scurry off in different directions, eager to explore the quaint, rustic cabin, while I stop in the entryway to make my own assessments.

From my standpoint, it appears to be one large square room, with a huge, double-sided fireplace built directly in the center. To my right is a wooden, "L"-shaped bench built directly along the front and side walls of the cabin with a matching wooden table placed alongside. To my left, also built into the wall, another long, continuous bench, only this one was much wider and had, what appeared to be, several mattresses set flush into it.

Slowly making my way around the room towards the right, I notice that on the other side of the fireplace is the makeshift kitchen. The cast-iron, freestanding, wood-burning stove is obviously where we can perform some limited cooking, as well as melt some snow for water. Running alongside it, up against the back wall of the cabin is a nice countertop with a stainless steel sink basin built into it. Although there is no plumbing or running water, the sink does contain a drainage system, making it quite possible to fill with water and then empty again.

Above the countertop are some cupboards, filled sparsely with eating utensils and cast-iron kettles, pots and pans. Under the countertop, I find several bottles of stored propane. Although rugged, the cabin still contains many more conveniences than I had originally expected.

The most interesting room of all to me is the bathroom. It is located adjacent to the kitchen, but walled off from the rest of the main room for privacy. To the right is a big freestanding metal tub, elevated a good foot off the floor. Under the tub is a contraption, similar to a barbecue grill, complete with attached propane bottle. All one had to do was turn on the propane, throw in a match, and voila, a cozy little fire to burn conveniently under the tub. The wonders of modern technology . . .

Continuing on my little excursion, I notice a sink and mirror to my left, and a closed door directly in front of me. I open the door to discover it leads down a short, narrow walkway to an enclosed port-a-potty. Satisfied that my lodgings would be more than adequate, I return to the main room to join the others.

Vicki has already taken off her snowsuit and is sitting contentedly on one of the mattresses dressed comfortably in nothing but her baggy sweats. Nick and JD are still fully clothed, Nick making several trips back outdoors to gather firewood, while JD is keeping busy by filling containers with snow and then emptying them into the bathtub. They didn't stop until they had a fire burning in the fireplace, a fire burning in the kitchen stove, a fire burning under the tub, and everything possible completely filled with rapidly melting snow. Once they are satisfied that we are well provided for, they grab themselves a beer and join Vicki and I, well into an hour's worth of gossip and a dwindling six-pack of beer.

"What have you ladies been chitchatting about while Nick and I have been working ourselves to the bone, seeing to your comforts?" J D asks, good-naturedly.

"Oh, just girl stuff, nothing that you'd be interested in," Vicki replies with a wink.

"Don't be so sure about that. Men can learn a lot by eavesdropping on women's conversations," he whispers conspiratorially.

Glancing over at me, he bathes me in the heat of his sensual smile, connecting with me for the first time since our trip had begun. I try to ignore my sudden, irregular heartbeat, and cast my eyes downward, purposefully breaking the intangible contact. I needed to speak with Nick. He didn't tell me what any of his plans were for this trip, making it very awkward for me. Was this a platonic getaway, a chance to become reacquainted with old friends? Or was this an elaborate sham for a chance at some wife swapping? Nick, sensing my nervousness, quickly asks, "Anybody hungry yet? How about if Miranda and I whip up some quick grub?"

"Sure." is the unanimous response, as Nick reaches out for my hand and leads me away around to the kitchen.

"You look a little uncomfortable. Are you ok?"

"Well, yes, I'm fine, but I'm not quite sure what it is that you want from me?"

"What do you mean?"

"I'm not sure what game you're playing, Nick. I don't know the rules. Am I supposed to be flirting with him, or is this strictly a *friends only* encounter?"

Grinning in mischievous delight, Nick gently grabs my chin, running his thumb along my jawbone.

"What do you want it to be like, Miranda?" he asks seductively. "Do you want to have sex with one of my oldest and best friends, while his wife and I look on? I'm sure he wouldn't mind."

"Well, uh, I don't know, Nick. I've never thought about him in that way before. He's just always been our friend."

"I tell you what. Let's just play it by ear and see what happens. We won't plan anything."

"But, what do *you* want, Nick? If it comes down to it, would you rather I did, or didn't?"

"Miranda, I'd rather you just do what you want to do. If he turns you on, then go for it. If he doesn't do anything for you, then don't. It's quite simple. Just remember. There will be an additional swat each day if you do."

"What about Vicki? She'll hate me for life if she finds out her husband wants to have sex with me."

"Randa, somehow I don't believe she'd even be on this trip if she had a problem with it. I'm sure they've talked about the possibilities of this weekend.''

"Like we have?"

Again, the devilish smile. "You're so cute in your uncertainty, Miranda. I like to keep you off-balance."

"Ok, then, I'll take this as you don't care what happens this weekend."

"Help me with dinner, Miranda."

Pouting, I realize that I'm not going to get a definite answer from Nick, and silently begin to help him get our meal together. Before long we are all sitting around the table, feasting on cold chicken sandwiches and potato chips. Nick is sitting at the end of the table, with Vicki to his right, then JD and then me. I can feel the heat of JD's leg penetrating my own warm clothing, unnerved by the jolts that keep passing through me as his leg accidentally brushes up against my own. Trying to keep my breathing under control, I fight hard not to choke on my sandwich, keeping my conversation down to a minimum. Nick, Vicki and JD are completely engrossed in conversation, completely unaware of my own discomfort.

The next bite of my sandwich almost takes with it a portion of my tongue as I suddenly feel a very large and very masculine hand resting on my knee. My eyes widen in surprise, but other than that, I am able to keep my body language from exposing any of JD's wrongdoings.

His attention is still focused on the conversation, yet his hand begins to lightly caress my knee, slowly and carefully working its way up my thigh. Like Vicki, I too am wearing baggy sweats, but the heat emanating from his hand radiates through them as if I were wearing nothing at all. Time has stopped, my half-eaten sandwich forgotten, as my concentration centers on his hand inching its way further and further up my leg. It takes all my willpower not to make any sound, torn between wanting to push his hand away and spreading my legs a little wider.

Panicking, certain that I will not be able to keep my rising desire in check much longer, I discreetly move my left hand under the table to rest on top of his. His hand has made its way to the very top of my thigh, resting in the crease, his pinky finger no more than a millimeter away from grazing the outer lip of my sex. I apply pressure to his hand, implying that I don't want him to go any further, to stop, but he ignores my plea. Instead, he reaches his pinky outward to gently snake across the folds of my pussy. Sucking in my breath, realizing that the only way to stop him is to blow his cover, I relax my grip on his hand and succumb, allowing him full access to my secret treasure.

Unhindered now, fully aware that I will not give him away, JD continues to masterfully manipulate my pussy through the fabric of my sweat pants, caressing and stroking it in all the right ways. Struggling to keep my composure, it is impossible to stop the rosy glow from reaching my cheeks, as well as the slight ripples of pleasure that continue to work their way up from my legs to center on my nipples. His fingers settle on my clit, rubbing relentlessly in circles, determined now to masturbate me to orgasm. The ripples begin to build and build, evolving into spasms as my body finally yields to his ministrations and begins to convulse mercilessly.

In a fit of coughing, I attempt to disguise my plight as I ride my climax out to its bitter end, excusing myself and hastily leaving the table without making eye contact with anybody. "I'll make sure she's ok," JD offers, as he follows me around the fireplace and into the kitchen area.

My "How could you?" is immediately cut off as JD rounds the corner, pulling me into his powerful embrace as his lips desperately seek out and find my own. Kissing me passionately, he pushes me backwards until I am pressed up against the hard rock of the fireplace wall. Whimpering, I kiss him back, my hands reaching behind him to entwine in his hair. He takes my legs, one at a time, and wraps them around his waist, so that I am no longer standing on the floor, braced up against the fireplace, depending solely upon him for support. He grinds his hardness into my crotch, making me all too aware of his consuming desire for me.

Gasping as he pulls his lips from mine, he whispers, "God, Miranda. I've wanted you for so long. Your body ... it responds to me ... beautifully. I want to do that again, but with my lips ... my tongue ... my mouth. I want to hear you cry out my name the next time I take you there."

Panting, I unfold my legs and regain my footing, standing solidly once again on the floor. "No ... not now, not yet ... we can't ... somebody might come. We'll get caught," I stammer, confused, still not completely back in control of my senses. Get caught by whom, I wonder silently as I push JD away, and begin to walk back toward the others.

"Sorry, guys," I apologize. "I choked on a piece

of my sandwich, but I'm okay now. Who wants to help me with the dishes?'' I ask with false bravado.

"I will,'' says JD, standing directly behind me, and begins to gather things from the table.

I risk a direct look at Nick, and his smile confirms my suspicions. He knows.

"Thanks, JD. I'll keep your lovely wife company while you and Randa clean up.''

Offering Vicki his hand, he escorts her over to the other side of the room where they sit in comfort once again on the soft mattresses provided.

After quickly gathering what's left on the table, I return to the kitchen with JD hot on my tail. Setting down the trash, I am dismayed to find JD standing directly behind me, holding me trapped against the edge of the counter with the weight of his body. His pile of trash joins mine, and I hold my breath waiting for his next move. My senses have come alive and I can hear and feel everything exaggerated one hundred times over. I begin shivering as I feel him place his hands gently on my upper arms, slowly sliding them up and down.

"What's going to happen tonight, lovely Miranda?'' he whispers into my ear.

"Nothing, nothing's going to happen . . .''

"Why don't you want me, Miranda?'' he asks, his voice darkening dangerously as his hands slip from their place on my arms to rest on my waist. His thumbs begin to delicately massage the small of my back.

"I . . . it . . . it's not that I don't want you, JD, it's just that . . . that now is not the right time.''

"Now may be the *only* time, Miranda. Want to

know how easy it would be?" he asks as he slowly turns me around to face him.

"In a single movement, I could have your pants in a pool at your feet."

I gasp in fright as I feel him jerk my sweatpants to my ankles, leaving me with just the modest coverage of my black cotton panties.

"Then, I could pick you up and sit you on the edge of the counter like so. . . ."

Another tiny shriek escapes as I find myself lifted from the floor and abruptly deposited on the countertop with a thud.

Then he holds me tightly as he scoots my butt to the very edge, thrusting his pelvis into my crotch, saying, ". . . and fuck you," immediately stopping the thrusting and releasing me only to kneel before me with his face between my legs, "or . . . suck you . . ." He presses his face forward until I feel his mouth, teeth and tongue probing at my pussy through the dampened fabric of my panties, soaking them with his saliva. ". . . and nobody would be the wiser . . ." He stands back up to face me, holding my head stationary so that I'm forced to look him deeply in the eyes.

My mouth hangs open in shock as he once again savagely kisses me, then pulls away and leaves me alone in the kitchen to join Nick and Vicki in the other room.

Guiltily, I jump from the counter and hurriedly pull up my pants, leaning against the counter with my hand pressed against my chest trying to get my emotions in check. Well, if I had any doubt that I was attracted to JD, it was gone now. Shit, what was I going to do? Grabbing another beer from the ice chest, I guzzle it down in two long gulps, then reach for another. After several minutes of quietly composing myself and unnecessarily cleaning up in the kitchen, I am ready once again to face the others. Grabbing a full six-pack of beer, I carry it with me to take to the group.

JD's eyes never leave my body as he watches me enter the room, following me as I offer a beer to everyone. Nick's interested eyes continue to waver back and forth between JD and me, knowing full well what is unfolding before him. Vicki, whether on purpose or just from not being very observant, appears to be blissfully ignorant of any sexual tension developing, happily caught up in the conversation and her own "beer buzz."

I decide not to risk sitting by JD again and plop exhaustedly down beside my husband. Leaning over, he whispers into my ear, "So, he's finally getting to you, isn't he?" Laughing when I refuse to answer him, he moves away as I look to the floor in embarrassment.

"Hey, I've got a great idea! Let's play Truth or Dare!" JD announces as if for all to hear, but continues looking only at me. Looking up, I can see the hint of a challenge in his eyes, wondering if I have the balls to play the adult version of my favorite childhood game.

I look over at Nick and Vicki who are shrugging, saying, "Sure, why not? That sounds like fun."

Meanwhile, I still haven't answered, meeting JD's eyes once again, realizing that I was already playing the game, and this was my first dare.

"Well, Miranda? You're not afraid of a harmless little game, are you?"

"No, of course not. I'll play your game."

"Excellent! Ok, here in my pocket, I have a die. Nick, pick a number from one to six."

"Two."

"Vicki?"

"Um, I'll have number three."

"Okay, Miranda, what number do you want?"

"I'll take six."

"Great, and I think I'll take number one. What we'll do is take turns rolling the die. Whatever number you roll is the person you have to ask the truth or dare of. Simple enough?"

"Sounds fair to me," I chip in, wanting to sound as nonchalant as possible. "Who goes first?" "Whoever rolls the highest number."

Well, as luck would have it, I rolled a six and got to go first. I rolled a five.

"Now, what? Nobody has number five."

"Just keep rolling it until you do land on somebody's number, other than your own."

After three tries, I finally roll a one. Looking up victoriously at JD, I ask him, "Well, JD, truth or dare?"

"Truth."

Ok, great. Now what? What did I want to ask him? It was his game, after all. I hadn't even given it any thought. Finally, I decide what I want is revenge, and I take the lowest shot possible.

"Ok, JD. How many women, other than your wife, have you had sex with since you've been married?" I ask as innocently as possible.

JD's eyes narrow into dangerous little slits as Nick coughs and sputters on his beer.

"You can't ask him that, Miranda. That's none of *our* business," he says with his eyes shifting in the direction of Vicki.

"Well, then, maybe someone ought to lay down some ground rules."

"No, I think there shouldn't be any ground rules," Vicki pitches in. "Besides, I'd like to know the answer to that one myself."

Turning a sarcastic smile towards her husband, we all wait expectantly for JD to answer.

"Ok, Miranda. You've just declared war. I hope you're prepared. Ten, I've had sex with ten women since I've been married."

Vicki looks over at her husband with an expression of surprised amusement and smiles, but says nothing.

"Ok, Vicki, it's your turn."

Vicki rolls the die until it lands on six. Looking over at me, she asks, "Truth or dare, Miranda."

"Truth."

Bluntly she asks, "Have you ever made love to a woman?"

Just as brazenly, "Yes, I have Vicki." We both smile in spite of ourselves.

Now it was JD's turn. I could hear him silently wishing for a six, praying to be able to get back at me for the awkward position I put him in earlier. No such luck, he rolls a three.

"Well, darling, truth or dare."

Vicki, trusting her husband completely, responds, "Dare."

"Thought you were out of the woods, didn't you,

Miranda? You're going to find out that no matter who's number I roll, you'll be my target. Vicki, I dare you to kiss Miranda. A long, slow, French kiss.''

"Hey, now. That's not fair. One person's dare shouldn't include another.''

"Miranda,'' Nick explains, "You're the one that started this, down and dirty with no rules, remember? Now you have to play along.''

Now it was my turn to narrow my eyes, at both JD and Nick. Reluctantly, I turn toward Vicki, watching her scoot closer and closer to me. We face one another with our profiles offered for the guys to watch. Gently she takes my face into her hands and holds it still while she formulates her strategy. Making quite the display of licking her lips, slowly and sensually running her tongue along the edges of her mouth, she stops only when they are completely wet and glistening. Then she begins to close the distance between our faces, keeping her eyes wide open and watching until the tips of our noses touch, then fluttering them closed.

Finally I feel her soft lips press against mine, mingling with them, coaxing them open until she has caught and claimed them. Our lips connect, her tongue enters and traces the edges of my teeth, pulling my tongue into her own mouth and suckling on it like a small penis. The kiss goes on and on, parrying back and forth until the agitated coughs of our spectators regain our attention. Finally, she breaks the kiss, and we turn to face the flabbergasted expressions of our husbands.

"Was that ok, JD?'' Vicki asks, playfully.

"Oh, yes," JD barely manages to croak out. "Nick, your turn."

Nick rolls and gets a one. "Truth or dare, JD?"

Confident that his buddy wouldn't betray him, JD answers, "Dare."

"Hmmmm . . . JD, I dare you to drop your drawers and moon everybody."

Laughing, Vicki and I start taunting JD. "Woo, woo. Come on JD, show us what you've got."

Laughing himself, JD turns to Nick and says, "Thanks, man. I thought you were my friend."

Standing up, he turns around and whips down his pants, giving an exaggerated shake of his bare ass to his enthralled audience. After pausing just a few seconds, he reaches down to pull his pants back up. Vicki and I whistle and clap enthusiastically until he is seated back down again and it is my turn to roll the die.

I roll a two and ask Nick, "Truth or Dare, honey?"

Being somewhat on the conservative side, Nick opts for truth.

"Ok, would you like to see Vicki's naked breasts?"

Grinning, Nick replies, "That's an easy one. Who wouldn't want to see them. I'd love to see Vicki's naked breasts."

We all look over at Vicki to find her blushing furiously. Then she surprises us all by reaching for the bottom of her sweatshirt and pulling it up and over her head, taking it completely off. The only barrier concealing her naked breasts from three pairs of appreciative eyes is the tight white sports bra she has on underneath. Worried that she'll continue, JD interrupts, "Honey, that wasn't a dare for you. That was just a truth for Nick."

"I know," Vicki states unconcerned. "I'm just getting a little warm is all. My turn."

Vicki rolls a one and asks her husband, "Truth or dare, stud?"

Grinning, JD answers, "Ah, I'm gonna have to go with dare."

Obviously in cahoots with her husband, Vicki looks over at me, then back to JD and then back to me again.

"Ok, JD. I dare you to suck on Miranda's toes, all ten of them."

"At once?" JD asks in mock horror, but eagerly starts moving in my direction.

"However you'd like."

Uncomfortable having JD touching me again, especially when my reaction would be witnessed by both of our spouses, I instinctually begin scooting backwards and away from him. My progress is halted immediately as my back bumps up against the wall, and I have no choice but to sit there and offer my foot to JD. He takes one foot in both of his hands and cradles it gently. He gives it a mini-massage as he works to get my sock off, dragging it out for several moments longer that it should have taken. Finally, he is staring at my bare foot, and leans his head down to honor it.

At first, he gently kisses the tip of each toe, then changes to a slight grazing with his teeth, nipping at each one individually. Once he feels he has awakened them properly, he begins to fully immerse each toe completely into the warm, wet cavern of his mouth.

His tongue snakes in and around each toe, bathing them completely, tickling them, sucking them, biting them.

I have trouble resisting the pleasurable sensations as I lean my head back and close my eyes and moan out loud. I can feel the magic of his tongue and imagine it working on other areas of my body, my breasts, my pussy. Oh, yes, I can feel him there, probing, entering, sucking, licking. Mewling, whimpering sounds are torn from my throat, and I am jarred back to the present as Vicki's soft voice intrudes.

"I think you'd better stop working on that foot for now and move on to the other before you bring her to orgasm, JD. She looks like she's getting ready to blow!"

Mortified, I open my eyes to see everyone staring at me, JD included.

Trying desperately to preserve any shred of dignity I have left, I joke, "My, my, my, Vicki. That's some tongue there. You're a very lucky lady."

Preening, Vicki croons, "Yeah, he has his talents."

"Let's see if I can keep myself together for the next foot."

Pulling my bare foot from JD's grasp, I offer in exchange my other foot. He removes the sock from it and begins the sexual slaughter of that foot as well. This time I am better prepared for the sensations and am able to keep from embarrassing myself any further. After several minutes, JD releases my foot and the game continues.

JD rolls a two and looks over at Nick. "Well, buddy, truth or dare?"

"What the heck. You owe me one. Dare."

With an evil twinkle in his eyes, he demands, "I dare you to tickle my wife until I tell you to stop."

Vicki's shriek is immediate. "No, JD, you can't!"

"Sorry, love, I just did."

"But . . . but, JD, you know what that does to me," she hisses back.

"Yeah, I know. Go on, Nick, and you have to tickle her hard. No sissy tickles . . . until I stay to stop."

Nick, eager to finally get some action, scoots over to where Vicki is sitting. Pushing her down flat onto the mattress, he places himself above her and sits on her pelvis. Then, without any further encouragement, begins to tickle her relentlessly.

Vicki begins shrieking and laughing, alternating between cursing and begging, helplessly kicking her feet to no avail. She begins struggling with him, trying to fight him off, but Nick appears as though he doesn't even feel it. Nick, originally just fulfilling the obligations of the dare, is now getting into it, receiving great satisfaction from Vicki's futile struggles.

He renews his attack with vigor, allowing his hands to grope at her breasts, camouflaged in the name of tickling. Finally, JD calls out to stop, and Nick rolls off of Vicki, exhausted. It takes several minutes for them to recover, and when they do, their eyes are glazed over with passion. Satisfied with the results of his tickle torture, JD leans back and grins lazily. The night is going much better than he had anticipated.

We decide to take a small break, get some more beer and light the lanterns. We suddenly realize that it has gotten dark outside and we were playing solely by the light of the fireplace. JD runs outside to acquire more snow for the tub, while Nick turns off the propane, the tub now half full of boiling water. Once the fireplace is stoked and burning brightly, the tub is full with more melting snow and the lamps are all lit, we sit down for another round.

"Nick, I do believe it was your turn," JD offers, excited to get back to the game.

Nick rolls a three and looks over at Vicki. It is obvious that JD's little trick had created some serious sexual tension between the two of them, and they were finding it very difficult to deal with. "Well, Vicki, truth or dare?"

"I think I need a truth right now. I still haven't fully caught my breath."

Nick gazes thoughtfully into her eyes, then asks, "Ok, Vicki. What are you thinking about right now?"

"About how much I want to fuck you," she replies, without so much as a blush. Looking briefly in my direction, she also states, "Sorry, Miranda. Hope that didn't bother you."

"Don't worry about it, Vicki. I quite understand that attraction."

Vicki and Nick remain visually locked together, while I chance a glance at JD. He is smiling, quite proud of himself, waiting for me to roll the die.

"Go on, Miranda. Your roll."

I roll a one, and grin back toward JD. "Well, stud," I start, mocking Vicki's reference to her husband earlier, "gonna brave another truth, or would you rather have a dare this time?"

Rising to my challenge, he simply states, "Dare."

Thinking of the perfect dare to take care of his smug, overheated body, I order, "Ok, JD, I want you to strip, then walk outside and make a snow angel while you're completely naked."

"You are heartless, you know that. I change my mind. I want a truth."

"Too late, buddy. You have to do it or the game ends, and you're the big loser."

"You are so dead if I ever roll a six," JD grumbles, as he starts to begrudgingly remove his clothing.

Nick and Vicki finally have the inspiration they need to become distracted from one another. A stark naked JD is hard to miss and they both glance up at him with curiosity.

"What are you doing, JD?" they both ask simultaneously.

"Well, obviously you guys haven't been paying attention. Little Miss Black Heart over here dared me to go outside naked and make a snow angel."

Unable to contain themselves, Nick and Vicki burst out laughing.

Vicki turns to me and says, "Way to go, Miranda! He deserves at least that after having me tickled."

"Out the door, cowboy," I continue with no compassion.

JD slowly makes his way to the door, pouting. "This is gonna suck!"

"Out!" I order, one last time.

Nick, Vicki and I all watch from the open doorway as JD wanders outside, cursing and dancing as the freezing snow touches his feet. He finds the first fresh patch of snow he can, lays down, whips his arms and legs up and down, in and out, then comes jumping up and racing towards us yelling curses the entire distance. He runs past us to his sleeping bag, pushed in a corner on the mattresses, wraps it around himself, then goes and stands by the fire.

"Dead, Miranda, dead!" he threatens between shivers.

I would have almost felt sorry for him if it wasn't for the knowledge of what he had gotten away with earlier at the dinner table. Revenge is sweet.

After about fifteen minutes, JD has his shivering under control and gets dressed once again. He sits back down to join us for the remainder of the game, but his disposition has somewhat soured. Grumpily he watches as Vicki rolls the die. Breathlessly, she looks at Nick as she realizes that she has rolled a two. She can barely get the question out.

"Truth or dare?"

Without realizing it, Vicki leans slightly back, her chest thrust forward in anticipation of Nick's answer. Her lips are parted and she can barely keep from squirming.

"Dare," Nick croaks out.

"Kiss me."

Plowing through me to get to her, Nick hurdles past to land on Vicki. Knocking her flat on her back, he begins to kiss her fervently, refusing to break contact even for a moment to come up for air. His hands are all over her, touching her everywhere, while they are rolling around together on the mattresses. JD looks at me with disgust.

Having witnessed enough, JD yells in an unsportsman-like manner, "Enough all ready!! We have a game to play."

I smile at him deviously, pleased with his discomfort.

Finally Nick and Vicki untwine themselves and sit up, only Nick decides to remain sitting next to her. Well, that's going to screw up the whole order of the game, I think irrationally. Chances are good that the game will be over quickly enough anyway, the way Nick and Vicki can't keep their hands off one another. JD grabs the die and throws it, watching unbelievingly as it lands on a six. He jumps up and begins to hoot and holler, while I sit there looking at him quite amused.

"What are you so excited about? I can always choose truth."

"Goddamn it, Miranda," he curses as he heads in my direction. "You'd better not pick truth. You owe me!"

Pouncing on me, he knocks me over and begins to tickle me as Nick had done earlier to Vicki.

Screeching, I begin to yell, "No! No . . . no . . . no . . ." Laughing hysterically between each no, I beg him to stop. "Please, JD, stop!"

"Pick dare, and I'll stop. Pick truth, and I swear I'll tickle you until you pee in your pants!"

"Ok . . . ok . . . ok . . . dare . . . dare . . . Dare!!!!"

JD chivalrously keeps his promise, and immediately stops tickling me. Needing a minute to recover, I remain lying flat on the mattress, wiping the tears from my eyes. I look up to see JD smiling once again.

"Ok, Miranda, I dare you to go into the kitchen with me, alone." Then, looking at Nick and Vicki adds, "And you two have to stay put, no matter how much she screams."

Nick and Vicki, relishing the opportunity to finally be alone themselves, make no objections.

"Now, Miranda!"

Getting up quickly, I scamper barefooted into the kitchen, a vengeful JD right behind me. As soon as we get around the corner of the fireplace and out of sight, JD grabs me and pulls me close, suffocating me with a spine-crushing kiss. His hand works its way deep into my hair, twisting it painfully as he backs me up against the kitchen counter.

"God, Miranda, you torture me," he mumbles between kisses. "I'm going to have you, now."

Taking his hand from my hair, he places both hands on the waistband of my pants and yanks them down. Grabbing the cheeks of my ass through my panties, he crushes me up against him, and again I feel his hardness press insistently up against me. He continues to kneed my ass, gripping it tightly, still kissing me all over my face and throat. I begin to feel his fingers work their way into the elastic band of my panties, pulling them away from my skin and then downward, much more slowly than he did my pants. I feel every inch slide as they are removed from my body, revealing more and more bare skin with each passing second. Finally, they join my pants, swirled in a heap at my ankles.

"Step out of your pants, Miranda," JD urges between several more sensual kisses. Not able to resist, I step out of them and kick them aside, wondering desperately what comes next. Without warning, I am lifted and placed on the counter. The coolness against my bare ass is exhilarating, and I find that I'm arching my back in spite of myself. JD scoots me up to the very edge, then, with his hands, gently coaxes me to spread my legs until they are wide apart and dangling. My hands are gripping the edges of the countertop to keep myself from falling off, my head leaning back and against the cupboards. I close my eyes, not wanting to witness his intense scrutiny of my pussy, but he demands that I keep them open.

"I want to see your face while I fuck you, Miranda. I want to see your eyes. Keep them open."

JD kneels down on the floor, his face eye level with my exposed crotch. I can feel his warm breath blow softly across the folds of my pussy, teasing me. Finally his mouth closes against my lips, and I stifle a zillion tiny shudders and his mouth and tongue begin to work their magic. Wetness is everywhere, his tongue sliding effortlessly between all my folds and creases. His mouth is warm and soft and consuming, keeping my pussy entombed in pleasure. His tongue buries itself deep inside me, then returns to the surface to toy with my clit. I am cooing in bliss, not wanting it to ever end, knowing in all certainty that it will, as I feel the first ripples beginning to build into the tidal wave that will carry me to the brink. Unable to hold back any longer, I release a sharp cry as I move my hands to his hair and hold on, riding the swells of ecstasy to completion.

Once I have stopped convulsing, JD removes his face from between my legs and stands upright. Never taking his eyes from mine, he begins to remove his pants, then kicks them aside. Next, he removes his shirt, until he is standing gloriously naked before me. I allow myself more time to take in his masculine beauty, too bent on revenge earlier to notice. Wide shoulders, broad chest, generously covered with thick, curly hair, thick, muscular legs, and a very impressive penis.

He reaches for me again, this time to remove my sweatshirt. Over my head it goes, my breasts instantly protesting the sudden cold. He pulls me tightly to him, rubbing bare chest to bare chest and begins to kiss me once again. The feel of him is heavenly. I can feel his cock poking at me, level with the countertop and the entrance to my pussy. It is covered in moisture, sliding possessively between the folds, making me squirm. I want him inside me, and I begin to wiggle to press him inside. JD, knowing he has waited for this moment for years, struggles to hold back, to make it last, but finds he cannot, and thrusts himself deeply inside.

A small, rapturous sound is ripped from my vocal chords as JD plunges his cock to my depths. Again and again he thrusts into me, fucking me, harder and faster with each stroke. He has to kiss me to keep me from yelling out loud, very aware that the other couple may come to investigate the noise. Thrusting into me, over and over again, deeper and deeper until I am mindless, he continues, slowly working his way to his own, ferocious climax. One final thrust and he is there, groaning into my mouth all the pleasure of his intense release.

He collapses against me, muttering, "Oh God, Miranda. Oh God."

When we are able, we pull ourselves back together and peek awkwardly around the corner of the fireplace. The sight that greets us, however, absolves us of any guilt we may have felt over our climatic rendezvous.

There, on the mattresses, are a naked Nick and a naked Vicki, both on all fours with Nick currently fucking her from behind. Very quietly, JD and I continue to watch until they both sprawl out flat on the mattress, thoroughly spent from their own encounter. JD is ecstatic, always hoping to be able to witness his wife fucking another man, especially without her knowing about it. We walk back into the room as Nick and Vicki scramble to get back into their clothes, and all fall into a pile on the mattresses. Exhausted, we are sound asleep in minutes.

The next morning, we all wake up slightly embarrassed by the previous night's escapades. Nobody really seems eager to address it until Nick calls for me.

"Yes, Nick, what is it?"

"Time for your daily spanking, my dear."

"In front of the Masons?! Can't you just give me two tomorrow? Please?!"

"Sorry, love, no can do. So . . . how many swats is it going to be today?" Nick asks viciously.

"You asshole. You know how many."

"How many, Miranda?"

"Thirteen."

Grinning, Nick says, "That's what I thought. JD, Vicki. Can you come here for a minute. I need your help with something."

Panicking, I grip Nick's arm and begin to beg him. "Please, Nick, please. Don't spank me in front of them. I swear I'll die if you do!!!"

"Always so dramatic. You'll survive. Now where's my paddle?"

Nick digs out his paddle just as JD and Vicki arrive to join us.

"What's going on?" JD asks curiously.

"Miranda's been a naughty girl. I need your help holding her while I spank her.

"Oh, yeah! I was hoping I'd get to witness her punishment."

"Oooooo, Miranda. Shame on you! Ah, what did she do?" Vicki asks guiltily.

"She's been unfaithful. She gets spanked every day, one swat for each person she'd had sexual relations with other than myself. She's up to thirteen swats today."

"Thirteen! I thought you were only up to six." JD mentions accusingly.

"A lot has happened since we chatted, JD."

"No kidding." Then coming up to whisper into my ear, "Are one of those swats for me?"

"Yesssss," I reply with a less than pleasant growl.

"Ok, Miranda. Strip naked."

"Oh, God, Nick. Isn't it bad enough that you're going to spank me in front of these guys, but I have to strip naked, too?"

"Oh yeah. Might as well go for the whole tamale."

"You're a bastard, Nick."

"Aw shucks, Miranda, but sweet-talking me isn't going to get you out of it. Strip, please. Don't make me have to do it myself."

Drowning in embarrassment, I begin to remove all of my clothing, until I am standing cold and naked for all to see. Sitting down on a section of the bench cushioned with mattresses, Nick pats his knee, motioning me over to join him.

"Over my knee, sweetie."

"Nick . . . please . . ."

"Now. Over my knee."

Hopelessly, I place myself over his knee, my arms and head dangling down on one side, my legs on the other.

"Vicki, would you be so kind as to hold her hands and arms still?"

"Sure, my pleasure."

"Now, JD, how would you like to spank my lovely wife yourself?"

"Me? Are you kidding? After what she put me through last night? I'd be ecstatic to!"

"Great. The angle isn't good enough for me to be able to give her full swats. Here you go, buddy. She has to cry out the name she is getting spanked for before you smack her though, so wait for that. Oh, and JD, no sissy ones, ok?"

"Deal! Ready, Miranda? Call out the first name," JD demands.

"Adam!"

SMACK!!!

"OWWW . . . Wit!"

SMACK!!!

"OWWW . . . Not so hard! . . . Rachel!"

SMACK!!!

Gasping . . . "Please . . . not so hard . . . Angela!"

SMACK!!! "Oh, Jesus, Nick. This is giving me a fucking hard-on. I'm going to have to start doing this to Vicki!"

"I don't think so," Vicki replies with a murderous look in her eyes.

"OWWW . . . Goddamn it, JD! . . . Robert!"

205

SMACK!!!

Whimpering . . . "Russ . . ."

SMACK!!!

"Eeeeeeeaaaa . . . Bill . . ."

SMACK!!!

"Owowowowowowow!! . . . Jake!"

"Oooo, look how red her ass is getting, JD," Nick adds, helpfully.

SMACK!!!

"KKKKevinnnnnnnnnnnnn!"

SMACK!!!

"Jeromeeeeeeeeeeeeeeee!"

SMACK!!!

Sobbing . . . "Celeste . . ."

SMACK!!!

"Tim . . . Tim . . . Timmmmmmmm!" I scream out.

SMACK!!!

"One more baby," JD taunts. "Who is it? Who is this last spanking for?"

"Yooooouuuuuuuuuuuu! You asshole!!!!!!!!!"

"Say my name. I want to hear my name."

"JAYYYYYYYYDEEEEEEEEEEE!!!!!!!"

SMACK!!!!!!

Sobbing, thoroughly ashamed and humiliated, I remain lying across Nick's legs for several moments as he touches my hair and whispers words of encouragement to me.

"Ah, that wasn't so bad. Most of that screaming was from embarrassment, not pain. Just think how much easier it will be tomorrow."

Oh, God . . . tomorrow. I will have to go through

this all over again tomorrow. Maybe Vicki could wield the paddle tomorrow.

Once I have recovered, my first and foremost priority is a nice hot bath. The tub is full of water, but it is cold. After lighting the fire, I let the water heat up for a half hour and then turned off the propane. Sighing contentedly, I immerse myself into the delightfully warm water and quickly scrub myself clean. As soon as I exit, Vicki walks in, perfectly happy to share the slightly used water. Even the boys help themselves, everybody acting as if the events of this morning had never taken place. By noon we are all clean and ready to go outdoors and play.

The afternoon is spent building snowmen and snow forts, snowball fights, and a little bit of cross-country skiing. All in all, we have an absolute blast, and before we know it, it is starting to get dark. We go back inside and set up for a new night, refilling the tub with more snow, relighting all of the fires and lamps and snuggling down to another picnic dinner.

JD pretty much keeps his hands to himself, the thrill of the chase now behind him. After all, he had the added pleasure of spanking my behind, a "bennie" he hadn't counted on. He did, however, engage Nick in quite the confidential conversation, and I was dying to find out what he had said. Neither are talking, however, leaving me unable to appease my curiosity.

After dinner and cleanup, Nick corners me in the kitchen while JD and Vicki go sit together in front of the fire. "I want you to do something for me tonight."

"What?" I ask, suspiciously.

"I want you to seduce Vicki so that JD and I can watch."

"Is that what you guys were talking about earlier?" I accused.

Grinning, Nick states, "Possibly. Will you do it for me?"

"No way, Nick! . . . I'll be up to fourteen freaking spankings a day!"

Holding my chin, Nick looks at me and says, "Let me rephrase that. You *will* do that for me, or else."

"Or else what?" I query bravely. What could be worse than fourteen swats with the paddle?

"Or else . . . I'll loan you to Russ for a day."

Gulping, I acquiesce. "Ok, honey. I'll do it for you."

"I though so," Nick states affectionately with a wink.

The next hour passes with us exchanging small talk, me wondering how on earth I'm going to initiate the seduction of Vicki. Nick, looking rather restless, continues to send me impatient glances. Finally, an idea comes to mind and I look over to Vicki who is sitting alone on the mattresses. The rest of us have decided to sit on the floor in front of the fire.

Getting up, I head in her direction.

"You're looking a little sore this evening, Vicki! Do you want me to give you a massage?"

Nick and JD exchange glances, knowing that the fun is about to begin.

"Oh, Miranda, that sounds wonderful. I am a little sore after all that playing this afternoon."

"Ok, scoot over and let me get behind you."

After Vicki readjusts herself on the mattresses, I climb up behind her and begin to massage her shoulders. Within seconds she is moaning helplessly, relaxing into my healing hands. I try to make the massage as sensual as possible, going slowly and gently, caressing up her neck and into her hair. I attempt to lose myself in the caresses as well, marveling in the feel of her skin, her smell.

"God you have beautiful hair, Vicki . . . so soft."

"Mmmmmm," is her only reply.

"And it smells so good . . . so feminine," I whisper hoarsely, as I burrow my nose into the softness of her hair.

"Mmmmmm."

"And it tastes so good," I finish, as I press tiny kisses all over her head, moving down to her neck to nip at the fine hairs resting at their base.

She begins to arch and squirm as I center my attention on her neck, and I know I have her.

"Sweetie," I whisper into her ear, "let me take off your sweatshirt. It's getting in the way of the massage."

"Ok . . . ok." Lifting her arms, she allows me to remove her top, exposing a white sports bra once again.

"Your pants, too."

Nodding, she lies back as I move around in front to remove her pants. I leave her panties intact, for now. She is oblivious to everything, her eyes closed as she waits for me to return to her. I take the opportunity to remove my own clothing, leaving myself clad only in panties. My breasts are completely bare.

I pull her by the arms so that she is sitting up again, and place myself on her lap, facing her. She opens her eyes in surprise at my lack of clothing, then smiles.

I continue to massage her, focusing on her throat and collarbone as we stare at one another. The message is clear, and she reaches her arms around the back of my head and pulls my face towards her, capturing my lips with her own.

The kiss is heady, sensual, long. Our hands take the opportunity to find each other's breasts, mine stroking her nipples through the fabric of her bra, hers milking mine in deep caresses. Our pelvises are squirming, grinding against the other, pushing, rubbing, begging to be sated. I hold her arms upward, pulling them from my breasts only momentarily, as I remove her restricting bra. Equally bare, I pull her close and begin to rub our breasts together.

We are both enjoying this immensely with our heads thrown back, hair cascading downward, nipples still touching. We rub our bellies together, enjoying the feel of one another, never once glancing in the direction of our husbands. She straightens slightly and presses me further back, my feet bent under my legs as my torso arches backwards.

Then her lips lower to capture a nipple in her mouth, and she begins to suck on it. Teasing it, she alternates between biting, licking and sucking, causing me to moan and squirm restlessly. She switches to the other nipple, then removes her mouth altogether, pulling me back up and offering herself to me.

I return the favor, descending my head to her breasts and making a feast of her nipples. I feel them grow harder and longer in my mouth as I alternate back and forth between them. She begins to moan and rock, her body begging me for more. Deciding that it was time to move onward, I push her back until she is lying flat on the mattress and move away from her. I quickly dispense with my panties, then remove hers. She raises her hips, allowing me to strip off her panties unhindered.

I move around to sit at the top of her head and look down at her. She nods and says, "Sit on my face, Miranda. I want to taste you."

Pleased, I scoot forward until my pussy is hovering just above her face and slowly lower myself down until I can feel the warmth of her mouth surround me. Sighing in delight, I lean over until I am laying flat on top of her, my mouth centered on her pussy now, busy with the task of bringing her absolute pleasure.

We remain in the "69" position for what seems like close to a half hour, licking and sucking, probing, entering, retreating. At one point I feel her fingers worming their way inside me to finger fuck me as she eats me to orgasm. I reciprocate, entering two fingers into her pussy and stealthily sneaking one into her ass. She gasps, but allows the intruder to remain. We are both bucking wildly now, ready to come, ready to explode. I feel Vicki start to shudder and convulse beneath me just seconds before I succumb to my own internal release. With small cries of surrender, we allow the spasms to take us on a glorious ride starting at the tips of our toes and exiting through the tops of our scalps.

Collapsing against one another, we are rudely awakened from our sexual reverie by two horny husbands with massive erections to attend to.

Nick pulls me from Vicki and away so that my torso remains bent over the edge of the mattresses, but my legs are over the edge and my knees on the floor. I am facing the wall with him on the floor behind me, and I watch as JD positions Vicki exactly how I am. Together, they fuck us in unison, thrusting in and pulling back all at the same time. Vikki and I are thrilled by the aggressive fucking, and urge the guys on. JD and Nick reach their climaxes simultaneously, falling across our backs in mindless heaps. Resting peacefully, we remain in those positions for quite some time.

The next morning, Vicki is just as unforgiving with the paddle as JD had been the day before, excited to be the reason for the fourteenth swat. I am better able to deal with the situation, realizing that the Masons have witnessed me stripped bare, both outside and in. I had nothing to hide from them, leaving me with a wonderful sense of freedom.

Unfortunately, the hut trip had to end and the Masons had to return home, but they left behind, bizarrely enough, a stronger and deeper friendship than what had existed before. I am uncertain about what the future has in store for Nick and I, but remain committed to repairing and strengthening our relationship. Although Nick's need for revenge seems to be appeased, I am willing to do whatever he asks of me to prove my devotion. He no longer finds any personal satisfaction from sharing me with his friends, much to Russ's chagrin and my relief, reminding me of the way it used to be, before . . .

CHAPTER 9

■

ENDINGS

I think you have another winner here, wife."

"Well, thank you very much, husband. I'm glad you enjoyed reading it."

"Very much so . . . but . . ."

"But what?" wife asks, annoyed.

"But . . . next time, I think you should write it from Nick's perspective, rather than Miranda's."

"Oh, really now? Well, that is a thought, but rather difficult considering the circumstances."

"What circumstances?"

"Oh, simply the fact that I'm a woman. I wouldn't have the foggiest idea of what a man's perspective would be. Perhaps *you* should write the next book?"

Looking startled, husband replies, "Me? Hmmmm, that is a thought, but . . ."

"But what?"

"But I'd have to do some serious groundwork and put in several hours of investigation before I'd be ready to put it all down on paper. Now let's see, where's that hot, melted chocolate?"

OBSESSIONS

CHAPTER 1

∎

CONFESSIONS

Obsessed. That's the only way to describe it. Russ is completely and utterly obsessed, the desire to have his way with me consuming every waking moment. It wasn't always like this. Russ used to be a good friend, well, of my husband, happy go lucky, yet always with a perverted twist. Never were his sexual advances directed at or towards me, not until the poker game, that is. Ever since that poker game . . . ever since he *lost* that poker game, things have been different.

It wasn't your usual game of poker by far, but a rather unorthodox one with yours truly as the grand prize. Although it was exciting at the time, it is an experience I'd rather not repeat. The winner of each hand was allowed only a minute to use and fondle my body at will, the only stipulations being no penile penetration and nothing that was harmful or dangerous. Although Russ did manage to win a couple of hands, he was not the big winner of the night.

*   *   *

Jerome . . . big, black, beautiful Jerome came out on top and was offered my services for an entire hour. This time, fucking was allowed, and Jerome took me every which way imaginable, a sight which proved to be more than Russ could handle. He left that night very disgruntled and agitated, and let Nick and I know on a daily basis how wronged he felt. After all, Nick and I have a very open marriage, and if I am allowed extra-marital affairs, why couldn't he be one of the recipients?

Now, six months later, I am still receiving bizarre e-mails from Russ, only this one a little more threatening, a little more menacing. Unable to keep the shivers from climbing up my spine, I read his chilling words once again . . .

Miranda . . . I keep remembering how your body swallowed up Jerome's cock, and how I wished it were mine instead, ramming mercilessly into you. Oh, and that ass . . . that sweet, fuckable ass was meant to be mine. I shall have it someday.
I've been watching you dress . . .
The arms you caress . . .
As you try to decide what to wear.
I've been watching the way . . .
You get ready each day . . .
The results are most charming, my dear.

A blouse made of silk . . .
Covers shoulders of milk . . .
But can never disguise what's beneath.
And panties of floral . . .
Can't hide what's immoral . . .
A hot wanton womanly sheath.

And you stroke oh so tender . . .
Long legs, smooth and slender . . .
Each time that you put on your hose.
And with earnest precision . . .
Your skirt has arisen . . .
Revealing a dew-moistened rose.

Slowing turning around . . .
To reach for the ground . . .
Rewards me with one tiny peek.
A glimpse of a thigh . . .
As it stretches . . . my, my . . .
And the bottom of each little cheek.

You are heaven in motion . . .
Causing quite the commotion . . .
To not touch you is physical pain.
The sensuous way . . .
I watch your hips sway . . .
The pleasure is mine soon to gain.

I've been watching you dress . . .
And my cock I caress . . .
As I dream of the day I shall have you.
All twisted in passion . . .
My own special fashion . . .
In a dungeon I've built to contain you.

When I finish my game . . .
My mark will forever be left upon you.

Dear God . . . the man is insane.

*   *   *
_____

3

"Nick!"

"What?! What is it Miranda? You sound panicked."

"I am . . . oh, God . . . read this latest e-mail from Russ. I think he's gone over the edge."

"Wow. I didn't know he was a poet!"

"God damn it, Nick! That's not what I'm talking about. I'm truly scared!"

"Sorry, sorry. Just trying to lighten the moment with a little humor, that's all. Want me to have a talk with him? Tell him the game is over and to quit pestering you?"

"Do you think that will work?"

"Yeah . . . Russ isn't dangerous. He's just a pervert. I think he's trying to talk your language to entice you. I believe that he thinks this letter will turn you on. Did it? Maybe just a little?"

"Uh . . . what a fucked up question, Nick. No . . . no . . . Of course not!"

"I don't believe you."

Without warning, Nick grabs the rear of my chair and begins to roll me backwards, away from the computer desk, then swivels me around to face him. Searching my eyes deeply, he asks again, "Are you sure you're not even remotely excited by that letter?"

Nervously I answer, "No. For Pete's sake. I said I wasn't, now let's please just drop it."

A malicious grin slowly spreads from ear to ear across his handsome face.

*   *   *

"If I find out that you're lying to me, Miranda, I'm going to have to spank you," he warns teasingly.

With his eyes never leaving mine, he crouches down in front of me and places his hand on my bare knee. Slowly, he begins to move his hand upward along the inside of my thigh, causing me to shiver and gasp at his intentions. His hand disappears under my short skirt to moments later confront the evidence I can no longer conceal.

"Tsk, tsk, tsk, Miranda. Your panties are soaked! I'd say Russ's letter did a mite more than you admitted earlier. Now answer me again. Does the thought of being taken into Russ's dungeon excite you?"

My words are cut short as I feel Nick's fingers begin to stroke me, swirling themselves around on my drenched panties, rubbing in circles across the satin barrier. Back and forth his fingers travel, starting up high at my clit and circling down to my opening. Forgetting that I am supposed to reply, I moan and lean back in the chair, closing my eyes, surrendering to the sensations of his expert fingers. Nick continues to masturbate me gently, his thumb now taking over, still taking care to remain above my panties.

"Oh yes, I'd say that it does, my little whore wife."

Shaking my head, I try to deny it, but am unable to speak the words. My hips begin to rock and thrust upwards, begging for something more.

*   *   *

"Please, Nick, please . . ."
　"Please, what, baby?"
　"Please take me there. . . ."
　"Not until you're honest with me."

Still, his thumb continues its gentle assault, stealing yet more moisture from my throbbing pussy to become absorbed into the already dripping crotch of my panties. Back and forth, up and down, gentle circles teasing, causing me to buck wildly. With my head thrown back over the top of the chair, my hands assume a death grip on the handles.

Panting now, I beg him for release.

"Please, Nick. I . . . need . . . more."

"What are the words I want to hear, my little whore wife? What are they?"

Breathless . . . "Okay, okay. . . . Yes, ohhhhh, yes, Russ's letter turned me on. I admit it. Now please . . . "

"Not yet, sweetness. What about Russ's letter turned you on?"

"Ohhhh, Nick."

"Come on, now. I want to enter that depraved little mind of yours. Tell me."

Nick's thumb continues its torturous course, never increasing in speed or pressure, just slowly and methodically working to maintain a high state of arousal, yet allowing nothing more. I wrap my feet behind the wheels of the chair to keep my legs from closing, relishing in the feeling of simulated bondage.

"Oh God, Nick. The thought that he watches me dress and undress. The thought that he witnesses my most private moments."

"My little slut enjoys putting on a show, doesn't she? What else?"

Nick's thumb picks up a little speed as a reward for my cooperation.

"Uh . . . oh, yes. . . . Uh, the thought of him taking me against my will."

"Oh yes. The infamous rape fantasy. How do you want it to happen?"

"I don't . . . I don't . . . want it to happen. . . . it's just a fantasy."

Nick applies more pressure as his own excitement begins to build.

"That's a cop-out answer, Miranda. How? Do you want him to rip your clothes from your body, or fuck you with them still on?"

"Yes . . . oh yes . . ."

"Do you want to feel the head of his dick ramming through your panties, pushing them way up inside you, like this?"

"Eeeeeeeeyyyyyy! Yesssss, yessssss!"

Nick's thumb forces the fabric of my panties as far deep into my pussy as it can reach, stretching the delicate elastic to its limit . . . Then he reaches up with his other hand and grabs my hair, pulling my head back even further and holds it immobile. Choking, I gasp at the aggressive turn this encounter has taken, as his thumb begins to relentlessly penetrate and withdraw from my aching hole. My legs and arms remain rigid and solidly affixed to the chair as if indeed, they truly were bound to it.

"What else?" Nick grunts out through clenched teeth, almost angrily.

"Nothing . . . there's nothing else," I manage to wheeze out despite the angle of my out-stretched neck.

"Nothing? Not even curious about this dungeon he mentions?"

"Oh yes . . . yes the dungeon, too. . . ."

"What about the dungeon excites you, Miranda?"

Nick continues to vigorously fuck me with his thumb, while his hold on my hair remains firm. Just as I begin to answer him, his teeth clamp on to my right nipple through the thin fabric of my sheer blouse.

"OWWWWW!" I wail in protest, but his bite stays constant.

"Go on," he mumbles as he begins to chew and feast on his newest target.

"The. . . . b. . . . bondage . . . the. . . . re . . . restraints . . . all of it. The whips. . . . the paddles . . . everything."

With this last admission, Nick begins to masturbate me with a purpose, no longer content to just play with me. His thumb continues to fuck me while his other four fingers manipulate and rub circles over my throbbing clit. The sensations are compounded by his teeth viciously twisting and pulling at my nipple, taking pleasure in my small little yelps of objection. The pain is not enough to take away from my rapidly approaching orgasm, in fact, only serves to heighten it. Suddenly, I am completely and thoroughly consumed by rapturous spasms and paralyzing convulsions.

As I cry out my release, Nick relinquishes his hold on my nipple and stands to passionately fuse his lips with my own. Kissing me through my final shudder, a disheveled Nick finally takes a step back and begins working on his own problem. The front of his boxers are stained with his arousal, while his raging erection pushes angrily outward. Upon release of his rigid member, Nick once again grabs my hair at the back of my head, forcing me to sit up straight and remain at eye level with his engorged penis. Wrapping his hand around the base of his cock, Nick begins to stroke it and pump it up and down, keeping it within inches of my face. I watch as he jacks off at a fast and furious pace, impatient to reach his own climax. I acknowledge the inevitable swelling of his prick only moments before globs of sticky white cum shoot out and splatter across my face, just as his own satisfied grunts fill the room. He finishes by rubbing his still semi-erect cock all over my face until every drop of his cum is absorbed into my skin.

"Oh, God, Nick. What the hell was that about?"

"Fun, wasn't it?" he answers, mischievously. "But I'm not quite through with you yet. I still owe you a spanking for lying to me."

As a feeling of dread washes over me, I try every tactic I can think of to dissuade Nick.

"I'm sorry, Nick. I didn't mean to lie. I didn't know I was aroused until you discovered it."

*   *   *

9

Nick raises his eyebrows in amusement, but says nothing.

"Really, Nick. I thought I was just scared. I guess there's a fine line separating the two. I didn't realize . . ."

Still remaining silent, Nick crosses his arms and waits for me to continue.

"Uh . . . now I know . . . now we both know. What's the big deal?"
　"You are so delightful when you panic, Miranda, but a lie is a lie. If you didn't know, you should have just said that you didn't know. Now get up out of that chair and follow me over to the couch."

Nick perches himself on the edge of the couch to wait for my less than enthusiastic arrival. Damn, what is the matter with me? I've been spanked by Nick hundreds of times and I've survived them all blissfully intact. What is it about the threat of a spanking that can reduce a grown woman to a trembling pathetic little waif? As if a spanking was the most horrible torture ever devised! Even rationalizing this has no effect as I close the distance between Nick and me, trying one last desperate plea.

"Please?"
　"Miranda, the longer you stall, the angrier I'm going to get. Now get over my knees."

Pouting, I lay myself across his knees, my belly firmly supported by his thighs, my head and arms hanging over one side while my legs dangle over the other. Shifting, he readjusts me so that he is able to lift my skirt completely up and over my ass, unhindered. Mortified, I feel the blood and heat surge to my face. Nick takes his time, dallying to prolong my humiliation, making comments about my ass.

"Mmmmm, no wonder Russ is obsessed with your ass, Miranda. It is beautiful . . . intoxicating . . . especially the way it quivers right before a spanking. I think I'll spank you until I'm hard again, and then fuck you between those rosy red cheeks."

"Oh, God, no, Nick. They'll already be so sore. . . ."

Gently slipping my thong panties down and off my ass and legs, Nick wads them up and stuffs them into my surprised mouth.

"You talk too much. These should help keep you quiet."

Outraged, I begin to kick and squirm, my muffled protests falling on deaf ears.

"That's it, baby. Fight me as I spank the hell out of you. Let's make this interesting."

Soon his hand is rising and falling in rapid succession, giving me little to no time to recover from each swat. Within seconds, my ass is on fire, Nick's large hands leaving lasting imprints on my backside. I continue to kick out and squirm, unable to make my hands of any use. This only goads Nick on, fueling his fire.

"Come on baby . . . where's your spunk? Oh, look at that rosy ass. Mmmmm, mmmmmm. I'm going to enjoy fucking it. What's that? A squeal? Hmmmm . . . does that hurt, my little whore wife, or does it make you wet? Seventeen . . . Eighteen . . . Nineteen . . . Twenty."

As tears begin to flow freely down my face, Nick pauses to check on his progress. Slipping a finger easily inside my well-lubricated pussy, he comments on his findings.

"Ah, yeah . . . that's it, my baby. Nothing like a good spanking to get those juices flowing freely again. As much as you fight it, you want it."

Removing his finger, he resumes the spanking.

"Twenty-one . . . twenty-two. . . ."

By thirty, I am all but bucking on his thighs, his erection now very noticeably poking me in the side. By forty, Nick decides that I've had enough and stops the spanking just long enough to pull me to a standing position. He kicks off his boxers and then orders me to bend over and grab my ankles. Assisting, he helps to speedily fold me in half, pressing my shoulders over and down. Still not fully recovered from the spanking, I continue to sob and moan as I'm forced to, once again, offer my ass.

Nick's fingers waste no time gathering lubricant from my dripping pussy to spread generously on, around and in my tight little ass. I suck in my breath as I feel the head of his dick press cautiously against it, slowly coaxing it open. I have never before been taken anally in this position, and the sensations are all new and quite thrilling. Suddenly, the stinging heat of my ass is forgotten as I lose myself in the splendor of Nick's cock slowly entering my ass. Nick holds tightly to my hips to keep me from toppling over as I will myself to relax and open for him. Slowly he guides his entire length deep inside my ass and holds still for a few moments so that I may grow accustomed to the intruder.

"Mrrrrumph . . . mmmmmrrrrumph"
  "Yeah, baby. I know."

Nick waits to continue until he is quite certain that I am relaxed and ready, spurred on by the persistent wriggling of my hips. Then he begins to withdraw only to drive back deep into my bowels on the next thrust. Nick fucks my ass over and over again, picking up a little more speed, pulling my hips back towards him as he rams his own cock forward. In and out, in and out, back and forth, back and forth. As the frenzy of the pace increases, so do the groans being torn from Nick's throat.

"Ahhhhh, yeaaaaaah, baby, I'm gonna cum. I'm gonna cuuuuuuuuuummmmmmmmmm.
AHHHHHHHHHHHHHHH!!!!!"

With one final thrust, Nick buries his dick to the hilt and explodes deep in my ass, losing himself in ecstasy. Still gripping my ankles, I wait for him to recover and extract his slackening penis, which slips easily from my well-used anus. Breathing a sigh of relief, I am happy to discover that I have survived yet another one of Nick's terrifying spankings.

Once the sexual tension of Russ's e-mail finally dissipates, Nick and I are able to resume some sense of normality. I return to the computer to finish checking my e-mail, while Nick busies himself with his own little chores. Keeping the conversation light, Nick asks, "Hey, who was the other e-mail from? I noticed you had two of them."

"I'm not sure yet. I'm just now reading it."

Meet me in the chat rooms tonight.

SeaNymph

"Well, I'll be! I think it's from Angela! She must have finally gotten her own computer. She wants me to join her tonight in the chat rooms."

"Angela, the hot redhead? The exotic dancer?"

"Yes, and one of my best friends. Gosh, I haven't heard from her since I've been back home. I feel terrible for not keeping in touch with her!"

"Well, if you'd like, I can explain to her how I've kept you *tied up* since you've been home, allowing you little opportunity for correspondence."

"Depending on how mad she is, I just may have to take you up on that. What a selfish, selfish husband you've been, not letting me stay in contact with my friends."

"I don't think selfish is a subject you should be bringing up at all, Miranda," Nick chastises playfully.

"Touché!" I reply, somewhat embarrassed.

Eager to hear what Angela's been up to, I hurriedly enter the chat rooms and search for her nickname. I locate the *SeaNymph* instantly, and invite her into a private chat.

<Aphrodite>   I Angela! How are you? I was so happy to
                 get your e-mail!

14

\<SeaNymph\>	I	Doing great, Randi. I have so much to tell you.
\<Aphrodite\>	I	I'm all ears.
\<SeaNymph\>	I	Well, as you can guess, I finally bought my own computer. I've become totally enslaved. It's all I do now when I'm not dancing!
\<Aphrodite\>	I	Oh, I know how that goes, believe me. Been there, done that. But don't worry. It will pass soon enough.
\<SeaNymph\>	I	And do you remember Antonio? Or should I say, Poseidon?
\<Aphrodite\>	I	How can I forget? He was your first on-line orgasm, if I remember correctly.
\<SeaNymph\>	I	\<blushing\> You got that right! Anyway, I've been hooking up with him almost daily in the chat rooms. Apparently, he is a big computer guru who spends most of his time down in Mexico. He's filthy rich from inventing some type of highly advanced Virtual Reality suit.
\<Aphrodite\>	I	I don't know, Angela. I think "VR" has been around for a while. Are you sure he invented it?
\<SeaNymph\>	I	Maybe not the original design, but he's perfected it. His specialty is "Sex in VR."
\<Aphrodite\>	I	Oooo, now that's intriguing. I haven't heard much more than being able to see in 360 degrees. Sex, huh?
\<SeaNymph\>	I	Oh yeah. And he builds programs to work in conjunction with the suit. He creates the virtual worlds needed for ex-periencing the virtual sex. He's a freak-

ing genius! And he's all mine!

<Aphrodite> | Wow! And of course, Virtual Sex automatically made you think of your good friend, Miranda!

<SeaNymph> | But of course, dahhhling . . . don't be ridiculous. Two peas in a pod!

<Aphrodite> | I'm flattered. So have you tried it out? How does it work?

<SeaNymph> | No, not yet. I'm afraid to. What if I get stuck in the program or something and my brain fries in real life and turns to mush? Antonio wants to meet me for the first time in VR. I'm scared to death. I had to send him all sorts of information about myself, as well as several nude pictures taken from all angles. He now knows everything about me from the circumference of my head to the color of my toe nails!

<Aphrodite> | Wow! It sounds spooky. He can totally re-create you now in a computer image. I don't blame you for being hesitant.

<SeaNymph> | But I want to meet him and experience VR so badly. It's tearing me up. Even you and I could meet in person in one of his worlds. (Sex optional, of course! <evil grin>)

<Aphrodite> | It does sound fantastic. Promise me this, though. If you decide to do it, don't do it alone. Invite Robert or one of the other dancers over and give them explicit instructions on when to interfere. Set a certain time limit, and if you haven't come out on your own by that time, have whomever shut down the computer. Once the computer is off, I'm sure you'll be able to come out of it instantly. Just as a precaution. I'm sure you won't have to resort to that. Just inform Antonio of your time restrictions in advance.

<SeaNymph> | That sounds plausible. Oooo, I knew you'd understand! Hey, can I e-mail you one of Antonio's VR questionnaires? You know, just in case you ever want to join in the fun? It's quite extensive and will most likely take you weeks to complete.

<Aphrodite> | Sure, but I doubt that I'll be able to afford to buy one of the suits. As technical as it all sounds, it probably costs a fortune.

<SeaNymph> | Well, right now we can get in for free, because he is still in his testing phase. He needs guinea pigs to help discover any glitches. Once it is out there for the general public, you can bet it's going to cost a pretty penny. He's assured me over and over that it is completely safe. He just needs confirmation that the experiences and sensations felt in VR closely resemble those of the real world.

<Aphrodite> | Well, if we are ever going to do it, it might as well be now while we can afford it. Go ahead and send me that application or whatever it is.

<SeaNymph> | Ok, it'll be in your e-mail box by tomor-

```
                        row. I have to go now and explain
                        things to Antonio. Oh, Randi, I'm so ex-
                        cited.
    <Aphrodite>    |  Well, I'm not going to get in a tizzy until
                        I'm dressed in the suit and ready to
                        press the "start program" button!
    <SeaNymph>  |  Ta ta. . . . I'll keep in touch with details!
                        Until we re-unite in VR!
    <Aphrodite>    |  Ta ta. . . . See you in VR!!!
```

What a nut. As much as I'd like to think that Virtual
Reality Sex is a possibility, I'm far too skeptical to be-
lieve that it truly can work properly. Too many variables
exist that are too complicated to recreate. I'll fill out
Angela's questionnaire, but with minimal expectations.
At the very least, it was great to hear from her again.

Just as I'm about to click out of the chat rooms, another
name invites me into a private chat.

```
    <DarkShadows>  |  Beware of where he lurks . . .
                          Cause despite his many quirks . . .
                          He is hell bent to possess you.
    <Aphrodite>       |  Excuse me?
    <DarkShadows>  |  Be careful where you strut . . .
                          For you see my little slut . . .
                          He knows you as so few do.
    <Aphrodite>       |  Who is this?
    <DarkShadows>  |  Be careful where you roam . . .
                          Don't you wander far from home . . .
                          He might get you if you do so.
    <Aphrodite>       |  Russ? Is that you? Come on, this isn't
                          funny.
```

\<DarkShadows\>	Every night and every day . . .
	You'll be forced to play my way . . .
	Putting on a pretty show.
\<Aphrodite\>	Russ. It doesn't have to be like this.
	Let's talk, please.
\<DarkShadows\>	Beware of where he sits . . .
	For you know he never quits . . .
	Not until he's won the grand prize.
\<Aphrodite\>	Come on, now, you're scaring me.
	We're friends, remember?
\<DarkShadows\>	Beware my little lass . . .
	Soon I'm gonna fuck your ass . . .
	To surrender would be so wise.
\<Aphrodite\>	I surrender! I surrender! What do you
	need for me to do?

Chat ended.

Damn, damn, damn! Do I tell Nick about this, or will it turn into another spanking session? Wrought with fear and uncertainty, I snuggle up extra close to Nick after climbing into bed, surrounding myself in the safety and protection of his loving arms.

CHAPTER 2

■

DECEPTIONS

A man left incomplete . . .
May wander down the street . . .
Devising evil plans.
A man left on the brink . . .
Has lots of time to think . . .
How he'll use you in his hands.

"Nick! Russ is still at it! I just got another threatening poem from him. I want you to talk to him."

"Ok . . . I'll talk to him. Let me know if you get any more of them."

"You'll be the *first* to know . . ."

Well, at least he waited a week before e-mailing this one to me. For a while there, I was getting them almost daily. He must have just gotten back from a vacation too remote even for his laptop. It's also been almost a month since I returned Antonio's VR questionnaire back to Angela, and am waiting with bated breath for the arrival of my suit. She assured me in her last e-mail that it would be sent within a couple of weeks. The realization that I may soon be participating in Virtual Reality Sex . . . taking place in a make-believe world . . . is finally beginning to pique my curiosity. I can't wait.

"You know, Miranda, I was thinking."

"Yes, Nick."

"How would you feel about getting a job, even if just part time? I think it would be good to get away from the computer and all those psychotic e-mails for a while. They are beginning to consume your thoughts, and I hate to see you so unnerved all the time. It's just a suggestion."

"You know, that's not a bad idea. I've been thinking about it too, but because of Russ, now I'm *afraid* to leave the house. I feel like he's going to follow me and whisk me away at the first opportunity."

"Miranda, if he really wanted to kidnap you, he knows where to find you. I'm gone most of the time and you are left home alone. Coming here would be the easiest way to snatch you up. I told you, he's not dangerous. He's just messing with your head to get back at you for rejecting his advances."

"You really think so?"

"Yes, I really think so. Otherwise, I'd have had him arrested by now for harassing you."

"Well, if you really think I'm safer out in the workforce . . ."

"I think it will improve your peace of mind immensely, not to mention help your social life. Your computer friends are fine, but some real interaction wouldn't hurt you any, either."

"Have anything in mind?"

"Hmmmm . . . just off the top of my head I can tell you that they are looking for a receptionist for that new office building at the corner of 6th and Main. You could easily walk back and forth to work each day."

"That's sounds perfect. I'll call them."

It feels strange being back in the formal nine to five atmosphere. Although it is just the interview, I feel as if I already have the job. I glance around the reception area, beautifully decorated and spotlessly new, but sorely neglected. The coffee pot is almost empty, with the remaining contents close to burning. Newspapers and magazines are haphazardly scattered about. The plants are drooping, positively dying from thirst, and the phones keep ringing, unanswered. Well, if not me, they'd better hire someone fast before they lose tons of business.

I take it upon myself to begin straightening things out while I wait. A kind man informs me that "the boss" will see me shortly, and that he is still with a previous applicant. He also apologizes for having to immediately abandon me, but he has a quick errand to run. Of course, I am to make myself comfortable in the interim.

First, I quickly organize the magazines and arranged them neatly on the table. Then I toss out all the old newspapers, keeping only the ones from today. Next I wander over to the coffee and sink area and begin to brew a fresh pot. Finally, I find an empty glass and use it to water the poor, overlooked plants. I find myself tempted to answer the phones as well, but struggle to curb that urge. I'm not even sure of the name of the company . . . how can I possibly answer their telephone?

* * *

Sitting back down once again, I glance at my outfit. I had chosen a basic black skirt, mid- to upper-thigh length, accented by a pale pink silk blouse. I am also wearing black thigh high stockings and a pair of classic black heels. The outfit isn't anything too fancy, just a nice, professional look. I also chose to wear my hair down, not wanting to give the impression that I was too severe or rigid. Intent on removing a piece of lint from my skirt, I miss his entrance.

"Uh hum . . . excuse me . . . ma'am?"

"Oh, hello. Sorry, I never knew a piece of lint could be so fascinating," I offer humorously.

Smiling, he says, "My name is Wesley. Mr. Miller will see you now."

"Hello, Wesley. I'm Miranda. Pleased to meet you," I respond, as he gallantly shakes my extended hand.

I follow him down several corridors until we stop outside a closed office door.

"Just a word of warning. Mr. Miller is a very nice man, but he's a little out there."

"What do you mean?"

"He doesn't ever let anybody see him. A curtain separates his desk from the rest of his office and he sits behind it while he conducts meetings and interviews. Rumor has it that he suffered a terrible injury that left him physically deformed."

"Oh! The poor man! It must be horrible to have to live your life like that! He should just come out and face it. People would accept him more readily than he thinks."

"Rumor also has it that he is very vain. Nobody has ever seen him, yet he runs his companies flawlessly."

"He has more than one?"

"Yes, several. He spends a couple of years setting them up and making sure they are running properly, then goes off to buy another one." Whispering conspiratorially, "And. . . . they say he travels only at night. . . ."

"Ohhhh . . . if you don't mind my asking, what exactly is the name of this company and what does it do?"

"It's called *Handymans*. Basically, it's a service used mostly by women to hire a man to do things around the house that she herself doesn't feel comfortable doing . . . or just plain doesn't want to do. You know, things like mowing the lawn, putting up shelves in the kid's room, taking the car in for a service, shoveling snow, those sorts of things. Our fees are very reasonable, and already hundreds of calls have come in. We've only been here a month, but it's been long enough to get the word out. Mr. Miller is still trying to hire enough men to fill all of the requests. As you can see, we need a receptionist very badly."

"Sounds like it would be a lot of fun to work here. I can't wait to chat with Mr. Miller."

"Right this way."

As I step inside his office and the door shuts gently behind me, I look around hesitantly. Am I alone? It's a little on the dark side, Mr. Miller's preference for artificial light quite apparent. Although he has windows, every blind is shut tightly. Wesley was right about the curtain. There, in the middle of the room, is a curtain the likes of which you would expect to see in a hospital room separating the different beds. The curtain completely conceals the desk on two sides, while the back and left sides of his secret area are barricaded by walls.

I head for the chair situated directly facing the curtained-off desk, but am halted.

"No, please, stay standing for a moment."

"Oh, hello. I'm sorry. I didn't realize you were in here."

"That's quite alright. Now, if you wouldn't mind, please turn around, slowly if you will."

"Excuse me?" I can't possibly have heard that correctly.

"Humor me. Just turn around. . . . slowly."

"You can see me?"

"Oh yes, very clearly."

"Uh, ok, but why do you want me to turn around?"

"My secretary has to be very pleasing to the eye. It's a prerequisite."

"You can't be serious. That's against the law."

"Don't worry. I don't tell the ugly applicants that."

Unable to believe my ears, I continue, "*You*, of all people, shouldn't judge a person by looks!"

"And why is that?"

"Um, well, you know . . . because of the accident and all."

Booming laughter fills the room. After he has settled down, he asks, "Is that what people are saying? That I've been in an accident?"

"Well, yes . . . haven't you?"

"I assure you that I haven't."

"Then why the curtain? Why don't you want people to see you?"

"Let's just say, I've been cursed with these looks since birth, but I certainly didn't have any traumatic accidents. I don't need my features distracting from my professional dealings. I prefer to conduct business in this fashion. Well?"

"Well, what? If you ask me, the curtain is far more distracting."

Chuckling, "I didn't ask you. Now, are you going to turn around for me, or is this interview over?"

"I'm not so sure I want to work for a pervert, Mr. Miller."

Again laughter drifts from behind the curtain.

"My sexual perversions run no deeper than voyeurism, Miss. . . . ?"

"It's Mrs. . . . just call me Miranda, thank you."

"Ok . . . Miranda. Due to my unusual circumstances, I allow nothing else. You have nothing to fear from me in that department. I will never lay a hand on you."

"Oh, my. You don't ever have sex?" Before I can stop myself, the words are blurted out and I turn several shades of crimson, horribly embarrassed. "I'm sorry. That was out of line."

"No more out of line than me asking you to turn around. No, I don't ever have sex. Now can you please take pity on my poor soul and allow me to see your full beauty?"

Feeling so sorry for this unfortunate and lonely man, I decide that allowing him to look at me isn't such a big

26

deal. Hell, men look at women every day, and vice versa. What's the difference just because someone asks first?

"Ok, I'll turn around for you."

Slowly I begin to turn, yet, instead of feeling degraded, I feel more like I'm performing a kind act of charity. This is all this man ever gets. It's the least I can do for him. I resist the urge to offer to return every day, regardless whether or not I get the job.

"Thank you. Now please, have a seat."

"You're welcome."

As soon as I sit, I begin to fidget. This is right up there with my most strange experiences, and Lord knows, I've had my fair share.

"By the way, thank you for straightening out the lobby."

"Uh . . . oh . . . you're welcome. I was just passing the time."

Shit, how did he know that? . . . . I glance around nervously.

"I assume Wesley filled you in on the type of business we conduct here?"

"Yes, he did. A handyman service. I think it is a wonderful idea."

"Thank you. It does very well in areas such as this one . . . lots of wealthy divorcées. I would love to be able to incorporate women for hire as well, but there is more risk involved and not many women are willing to chance it. They assume that the men who hire them will expect sex."

"Hmmm . . . I can see that point. Do the men ever get asked for sex?"

"Not to my knowledge. However, I hear the tips are great."

"Oh. Then I suppose you only hire men that are pleasing to the eye as well?"

Chuckling, "I like your frankness, Miranda. Coincidentally, all of the men that work for me *are* rather good looking."

"I suspected as much. Anything else you'd like to tell me about?"

"Not for now. How about you? What is your work history? Are you currently employed?"

"No, I haven't worked in a few months. I had a pretty good career going, but decided it wasn't worth the stress."

"I see. Your application says you worked in a night club in California. Tell me about that."

I should have just left that off of the application.

"Oh, nothing much. It was just an odd job I stumbled upon to pay the bills. I mostly served cocktails."

"Interesting. With legs like yours, I would have figured you for a dancer."

Thunderstruck, I just about fall from my chair. Oh my God, he knows! He can't possibly know. Trying desperately to keep from hyperventilating, I struggle to regain my composure.

* * *

"Thank you," I manage to sputter out.

"Are you okay?"

"Yes, I'm fine . . . fine . . ."

"Well, let me explain what will be required of you if I offer and you accept this position. Of course, you'll be responsible for answering the phones and making appointments for the men. You'll also be expected to keep the lobby clean and coffee going, which I am already aware that you do quite well. The majority of your time will be spent attending to me."

"Just so there is no confusion, please define *attending*."

"I don't leave this office much during the day. I may need you to run errands for me, bring me coffee, and of course, be available for me to look at."

"Just look, right?"

"Just look."

"And how much do you intend to pay me for just looking pretty?" I ask, sarcastically.

"How does twenty dollars an hour sound to you?"

"Mr. Miller. You have yourself a deal, but at the first sign of any monkey business. . . ."

"You have my word, Miranda. You just make sure that you look your best each time you walk into this office."

"When would you like for me to start?"

"Can you finish out the day?"

"As a matter of fact, I can."

The remainder of the day passes without any glitches. Mr. Miller must have had his fill of looking, because he doesn't ask for me again. I basically have to teach myself the job, or more accurately, create the job. Since nothing has been set up beforehand, it is up to me to run the front desk how I see fit. Thrilled, I begin to organize the appointment book.

Each day is divided into twelve columns, and at the top of each column are the names of the handymen. The men all go by fictitious names, just in case one of the ladies gets too attached. Next, I review all of the messages on the answering machine, returning phone calls and setting up appointments. Each handyman has his own voice mail box where I am to leave and update all of his appointments. Once that is complete, I intercom Mr. Miller to ask if he needs anything else.

"No, thank you, Miranda. You've been a great help today already. It's almost five now. If you'd like, you can leave a little early. I'll see you back here at 9 AM sharp."
   "Ok, then. Goodnight, Mr. Miller."
   "Goodnight, Miranda."

I race home to fill Nick in on the events of my day only to be disappointed by his absence. Knowing that he will be home shortly, I pass the time checking my e-mail. Sure enough, another threatening poem is waiting for me.

   Beware of where he goes . . .
   For nobody ever knows . . .
   Which day he'll plan to strike.
   Beware of where you stand . . .
   Cause you're putty in his hand . . .
   He knows the things you like.

Darn it. Nick was supposed to speak to him about this. More annoyed than frightened, I quickly close the bothersome letter and move on to read the rest of my mail. There's one from Angela informing me that my VR suit is on the way and should be arriving in a day or two. Other than that, my box is disappointingly empty.

At dinner that night, I replay the events of the day for Nick to mull over.

"Mr. Miller does sound a bit weird. Be careful around him. Carry some mace or something."

"Don't worry. He promised me that all he wanted was to look, and that he would never attempt to touch me."

"Ah, my sweet. He does not know the power of your charms. He's doomed to break his promise . . ."

I positively purr, "Aw, Nick. I bet you say that to all your wives."

"Damn straight I do. Let's go upstairs. I'm feeling frisky. Shall we play a game?"

Giggling, I ask, "What's it to be tonight? French Maid? Airline Stewardess? Cave Woman?

"Nah, I think I want to see you dressed up all slutty, with me having to pay for it, no strings attached. I'm in the mood for the *streetwalker*."

"Oooo, baby. Let me go get ready."

Thirty minutes later, I descend the stairs looking like a harlot . . . cheap and tawdry but, ohhh so sexy. My hair is teased up big and poofy, held in place with industrial-strength hairspray. I went overboard on the makeup, painting my lips a sultry bright red, and adding false eyelashes for a more dramatic affect. I also couldn't leave out the authenticity of the moment, and doused myself with inexpensive perfume. The outfit I put together is just as sleazy, perfectly matching your typical

---

31

stereotype prostitute. The fishnet stockings have a few extra holes in them, while my short, red, spandex skirt clings obscenely to the contours of my ass. I chose a black and red halter top accented with lace to complete the outfit, as well as a pair of five inch high, red spiked heels.

I strut in front of an appreciative Nick for several minutes before I turn to him and ask, "Looking for some action, sugah?"

"Wooooeee! How much is this action going to cost me?"

I answer his question while loudly chewing and popping my gum.

"Well, let's see. Depends on what you're looking for."

Slowly, I pull my gum out of my mouth and begin to twist it around my finger, the other end still clenched tightly between my teeth.

"What will twenty dollars get me?"

"Twenty dollars gets ya a blow job."

"Forty dollars?"

"Forty dollars gets ya straight sex, missionary position, no kink."

"One hundred dollars?"

I saunter over to him very suggestively and place my arms around his neck. "Sugah, for a hundred dollars, you can have whatever your little ole heart desires . . . for two straight hours."

"Anything?"

"Within reason of course. Just so long as you don't get carried away."

"Will you call me. . . . HumpDaddy?"

Unable to contain a snicker, I reply, "Oh, yes, but first, let's see the hundred."

Nick whips out a hundred dollar bill from his wallet. Without a moment's hesitation, I take the bill from him and stuff it into my cleavage, taking his hand and leading him up the stairs.

"Take me home, HumpDaddy. I've been a very naughty girl."

Before we even reach the top of the stairs, Nick's hands are all over me, fondling and groping anything he can catch hold of. He passionately kisses my entire face while whispering, "Oh, God, Randa. You look so fuckably nasty. I love it!"

"Now, now, big HumpDaddy. Settle down a bit. We want to be able to last the two hours, don't we?"

"That's not going to be a problem. Get in the bedroom."

Nick begins pulling devices out from all corners of the room. I watch in wide-eyed surprise as vibrators, whips, paddles, handcuffs and leather shackles go sailing through the air to land on the bed.

"Now, HumpDaddy, don't you go forgetting what I said about getting carried away. I'm seeing an awful lot of bondage and torture toys lying about."

Smiling, Nick explains, "Oh don't worry. We're going to do something different this time. I want *you* to tie *me* up and be the dominant little slut. And these can be some of your accessories."

Grinning wickedly, I remark, "Well, well, well. It looks like *HumpDaddy* has been the naughty one. Come over to me this instant. And bring that cat-o-nine tails with you!"

"Yes, ma'am!"

Nick scurries to obey my order, thrilled that I'm jumping into the game with both feet. When he is standing before me, I yank the whip out of his grasp with one hand, while the other hand dives for his crotch.

"What do we have here, you naughty boy? I didn't say you could have an erection. You're going to have to be punished for this. Take off your clothes! Now!"

While Nick hurries to disrobe, I survey all of the goodies scattered about the bed. I select the few items that I'll need immediately, then return to face a naked Nick.

"Stand up straight! Put your hands behind your back! Nice. . . . very nice," I coo, as I walk around him to inspect my new plaything. Pinching his ass I say, "Oh, we're going to have some fun with this delectable piece of meat tonight. Did I mention that I like my steak rare and bloody?"

Before he has time to react to my question, I have his hands cuffed securely behind his back. I walk back around to face him and notice that his erect cock is twitching excitedly, and his pulse seems to have quickened.

* * *

34

"Ah, you like the thought of what I'm going to do to your ass, don't you? Now, spread your legs wide and keep them there."

Bending down, I fasten a spreader bar between and to his ankles. His legs are rendered helpless and immobile. Next comes the collar, a wide leather band with several silver spikes and loops jutting outward. Taking down the end of a chain already attached to the ceiling, I clamp it to one of the front loops on Nick's collar, tethering him to the ceiling.

"Oooo, my pet. I sure am enjoying the way you look all trussed up. It's just making my pussy all mushy inside."

Nick groans and rolls his eyes back into his head, totally enraptured by my nasty words.

"You like it when I talk dirty, don't you, my pet? Answer me!"

I raise the whip and bring it down sharply across Nick's erect penis.

"Ow, God damn it, Miranda. Not so hard."
"Oh, this will never do . . . never, never do."

I take from my pile of goodies, a penis gag and shove it into his protesting mouth, then affix it around the back of his head, compliments of the nifty velcro closure.

"Much better. Now I can dish out this part of your punishment without getting interrupted. Try not to move too

---

much, lest you inadvertently choke or hang yourself," I warn.

Nick flinches as the whip comes down across his cock once again. Angrily, he tries complaining, but nothing other than muffled puffs of air are expelled. Again, WHACK.

"This is for getting an erection without permission."
WHACK.

"This is for not getting undressed fast enough."
WHACK.

"This is for not immediately answering my questions."
WHACK.

"And this, is for speaking out of turn. You must always have my permission before you can speak. And you will address me as Mistress. Is that clear?"
WHACK.

Nick nods his head as best he can in his tethered state and moans excessively trying to convey his understanding. By the last stroke of the whip, Nick's cock has sadly gone flaccid.

"Ok, you naughty boy . . . Now I'm going to whip your ass. You now have my permission to achieve an erection. But, first, let's get it all nice and ready."

Momentarily setting aside the whip, I reach for the baby oil and petroleum jelly. First, I pour a generous handful of the oil into my palm and rub my hands together. Next I begin to massage it onto Nick's tight buttocks. I take my time, savoring the feel of his clenching butt muscles, slipping a finger into the crack of his ass every so often, then reaching my hand down between his legs to cup his balls from the other side. When I am satisfied that his ass is well oiled, I dip a finger into the petroleum jelly and scoop some out. I move around so that I am perpendicular to his left side, his arm evenly dividing my breasts. My right leg and arm are behind him, and my left leg and arm are in front of him. I press up against him and grind my pubic bone into his hip as my left hand begins to massage his cock back to life and my right finger slowly works its way into his ass.

Nick begins to squirm and moan as my finger enters him deeper. His cock is back to a raging hard-on within seconds, and I continue with the hand-job as my finger fucks his ass.

"Does the naughty boy want to cum?"

"Mmmmpfff, mmmmmpffff, mmmmmpffff."

"Oh, that's too bad. The naughty boy can't cum. That would be a no-no."

Even as I am saying it, I don't relent in my stimulation of his genitals. I continue to work his cock and finger fuck his ass deeply until he groans and his cum is shooting out across the bedroom. Although thoroughly impressed, I pretend to be offended.

"You just can't help yourself, can you? What a bad, bad boy you are. I'm going to have to teach you a serious lesson."

I remove my finger from his ass and release my grip on his cock, then move behind him and pick up the whip. I begin to whip his shiny ass with much more force than

I used on his prick, until I hear him start to whimper. I move around to face him, surprised to see tears welling up in his eyes. Shit, I am going to be so dead once I let him go. . . .

"Has the naughty boy had enough?"

Nick answers with a murderous glare. Continuing on undaunted, I remark, "That expression doesn't look to me like you're the least bit sorry for your horrid behavior. I'm afraid we are going to have to continue your punishment, but I think I'll reposition you."

Unhooking his collar from the ceiling, I carefully push him backwards so that he is sitting at the foot of the bed. Then I remove the collar completely. Nick appears to breathe a sigh of relief.

"Ah, not so fast. I'm not done with you, pet. I want you to scoot back to the middle of the bed and then roll over so that you are lying down on your stomach. Then I'll release your hands."

Warily, Nick does as he is told, fully aware that I am still in possession of the whip. Patiently, he waits for me to make my next move. I take another pair of handcuffs out from the pile of goodies and connect a chain to it. Then I clamp one side of the cuffs to his right wrist, while connecting the chain to the headboard. I do the same with the cuffs that he is still wearing, chaining the left side to the headboard. Certain that he won't be able to get away, I unlock the cuffs holding both his wrists together. He attempts to break free, but is unsuccessful. Chastising him once again, I rearrange his arms so that they are now spread-eagled out in front of him and then shorten the distance of the chains locking his wrists to the headboard. I decide to leave his legs as is, nice and wide, held apart by the long metal bar.

"Let's see now. I bought you a new toy the other day. I think now is the perfect time to break it in. It's called a "cock taco" but I like to think of it as a "cockdog bun." It's so smooth and soft, flat and rubbery, perfect for cradling that naughty cock of yours while you're in this position. Now, I'll fill it with lots of lubricant so we can take your cock for the swim of its life. Lift your hips up, baby. That's it. Here you go. Now lower yourself down. How does that feel? Yummy?"

"Mmmmmmmmmmmmmmmmmmmmmmmmmmmmmmmm."

"Oh, yes. I thought you'd like that. Your cock surrounded in slick, slippery wetness. How does it feel when you squirm around?"

Nick rocks his body up and down to test the feeling.

"Mmmmmmmmm,Mmmmmmmmm,Mmmmmmmmmmmm-mmmmmmmmmmmmm!"

"Perfect. Now every time I smack your ass, it will cause your dick to slide up and down, back and forth. Won't that be divine?"

Nick starts to make a racket, wiggling and squirming all over the place. Soon he has himself groaning as the wonderful sensations of his dick slipping through the lube register. Defeated, he stops and waits for the inevitable.

* * *

"I think I'll change to the paddle for the rest of your punishment. Twenty more swats ought to do it. One . . . SMACK . . . Two. . . . SMACK . . . Three. . . . SMACK. . . ."

Nick whimpers and gasps . . . then moans throughout the rest of his spanking. By the twentieth swat, he is humping away at the bed like a madman, trying to get the friction he needs to cum again. With one last thrill in mind. . . . I take one of my vibrators, grease it up, turn it on low, then place it under Nick's balls. Then I take a second vibrator, a bit larger, and really lube it up. Turning it up to high, I again begin to talk dirty to Nick.

"Oh, Nick. Now you're going to know how it feels to have a dick up your ass. I'm going to fuck you just like a woman, Nick. What do you think of that?"

I slowly start to insert the penis shaped vibrator into his ass. He begins bucking wildly. . . . stimulated fully in all areas. As his ass stretches to accept the entire length of the plastic shaft, I reach around to increase the speed of the vibrations under Nick's balls. Soon I am fucking his ass in time with his desperate thrusts against the "cock taco" still snuggled tightly beneath him. Repeatedly, I plunge the phallus into his ass, deeper and deeper. His moans are constant, grunting, groaning, wheezing, whimpering, until finally his whole body seizes into one big contraction. Convulsing into the sheets, Nick finally collapses and remains still.

"Nick? Are you okay? Nick?"

*   *   *

Oh God, I killed him. Worried that he is truly hurt, I hurry to release him. Finally, his arms are free and I quickly go to work on his legs. Once he is completely loose, I ask him again if he is alright. Slowly he rolls over onto his back, his belly a slimy mess, and looks up at me.

"Miranda, I'd beat you senseless except for that was the most fucking intense orgasm of my entire life."

The next minute, Nick is fast asleep.

CHAPTER 3

∎

DEVIATIONS

"Miranda, can you please come see me in my office? I need to speak with you."

"Certainly, Mr. Miller," I reply into the intercom. "Can I bring you some coffee as well?"

"No thank you. Just your lovely self."

"I'll be right there."

I take a detour into the restroom to touch up my make-up. So far, Mr. Miller has been quite pleased at how flawless I've been keeping up my appearance. The last thing I need is to become complacent, jeopardizing my cush cush position here. And I thought dancing was easy money. Satisfied, I continue on down the hall and knock softly on Mr. Miller's door.

"Entre vous."

"Good morning, Mr. Miller. What can I do for you today?"

"Miranda. Come in and lock the door behind you. And

enough with the Mr. Miller formality. You can call me Beau."

Giggling, "Beau?" Unable to stop myself, I continue to snicker.

"May I ask why you find my name so humorous?"

"I'm sorry." I sputter out between my laughter. "It's just the way my mind works. I was just thanking God that your last name isn't Weevil."

Not amused, *Beau* asks me to have a seat.

"How long have you worked for me, Miranda?"

"After tomorrow, it will be two weeks, why?"

"Have you been enjoying your work here?"

"Immensely."

"Have you been enjoying my companionship as well?"

"Oh very much so. You are most interesting and entertaining."

"Hmmm . . . I was thinking the same of you . . . Anyway, have I, at any time, made you feel uncomfortable?"

"Other than my initial interview? No. I feel very comfortable in your presence."

"I'm glad to hear that. How does it make you feel to know that I'm watching you all the time?"

"Like I'm doing a good deed. . . ."

"Does it make you feel sexy?"

"Well . . . yes. I'm flattered that you selected me."

"Do you like to feel sexy?"

"What woman doesn't?"

"Do you like showing off your body for me?"

"Mr. Miller. . . ."

"Beau."

"Beau. Why are you asking me all of these questions? Now you are beginning to make me feel uncomfortable."

"I just want to know where your mind is before I ask you to do me another favor."

"What's the favor?"

"I purchased you some new clothes, ones that I would like for you to wear while you are alone with me."

"You're not happy with the ones I usually wear?"

"Oh, they're fine . . . acceptable. But they don't necessarily accentuate your figure as well as they could. What are you, about a size six?"

"Yes. Exactly, in most things, anyway. Sometimes a five, sometimes a seven, just depending on the style. You've got a pretty keen eye, Mr. Miller."

"Beau! Beau, Beau, Beau! My name is Beau. If you call me Mr. Miller one more time, Miranda, I'm going to have you thrashed!"

Tauntingly, I reply, "Ah, but, *Beau* . . . you promised never to lay a hand on me. You'd be breaking your promise."

"I never said I'd be doing the thrashing, Miranda. I'll just be watching. Don't be so smug."

"Ooookay then. How much skin do these new clothes reveal, *Beau*?"

"More than what you are accustomed to."

"Can I see the clothes before I make my decision?"

"Every day I'll have something new set aside for you to wear. You may decide at that time. If you choose not to wear them, then you are dismissed for the day."

"Uh, but you need me here. It doesn't make good business sense to send me home."

"No, it doesn't, but those are the conditions. Would you like to see what I have set aside for you today?"

"Do I have a choice?"

"Of course you have a choice, Miranda. You may leave for the day if you'd rather."

"No . . . no . . . no. Some choice. Where are the clothes?"

"They are in my private bathroom off the other end of my office. Remove all of your clothing and only put back on what I've set aside for you."

"I'm not saying that I'm agreeing to anything. I'm just willing to look at what you brought, that's all."

"Of course, Miranda. You'll find what you need in the bathroom."

I begin to sift through the delicate clothing stacked on the counter with trepidation. Everything is white. A white spandex dress with a white lace overlay, a white garter belt, a pair of white stockings with a white seam running up the back of each one, a pair of ridiculously high white heels, a white veil, and . . . Oh my God. A chastity belt.

What the hell? And why does it feel so deliciously kinky? For goodness sake, I wear less each time I visit the public swimming pool. Is it the idea, the symbolism that makes it feel so wrong, so twisted? As much as I try to reject the exquisite clothing, I can't resist the urge to try them on.

Several minutes later, I am completely decked out in my new costume, and the sight is breathtaking. Any woman would have looked just as devastating in such an outfit. Such pure, wanton sexual lust disguised in an aura of innocence. I still can't believe that I'm looking at my own reflection. I feel so beautiful, so provocative and so aroused. The dress, worn without a bra, is extremely tight, accentuating every curve. It is also so short that my cheeks hang out slightly, even standing as tall and straight as possible. The stockings only reach to mid thigh, hooked to the garter that continues up to eventually disappear beneath the dress. Loving the sight in front of me, I decadently run the palms of my hands up my rib cage to grasp and squeeze at my swollen breasts. I want to be ravished, right here, right now, in this outfit. Looking down, I notice the chastity belt still sitting suggestively on the counter. I pick it up and begin to examine it, never having seen one up close before. What an intimidating piece of equipment. Sighing, I slip it on and lock it up tight. God help me if I lose the tiny silver key. Adjusting the veil one last time, I prepare to make my entrance back into Beau's office.

I open the door quietly, still a little shy about what I'm doing. Hesitantly, I begin to walk toward his desk, unnerved by the suffocating silence.

"Stop. Don't move."

Startled, I freeze in my tracks. I stand for what seems like hours in dead silence, unsure of what to do.

"Beau?"

"Shhhhh. Just stand there. I've died and gone to heaven."

Relieved that he likes what he sees, I begin to relax as I innocently pose for him.

* * *

_____

46

"Can a slut be a virgin? That's what you look like. A virginal slut . . . a virginal slut nurse to be exact. Turn around and face the wall. I want to look at your backside for a while."

My pulse quickens at his words as I slowly turn back to face the direction of the bathroom. Oh God, I moan, as a warm gush of fluid rushes down to settle in the bottom of the chastity belt.

"You are stunning, Miranda. Lift the bottom of your dress up a little higher. Please? Just a little higher. Why hide such a beautifully round and sexy ass? Show it to me."

Swooning, I do as I'm told, enjoying the display almost as much as he. As I hike my dress up a couple more inches, another wave of moisture finds its way down into my chastity belt. I hear Beau groan from behind the curtain as he begins to fumble around.

"Oh, yesssss. Now spread your legs wide and lean over . . . just a little. Oh yes, just like that. Stay like that. Oh, Miranda. I'm taking my cock out and I'm going to masturbate while I look at you. Does that turn you on to know that I'm back here, beating my meat, all on account of you? Huh, can you hear it? Can you hear my hand sliding up and down my cock? Can you hear how fast I'm pumping it, Miranda. Oh, yesss. Oh, God, yessss . . . I'm going to cum in a minute. I'd love to spurt my seed all over that ass, but I made you a promise, didn't I? Ohhh, Ohhh, Ohhh yeah, yeah, yeah. Wiggle your ass for me. Sway it gently back and forth. Ummmm, yessss, just like that. What a peach. I'd love to take a bite out of that peach. Just a little longerrrrrr. I can feel my balls boiling, Miranda. I'm getting ready . . . ready. . . . Ah . . . ah . . . ahhhhhhhhhhhhhhhhhhhhhh . . . AAAAAHHHHHHHRRRGGGGGGGG!!!

Flushed, I stand there, swaying, barely able to keep on my feet. I am so wet and horny, dying to be fucked. Oh God, I wish Nick were here. I'm half inclined to beg Quasimodo to come have his way with me, needing desperately to assuage the ache that has begun spreading.

"You're horny, aren't you? I can hear your tiny whimpers. You'd give anything to be able to touch yourself right now, wouldn't you, Miranda? And that mean, nasty belt is in your way. Tomorrow. Tomorrow we're going to do this again, but tomorrow there won't be any belt. Tomorrow you're going to masturbate and get yourself off for me, isn't that right, Miranda?"

"Yes . . . yes . . . whatever you say. . . ."

Just then a steady three knocks sound out as the door to Beau's office flies open.

"Mr. Miller, I . . . "

"For God's sake, Dante! I'm in the middle of something. Close the door immediately!"

I turn to look over my shoulder, mortified that someone should catch me in such a compromising position. My horror intensifies as my gaze takes me directly to the brilliant sky blue eyes of none other than my tormentor, Russ. Squealing, I yank my dress back down to cover my bottom as I stand to confront him. His face registers bewilderment, then shock, then amusement . . . and then pure evil.

* * *

"Dante, remain inside and close the door please."
  Dante?

"Well, if Miranda had locked the door like I had asked her to, we could have avoided this little bit of embarrassment. Dante, I'd like for you to meet Miranda. She started working here about two weeks ago as our receptionist. Miranda, this is Dante, one of my handymen."

Unable to speak, I just gape at Russ. Russ, highly amused, informs Mr. Miller that we already know each other, quite well, in fact. Oh God, no, Russ. Please don't tell him about the poker game. I shake my head and silently plead with him not to say another word. He just continues to grin. Never have I wished more fervently for a swift and painless death as in this moment.

"I apologize for interrupting you, Mr. Miller. I didn't realize that you weren't alone. I'll let you get back to ... uh, whatever it was you were doing. My problem can wait."

Snickering, Russ gleefully leaves the office. Shattered, I slump down into the chair waiting for Beau to let me have it.

"Miranda, you have put me in a very bad position. Why didn't you lock the door when I asked you to?"
  "I think I got sidetracked ..."
  "Yes, you were too busy laughing at my name, as I recall, to follow a simple instruction! I'm absolutely

livid. I have half a mind to fire you on the spot!"

"Go ahead. That's the least of my worries at the moment. I can't work here knowing that Russ works here too."

"Dante could make serious trouble for me if he wanted to because of your carelessness. You're not getting off that easily. You *will* continue to work here, even if it means I have to share you with him to keep him quiet."

"NOOOOOOO! God, no! You can't do that! And his name is Russ. Stop calling him Dante! It's driving me crazy."

"Miranda, you need to calm down and get a hold of yourself. I'm the one in jeopardy here. Pour yourself a drink. I have liquor in the cupboard above the filing cabinets. I need to think for a moment."

Needing no further encouragement, I bolt for the liquor and begin to slam down shots of tequila. After the third one, I pause to catch my breath, just in time for the nasty taste to hit me as zillions of shivers consume my body. Ok . . . that was stupid . . . and I slowly wander back to the chair.

"How do you know Russ?"

"Huh?" I ask, alarmed.

"Why can't you work here if Russ works here? What's up between the two of you?"

"It's a long story, one I'd rather not tell, if you don't mind."

"I do mind. I'm directly involved now. My company is at stake. I need to know. If you don't tell me, I'll get the story from Russ, and I'm sure he'll paint a different picture."

Defeated, I spend the next ten minutes explaining to Beau the events leading up to, during and after the poker game, as well as informing him about the threatening poems being sent to my e-mail.

"My, my, my. I do believe I am seeing you in a different light. But, I do understand the problem now."

Then, without warning, he bursts out laughing.

"I'm sorry, Miranda. I know this is serious, that he's threatened to harm you, but of all the people to walk in on us and catch you with your ass hanging out like that. It's too . . . too . . . much!"

"Laugh all you want, but it isn't funny. I'm gonna be sick."

I stand up to leave, heading in the direction of the bathroom.

"Where are you going?"

"I'm changing, and then I'm going home."

"Wait, wait. Don't be so hasty. I promise you I'll take care of things. You won't have to worry about running into Russ. I'll make sure he stays very busy . . . and distracted. Now, please make sure the door is locked so that we don't get interrupted again."

"It's locked, but I'm not in the mood to play anymore. I want out of these clothes."

"Well, Miranda, *I* still do want to play. You have no

idea how sexy you look right now in your disarray. Let's just forget this whole incident ever happened. Have another shot of tequila."

Shivering, I politely decline, as the warmth from the first three shots slowly begins to seep magically into my bloodstream. The affect is calming, and soon I am relaxed and accepting, no longer intent on fleeing.

"Open the bottom drawer of my filing cabinet. It's locked, but the key is in it."

I open the drawer suspiciously, and with good cause. Inside I find an extensive array of sexual toys, ranging from handcuffs to rope, from dildos to paddles.

"You sure have quite the collection of kink for somebody that never has sex," I comment as bravely as possible. What have I gotten myself into?
    "There are many ways of achieving sexual gratification, Miranda. Take out the pair of handcuffs with all the fur around them."
    "What do you want me to do with them?"
    "Put them on. Not too tightly, but tight enough so that your wrists can't slide out of them."

"You're scaring me. I'm beginning to think I don't know you at all."
    "You have nothing to be afraid of. I promised not to touch you and I won't. I like the way a woman looks when she's bound and helpless. The key will remain within your reach to unlock when the time comes."

———

"Do you promise that you're not going to invite Russ back once I'm vulnerable?"

"I promise. If I had known about Russ earlier, I never would have threatened to share you with him. That was anger talking. I'm truly not *that* wicked."

"Okay, the cuffs are on as tightly as I feel comfortable making them."

"Just set the key on top of the filing cabinet and then step back into the middle of the room."

A strange noise directly behind me causes me to jump as I toss the key down and search for the source. There, being lowered from the ceiling by a thick chain, appears to be a mini trapeze bar with a metal clasp on the bottom of it.

"Hook the middle of your cuffs to the clasp at the bottom of that bar, and then face me. Now, grab the bar. You're going for a ride."

Slowly the chain begins to recede back into the ceiling, pulling my arms up with it. Soon I am on my tip toes, grasping the bar for dear life. The chain stops, momentarily.

"I also like the way a lady looks when she's all stretched out. Very fetching, indeed. How do you feel?"

"Probably the way you want me to feel. I'm not comfortable, if that's your point."

Laughing, he informs me, "This is going to be your resting position. And this. . . ."

The chain begins to move upward again until my feet are no longer touching the floor.

53

* * *

" . . . is how you'll hang for the remainder of the time. When your hands get tired of holding onto the bar, you can let go and dangle from your cuffs. When your arms start to hurt from holding your body weight, then you can grab hold of the bar again. And, when I think you need a break, I'll lower your feet back onto the floor for a small rest."

"Why are you doing this?"

"Because it pleases me. . . . and because I'm still pissed that you left the door unlocked. I wasn't going to show you that drawer for a couple more weeks, but the admission of the types of situations you were involved with in that poker game led me to believe that you were ready now."

Groaning . . . my arms already beginning to protest, "What . . . I'm not as sweet and pure as you had first thought?"

"Your face is deceiving. Very wide, expressive, innocent brown eyes. And your body screams, 'fuck me,' leaving me with quite a challenge on my hands. How many times since you've started working here have you wondered what it would be like to fuck me?"

Gasping, shocked, "What kind of a question is that?"

"A very straight forward one. Now I'd like an honest answer to it."

"I imagine you horribly disfigured. What makes you think I've thought about it even once?"

"I'd bet my life on it. Now, how many times?"

Struggling, my grip starting to weaken, I beg, "Please let me down. My arms are getting sore."

"Not yet, my sweet. You don't know the meaning of sore. How many times?"

54

"God damn it! You're beginning to tick me off!"

"Temper, temper. How many times?"

During my struggles, I manage to somehow get myself twirling slowly in a clockwise position. Finally my hands give up and I feel a mild jerking in my shoulders as the burden of my weight is transferred. It doesn't take long before I feel the cuffs digging into my wrists, despite all the padded softness of the fur.

"Please, let me down. This hurts."

"Answer my question and I'll let you down for a while."

"Okaaay . . . Once, just once," I practically whine.

"When?"

"Uhhh . . . please! . . . Today . . . in the bathroom . . . when I first put on the outfit. I wanted so much to be fucked in this outfit."

Immediately, the chain begins to lower until I feel my toes touch the floor. He stops the chain so that I have to remain on tiptoes, even in the outrageous heels. Relief floods through me as my arms begin to relax a little, my legs now carrying the load.

"You wanted to be fucked by me?"

"I wanted to be fucked by anybody. You were just the closest. I was actually hoping for my husband."

"Tell me about your husband."

"Can you lower me a little more, please, so that I'm not on my tiptoes?"

"In a moment. When your thighs start to quiver and shake."

"Damn, you're a bastard. . . ."

"Careful, I can hoist you right back up there . . ."

"Why do you want to know about my husband?"

"Just curious. What is he like?"

"Well, he's only the most perfect man on the face of the planet. Perfect *person* to be exact."

Chuckling, "Well, it's obvious you adore him. What makes him so perfect?"

"I don't know, exactly. It's kind of like his sole purpose in life is to please me. Everything he does is with respect to how it will affect me. I didn't ask him to be that way. He just is, and sometimes I feel so guilty, like I don't deserve him. But it makes *him* happy to be that way, so I guess we both win. Like I said, he's perfect."

"Does he satisfy you sexually?"

"Oh, God, yes. Satisfying me sexually is what he lives for."

"That must be quite a job, satisfying a nymphomaniac."

"That's not fair. I'm not a nympho."

"Oh, no? What would you call yourself?"

"I'm. . . . just. . . . very sexually aware, that's all."

"So sexually aware that he has to share you with his friends to keep you satisfied? I'd call that a nymphomaniac . . . "

"It's not like that. He doesn't *have* to share me with his friends. He wants me to be able to live out as many of my sexual fantasies as I can. He realizes that some fantasies he just cannot fulfill. That's why he staged the poker game. Not because he had to."

"He's a very generous man. If you were mine, I don't think I'd want to share you."

"He's just very secure and knows it is only he who

---

holds my heart. No matter what happens, I'll always come home to him."

"Does he know about me?"

"Yes. I told him that I was hired because you found me attractive and wanted to spend your days looking at me."

"Are you going to tell him about today? By the way, how *are* your legs faring?"

"They're shaking quite nicely, thank you. Care to let me down?"

Beau lowers the chain another inch or two, allowing my whole body time to recover. My arms are still stretched above my head, but not pulled tightly.

"Oh, thank you. I've learned not to keep any secrets from my husband. I'll tell him about today."

"Hmmm. I hadn't counted on that. Will he come after me?"

"No. He'll get me to admit that I was turned on by the whole experience and then fuck my brains out."

Laughing, "Your husband sounds like a man after my own heart. I do believe I would like to meet him someday."

"Would he get to see your face?"

"Nah, I'm afraid not. Nobody gets to see my face. Not yet, anyway. Perhaps someday."

"I'm sure you're not as ugly as you think you are. You *sound* handsome."

"Charming . . . A modern day Beauty and the Beast. Perhaps if you kissed me, I'd change into a handsome prince? Ah, a man can dream. . . ."

"I would kiss you, you know, if I thought it would help. You could blindfold me."

"I don't want your kisses of pity, Miranda, but the offer is sweet. Now, I think you've had a long enough rest, time to hoist you back up. Hold on."

"Uuhhhhhhh . . . "

I spend the remainder of the day hanging in limbo. Beau continues to ask me questions about my life and my relationship with Nick. He masturbates twice more, both times while I am hanging and pleading with him to release me. He finally allows me down for good around 4:30, reminding me before I leave for the day what he promised would happen tomorrow.

On my way out the door, I feel a tug on my arm and turn to see a grinning Russ.

"Mind if I walk you home?"

"Hell, yes, I mind. Leave me alone, will you?"

I continue walking, picking up the pace, making sure I stay well out in the open. Russ wouldn't dare make a move with all these people as witnesses. Russ continues to walk right alongside me and starts to singsong:

"You should finish what you start . . .
Cause you know deep in your heart . . .
That you crave a wild conclusion.
Such a shameless, pretty face . . .
Shall be put back in its place . . .
To avoid any confusion."

*   *   *

"Damn it, Russ. Stop that!"

"That was a mighty pretty sight I walked in on this morning. Are you doing Mr. Miller?"

"No, I'm not *doing* Mr. Miller. He just likes me to dress up for him. You know he's deformed."

"So I've heard. So, how come you'll play with everybody but me?"

Russ grabs my arm and turns me to face him.

"Let. . . . Go . . . Of. . . . My. . . . Arm! If you try anything, so help me God, I'll scream my head off."

Angrily,

"The time just isn't right . . .
Though I do enjoy the sight . . .
Of your sweet lips as they quiver.
Turn around and walk away . . .
But the sight of me today . . .
Will leave you cold to shiver."

Russ thankfully stomps off in the opposite direction.

"Nick! You are never going to believe the day I had."

CHAPTER 4

∎

EXPLORATIONS

"Miranda. A package just came for you."
   "Is it from Angela?" I ask, expectantly.
   "No, but it is from Mexico. Isn't Angela's friend from Mexico?"
   "Yes! Yes! That's got to be it! Give it here!"

I tear open the package and examine the contents inside very carefully. The first thing I remove is the head gear. It looks mostly like a pair of goggles and headphones with a very extensive mouth and chin piece. All in all, it's quite light and non-cumbersome. What I pull out next resembles a ski mask, all in black with holes cut out for the eyes, ears, mouth and nostrils. It is made of an extremely luxurious, suede-like material, making it very pleasing to hold against my face. At the bottom of the neck are connectors, which I assume must fasten to the rest of the suit. The suit itself is made of the same material as the ski mask, and all one piece including the gloved hands and feet, zipping closed in the front. It reminds me of something "Catwoman" would wear, very sleek and sexy, except for the fact that the entire crotch area is missing and tiny connectors are visible around the edges.

I dig deeper into the box and find the missing crotch piece. It is made of sturdier material, more like that of the head gear, and it is quite clear how it works. There are two very distinctive "nubs" which are to be placed directly on the vaginal and anal openings, then the device can be fastened to the rest of the suit by the connectors. Well? It is a sex suit, after all . . . and the piece is removable, making sex in VR optional. I don't *have* to wear it.

The very last item I remove from the box appears to be a swing, a very strange looking swing. It looks more like what you would wear if you were jumping out of an airplane, what the parachute is attached to, only no parachute.

"Ok, Nick. Here are the instructions. Want to help me set it up?"

Two hours later, the swing is in place and the software installed. Apparently, when in VR, you need to be safely secured in the swing to avoid injuring yourself. Nick installed the swing to tilt backwards, so that when I am sitting in it, I will be comfortably reclining. Eager to begin, I ask, "Now what? I just can't go in there, can I? Don't I need to set up a time so that I am not all by myself?"

"Probably. Why don't you send Angela an e-mail letting her know that you're already to go and see what you need to do from here."

———

```
<Poseidon>    | Hello, Aphrodite.
<Aphrodite>   | Hello there. Where did you come from?
```

"Nick, come look at this!"

```
<Poseidon>    | This is the Virtual Reality chat room
              | which automatically activates when
              | your computer goes online. It was in-
              | stalled when you downloaded the VR
              | software. This is where we arrange our
              | VR scenarios.
<Aphrodite>   | How many others besides Angela and I
              | have suits?
<Poseidon>    | Yours is the 20th.
<Aphrodite>   | Are the suits working the way they're
              | supposed to? Have you had any prob-
              | lems?
<Poseidon>    | A glitch here and there, all of which
              | have been worked out. My "guinea
              | pigs" are thrilled with their VR experi-
              | ences.
<SeaNymph>    | Hey you two!
<Aphrodite>   | Angela! Hi there. I have my suit. I'm al-
              | ready to go. Have you tried it yet?
<SeaNymph>    | No, I've been waiting for you.
<Poseidon>    | Would you ladies like to try it now?
<SeaNymph>    | Sure, I'm game.
<Aphrodite>   | Me too. I'd like it short and sweet
              | though, so I can test the waters. And I
              | most definitely don't want to experi-
              | ence sex my first time in Virtual Reality.
              | Can we make it nice and platonic?
<Poseidon>    | Absolutely. Where would you like to
```

meet? As you can see when you open up the VR program, it gives you a list of locations. Choose one.

<SeaNymph> | Randi, you party pooper! Antonio, I'm still game for sex. I'll be wearing my crotch attachment.

<Poseidon> | Ah, Angela. You're shameless. That's what I love about you. Even in platonic VR, I would still highly recommend wearing your "crotch" attachment, as Angela so eloquently put it. Otherwise, it could get a bit drafty, not to mention, if you change your mind, you'll have to exit the program to go and retrieve it.

<SeaNymph> | Well, what's it called then?

<Poseidon> | It's simply called the "sex insert."

<Aphrodite> | I kind of like the looks of the private yacht for a location. What about you, Angela? Any preferences?

<SeaNymph> | Oooo, that sounds heavenly to me. Antonio?

<Poseidon> | The private yacht it is then ladies! How about if I have us sailing around the Hawaiian Islands?

<Aphrodite> | Oh my God . . . this is sooo cool. I can't wait.

<Poseidon> | In 15 minutes, I'll have the program ready to go. You can access it any time after that just by clicking your mouse on the location icon. Then, take your place in the swing and put on the head gear. There is a small knob above the right ear which activates the helmet. Turn it on

and then sit back and enjoy the experience. See you soon.

Oh my goodness. I can't believe it's actually going to happen.

"Do you think you'll need any help getting into this suit?"

"Yeah, stick around and make sure I do this right, ok?"

The suit is tricky, but is soon on and fitting like a glove. Each finger and toe are wrapped snugly in their own little section of the suit, as well as my breasts being sucked up into the built-in bra cups. Next I slip on the "sex insert," making sure that the two little nubs are well lubricated before I clamp them so near and dear to my delicate openings. I wriggle around a bit, enjoying the feel of the sturdy piece between my legs. Next, I pull back my hair and slip the hood over my face. Nick helps me by attaching the neck to the rest of the suit. Oh, God. Almost time.

"Why don't you go get comfortable in the swing? I'll click on the location when it's time."

"Ok, but I'm a little scared. You won't let anything happen to me, will you?"

"Of course not. Want to set a time limit? I'll exit you from the program at that time if you haven't come out on your own."

"Yeah, let's do that. Just in case. How about 30 minutes?"

"Ok. If you're not back in 30 minutes, I hope you're not doing something fun when I shut you down!"

Laughing, "For your information, I'm keeping my first VR experience G-rated!"

"Okay, but I know women. They're famous for changing their minds!"

"I'll risk it."

I climb up into the swing and relax.

"Ah, this is nice! I feel weightless."

I let my legs dangle freely as I lie back into the comfortable back support.

"I could stay in this all day! We need to get you one. They'd be great outside, even better than a hammock."

"Well, don't fall asleep and miss all the fun . . ."

"Has it been 15 minutes yet?"

"Yup, 17 to be exact. Want me to fire it up?"

"Yeah, but come give me a kiss first, just in case I come out of this and my brains are scrambled. I may not recognize you."

"I doubt that . . . but I'll kiss you anyway, assuming I can find your lips around all that mask."

"They're right here. See? They have to be accessible . . . you know, so that I can talk . . . and stuff."

"It's the. . . . 'and stuff' that I want to know about!"

"I promise to tell you all about it. Now come give me that kiss."

After Nick kisses me and clicks on the yacht icon, I don my headpiece carefully, making sure my headphones are directly over my ears, and my mouth is placed flat up against the mouth piece. With a few minor adjustments, the helmet is on snug and secure. Taking a deep breath, I cautiously turn the knob over my right ear.

Immediately, soothing music begins playing in the headphones, helping me to relax, while my eyes behold a subtly increasing hue of swirling colors. Soon the music changes to the sounds of birds and a startling bright blue dominates my vision. I get the sensation that I'm flying as I begin to see the birds that I have been hearing, and white puffy clouds splattered sparingly throughout the wide expanse of blue sky. The sun is brilliant, and I can feel it slowly warm my body as I continue my journey. No longer afraid, I begin to move and turn my head in all directions, marveling at this incredible experience. Even if VR went no further than this, I would be thrilled just knowing what it feels like to fly. Thank you, Angela.

I can see the yacht that I assume I'll be "landing" on sitting prettily alongside one of the Hawaiian Islands. Everything is so colorful, the vegetation lush and green, fruit so ripe I can almost taste it, and the smells. . . . ah, I can smell everything. Clean, crisp, fruity, earthy and moisture. As I float closer to the ship, I can hear the ocean, hear the waves as they crash against the surf, watching the impressive yacht bob up and down with each passing wave. It's incredible, and so easy to forget that I'm not actually here.

I hold my arms out in front of me, taking on the "Superman" pose, expecting to see my gloved fingers, and become startled by the sight of flesh. What I see are my very own hands, with one heck of a nice manicure, nails painted a pale pink. My wedding and engagement rings are right where they belong, as well as the class ring that I wear constantly on my right, middle finger. This is too much . . . Every last detail appears to be taken into account. Amazed, I continue to gaze at my hands, flipping them over and over until I decide to take the real test. Apprehensively, I take my right index finger and stroke it along the inside of my left palm. I feel it! I can feel the soft, tickling sensation, and decide to add more pressure to see if the sensation changes. Thrilled to find that it does, I scratch at my palm with my nails. Not only is the sensation accurate, I begin to notice a slight reddening of my palm and a mild burning from my curious abuse.

Forgetting my hands for the moment, I concentrate on where I am being taken. I am getting very close to the ship, serenely afloat and picturesque in the tropical setting. Although I see and hear many things, none of them are human. I haven't seen any people, on the island or on the ship—no cars, no traffic, nothing to disrupt the peaceful tranquility of the setting. It's positively heavenly. Who needs a vacation when there is VR?

The landing on deck is very gentle, like I had been placed there by a set of invisible arms, very controlled and steady. Looking around, I see that I am at the back of the yacht and all alone. The deck is beautiful, with a built in swimming pool occupying at least one-third of the space, surrounded by a few lounge chairs and umbrella'd tables. At the very end is a cocktail bar decorated as a Tiki hut, complete with a grass roof.

*   *   *

I walk around and begin to touch things, comparing them to the real world. I touch a table, drag my fingers through the water in the pool, move a chair and then walk on over to the bar. I begin to notice that my feet are getting warm and look down to see that I am indeed, barefoot. I also notice for the first time that I can see my bare legs and most of my body, covered in nothing but a skimpy pink swimming suit. Smiling, I turn to head back toward the center of the ship, hoping to find Angela.

"AYYYYYYYEEEEE," I screech, very unladylike. "You scared me!"

Chuckling, the handsome man extends his right hand and introduces himself.

"I apologize, Miranda. I did not mean to startle you. I am Antonio. It's a pleasure to finally meet you."

"You, as well. Whew, it's going to take me a minute or two to get my wits back together. I was beginning to think I was all alone on this ship."

"I'm a little mischievous that way," Antonio replies. "I like to watch people when they think they are by themselves. But I truly didn't mean to frighten you."

"Mmmmm Hmmmm. I'm not so convinced."

"Since we have some time to kill waiting for the others, would you like for me to show you around the yacht?"

"Sure, that would be wonderful."

I take a few minutes to size up my host as he busies himself with the grand tour. Now that my nerves are back in check, I am able to really get a good look at him. I was expecting more of a "Mr. Ruark—Welcome to Fantasy Island" type of man, not something right out of Playgirl magazine. He appears to be in his early to mid thirties, not so much because of his looks, but more from his air of confidence. It's quite obvious, too, that he either comes from or has access to lots and lots of money. He is about six feet tall, with a strong and healthy appearance, not overly muscular, but very sinewy. Black loose curls adorn his head and neck, tapered to lay gracefully between his shoulders. His eyes are killer, a deep jade green, almost teal at times, and they possess a naturally lazy bedroom droopiness to them. His nose is very aristocratic and his lips have that puffy "kiss me" look to them. Overall, his looks are almost too perfect, too pretty, but with just one smile, I can see how he could charm the pants off of anything. . . . man or woman. This man is way too sexy for anyone's good. Angela will positively drool when she meets him.

"And this is your stateroom. Would you like some time to freshen up before Angela arrives?"

"She'll be here soon, right? I can only stay for thirty minutes. My husband is going to disconnect the program if I take any longer. We set that up in advance, just as a precaution."

"I understand. She should be here any time, but even if you get plucked from the program, you can always return. Speaking of which, there are several pull stations that look like fire alarms located in every section of this ship. If at any time you want to exit, just pull one of them. It immediately disables your headgear."

"That's good to know. Thanks, I'll only be a minute. Where should I meet back up with you?"

"By the pool is fine. Now, let's see if I can go sneak up on Angela!"

With a wink, Antonio disappears and I am left standing in complete luxury. Only the gentle rocking of the room reminds me that I am not in the Presidential Suite at a 5-star hotel. Everything is decorated in gold and white, from the comforter of the king-size bed to the fixtures in the bathroom. There is a sliding glass door leading to a balcony overlooking the edge of the ship and into the pristine waters below. The mirror is what I am most concerned with at the moment, dying to get a peek at what I look like in VR.

Whoal! I've never looked so good. I'm sure Antonio must have shaved a couple of pounds off as he recreated my image in VR. Turning, I'm pleased to see that not an ounce of cellulite exists at the tops of my thighs, while my breasts seem to have increased a cup size. My face is flawless . . . not a wrinkle, not a blemish—smooth, even color. I wipe my hand against my cheek to see if it's covered with makeup, but nothing comes off. No wonder he looks so pretty. He can fine-tune any flaw or even make it disappear. I love the little pink suit that he had picked out for me, and satisfied with my appearance, return to the pool deck.

Quickly, I duck back around the corner and out of sight as my brain registers the intimate scene I had just unwittingly intruded upon. Angela is there alright, but must have been very anxious to try out her sex insert. Embarrassed, yet too curious to stop myself, I slowly steal another peak around the corner. Oh my God . . . to witness such unleashed passion, so beautiful, so erotic. Angela and Antonio are completely nude, the remains of

Angela's suit piled carelessly at her feet. The sun is beating off of their already hot and sweaty bodies as they continue to thrash and kiss torridly. Finally Antonio has Angela backed up against the Tiki Bar and pushes her down backwards to lie across it, wrapping her legs around his waist. Without any further preliminaries, Antonio inserts himself and begins to thrust into Angela like a wild man. I watch in awe as the strong muscles of his ass flex with each savage plunge, suddenly wishing that I could trade places with her.

My God. . . . how can such a primitive coupling as this be so artistic? I can't tear my gaze away! I've never seen such a fierce and frenzied assault as this, and Angela appears to be loving every minute of it. Such a contrast to hear her sweet melodious voice screaming. . . . "Fuck me harder, you bastard! Oh, God, Yes, Antonio! Yes! Hurry . . . I'm there! YYYYEESSSSSS!" Antonio shouts out his own release, only in a language that I'm not at all familiar with. Still, it sounds so hot and sexy, my own blood begins to boil.

Breathing heavily, I close my eyes and lean back against the wall, no longer spying on the rutting couple and wishing I had never seen it. How can I face them now, especially when all I can think about is receiving the same ravishing treatment from Antonio myself? I'm going to have to get out of here and back to Nick, and soon.

As soon as I open my eyes, I again almost scream as I find myself nose to nose with none other than Antonio. His hand quickly covers my mouth to stifle any noise, and makes a shushing sound. Convinced that I have recovered from my shock, he removes his hand.

"How . . . ? Angela. . . . ? But . . . ?"

"Spying is not very nice. Just wait till I tell my brother. . . ."

"What . . . ? Who . . . ? Oh God . . . "

Smiling, he enlightens me. "I'm Lucas, Antonio's twin brother. He asked me to keep you company if he and Angela got carried away and neglected you. It looks like they're working on it, doesn't it?"

"Um. . . . I think it was just poor timing on my part. I think . . ."

"Did you get off watching them? They are a sexy couple, I'll have to admit."

"Did I get off?. . . . How long were you watching me?!?"

"Long enough," he grins wickedly.

"You must be the evil twin. . . ." I whisper under my breath.

"What was that?"

"Nothing. Shall we go join the lovebirds?"

"Hmmm . . . let's give them a few more minutes to get themselves together. Besides, I'm more interested in getting to know you."

"I'm married. Sorry to dash your hopes."

Lucas begins to laugh and then completely falls into hysterics.

"What is sooo funny?"

"This is VR, baby. You can't be unfaithful in VR! It's not even really happening. For instance, when I touch your bottom lip with my thumb, it's not really happening."

I feel a sudden, electric jolt as Lucas touches my lip . . . an all-too-familiar sensation that seems to be directly connected with my already over eager sex.

"Or, when I slip your bikini straps off of your shoulders . . . it's not really happening."

Oh God, here we go. Goosebumps rise as he slowly drags the straps and his fingers across my shoulders and down my arms. Moaning internally. . . .
    "Or when I kiss the hollow of your throat, it's not really happening. . . ."

Whimpering, I get lost in the warm wetness from his mouth and tongue on my throat, moving slowly further and further down. Lucas stops at my nipple, still covered by the swimsuit top, and then takes a frisky nip at it, softly grinding it between his teeth.

"Ouch!"
    "And that didn't really happen either."

As he straightens himself back to his full height, he doesn't pass up the opportunity to swipe the entire right side of my face with the length of his long, wet tongue.

"Pretty tasty for something not really here."

A scream from the deck momentarily distracts us as we both rush in the direction of the pool. We are just in time to see Antonio hoisting Angela up into his arms to throw her into the swimming pool. Another scream follows as she goes sailing through the air to become submerged. Lucas, not about to be undone by his brother, follows suit, and soon I am gasping and choking in the pool right alongside Angela. Thrilled to finally see one another again, Angela and I hug and start chatting, totally willing to forgive the boys for the unmerciful dunking.

For the next ten minutes, we all make ourselves comfortable on the lounge chairs, mine positioned between Angela and Lucas, while Antonio lies peacefully on the other side of Angela. Amazingly, ten minutes is all Angela and I need to catch up on everything, which is perfect since my thirty minutes of VR are just about up. Begrudgingly, I glance over at Lucas as I say my goodbyes, just in time to catch him stroking himself through his swimming trunks. He grins suggestively as he continues to play with his impressive erection. "It'll be waiting for you when you get back, baby."

Oh God, what a pig! "Don't hold your breath, Lucas. Ok, Antonio, how do I get out of here?"

As if by magic, everything disappears and I am groggily brought back to my basement and Nick.

After removing the headgear, I smile at my husband and say, "Oh, Nick. That was so awesome. We need to get you a suit!"

"Did you get lucky? You were moaning and groaning there for a while."

Blushing, I explain, "Well, not really. But it was close. Antonio has a brother."

"Ah, say no more!"

Giggling, I relate every tiny detail of my VR experience to Nick, from the thrill of flying to the feel of a thick, wet tongue against my cheek.

CHAPTER 5

∎

PERVERSIONS

"I'm pleasantly surprised to see you today. I thought for sure I scared you away."

"Well, if I had any sense at all, I'd quit this job. But my curiosity always gets the better of me. Hate to think I might miss anything. . . ."

"Did you remember to lock the door today?"

"Oh, yes. That's a mistake I won't make twice."

"Hmmm, I may have to find another reason to string you up, then. I found that far too arousing to do only once."

"Please, not too often. My body is still sore."

"That only excites me more . . . when you beg. Let me outline for you what's going to happen today. This first hour, I'll actually let you get caught up with your work. Make sure all the appointments are scheduled and calls returned. Then, for the remainder of the day, you will stay in my office and masturbate for me."

"All day?" I ask, incredulous.

"Yes, all day. How many times do you think you can cum in seven hours, Miranda?"

"Uh . . . I don't know. I never tried it before."

"Well, I'm hoping for ten, expecting seven but will settle for five. Anything less than five, Miranda, and you're going to have to call your husband and tell him you have to work late. Anything less is unacceptable. Understand?"

"Yes."

"See you in an hour."

The hour is plenty of time to get all of the appointments made and voice mails updated, but not near long enough to forestall the inevitable. Why do I feel like I'm on my way to the executioner's block, and why don't I just leave?

"Beau, I don't think I can do this."

"Your outfit is in the bathroom, Miranda."

Shit. Expecting the same white outfit as yesterday, minus the chastity belt, I am pleasantly surprised to see a whole new ensemble. Today it looks like Beau is going for the innocent schoolgirl look. He definitely has a thing for that virginal charm. The first piece of the outfit is a ridiculous looking white, long-sleeved, button down blouse with ruffles covering the buttons and surrounding the wrists and collar. Next is a short, plaid skirt, followed by white cotton panties, white knee socks, and black and white saddle shoes. This time, however, there is a plain white cotton bra as well, clasping in the front, nothing fancy and no padding. Set aside from the clothing are two red hair ties and a book. With a deep sigh, I begin to change.

*   *   *

The transformation is not nearly as devastating as yesterday's, at least not to me. Nor do I feel that same power of the irresistible temptress. Instead, I do feel more like a young woman, insecure and unsure of what to do next. Can a simple outfit mess with your head that much? Beau's voice startles me as it comes booming over the intercom in the bathroom.

"Please use the red hair ties to put your hair into two pony tails. Then grab the book and come out here. You are taking too long. I am getting restless."

I look up and around, searching for a camera or something, but can see nothing. He is either very intuitive or just damn lucky. Less than enthusiastic, I reach for the book and exit the restroom.

"You're a pervert. This isn't right."

"Excuse me?"

"I didn't know you were into little girls."

"I'm far from being 'into' little girls, Miranda. I'm into innocence, or at least the appearance of innocence, but I like the look on a hot-blooded woman like yourself. We all have our perversions. YOU just happen to be mine."

"I'm your perversion?"

"For the time being. I bought that outfit solely with you in mind, not because of a fetish for little girls."

"Oh."

"Now, if you are done insulting me, I'd like to get on with our game."

"What would you like for me to do?"

"You are going to read to me from that book. That's all."

"That's all?"

"Yes. I have every confidence nature will take its course from there. In case you haven't noticed, it's a dirty book."

Glancing down, I skim the title.

"*Sinsatiable Tales*. What's it about?"
    "It is a compilation of women's sexual fantasies."
    "I can't read this out loud to you!"
    "You can and you will. Now please have a seat in that chair directly across from my desk and begin reading to me, Miranda."

I start reading and immediately become enthralled with the first story. It's about a female prison guard getting overpowered and gang banged by several of the inmates. Not one to judge, I silently wonder about the woman who wrote down this fantasy. Halfway through the story, I begin to squirm uncomfortably.

"Getting a little warm, Miranda? Why don't you take off that blouse?"

Wishing I could make eye contact with the little pervert, I do as he requests. Soon I am sitting there in just the bra.

"How about those panties? Are they wet yet? Touch yourself. Tell me if they're wet."
    Surprised by how wet they actually are, I inform Beau, "Yes. . . . they are a little wet."
    "Just a little? We are going to have to fix that. I want you to rub your clit while you read the next few pages."

"Through my panties?"

"Yes, through your panties. Make yourself cum if you can."

Getting caught up in the story once again, I begin a tedious assault on my clit, teasing it slowly at first, and then becoming more vigorous and desperate as I near my climax. Soon it becomes too difficult to concentrate and read at the same time, so I let the book fall to the floor. My attention becomes focused completely on pleasuring myself. I throw my head back as my hips start to buck up out of the chair. With a few more magical strokes of my fingers, I reach my goal and gasp out my sweet release, feeling every clenching pulse of my pussy as it subsides. Exhausted, I look up, only to see a curtain and to hear Beau say, "Oh, baby, that was sweet. Do you like that book?"

With a slight glaze still lingering in my eyes, I nod and mumble a feeble, "Oh yeah."

"Good. Let's continue then. I want you to grab some extra cushions off of the other chair and pile them on the chair you are sitting in until you're elevated to the same height as my desk. Then scoot the chair closer until you can place the arches of your shoes on the edge of my desk with your knees bent up. Before you sit, remove your panties, but leave them resting around your ankles so your legs can only spread a short distance apart. Just pretend you're at the doctor, dear, preparing for your annual exam. Ah, I've always wondered what it would be like to be a gynecologist . . . Oh, and Miranda, be careful not to move the curtain around my desk. That would be unforgivable."

*   *   *

With the warning well understood, I begin to reposition the chair as instructed and sit myself back down, legs spread and feet resting on the edge of his desk.

"Raise your skirt up so that it's up around your waist. I want to be able to see that hungry little cunt clearly."

"Do you have to be so vulgar about it?" I pout, as I shift to get the short skirt up and out of the way.

"Yeah, I think I do. I think the nastier I talk, the more you like it. You'd like nothing more than to be used, as a piece of meat, over and over again, satisfying the sexual whims of anyone you came into contact with, would you, Miranda?"

I shake my head violently from side to side, ashamed to admit such a thing, even to myself. Am I that depraved of a creature? But even as I deny it, I feel my blood start to rapidly pulse and swell into the folds of my pussy, plumping up the already glistening lips. So quickly I find my body eager to respond to his lewd question, my mind close behind, clouded with images of hot, naked bodies intertwined in passionate embraces.

"Your head says, 'No,' but your body screams, 'Yes,' Miranda. Your body was made to fuck. What a damn shame mine wasn't. But I'm going to enjoy you just the same, because it turns you on to perform for me, doesn't it? Look how anxious your body is getting . . . already rocking, your thighs flexing in and then back out again, humping air. You want to fuck something, don't you, baby?"

*   *   *

Unable to answer, I continue to stare at the curtain in front of me with a pained expression on my face, whimpering tiny moans of discomfort.

"Unclasp your bra and play with your tits while your body continues to fuck that imaginary cock, Miranda. You're thinking about fucking me again, aren't you?"

Gasping, I cry out, "Yes . . . ohhhh, yes! Why won't you fuck me, Beau? I release you from your promise. I don't care what you look like. Please, come fuck me . . . please. . . ."

I hear his sharp intake of breath at my pathetic plea, begging him to have his way with me. "Oh sweetheart, if only I could. You have no idea what the sight of you does to me. But I can't. Play with them."

I fumble with the front clasp of the bra in my haste to please him . . . and to provide some stimulation for my aroused body. Finally my breasts spring free and I sigh as my hands cup their exquisite softness. I begin to squeeze and caress them, pushing them close together, pulling them apart and smashing them flat to my chest as my palms glide over my distended nipples. The sensations only cause my hips to rock more insistently, while my knees and thighs attempt to touch as they flex more boldly inward.

"Pinch your nipples, baby. Pull them out toward me. Imagine me swallowing them. Imagine the suction."

Whimpering, I pinch and pull at them, shooting shards of electricity right to the center of my pussy and my throbbing clit.

---

* * *

"Oh, God, please . . . take care of me. . . ."

"Reach down between your legs and spread your lips, baby. Open wide. I want to see deep into you."

Gulping, almost panting, I snake my hands downward to delve into folds of my sex. Intense heat and wetness surround them as I gently separate the fleshy lips and pull them apart.

"Further."

Digging my fingers a little deeper into my opening, I attempt to widen myself even more.

"I can't. . . . I'm too slippery."

"Oh, yeah . . . ok, baby. You're ready for me now. Lift the right arm of the chair and take out what's hiding inside."

Reluctant to remove any stimulation from my overheated body, I lift up the arm of the chair to find a carrot, a cucumber and two clothespins guiltily waiting inside. Curiously, I notice that there are two holes drilled near the ends of the legs of the clothespins with twine threaded through. Needy for anything, I grab them all and set them on my stomach awaiting Beau's instructions.

"Put the cucumber in your mouth and suck on it. Hold it there until I tell you to take it out."

What, is he crazy? Suck on it? I'll be lucky if I can even get it to stay in my mouth. Still, I'm desperate, so

I do as he asks. Slowly my mouth widens enough to accommodate the massive intruder. Although I am unable to officially suck on it, I hold it steady with my teeth while my tongue gently licks at the tip. Satisfied that the cucumber will remain in place, Beau then tells me to take one of the clothespins and clamp it to the inner, right lip of my pussy.

"MMmrrrrphhhhffff!"

"Afraid it might be painful? Oh, you'll feel it, but it won't hurt. Trust me. Then take the other clothespin and clamp it onto your inner left lip."

Hesitantly, I open the first clothespin and attach it slowly to a small section of my tender skin. There is a slight smarting initially, but within seconds it vanishes into a dull throbbing sensation, not at all unpleasant.

"No, hon. You need to get a good, meaty chunk clamped down. We're going to be pulling on those sweet lips, and we don't want those slipping off."

I re-adjust the clothespin so that it is now swallowing up a much larger section and position the other identically on the left side.

"Ah, that's more like it. Now, take the strings that are dangling down and pull them out to your sides. This will teach that naughty pussy not to open wide enough for me."

I moan in sweet torment as I begin once again to pull myself wide open for his inspection. I gasp as the cooler air rushes to mingle with my moist heat, trying to work its way inside me. Soon my pussy is resembling the mouth of a hungry baby bird, perched open to accept anything offered to it. It continues to slurp in air, mortifying me to no end with the embarrassing noises escaping it.

"Ok, baby. You can let go. Now I want you to pull your knees in toward one another. Leave your feet right where they are, but try to touch your kneecaps together."

I again do as I'm asked, desperately trying to ignore my tired jaw and the saliva beginning to seep out from the corners of my mouth.

"Keeping your knees together . . . grab the two ends of the string on the right clothespin and tie them tightly together around your right thigh. Ah . . . beautiful. Now the same with the left. Mmmmm . . . now, pull your legs apart, Miranda."

Of course, I knew what was going to happen even before I felt it. Every time I move my legs, even just a fraction, it feels like someone tugging at my pussy lips. The wider my legs fall open, the more they will be pulled and stretched. Mmmmm, it feels gloriously wicked. The rhythmic pulsing of my pelvis begins to increase in intensity, urged on by this newest form of stimulation.

"You're doing wonderfully, Miranda. It won't be long before I have you cumming all over yourself once again. Now, pick up the carrot and insert the larger end into your pussy and slowly fuck yourself with it."

Not needing any further encouragement, I pick up the carrot and examine it briefly before I lower it in place.

It's a decent size carrot, about the width of two fingers crossed together, but the intriguing part is the thicker bump about six inches down from the top running all the way around it. I can't help but wonder how that will feel as it crosses the threshold of my aching pussy. Eager to finally feel something enter me, I place the larger end of the carrot at my opening and slowly begin to penetrate it. Moaning with pleasure, I close my eyes and lay my head back while I insert it the rest of the way, gasping as I am stretched further to accommodate the extra large bump in the middle. Once the knot passes beyond, I feel my body suck up the carrot and close around it. Slowly I pull it back out, once again marveling at the added sensation the bump provides as it pauses briefly at my opening to hold me open. Soon I begin to pick up some speed, driving the carrot in and out at a faster pace. I have become even more aroused, my juicy secretions beginning to ooze freely and overflow down between my cheeks and into the cushions. I attempt to squeeze the walls of my pussy tighter, trying to grasp and pull at the carrot, but immediately become frustrated. I want more, something thicker. I want to feel full. I want the damn cucumber to replace the carrot, can't he see that? My body quickly becomes agitated and my whimpering in-creases.

"What's the matter, baby? Isn't that carrot big enough for you? Do you want more, Miranda?"

I begin to nod frantically, blushing at his sudden chuck-ling.

"Ok sweetheart. Take that juicy carrot out of your pussy and let's see you take it into your ass. I know from your earlier confessions that this is not something new to you. I want you to push it up until your ass closes over and around the nub in the middle of the carrot. Understand?"

I nod my head in acknowledgement, saliva now totally coating the cucumber and dripping down my chin and chest. I remove the carrot and begin to insert it into my ass, a bit impatient to move on to the cucumber. My ass greedily sucks it up a good six inches then pops tightly closed around the bulge, temporarily imprisoning the carrot. Only two inches are left hanging from my bottom. I begin to shiver at the sensations . . . the carrot wedged deeply into my ass, the clothespins constantly tweaking and twisting my pussy lips . . . and thoughts of where that cucumber is sure to end up. . . . My squirming increases as do the chuckles from behind the curtain.

"That cucumber looks nice and lubed up. Why don't we see how much of it you can take. You can remove it from your mouth now, but hold it right at the entrance to your pussy. Don't push it in yet."

"Oh God . . . oh God . . . oh God . . ." I manage to whisper, as I remove the massive instrument of discomfort. Oh my aching jaw . . . Gasping and slurping, I try to regain control over my mouth as I wipe myself up with the back of my hand.

"No . . . leave your face like that. I like it all wet and shiny, slick and slippery. Makes me envision something else moist and creamy adorning those sexy lips."

In no position to argue, I leave my face as is and direct my attention to the cucumber. Anxious to feel it between my legs, I guide it hurriedly downward to poise waiting at the entrance to my insatiable sheath. The cucumber is huge, probably three inches thick in the center, yet this fact does not discourage me at all. Right now I am so hot and wet that I have no doubts that I'll be able to take it all.

"Hungry, puss?"

"Yes, oh, yes. Let me do it. I need to do it."

"Do what, puss?"

"Push it inside. I need to feel it inside me now."

"Go ahead, Miranda. Fuck yourself with that cucumber until you cum. Do whatever you need to do. I'm ready to watch you have another orgasm. This time, I think I'll join you."

Just as I start to slip the head of the cucumber inside, I hear the unmistakable sound of a zipper being lowered. Smiling knowingly, I return to the task at hand. Slowly I start to work the cucumber in deeper, sighing at the overwhelming feelings. I feel the pressure from the carrot, still wedged deeply in my ass, as it rubs up against the cucumber in the neighboring passage. Unable to keep still, I begin to hump wildly, pushing the cucumber further and further in . . . stretching me to my limits . . . tiny pinches reminding me of the ever present clothespins. The cucumber meets with little resistance as it becomes surrounded by generous amounts of my natural lubrication, sliding in another inch until a squeal of utmost pleasure is ripped from my throat. I begin to work it now, needing sexual release almost as much as air. I slide the cucumber back out, only to plunge it in even deeper in one, swift thrust. Again a cry escapes . . . but

I continue with the vicious assault of my own body, craving the mixture of pleasure and pain.

My other hand finds my unnaturally distended and swollen clit, probably made more apparent as the protective lips are now pulled away to the sides. It is extremely sensitive, and the first touch almost sends me over the brink. . . . but I resist, wanting this to last as long as possible. I continue to fuck myself ruthlessly with the cucumber while rubbing my clit and bouncing on the cushions, thrusting the carrot upward with each landing. Finally I can hold back no longer and buck wildly as the spasms consume me, leaving my body stiff and contorted for several seconds as the convulsions sweep through me. Before I am able to get my breathing somewhat under control, I hear several more grunts and groans followed by a long, "Aahhhhhhhhhhhhhhhhhhhh," as Beau also reaches his own climax. Satiated, I lie back, contemplating a small nap in the overstuffed and comfy chair.

"Don't get too comfortable, doll. It's one o'clock and you've only come twice," Beau croaks out unsteadily. "You've still got some work ahead of you if you're going to make the deadline by five."

"I'm exhausted, Beau. I don't know if I can keep up this kind of pace."

"Go freshen up. When you come back, I want you completely naked."

"And you call *me* insatiable. . . ." I mutter, as I trudge off in the direction of Mr. Miller's private bathroom.

* * *

I spend ten minutes revitalizing myself, then return to the room wearing only my birthday suit.

"Ok, now what would you like for me to do?"

"Miranda . . . ah, what a lovely sight you are. How is it that you manage to look more exquisite each time I see you?"

"A curse, I can assure you."

Laughing, Beau asks me to sift through the contents of his bottom file cabinet until I've found a vibrator and a long string of anal beads.

"Take them back to the chair with you . . . and grab the book on the way. I think it's time for more reading."

I settle myself back into the chair in much the same position as before, only this time my ankles are not restricted by the panties, and I can part my legs as wide as I like. They are still bent, and my feet are still resting on the edges of his desk, but I have since done away with the carrot, cucumber and clothespins.

"Before you start reading, I want you to insert those anal beads. There should be eight of them attached together on that string. That should be enough to keep you feeling pleasantly full."

Totally without inhibitions and reservations, I spread my legs wide and begin to press the anal beads into my ass as if it were the most natural thing in the world for me to be doing. Although I have cooled down a bit, I am still overstimulated and looking forward to giving Beau a show. Again my ass becomes a creature all its own and sucks in each and every last bead offered to it, pouting when they have all been eaten.

"God, Miranda. Your ass loves to be fucked just as much as your pussy does."

Sighing, I squirm down into the cushions, relishing the feeling as the beads shift and move around inside me. Finally settled, I begin to read another erotic story. Within a half of an hour, I am once again aroused and looking forward to another orgasm. This time Beau has me turn on the vibrator and use it only on my clit, not allowing it to penetrate me. I continue to read as sweat begins to bead up on my forehead from the constant vibrations coursing through my body at my clit. When I can no longer concentrate on the words I am reading, I cast the book aside and begin to remove the anal beads while the vibrator continues to happily buzz along my clit. As the last bead is removed, my body is thrown into its third orgasm of the day, this time visibly squirting liquid outward with each separate convulsion.

"Oh my God, Beau . . . that's never happened before . . . I've never . . . ejaculated before . . . I . . . I'm. . . . Oh, God . . ."

"Oh baby! I've never seen a woman do that before, either! What an incredible turn on! I'm never going to be able to let you go . . . "

Gasping, I try to relax back into the cushions, watching and feeling the goosebumps slowly recede, amazed that even my scalp came to life and tingled throughout that last orgasm. "Beau, I can't do this anymore. My body is worn out."

"Miranda, there's nothing that turns me on more than a challenge. It's going to be all the sweeter when you do cum for me again knowing that you thought you had reached your limit. I want to enter your mind and control your body, bending and shaping it, molding and manipulating it. I want it to react to me and for me . . . and then I want to do it all over again."

"Beau . . . "

By five o'clock, as promised, Beau manages to extract from me yet another orgasm, relying solely on his own verbal skills and my practiced hands. For two hours he speaks dirty to me, invoking raw and primal images, carrying me to places I had yet to discover, drawing from me even more of my darkest thoughts. I am utterly spent, but still he is not satisfied, and won't be until I've shared my fifth and final orgasm with him. Reluctantly, I stumble out to my own desk to call the house and inform Nick that I will have to work late this lovely Friday night.

"Hello."

"Hi, hon. I have some bad news. I'm going to have to work late tonight. Mr. Miller needs my help getting some deadlines met. I'm sorry."

"No problem, Randa. I'll probably just head down to the pub for a couple of drinks. If I'm not home when you get home, look for me there."

"Okay, great. I'll be ready to have a few myself. It's already been a really long day."

"Tell me all about it when you get here, okay? I love ya."

"I love you too. See you soon."

The fifth orgasm is by far the most elusive, but by 9:30 PM, Beau is whistling victoriously, and I am vowing to never again touch myself for self-gratification. I agree to return to work Monday morning only after he promises me that the activities of today will never again be repeated. Exhausted, I exit the building, immediately perking up as I discover the beauty of the night. It is warm, yet refreshing, the air very fragrant with nature's finest scents, reminding me of why I moved to the small mountain community in the first place. Revitalized, I continue my short trek home.

CHAPTER 6

EXPLOITATIONS

I am disappointed to learn that Nick is not at home when I get there, but that quickly dissipates as I read the rather intriguing note left behind. Typed in all capital letters, it simply reads: MEET ME AT THE BASE-BALL DIAMOND.

Now what is he up to, I wonder with a large grin, another game perhaps? That's one we hadn't discussed before. . . . the baseball player and the ???? I can't even imagine what my role is supposed to be. Hmmm, maybe I am supposed to be the baseball player and he the ????? Excitedly, I hurry and freshen up, changing into a comfy pair of jeans, a long-sleeved T-shirt and a pair of tennies. Then, racing out the door, I head in the direction of the baseball diamond.

The ball field is located just a short walk from my house, actually on the local high school's property. It is situated way toward the back of the school, beyond the track in a very dark and secluded section. During the daytime, the location seems innocent enough, but at night, without any lighting to humble it, it seems dark and foreboding. Nick must have known that I would get a charge out of meeting him in such a creepy place. Immediately, my sexually fatigued body begins to awaken in anticipation for the unknown delights that Nick has in store for me.

The baseball diamond appears to be deserted when I arrive. No sign of any activity at all making it seem even more sinister.

"Nick?" I whisper. "Are you here? Yoo hoo, Nick?"
Immediately, a hand comes from behind me to cover my mouth, and a soft, "shhhhh" is whispered into my ear. I overcome my momentary panic and elect to play along as Nick guides me to the chain-link fence backstop. The backstop is about ten feet high and shaped like half of a hexagon. He walks me over to the far right of the fence and pushes me up against it whispering another "shhhhh" as he removes his hand from my mouth. He keeps one hand pressed into the back of my head, not allowing me to turn my face to look at him.

"Nick? What are you doing?"

Again, all I hear is another, "shhhhhh" accompanied by a blindfold being placed over my eyes. I shudder, despite the warm night. Confident that I cannot see, Nick turns me around so that my back is pressed flat up against the backstop, the metal chain somewhat uncomfortable. The next thing I feel is something soft and silky being draped around my neck and through the chain of the fence. My God . . . he's tying me to the fence by my neck! I feel him move around to the backside of the fence to complete the process, making sure I can go nowhere without strangling myself.

One simple maneuver. One simple knot, yet the havoc that it is creating in my mind is boundless. Immobilized by one tiny silk scarf! Unbelievable. The pressure against my throat, enough to remind me it's there, but not enough to choke me, not unless I struggle. Even with my hands free, it would take hours to maneuver my fingers successfully to untie the knot fastening me to the fence. Next, Nick takes my right arm and draws it out to the side, slightly lower than my shoulder with the inside of my wrist positioned down and against the fence. Subconsciously, my fingers reach out and grip a section of the chain as I feel another scarf binding my wrist to it. Nick does the same with my left arm and wrist, tethering me to the backstop completely with three gentle scarves.

"Nick . . . what if somebody walks by? Or worse . . . uh, sorry, officer. We're just trying to spice up our sex life a bit."

For an answer, Nick presses his body flat against mine. I can hear his deeply impassioned breathing, smell the slight odor of alcohol with each puff of air expelled. And then the kiss. . . . oh, so completely consuming, rocking me to my toes. A kiss that says, "You belong to me . . . you are mine . . . I own you body and soul." A desperate kiss . . . a hungry kiss . . . His hands stroke my body as he continues his onslaught, his chest rubbing into and across mine. His mouth leaves my lips to gently nip at the skin on my face, my cheeks, my chin, and then down my throat. I begin to moan, knowing that it is Nick's intent to take me . . . right there, against the backstop. Granted, the probability of getting discovered isn't great, but it still exists.

"Nick . . . Nick . . ." I gasp out between delicious waves of pleasure, "We can't do this here. Somebody is bound to catch us."

Again, Nick says nothing, but the kissing and grinding stop. I wait nervously, breathlessly, wondering what his next move is going to be. Did he finally come to his senses and realize that this was too risky? No such luck, I come to find out, as I feel the cool edge of steel placed against my slightly parted lips. A knife?!? What the hell is he using a knife for? I begin to shake in panic, afraid to even speak lest the blade accidentally pierce my lip. Instead, I whimper and subconsciously press my body deeper into the chain-link fence.

The blade leaves my lips and begins a slow, tickling descent, down my chin, down my throat, grazing the silk scarf before it stops to tease the hollow of my neck. I try desperately to reason with my fear, to calm myself knowing that Nick would never hurt me. It's a game. He's trying to help me live out that "rape" fantasy . . . that has to be it, and he's just making it as realistic as possible. The fact that I'm still blindfolded proves it. If I could see him, make eye contact with him, none of these feelings would be the same. I'd automatically feel safe and secure no matter what device of torture he held in front of me.

---

*   *   *

I suck in my breath as the knife leaves my throat, and I feel his other hand tug at my shirt. Unable to keep my knees from shaking, I try to stand perfectly still as my shirt is untucked from my jeans. Then I hear a soft tearing sound as the blade is inserted through the bottom of my shirt and begins to slowly travel upward. Terror consumes me as the knife begins to split my shirt in half, the warm night air rushing in to meet my belly, yet even as I cringe, my body begins to respond sexually. It has been awakened on a whole different level, by far the darkest yet. This supercedes any bondage game that Nick and I have played in the past. This is for real, and it's scaring the hell out of me. But it's also the most powerful aphrodisiac to date, arousing me more quickly and to new heights than I ever thought possible. Every nerve ending is awakened, every sense intensified, every breath magnified, every shudder electric. My body is being held in such a state that it is precariously close to short circuiting. A sharp cry is emitted as the blade slices through the final shred of cloth at my collarbone, and then dips back down to cut away the tiny patch of satin holding my bra together.

"Oh, God ..." I groan as my breasts spring free, my knees collapsing, only momentarily as a painful tug reminds me that the scarf at my throat is not quite enough to hold my weight. Grasping the fence, I quickly call on the strength in my arms to help steady my shaking limbs. Mewling, I sigh in disguised rapture as I feel soft, wet, warm lips make contact with my already responsive nipple. The mouth stays there, suckling gently, licking, feasting, concentrating on nothing else. No hands accompany it . . . just a mouth, an endless cavern of bliss. Each time my nipple is sucked in more deeply, another pulse of pleasure beats violently in my throbbing clit. Before I am even aware that it is happening myself, my body jerks forcefully as another orgasm seizes control of my muscles and sends catastrophic waves of exhilaration throughout my being, from the top of my head to the tips of my toes.

Nick doesn't let it stop there, but changes nipples and begins to suck more vigorously while rubbing at my clit and pussy through my jeans. Not only does my orgasm *not* subside, but it continues to build, the spasms and pulses becoming greater and more intense, releasing, throbbing, building, then releasing again. Over and over I peak then crash, only to immediately peak again. Unable to contain myself, I begin to scream out, only to have the sound cut off as Nick entombs my mouth with his own, swallowing any evidence of my audible elation and imprisoning it within the pit of his belly. When the last wave of ecstasy finally recedes, Nick is forced to hold me upright, certain that I'll choke to death if left to my own devices.

Tiny kisses on the top of my head are the first sensations to greet me as I begin to recover. As more of my senses become functional again, I realize that I had just had the most mind-blowing orgasm of the century, multiple orgasms at that.

"Oh my God, Nick. That was too unbelievable for words."

*   *   *

My hips and ass begin to gyrate backward into the fence as I relive the incredible encounter I just went through. And even though I am completely satiated, I want more. My pussy is begging to be filled. All that stimulation, all that pleasure, yet none of it directly involved the heart of my womanhood.

"Oh, Nick . . . I need to feel you inside me, right now. Complete me, please."

Instead of feeling his fingers on the buttons of my jeans, I feel them working on removing my blindfold. I guess now that the initial game of fear is over, it is okay to see him as he takes me on the remainder of this monumental journey. I want it hot, I want it rough, I want it frenzied . . . and I want it now. Urgently. As soon as my blindfold is removed, I gaze into Nick's sky blue eyes . . . wait . . . oh God . . . Nick's eyes are brown . . .

My bloodcurdling scream is immediately stifled by Russ's large hand.

"Jesus Christ, Miranda. You don't need to scream. I haven't hurt you, and I don't intend to. Re-fucking-lax!"

I am speechless for several minutes as my mind absorbs the implications of what I've just discovered. Russ! It can't be . . . it couldn't have been . . . Oh God . . . it was . . . Russ? Russ is responsible for all that glorious bliss I just experienced? Russ? Evil, perverted, scary Russ? It's not possible, but here he is, standing in front of me as cocky and proud as always. The son of a bitch! In this moment, I can't decide if I'm more scared, or pissed. . . . or . . . horny. Oh God.

---

* * *

Russ removes his hand from my mouth hesitantly, prepared to slam it back over if another peep should escape. My mouth remains poised open in a witless "O," but silent. He watches the confused expressions cross my face with amusement, then ventures, "Still want me to fuck you, Mirandaaaahhhhhh?"

"What have you done with Nick?"

"Nick's fine. I took him out drinking. He's sleeping it off in the comfort of his very own bed. Promise . . ."

"How did you know?"

"How did I know what, sweetums? How did I know you were going to have to work late tonight? I can just imagine what you were doing, too. I bet your cunt is dripping with Mr. Miller's semen right now, isn't it? You stayed late so you could boff the boss . . ."

"I did no such thing!" I reply, indignantly. . . . then calm myself as I remember exactly why I did stay late. An embarrassed flush spreads accusingly across my face.

"Yeah, I thought so. Nick called and invited me out for drinks to pass the time. He played right into my hands. I think he wanted to talk to me about not sending you any more e-mails, but he got a little sidetracked. It was perfect timing, and so easy."

"What are you going to do with me?"

"Are you a little scared, Miranda? Of little ole me?"

"Russ, quit toying with me! You win, you've got me. I just want to know what you plan to do with me."

"Oh, listen to the martyr. Just five minutes ago you were begging me to fuck your brains out. I know what seethes below the surface, Miranda, and I know how to awaken it."

101

"Russ . . . "

"I'm prepared to let you go right now. But I bet . . . if you dig deep . . . you'll discover that you don't want me to let you go. You want to ride this out and see what happens, don't you? Admit it, Miranda. The thought of what awaits you in my dungeon excites you. Nobody else can make you feel like this, Miranda, not even Nick. I promise to deliver you unharmed to your husband first thing Monday morning, but for the weekend you'll be totally and completely at my mercy. What do you say, Miranda? Shall I continue with the complete ravishment of your body?"

Oh heaven help me. . . . the fact that I'm even considering it proves that I need psychological counseling. I say nothing as tears well up in my eyes and my body breaks out into a cold sweat.

"Miranda. . . . you're thinking about it, aren't you? You want this to happen so badly, yet you can't give your consent. I need a, 'yes,' baby. I've never taken a woman against her will, and I'm not going to start now. But I would love to rape you, with your permission, of course. Give it to me. . . . say, 'yes.' "

"Russ . . . you're insane. I can't say yes to this."

"Yes you can. You want to, I can feel it. It's easy. Just say yes. One little word."

Russ reaches a hand to my face and squishes my lips and cheeks inward, making my mouth pucker up like a blowfish.

"Yyyyyyyes," he says again, mouthing the word while squeezing my lips. "Yes, Russ. I'd like nothing more than for you to have your way with me all weekend. Do it Russ. Come on Miranda. It's right there on the tip of your tongue. Let me help get it for you."

Russ again captures my lips with his own, extracting from them my resistance, making me respond to his kiss, and not to Nick's. Grabbing my tongue between his teeth, he begins to suck on it, pulling it into his own mouth, teasing it with his own tongue. He continues to toy with it, plundering my mouth, his tongue slithering down my throat, drawing the breath from my lungs, then moving deeper. I feel him in my gut, twisting lower, not satisfied until he tugs at my sex from the inside, gripping it, squeezing it, making it burn from a hunger left too long unfed. Gasping in resignation, I finally utter the word he wants to hear.

"Mmmonkey."

Releasing my lips, he gazes back at me. "Monkey? Close, but not quite." He continues to grin maliciously, knowing full well the word I had so painfully spoken.

"I said . . . okay. Okay, Okay, Okay!"

"My, my, my. Now we're a little over anxious, aren't we? Okay, what, baby doll?"

"Damn it, Russ! Don't mess with me . . . I'll take it back . . ."

Russ begins to stroke his finger lightly up and down my throat as if placating an angry kitten.

"Shhhhh . . . okay, what, baby doll?"

Ohhhhh . . . SEX . . . is absolutely dripping from his voice. What am I doing?

*   *   *

"O. . . . kay . . . I'll go with you for the weekend," I stammer out, feeling suddenly drugged.

"Nooooo. . . . I want to hear, 'Okay, Russ . . . yes, Russ . . . I want you to rape me. . . . I want you to use my body . . . I want you to take me to the depths of hell and then to the pinnacle of pleasure, all in the same moment. Yes, Russ.' "

"Yes . . . Russ . . ." I gasp . . .

"I give you permission . . . "

"I give you permission . . . " Oh, God . . . I can't believe I'm saying this . . .

"To use and abuse my body. . . ."

"To use and abuse my body. . . ." Whimpering. . . .

"I want you to rape me. . . ."

"Uhhhhhh . . . rape . . . me . . . "

Russ growls and in a matter of moments, he's possessed. Something gets shoved inside my mouth . . . another scarf, maybe . . . and then another is placed over my mouth and tied around my head and through the chain-link of the backstop, holding my head as still as my neck. With this aggressive turn of events, my natural instinct to fight takes over, and I begin to kick out at Russ, my legs being my only body part left free. He curses and shoves his knee into my crotch, then throws his entire body weight against me. Then he whispers dangerously into my ear, "God damn it, Miranda. I'm going to have you one way or the other. If you want there to be bruises, then keep fighting me. And . . . don't forget. . . . about my little friend here, Mr. Switchblade."

My eyes widen in surprise and terror as I come face to face with the knife I had felt earlier. It is ten times more menacing than anything my mind had envisioned, and I immediately cease my struggles.

"That's better."

He closes the switchblade and then places it in his shirt pocket. Pressed nose to nose, he begins to fumble with the buttons on my jeans.

"You smell like sex, Miranda. It's seeping from your pores."

Don't panic, don't panic, don't panic. He's not going to hurt me. I asked him to do this. Oh, God. . . . I'm even getting wet. Soaked. I'm soaked, I can feel the fluids gushing from my center. Oh, God, hurry. Get it over with. Please.

Soon he has my jeans unbuttoned and begins to yank them downward, taking my panties with them. Stopping at mid-thigh, his hand immediately reaches for my exposed pussy and grasps at it roughly. He never takes his eyes from mine, thriving on my reactions, my eyes revealing every thought, every feeling. He begins to work his fingers inside . . . two of them? Three? Oh. . . . could it be four? I feel them curl and then pull back out again, removing with them large amounts of my intimate juices. He brings his hand to his nose and takes a big sniff . . . closing his eyes in delight as he does so.

"Hmmmm . . . maybe you weren't fucking Mr. Miller after all. There's nothing here but sweet Miranda. Smell for yourself."

* * *

105

He shoves his fingers into my nose, and then begins to rub them all around it, leaving me with a permanent reminder of how hot and wanton I truly smell. The remainder of my flavor is sucked off of his sticky fingers as he eagerly inserts them into his greedy mouth.

"Oh yeah, oh yeah, oh . . . yeah. . . . ," Russ mutters between noisy slurps. "Time to lose the jeans."

Pushing himself off of me, he bends down and busies himself with the task of removing my shoes and then my jeans and panties. I assist him in every way possible, concerned that he may get frustrated and bring Mr. Switchblade back into the picture to cut them away . . . and then some. All goes smoothly enough, and I breathe a sigh of relief. A short-lived sigh, however, as my legs are immediately pulled out from under me to be cradled in the crooks of his arms. Then without any warning, I am skewered, impaled on his rock-hard cock to the hilt. If I could scream, I would, the shock so overwhelming. But not from pain. . . . Oh help me, but it's deliriously wonderful. Exceptional. Savagely, he thrusts into me, pulling my body away from the backstop, just far enough for me to feel the tug at my throat, and then slamming me back into it. Over and over he continues with the vicious assault, my body gladly taking it and then asking for more. Time stands still. Nothing exists but his cock relentlessly plunging into the depths of my sex . . . ruthless . . . sadistic. My body knows none of this, basking instead in the frenzied excitement, welcoming each brutal thrust with open arms. Finally he collapses against me in a fit of convulsions. . . . the first in a series of how many?

* * *

Stepping back, Russ studies me silently as he regains his balance.

"You liked that, didn't you? Miranda, you're a woman after my own heart. I'll bet you can keep up with me, kinky stroke for kinky stroke. I guess I'll find out this weekend, won't I?"

Unable to answer, I continue to stare at him, shivers returning. He stoops down to pull up his own jeans, which have managed to worm their way down to his ankles during the physical onslaught. Now that my initial encounter with Russ is over, I can release some of the fear I had been harboring over the last several months. All those threatening poems had been sending my imagination into overdrive. I'm not sure what I had expected would happen if Russ ever did manage to follow through with his plans, but intensely thrilling, wild sex was not one of them. Am I actually looking forward to being taken to his torture chamber?

I examine Russ more closely as he gathers up my things . . . my shoes, my jeans, and then begins to walk away into the trees behind the backstop. A momentary panic envelops me as I imagine him leaving me here this way, but the feeling soon passes. I gave him a weekend. He wouldn't pass that up, would he? Well, I could be in worse positions. At least I now know that Russ isn't going to hurt me. That's a huge relief. And, well, if you're going to be used and abused by someone for a weekend, it might as well be someone like Russ. Anyone that asks for your permission before he rapes you has to have some shred of a conscience, and . . . well, as much as I hate to admit it, he is definitely easy to look at. The contrast between those sky blue eyes and that jet black hair is pretty spectacular. He also has the physique of a body builder, only taller, and has managed to maintain his neck in the process. I attempt to shake my head in exasperation at the insanity of my thoughts, but the scarves still bind me tightly.

"What is going on in that pretty head of yours? Your eyes are going a hundred miles an hour. Were you worried there for a minute that I was going to leave you?" Russ taunts.

Asshole. My eyes narrow into slits. Russ walks back over to me, close enough that I can feel his body heat, smell his breath. He reaches into his shirt pocket with an evil smile on his face and withdraws the switchblade, holding it directly in front of my eyes. The blade pops up without warning, startling me to the point of tears, my heart plummeting to my stomach for immediate digestion. I close my eyes, a feeble attempt at reducing the menacing threat that the blade signifies. Russ only chuckles, and moves to the back side of the fence, cutting through the delicate silk ties imprisoning my face and neck. Russ removes the scarves and tucks them into his pants pocket while returning to the front to check on his progress. As soon as I am able, I spit out the wad in my mouth, hitting him square in the chest.

"An act of defiance, Miranda? Good. It'll make it all the more fun when I break you."

Another malicious grin. I look down in time to see the knife being slowly slipped between the back of my right wrist and the silk scarf securing it there. Russ makes a dramatic display, keeping me on edge far longer than is necessary, then boldly slices through it. Ah, at last my arm is free. I immediately pull it away and begin to shake it. Before Russ frees my other arm, however, my right wrist is greeted with the cold, clinking metal of a handcuff.

"I'm not going to make this too easy on you. I don't want you getting away."

"I promised to go with you, Russ, and I will. You don't need to handcuff me."

"Maybe not, but let's pretend I do . . . "

Rolling my eyes, I stand stoically by while Russ cuts the other arm away from the fence and then pulls both arms behind my back and cuffs them together. Russ then grabs the tops of my legs and lifts me up and over his shoulder, forcing all the air from my lungs. He quickly starts walking back into the trees and dumps me into the back seat of his awaiting Jeep. The vinyl is chilling as it makes contact with my bare ass, reminding me of how naked I am. Although I have what's left of my shirt still on, it is sliced clean up the front with my bra pushed around and to the back, and nothing below my waist except for my little white ankle socks. The ride to Russ's house is brutal, unable to ascertain which emotion is more prevalent . . . dread . . . or anticipation.

"Welcome to the dungeon, my little house of horrors, where you will be spending the remainder of the week-end."

*   *   *

I wander in with trepidation, gulping at sights I had only previously seen in pictures, and some I had never seen, or even heard of before. The room is square with mirrors covering all four walls from floor to ceiling. Half of the room looks clinical; white, tile, ceramic, tables, counters . . . and a huge floor drain right in the middle. The other half of the room is dark and wooden . . . wooden padded benches and a huge, free-standing wooden wheel that looks like something right out of a giant gerbil's cage. I glance around warily to assure myself that no oversized rodent lurked nearby. There are several ladders, most suspended from the ceiling, ropes, pulleys, and a wooden and glass display case flaunting an extensive array of whips and paddles.

Russ leads me around, gently guiding me by the elbow, as if giving a grand tour to the Queen of England herself. First he explains the devices and some of their uses found in the white section of the room. There is a counter similar to what you would see in a doctor's office, with a built-in sink and a carton of disposable rubber gloves sitting off to the side. Above the counter is a cabinet with glass doors, making the contents inside quite visible. There are several jars containing a wide variety of herbs, as well as creams, lotions and lubricants. Stupefied, I continue with the tour.

In the far back corner is the shower/bath area. The huge jacuzzi tub sits innocently enough against the far left mirrored wall. Facing the adjacent mirrored wall is what Russ refers to as his seesaw ladder. It looks just like a seesaw only shorter, wider, and in the shape of a ladder with rungs only located on the top third section.

All the rungs and sides of the ladder are made from white padded vinyl, and at the very top, closest to the mirrored wall, is a headrest like you'd find on a massage table. Russ is able to stabilize the seesawing action by a lever, permitting the ladder to be secured at any angle. The ladder is also built on a hydraulic base and can be raised and lowered to any height that Russ desires.

The next piece of furniture that Russ discusses at length is a white table with rounded edges and sides standing a little higher than waist high. On top of the table is a white stockade, with a hole cut out for the head, and two smaller holes for the wrists. It doesn't raise up very high off the table, and Russ explains that the women are usually kneeling on the table while enjoying the stockade, facing outward toward the "wooden" half of the room, her bottom facing the jacuzzi tub.

Directly across from the seesaw ladder, is nothing other than a doctor's table, complete with stirrups. The back of the table adjusts so that you can either be lying flat on it, or sitting up completely straight. I imagine this position would be somewhat uncomfortable if your feet were in the stirrups at the same time . . . shudder.

Next Russ takes me over into the wooden half of the room, allowing only some of my curiosities about the huge wheel to be appeased. Russ has me step inside it as I make my inspection. There is enough room inside for someone at least six and a half feet tall to stand upright. The depth of the wheel is probably only two feet deep, with four inch wide wooden slats spaced a half an inch apart running all along the inside of the wheel. The interior is very sturdy, quite capable of holding my weight several times over. I ask Russ what the wheel is used for, but he just grins and tells me that I'll find out soon enough.

There are also a few spanking benches scattered throughout the room, a swing similar to my virtual reality swing, only not . . . a thick beam off to the side running from ceiling to floor with a narrow metal bar protruding from it about twelve inches, and another wooden stockade, only this one taller and standing on the floor. The last thing he shows me is the bondage bed, which is pretty much a glorified air mattress, all in black, with extra reinforcements to house the clips, clamps and eyelets running along all four sides.

Russ looks over at me again as if trying to decide where to start. Unwittingly, I make his decision for him.

"Russ. I need to use the bathroom."
    "Certainly. But let's get you out of these rags, first."

Thinking this isn't going to be so bad, I relax as Russ undoes the handcuffs and then removes the rest of my clothing, socks included. When I am completely naked, Russ replaces the handcuffs and whistles appreciatively.

"Ah, yes, that's the body I remember so well from the poker game."

Why did he have to mention the poker game? I watch his features closely, wondering if those memories are going to make him angry, but they don't appear to. Relieved, I follow Russ back on over into the white room. He has me stand on the drain and then moves to get his rolling white stool and sits down watching me.

"What are you doing?"

"You said you needed to use the bathroom. There it is."

"This drain?" I ask incredulous. "You want me to relieve myself in this drain?"

"Yup." He says, with a nasty smile.

"While you watch?"

"Yup again. You don't mind, do you?" He asks as innocently as possible.

"Of course I mind, Russ. I can't go with you watching me."

"Well, you'd better get used to it, because what you see is what you get. I doubt you can hold it all weekend. Besides, this is just a mild humiliation. I've got more in store for you."

A cold feeling of trepidation begins seep through me. I had forgotten what this was all about. This isn't a game, and it's certainly not going to be played by my rules. I gave myself to Russ . . . to use, to abuse . . . to even rape. What the hell was I thinking? And this is Russ we are talking about. He is by far the most sexually deviant person I've even known, myself included.

"What if I change my mind? What if I no longer want to spend the weekend with you. You said you've never forced a woman before and never would."

* * *

113

Russ looks me over thoughtfully. "You've obviously already forgotten the excitement of the backstop, haven't you? I can turn your insides to mush with just a look, Miranda. You won't change your mind. You can't change your mind. You need this. Look at me."

I glance up and immediately get ensnared by the intensity of his eyes. They are hypnotic, and I am helpless to deny them.

"Now piss."

I remain frozen, rooted to the spot, unable to respond. Russ bends over and takes off his shoes and socks, then stands up and begins to remove the rest of his clothing. His captive gaze never wavers from mine as his shirt disappears, and then his pants. Within moments, he is standing as naked as I, challenging me to disobey him.

"Piss."

Still, I cannot move, my brain ceasing to function. This is the first time I have seen Russ completely without clothing, and he's quite the specimen. Perfect symmetry, a sculpture come to life. Even as he stalks purposefully toward me, I am unable to flee or even look away. He presses his naked body into mine and pulls my head backward by my hair.

"I said piss, Miranda. We're going to stay like this until you do."

Russ then lowers his head and begins to kiss me. Oh, God . . . how can he kiss like this? Sweet, tender, yearning, begging, pleading, coaxing . . . magical. His kisses are magical, and he knows it and uses them to manipulate. Right now he could be threatening me with a beating, forcing me with brute strength, yet his strategy is to softly but slowly wear me down, kissing away any shred of resistance. It worked at the ball field, and it's working now.

I feel his other hand dip down to nestle between my legs, gently fondling the folds of my pussy. He pulls his mouth away from mine occasionally to whisper words of encouragement, then immediately returns it to the task of seducing my heated lips.

"Come on baby . . . Piss on my hand . . . Just let it go. . . . Let yourself go . . ."

I whimper, torn between saving my modesty and succumbing to his wishes. I feel a long, strong finger enter me, and I swoon at the welcome invasion. Russ slowly and leisurely explores my volcanic interior, while his thumb absently rubs at my clit.

"Piss for me baby. I'm going to find your G-spot in a second, and then you won't be able to stop yourself."

Why do these words suddenly sound sexy to me? Is it the heated way in which he is mumbling them, against my mouth, my nose and my chin as he kisses me? And why do I have this unexpected urge to please him? It would be so easy . . . just to let go . . . and fill his waiting palm. Just as my decision is reached, Russ's knowing finger finds and puts pressure against my G-spot, massaging it slowly yet persistently. His thumb continues to work on my clit, the dual assault more than I can handle. In an instant, he has me convulsing in orgasm as I simultaneously release myself into his hand. Damn him, damn him, damn him! I feel his mouth stretch into a smile as he finally pulls away and breaks the compelling and persuasive kiss.

"That wasn't so bad, was it?" he asks, as he moves to grasp the retractable faucet built into the pedestal of the gyno table. Turning on the water, he rinses off his hand and then directs the spray toward the drain, washing away any evidence of my recent disgrace.

"Before this night is over, toots, I'm going to become very intimate with each and every one of your bodily functions. Now, you've got ten seconds to get that sweet ass of yours up onto that gyno table."

Wrought with apprehension, I jump up onto the table and face him. He adjusts his stool height so that he is pretty much eye level with my navel. Then he adjusts the back of the padded table so that it is resting at an approximate 45-degree angle. Next, one cuff is removed as I am gently coaxed backwards until reclining comfortably against it. Never would I have assumed that a torture chamber could be so cozy, and its master so gentle. Before long I feel my arms being pulled back and around the edges of the angled table to be once again cuffed behind it.

"Feet in the stirrups, baby."

* * *

Cringing, I resist. I don't want to be that open and vulnerable to anyone, let alone Russ. Shaking his head in mock disappointment, Russ pulls my legs up one at a time and places each foot into a stirrup, securing them there with vinyl straps. Testing them, I attempt to remove my feet, but they remain firmly locked in place. Unable to bear witness to this newest form of humiliation, I squeeze my eyes shut and refuse to even glance at Russ.

Russ, on the other hand, is unconcerned and walks on over toward the sink area, washing his hands thoroughly. I hear him digging through the cupboard above, and then whistle while preparing the next surprise he has in store for me. I risk a quick peek in his direction, my curiosity always getting the best of me, but am thwarted from seeing anything other than his broad back and shoulders. Again, I find my imagination my own worst enemy as I try to conceive what form of torture he's certain to use on my very exposed and very defenseless pussy.

Russ returns gently shaking a very familiar looking pink bag.

"I'm going to clean you up, inside and out, before I get you all messy again," he declares with a smile.

"What did you mix inside?" I ask, accepting my fate passively.

Grinning, he reveals, "Ah, only my most potent and special herbs. I'm going to make sure that I awaken your pretty pussy and that she's going to want to play all night long."

"I can't believe this! You're drugging me?"

"Drugging is such a harsh term, Miranda. It's more like I'm applying a topical . . . itch. An itch that's impossible to scratch, although we'll have fun trying."

"Russ, don't, please. I'm cooperating, just like I said I would."

"Forgive me if your submissive martyrdom isn't exactly what I was hoping for. This is guaranteed to unleash the wild beast I know you hide within. Here kitty, kitty. Come out and play. . . ."

Russ reaches up and yanks on a pulley, hanging the douche bag to it, then releasing it back upward. Then he sets the end of the hose and nozzle to rest in the crease of my leg.

"Hmmmm . . . let's see. You look too plain. We need to fancy you up a bit."

He leaves me momentarily, only to return with a stunning white rhinestone collar and two nipple clamps. The clamps have a pearl necklace draped between them, and a heavy looking crystal hanging down from each one. Russ cinches the collar around my neck without any fuss, but as soon as he approaches a nipple with a clamp, I begin to struggle and squirm.

"Russ . . . Russ . . . please . . . I've never worn that type of clamp before, and never with any weight to them. Do you have a different pair?"

Russ looks up in amazement. "Miranda, when are you going to learn that you are not running this show? These are the clamps you will wear, and by Sunday night, you'll have three crystals dangling from each, instead of only one."

I hold my breath, waiting for the excruciating pinch, only to feel his soft lips begin to gently suckle at my nipple. I sigh in relief and yield to the pleasant sensations as Russ begins to increase the sucking pressure. Soon I am moaning and yelping as the gentle suction has turned to pulling and biting, working my nipple and preparing it for the clamp. I screech as his mouth is removed and the clamp takes its place, trapping all of that blood into my distended nipple. Immediately, a surge of moisture floods my gaping pussy. Russ does the same with my other nipple and then takes his place between my outspread thighs. I rock my head back and forth moaning, alternating between hating the feel of those clamps and loving it.

Russ quickly gets my attention diverted back to him as I feel the stirrups slowly clicking their way outward. Horrified, I find my thighs, knees, calves and ankles widening with each clicking sound until they are held at an obscenely uncomfortable distance apart. Russ is gleeful as he lowers his head into my widely displayed crotch and begins to lick.

"My, my. You've already made quite the mess down here, haven't you? Are you enjoying this? Do you love being my little captive, at the mercy of my every whim?"

I only whimper in response, confused between the mortification I feel and the delicious sensations shooting through my nipples and now . . . my throbbing clit. Russ makes an exaggerated sniffing sound then buries his nose into my opening.

"Mirandaaaa. . . . I can still smell my fuck in you . . . "

I cry out . . . my shame increasing with each passing moment. Russ lifts his face from my crotch and takes the end of the hose, still nestled in the crook of my leg. Grinning lewdly, he slowly begins to insert the nozzle, while my traitorous hips instinctually rock forward to greet it. Then he releases the clamp, and I begin to feel the warm liquid penetrate and coat me. Russ moves the nozzle all around, making sure the herbs make contact with every inch of my satiny interior. Before too long, the bag is half empty and liquid begins to dribble out and down the table.

The herbs are already taking affect as I feel my insides pulsing with need. With each passing minute, the twitching increases, and my clit answers back with its own desperate throbbing. Russ empties the bag and then removes the nozzle, allowing the remainder of the douche to dribble out at will.

"Russ . . . oh God . . . Oh God, Russ. . . ."

"Ah, starting to feel it, aren't you? And it's going to get much, much worse before it gets better, hon."

"Fuck me . . . " I whisper, barely audible.

"Excuse me? I missed that, Miranda. Say it again."

Gritting my teeth, I force out, "I said. . . . Fuck me!"

"Hmmmm, you're not asking very nicely at all. Where are your manners?"

"God damn it, Russ . . . you know . . . what . . . this is. . . . doing to me. Please. . . . please help me."

"Oh . . . is Miranda uncomfortable? This is how my dick and my balls have ached for you every day since the poker game. I've felt this torture for nine months. Feel lucky you'll only feel it for two days."

"Russ . . . please, Russ. I'm sorry . . . it was . . . Nick . . . Nick's idea . . . in the first place. I . . . didn't know . . . you . . . didn't know . . . how. . . . it would . . . affect you. Ssssorry. . . . so sorry, Russ."

The herbs are setting me on fire, so intense I can barely breathe. I want to be fucked. I want to be fucked and fucked and fucked. Russ stands, wanting to punish me by only watching as my desire mounts, yet unable to deny himself the erotic delights on display as I continue to squirm and beg. Soon he gives into his own impulses and drives his imposing erection deep into the fury of my heat. Gripping my thighs for balance, he begins to plunge into me. With each punishing thrust, more water and herbs are pumped from me, the herbs certain to affect his libido as well. As if possessed, I begin to urge him on.

"Oh yeah . . . oh yeah . . . oh yeah. . . . Fuck me, Russ. Yes . . . deeper . . . oh God yes . . . harder . . . come on . . . fuck me harder. . . . Ohhhhhhhh. . . . yeah . . . yeah . . . fuck my brains out Russ . . . faster . . . Eeeeeaaaaaaaa . . . yes, Yes . . . YES . . . Ahhhhhhhh . . . "

Russ is unrelenting, perfectly happy and able to keep up with my demands. After twenty minutes of exhaustive stroking, Russ finally explodes into my depths, so powerfully that I gurgle, feeling as if his seed were gushing through me and out via my throat.

———

"No . . . no . . . no. . . . more . . . more . . . more . . . keep going. . . . please . . ."

Laughing, Russ explains, "All in good time, sweetie. Now we have to clean you out all over again."

Instead of refilling the douche bag, Russ reaches down to the base of the table next to where the retractable faucet is located. This time he brings up a retractable hose and nozzle, screwed directly into the plumbing. As he turns on the hot and cold water, a steady stream begins to flow from the nozzle. Once Russ is satisfied with the temperature and pressure, he inserts it and allows it to continuously clean and titillate me. I am in bliss as the gently pulsing waves repeatedly caress my ravaged interior.

"Okay, sweetie. I think we've outdone ourselves here. Let's move on. I'm getting antsy and those herbs have my cock twitching impatiently. I'm ready for the main event, now."

Oh God . . . main event? Russ removes the nozzle and turns off the water, slowly clicking the stirrups back to their original position. Then he releases the straps holding my feet and gets up to undo the handcuffs. Thankful for the momentary reprieve, I begin to move and stretch, getting the blood flowing back to all of my extremities. Russ helps me down from the table, and while doing so, playfully pinches my tightly clamped nipples. I gasp in surprise at their sensitivity, the ache rivaling a similar ache still building between my legs.

He leads me over to the table housing the stockade, but doesn't have me get up on it. Instead, he presses me up against it so that the edge creases my waist and then bends me over forward until my torso is lying flat on the table. My nipples are painfully pressed into the hard surface while the crystals dig themselves a cozy home in the underbelly of my soft breasts. Russ pulls my arms out well above my head and then flips up a set of wide, vinyl cuffs previously concealed beneath the table top. Once the cuffs are snapped into place, he opens them and locks my wrists inside, pinning me to the table. Another set of cuffs are flipped up and locked down, these to hold my biceps immobile. Lastly, my legs are pried apart and separated, the ankle of each strapped to a different leg of the table.

Russ begins to lovingly massage the cheeks of my ass, sighing as he grips and squeezes the fleshy mounds.

"Ah, at last. Do you remember the day of the poker game, Miranda . . . what I said to you when I first arrived at your house and saw you in that skimpy outfit? Do you remember what I said about your ass?"

"Mmmmhhhh, you said you were going to *have* it someday . . ."

"Someday is here, Miranda. This ass is now mine, and it will be mine for forty-eight more hours. I am going to use it over and over and over again."

"Oh, Russ . . . "

His erotic promise is too much . . . too much to handle in connection with the increasing inferno building in my pussy. My hips begin to gyrate and rub against the edge of the table, my frustration mounting when I realize that my clit will be left without stimulation. As hard as I try, I cannot get the edge of the table to rub anywhere near my throbbing button. Russ alternates between kissing and biting my ass, his lips and teeth touching every inch of my exposed bottom. Then he stands and moves away.

"I'll be right back."

Whimpering, I am abandoned, left to squirm helplessly on the cool, flat surface of the stark white table. I hear Russ moving about the sink area, much the same as before, the water running, rattling the bottles of herbs. Slowly but surely, my drug induced brain begins to figure out what's in store, as the sloshing sound from the douche bag once again reaches my ears.

"NO, Russ! Oh my God, NO! You can't do that, you just can't!"
   "Can't do what, darlin?"
   I begin to cry as I utter another feeble, "No . . . you just can't. . . ."
   "Poor, poor Miranda. You'll get used to it, I promise you. You may even grow . . . to like it."

Russ adjusts the stool height behind me so that his chest is level with my ass. Then he hangs the freshly mixed douche bag up on another pulley beside the table and sits down.
   Still unable to believe what he is about to do, I try to plead with him, but am unable to form a complete sentence.

"Russ . . . Russ . . . wait . . . you   can't. . . . why?. . . . how?. . . . Oh God, don't, please."

* * *

In response, I feel a slender nozzle begin to worm its way into my ass. NOOOOO!

It slips in smoothly and then widens, and then my ass closes tightly around it, securing it in place. Within seconds I feel the slow trickle of warm water begin to enter my bowels, terrifying me.

"What's the matter, Miranda? Hasn't Nick given you an enema before? No? I'm going to have to have a talk with that boy. He doesn't know what he's missing."

"Ruuuuuussss . . . you're . . . sick."

"Thank you, but trying to sweet-talk me isn't going to get you out of this. I've been fantasizing about this moment for months, and I'm going to make it last. I've got the hose clamped down to the slowest trickle. It's probably going to take a good fifteen minutes to get this bag emptied into your gut. Hope you're comfortable. Now, what can I do to pass the time?"

Panicking, I hear Russ behind me, lowering his stool until I feel his tongue snake out and strike my clit, jolting me as if electrocuted.

"No reason why we can't make your first enema experience a pleasant one. Think I can get you off before the bag is empty?"

Racing to beat his own challenge, Russ begins to noisily slurp and lick at my pussy. His tongue is masterful, experienced, and despite the degradation being done to my ass, I begin to respond eagerly. My clit plumps up to the point of bursting, my hips bucking out and upward, inadvertently thrusting the enema nozzle slightly deeper. I begin to feel the familiar sensations creeping upward from my toes and the intense swirling in the pit of my stomach. Unable to hold back any longer, I cry out my release and attempt to quell the shudders rippling throughout my body, petrified that my convulsions will somehow expel the plug wedged tightly in my ass. Russ continues to lick and slurp up all the nectar my body has to offer, then stands to check on the progress of the bag.

"Almost done, sweetheart. Just a couple more minutes to go."

Panting in between breaths, I attempt to communicate with Russ.

"I. . . . feel. . . . full. . . . cramps . . . I   feel . . . cramping . . . "

Russ strokes my back while trying to reassure me.

"Shhhh, just relax. That's normal. It will pass more quickly if you relax. We're almost done now."

When Russ announces that the bag is finally empty, I feel about to explode. Mortified over how I'm going to be forced to eject the contents of my intestines, I begin to shake as Russ slowly removes the nozzle. Moving quickly to the side, he hollers, "Let it fly, baby!"

Fate is cruel and takes this moment to slow down the hands of time. Each second of this most degrading act. . . . the worst I've ever had to live through. . . . freezes, and then stretches into a minute, an hour . . . a day. The delay is interminable, my suffering, my humiliation extended so that I can remember and relive each and every moment with startling clarity. Thoughts of how I will ever survive this are interrupted by a warm spray of water coating my entire backside and legs. Realizing that my gut feels empty and the purge is over, I wait, trying to make myself as small as possible, wondering at Russ's reaction.

I have no reason to feel disgraced. Russ is jubilant. I couldn't have given him a better gift. Unable to conceive where this desire stems from, I just accept it as fact and pray to move on. Once Russ has everything cleaned back up again, he comes over to press a delighted kiss on the tip of my nose.

"Thank you for that indisputable display of surrender. Not like you had any choice.... but ... "

Thinking the worst to be over, I ask Russ to unlatch me. Russ informs me, however, that I will be receiving two more enemas before I'll be released from the table, another cleansing enema, and then the final one containing milk and the ominous aphrodisiac herbs. Oh God ... with the heat from those herbs still increasing in my pussy, how ever will I handle the same fire burning out of control in my ass?

I survive the second enema with a tad more dignity than the first, and am beginning to appreciate just how uplifting a cleaned out colon can feel. Not that I would like to repeat the procedure in such a humiliating way, but under the right circumstances, in the privacy of my own home, this treatment may prove to be quite beneficial. I wonder what Nick would think if I sprung that one on him? Jesus! Were Russ's perversions rubbing off onto me so quickly?

"Okay, honey. Your reward for being such a good girl. Here's the fun one. A nice, soothing milk enema laced with an itch. You're ass isn't going to know what hit it."

I am already envisioning myself fucking the wide end of a baseball bat just from the fury still unleashed in my pussy . . . what will happen once my ass has the same cravings? God help me. I begin to feel the warm milk flow into me, and with it an immediate heat. Soon the walls of my rear passage are twitching expectantly, waiting for a stimulation that will bring sweet relief. Russ plays with the nozzle a bit, pulling it completely out so that the milk and herb mixture will spill out, and therefore affect, my anus, then plunges it back to wreak havoc inside.

My hips thrust out as far as my bound body will allow, wanting to take on whatever is offered. Even the milk slowly filling my bottom becomes an object of relief, the sloshing providing tangible pleasure. Soon I am again begging Russ to ease the ache and take me, my wanton juices slowly dripping from my pussy to land in a puddle on the floor. Russ needs no further encouragement, the stimulation from the herbs still affecting his cock, as well as the display of my complete surrender. Russ moves in behind me and extra slowly begins to guide his cock into my searing pussy.

Knowing that he is far from having another orgasm, Russ develops a leisurely rhythm, with long, slow strokes. The effect is devastating, my entire body quivering in response. The milk, still slowly being pumped into my ass, caresses Russ's cock through the thin barrier separating my two passages. Russ is in heaven, holding my hips as he savors each stroke. I am in heaven, being used over and over and over again, as nothing other than a sex object.

When the enema bag is finally empty, Russ hesitates before removing the nozzle from my ass, contemplating his options.

"I think I'll stay just like this, slowly fucking you while I take out the nozzle. I know you're all cleaned out. There's nothing left in there but milk and herbs. Sounds like a perfect spa treatment."

"No, Russ, no. Haven't you humiliated me enough?"
    "Come on, don't fret. And once all the milk is out, as a reward, I'm going to shove my nice, thick cock into your delectable ass and fuck it for an hour. Won't that feel good, baby?"

Suddenly I am very impatient to expel the milk and herbs, the thought of Russ taking me as promised in his threats . . . disconcertingly appealing.
    "Yes . . . yes it will. Pull the plug, Russ. . . ."

Certain that there is no liquid left remaining in my gut, an elated Russ removes his prick from my pussy and begins to slowly work it into my ass. It slips in easily enough without additional lubrication, the interior walls of my bottom still coated with a light film of the mineral oil used in the previous two enemas. Russ and I moan simultaneously.

"Ooohhhhh God, Russ. . . . fuck it. . . . scratch that itch. . . . stretch me. . . . punish me . . ."
"Ooohhhhh God, Miranda. . . . finally, your ass is mine . . . sweeter than the sweetest of my dreams. . . . No, Miranda. . . . I'm taking my time . . . I'm going to enjoy your ass thoroughly . . . and slowly . . ."
"No . . . " I moan out softly, "It'll kill me . . ."

But it doesn't kill me. Russ enjoys my ass with long, slow strokes, and is true to his word. For over an hour, he determinedly sodomizes me with excruciatingly tantalizing plunges. Unable to do anything but receive, I quickly transform into a blubbering pile of Jell-o, one moment begging him to stop, the next begging him to go deeper, the next. . . . completely incoherent and unable to do anything but moan. Russ uses one hand to stimulate my clit during his relentless plundering of my bottom, bringing me to yet another orgasm. Through the haze, I try to recall how many times I've climaxed within the last twenty-four hours, but am unable to come up with a number. Just as Russ releases another surge of semen, this time into my rectum, I succumb to the darkness and mercifully pass out.

I awaken in a daze, staring up into an unfamiliar ceiling. What the . . . ? Where the hell am I? As I ask myself these questions, I attempt to roll over but find I am pinned down. Suddenly the events of last night come rushing back as I happen to focus on the giant wooden wheel. Russ.

* * *

"Morning buttercup. I trust you slept well."

Oh God. I turn my head in his direction. He is smiling cheerfully, carrying a plate of delicious smelling breakfast.

"Hungry? Wouldn't want my beautiful captive to starve. You're going to need all of your energy and then some."

"What happened?"

"Last night?" Russ begins, as he takes a seat beside me. "Well. . . ." he goes on to explain through large bites of eggs and hash browns, "You passed out. Just as I blew my wad into your tight little ass. Out like a light. Kind of rude, if you ask me. Now, if I were a mean person, I would have revived you just so you could suffer through a sleepless night. . . . those herbs still going strong. I would have tied you down to this bondage bed wide awake, and then left you to moan and squirm and want. But, I decided that I'd rather have you fully rested so that you could keep up with me today. There'll be plenty of time to let you suffer later."

"Oh how chivalrous."

"Yeah, you'll be on your hands and knees later . . . kissing my feet . . . and eating those words, baby. Go ahead. Be a smart ass while you can."

I watch in amazement as Russ woofs down the last of his food.

"Hey! I thought you were going to feed me some. You just ate it all!"

"Yours is upstairs, honey, keeping warm. You've got

a few things to do first before you can eat."

Oh, no ... here we go again. "Like what?" I ask, somewhat resigned.

"Hmmm. . . . just some general hygiene."

The pure glee in his eyes contradicts the matter-of-fact manner in which he utters the innocent sounding statement.

"I just bet you need to use the restroom again, don't you?"

"Nnnnnnooooo, Russ, don't make me do that again, please. Isn't once enough?"

"Miranda, by the time you leave here Monday morning, it'll be second nature to you. Do you understand?"

"Why?! What is it that gets you so off about that? It's gross. It's disgusting."

"*That* is what gets me *so off*, Miranda. The fact that you find it so horrifying. I get a charge out of making you do things that appall you. It's a power trip, really. Revenge for what you put me through the last nine months."

"That was the last book."

"What?"

"Never mind. So ... what you're telling me ... is that ... if I enjoyed urinating in front of you, you wouldn't feel the desire to make me do it?"

"No, what I'm telling you is ... once you become comfortable with it, I'll change it in some way so that you find it distressing again."

"God damn it, Russ, you're an asshole."

"Yesterday, I was Mr. Nice Guy. . . . today. . . ."

* * *

Russ never finishes his sentence, preferring to allow me to come up with my own conclusions. Instead, he leans down and begins to release me from the bondage bed.

"First, I need you to call Nick and make up some excuse as to why you need to be away for the weekend. Then . . . we're going to go play on the seesaw ladder."

Nick accepts my lame excuse of a needy friend without too much difficulty, his immediate problem of having to deal with his hangover outweighing any suspicions he may have had about my whereabouts. Satisfied, Russ leads me over to the ladder and fastens me face down, probably three feet above the floor. My arms are bound to the sides of the padded ladder running above my shoulders and upward, the tips of my fingers almost reaching the mirrored wall. One of the horizontal rungs hits me at about my collar bone, the second at my rib cage, and the third, right at my hips. There are no more horizontal rungs below my hips. My legs are pulled outward and around, draping the exterior of the ladder as much as my flexibility will allow, and then fastened there securely with straps. Then Russ begins to raise the ladder up, until I can see the top of his head. The sensation is frightening, almost as if I could fall, even though I know that to be quite impossible.

"I . . . I . . . thought you were going to let me go to the bathroom first, Russ."
   "And you thought correctly, sweetums. Hang on a second. I'll be right back."

* * *

Oh God . . . oh God . . . oh God. . . . What's he going to do? I begin to panic. Russ comes back with the nipple clamps I had been wearing the night before and two matching devices that remind me of spatulas. Russ walks under my levitated body with ease, and begins to fasten the nipple clamps. This time there are no soft kisses, no foreplay, no preparation . . . just a cruel, heartless pinch and then Zzziiiinnnggggggggggg.

"Aaaahhhhhhhhhhhhhh . . . " I groan out in discomfort.

Russ attaches the other clamp, watching as my nipples get pulled downward from the weight of the crystals. The pain is bearable but not quite as pleasurable as the previous night. Then, in surprise, I watch as Russ attaches *another* crystal to the bottom of each one, yanking my nipples even further down.

"Owwwwwwww, Owwwwwwwww, Russ, Russ, that really hurts. Please, take them off."

Laughing, Russ replies, "Miranda, Miranda, Miranda. Your naivete is so sweet and appealing, that I'll tell you what. I won't remove them, but I'll do something that will help you find them more. . . . titillating."

Russ again walks away, this time in the direction of his sink and cabinet. He returns holding a tube of cream. Standing under me while looking up into my face, he explains, "This cream is made from those same herbs you found so stimulating last night."

Russ squeezes some onto his fingers and then begins to apply it to my nipples. Once both nipples are covered, he continues to rub the cream into the entire breast, leaving no patch of the delicate skin untouched. My breasts immediately begin to tingle and throb, the weight of the crystals no longer painful. As a matter of fact, I resist the urge to beg Russ to add a third . . .

"Is that better, baby?"
   "Oooohhhh yes, yes . . . much better."
   Chuckling evilly, Russ replies, "For now."
   Russ wanders back over to the sink area, and I listen with dread as he prepares the horrid pink bag. Thinking that I will receive the douche first, I cry out in surprise when I feel the small nozzle enter my ass instead. Then directly following it, I feel a larger nozzle coaxing my sleepy nether lips apart and slowly penetrate until it is well encased within the satiny walls of my pussy. Why does it come as such a surprise that Russ has two bags?

I feel the warm liquids begin to flow into their respective channels and swirl around, bringing with them the potent effects of the diabolical herbs. Whimpering, I can only let it happen, unable to stop the vindictive turn Russ's game has taken.

Russ moves aside and begins to remove his sweat pants. When he is completely nude, he grabs the two white spatulas and lies down on the floor beneath me, facing upward, only I am looking at his knees while his head is positioned between my widespread legs at the other end. Russ flips a switch on the floor, and the ladder begins to lower, stopping when I am only six inches away from his threatening body.

Russ has both bags clamped on the lowest trickle, but I am already beginning to feel water spurt out from my

pussy, dribbling down to land on Russ's chest. I begin
to panic anew as my filling cavities begin to put pressure
on my painfully full bladder. Whack!

"Ow! What was that for?"

"Let's see how long you can hold out. I'm going to
smack both of your ass cheeks with these paddles until
you piss on me."

"Oh God . . . you want me to piss *on* you now? Oh
God . . . "

Even though Russ's position doesn't allow him to get
any strength behind the swats landing on my bottom, he
is quick and repetitive, all the stinging smacks falling
exactly in the same location. Within five minutes, the
cheeks of my ass are smarting, my gut is full, my rectum's on fire, my pussy's on fire, my tits are on fire, and
I've relieved myself all over Russ's chest. All I can think
about is how I'm going to kill him when I'm finally let
free. The ladder begins to raise as Russ scoots out from
under it, stopping it at waist high. Then he removes both
nozzles and stands back to view the rest my demeaning
expulsion. Again, the hose is turned on and the floor and
my backside are rinsed clean of any evidence of foul
play. Finally, I am released from the ladder and carried
over to the tub.

Russ accompanies me into the tub, turning on the shower
and giving me a good scrub down. Reluctantly, he removes the nipple clamps and washes away most of the
cream from my breasts. No area of my body is left untouched, even the washing of my hair. When I am completely clean, he takes care of his own needs, seeing to

every crack and crevice. Finally, I am towel dried and guided over to the large, wooden wheel.

It is hard to concentrate as Russ gives me instructions, my need to hump something growing stronger and more persistent. My whole body is alive and waiting . . . for something . . . for anything. I am a huge mass of desire, craving any kind of attention. Russ smiles in satisfaction at my discomfort, somehow knowing the tortures I feel.

Again I find myself inside the huge wooden wheel. Russ asks me to spread my legs as far apart as possible, and then begins to fasten soft leather cuffs to my ankles and wrists. Once the cuffs are in place, rope is threaded through an eyelet on each one and then out through the wooden slats, knotted together on the outer side of the wheel. Russ has to use a ladder to fasten my arms to the top of the wheel, a small price to pay for the end result. When he is done, I am tethered to the wheel, spread-eagled, as wide as my arms and legs can possibly be forced apart.

The intense burning in my two most private orifices is not enough to console a bitter Russ, and he leaves to retrieve the tube of magic cream that he had used on my nipples and breasts earlier. He also has with him the frightening nipple clamps. He sets to work massaging the cream into my breasts once again, but doesn't stop there. He goes lower, coating my ribcage, belly and thighs, then to the rear, attacking my buttocks and back with the doctored balm. He makes sure that my anus and pussy are generously attended to, then stands to rub the remaining cream on the lips of my mouth. I howl in pure sufferance, my body begging for appeasement.

"Time for your breakfast, toots. I'll be right back."
   "Russ . . . please, do something. I need to be touched. Don't just leave me here to suffer."
   Russ only smiles, returning with another plate of piping hot food and begins to hand feed me.

"Eat slowly . . . wouldn't want you getting a tummy ache."

I find that I am ravenous and soon have all the yummy eggs and shredded potatoes devoured. I continue to lick my mouth far after all tidbits of food are gone, the pressure against my drugged lips too sensual to resist. After the distraction of breakfast has passed, my neglected body again begins to demand attention.

"Russ. . . . please . . . now. . . . touch me. My body is aching . . . on fire . . ."
   "As you wish."

Russ walks on over to the cabinet housing the whips and paddles. I begin to tremble with anticipation, thankful for any type of reprieve, even a painful one. Russ brings back a cat-o-nine tails and a riding crop and then asks me where I'd like to feel it first.

"Oh God . . . my breasts."

The cat is whisked briskly across my breasts, tearing from me a scream of ecstatic agony.

"Yyyyyyyeeessss . . . Again . . . !"

Not one to deny his lady captives, Russ keeps the whip moving in time with my demands.

"Ahhhhhh. . . . more. . . . my stomach. . . . YES! . . . my thighs . . . my thighs next. . . . Oooooh God . . . again . . . harder . . . Yes . . . Again . . . Again . . . faster Russ . . . whip me . . . everywhere . . . Oh MY GOD . . . "

The whip keeps flying, although Russ remains very much in control and does not allow any one spot to be abused. The biting strands of the whip feel heavenly against my excited body, soothing and tormenting all at once. My arousal intensifies with each lash, and I cloudily wonder if I'll somehow be brought to the point of a masochistic orgasm.

"My back now, Russ. . . . my ass. . . . whip my ass. . . . yes, oh yes . . . Mmmmmm. . . . Eeeeeowwww. . . . Ooooooo . . . more . . . the back of my thighs . . . God damn you, Russ, for doing this to me . . . Ahhhhhhhhhh. . . . keep going . . . again . . . "

When my body has a nice rosy glow from shoulders to knees, Russ stops the whipping, only to have me squirming and mewling for more.

"Sorry, Miranda . . . I want you tenderized, not filleted. This is all for now. I've got more treats in store for you. You won't go without. . . . for a while, that is."

My moans are pathetic, pleading . . . but Russ appears immune.

"Time to cool you off a bit. How about some ice for those sore, hot nipples?"

Out of nowhere, Russ's hand appears with a cube of ice. He slowly places it on the tip of my left nipple and begins to rub it around, watching my nipple bloom around the meltdown. When my nipple seems to raise up as taut as possible, on goes the nipple clamp, complete with two dangling crystals. I suck in my breath and grit my teeth, as I become accustomed to the severe sensations ripping through my torso. Ice and the adjoining clamp are applied to my other nipple, and soon I am gasping in painful delight as I pull and struggle against my unyielding restraints.

Russ steps back to admire his handiwork, and then starts to singsong:

"Miranda loves to tease . . .
Now I'll use her as I please. . . .
Her fate rests in my hands . . .
Miranda loves to flirt . . .
I so crave to watch her hurt . . .
She'll fulfill all my demands . . ."

"Ohhhhhhhh . . . Russ . . . "
"Hot . . . cold . . . hot. . . . cold. . . . guess it's time for hot again, sweetie."

Russ goes over to his whip and paddle case and opens a drawer. He pulls out two strange looking candles and a book of matches. I watch apprehensively as he walks back toward me and sets one of them down. Each candle looks like two candles fused together in the center by a flat, oval base. One end of the candle is black and quite phallic looking, while the other half is cherry red and in the shape of your typical candle. One candle is also slightly thinner than the other. I shudder, already aware of where the candles are going to end up.

Russ lights the red end of one of the candles and steps up next to me in the wheel. He grasps my hair with one hand and pulls my head back to keep my face from being scorched as he places the candle a few inches above one breast and then angles it to drip directly onto my already tortured nipple. I screech as the first drop of wax lands to encase my nipple, several more soon to follow. Russ doesn't stop until the top and sides are completely entombed in several layers of wax. He moves to the other side and covers that nipple as well, sheathing it in a casket of red.

When he is content with his artwork, he blows out the candle, lets go of my hair and steps from the wheel. Then, he releases a lever and the wheel slowly begins to rotate. I panic as I am thrown off balance, but my cuffs are held secure and I stay in place, even though the weight of my body begins to shift. Soon I am completely upside down, crying out once again as the crystals from the clamps topple over, wrenching my nipples from a new angle. Some of the wax begins to crack, but miraculously stays put. Russ once again lights the red end of the candle and bends down to finish covering the under side of each nipple. When he is done, he takes the still lit candle and moves it between my wide open legs.

Without so much as a warning, I feel the penis-shaped bottom half of the candle being inserted into my honey-drenched cavern, helping to ease the fires raging within. I can feel the heat from the flame as it spreads outward, warming the insides of my thighs. Afraid to even breathe, I watch in horror as Russ picks up the second candle and walks around to the back of the wheel. Before long, I feel the shapely head of that candle commence to worm its way deep into the warm sleeve of my ass, and then the heat to emanate as Russ maliciously lights the accompanying wick.

"My . . . God. . . . Russ. . . . what are you doing?" I whisper, afraid to even raise my voice.

"Just a little mind fuck, Miranda. Are you scared that I'm going to let you burn?"

"Yeeeeesssss. . . . Oh please, Russ . . . this is dangerous. Blow them out . . . please!"

"Not quite yet. I've got a few things I want you to do for me before I do. Just don't move too much, and you shouldn't have any problems."

Russ begins to laugh out loud at that suggestion and wanders away. I, on the other hand, am immersed in sensory overload. The blood has begun rushing to my head, making me quite woozy. My body is still craving stimulation . . . of any kind, itching to be touched, prodded, poked . . . anything. The flames burning treacherously close to my thighs and my most intimate areas are petrifying me, yet I cannot help but to squeeze wantonly at the devices responsible for holding them in place. Please . . . if I can just keep myself from moving.

Any hope of remaining still is immediately dashed as Russ returns carrying with him a bag of clothespins and a heavy duty vibrator.

"Now, sweetness. I want you to shower me with praise, and I want you to make it believable. I'm going to put clothespins all over your body, and after each one, say something nice about me. If. . . . you do a good job, I'll let you cum and then blow out the candles. If. . . . you don't. . . . your cunt, ass and thighs will suffer. Ready?"

Russ begins clamping the pins to my already inflamed skin, his first area of concentration being my quivering belly. Desperate for the attack to end, I shout out anything and everything that comes to mind.

"Oh God Russ . . . you know how to please a woman . . . what turns her on. You have the best cock . . . the best fuck around. Sssssssssssssssss. . . ."

I try to keep up with Russ's momentum, but he is applying the clothespins much too quickly. Soon my belly and thighs have wooden legs sticking out from all angles, and he moves around back to repeat the damage. Unable to keep my body from jerking as Russ attaches the pins, I soon have hot wax splattering against the tender skin of my inner thighs. I begin to screech as each little fireball lands, some now dripping onto the lips of my pussy and all over my crotch area. Even my clit is not to be spared, wrenching from me another scream of anguish.

143

"Miranda . . . you've stopped talking. Keep talking or you're going to lose."

"Ruuuuusssss . . . you are masterful . . . and so. . . . hand . . . some . . . Eeeeeeeee . . . those blue . . . eyes . . . can melt a glacier . . . and your kisses . . . are hypnotic . . . I crave them . . . I want to be kissed . . . Ooouuuch . . . by you . . . Ohhhhhh . . . over . . . and over again. Your body is beautiful . . . muscular and sooooooooo owwwww . . . strong. . . . please Russ. . . . stop now . . . "

"More."

"You are so sssssmmmmmart. . . . eeeeechhhh . . . and patient . . . and . . . "

Russ stops with the clothespins and picks up the vibrator, coming back to the front to place it directly on my swollen clit. He turns it up full blast sending several jolts through my body, my muscles now in constant spasm. Russ blows out the candles for the remainder of this torture, the hot wax still being thrown in all directions as my shuddering body reacts to this new stimuli.

"Ok . . . you cock-teasing bitch . . . now, when you start to cum, I want you to say. . . . *Master Russ, I adore you. You rule my sex.*"

Already feeling the beginning pulses of my approaching orgasm, I scream out . . . "Mmmmaster Ruuusss. . . . I yeyeyeyeee . . . a . . . a . . . adddd . . . adddore . . . you. . . . Yyyyou . . . rrrruuule. . . . mmmy. . . . ssssSEXXXX!"

My body collapses in a fit of convulsions while Russ turns off the vibrator and slowly begins to rotate the wheel so that I am positioned upright. In danger of losing consciousness, I struggle to keep aware, concentrating on my breathing as the blood quickly drains from my face. I don't even notice the pain in my nipples as the crystals are flipped around, and then released, as Russ removes the clamps entirely. The clothespins quickly follow suit, as well as the candles, until I am left void of stimulation, only the patches of caked-on wax remaining to remind me of my ordeal.

"Was it like I promised, Miranda? Did heaven and hell collide? Are you able to tell the difference, baby . . . or *is* hell. . . . heaven?"

Russ exits the room entirely, leaving me alone to contemplate my predicament. My body is still too exhausted to react to the effect of the herbs, a tiny blessing, but my brain and my thoughts are still quite active. Russ is definitely agitated today, a big change in his demeanor from yesterday. Yesterday, he seduced me. Today he's terrorizing me. The end results, however, are both the same. . . . mind-altering exhilaration. I can't remember my body feeling this alive, thriving on the endless stimulation, pulsing with anticipation. Is this going to be Russ's true revenge . . . exposing and igniting these masochistic cravings, only to release me knowing my need to return will soon fester into an undeniable obsession?

Hours must have passed before a stark naked Russ saunters back into the room, sporting a fierce erection and a wild gleam in his eyes. My arms and legs are dreadfully sore, and I silently plea that Russ's first order of business will be to release me. Unfortunately, Russ has his own ideas. Russ takes his right hand and wraps it around his erection as he walks closer, masturbating to the sight of my spread-out body.

"How are you feeling, baby?" Russ asks, with exaggerated sweetness. "Getting a little bit tired of holding that pose? Somebody has been thinking about you for a while and would like to show you how much."

Referring to his penis, he looks down as he continues to casually stroke himself. Then he steps up into the wheel to stand directly in front of me and begins to pick up the pace, increasing the friction on his rigid prick.

"Oooooo, baba. . . . he likes what he sees. Oh yes . . . oh yes. . . . his horny slut, spread out and waiting for him. He finds that só exciting. Look . . . he's starting to cry, he's so happy . . ."

Now Russ starts to gently slap his cock up against my belly . . . Ooooing and Ahhhhhing the whole time while sucking air between his clenched teeth.

"Oh yes. . . . he's going to kiss you here in a minute . . . "

Russ stops the cock spanking and resumes stroking, pumping his hand up and down much faster while his other hand cradles his balls.

"Oooooo . . . Mirandaaaaa . . .
AAAAAAARRRRRGGGGGGHHHHH!"

Russ aims the powerful spurts of his hot, creamy cum directly at my slit, bestowing me with that kiss that he

146

had promised just moments ago. When the last of his load is deposited between my pouting lips, he takes the head of his still erect cock and begins to rub it around the folds of my pussy. My body reacts automatically, instinctively, and my hips begin to thrust outward, inviting the object of my lust to enter. Enter it does . . . swiftly, fluidly, sensually . . . taking on its own identity as it begins it's sumptuous rhythm.

I begin to coo. . . . purr . . . at the delightful impalement, feeling every pulsing throb beating in his masculine shaft. He reaches around to hold me tightly, then descends those luscious lips to meld with mine. I sigh in heavenly bliss at the return of the erotic, gentle master, wooing his captive into submissiveness rather than resorting to coercion. Lost in his kiss, I could promise him anything.

Russ leisurely fucks me while his lips remain locked with my own. His arms and hands are constantly roving, alternating between gripping my ass and caressing my breasts, coaxing contented sighs from my gurgling throat. After several minutes, he withdraws and picks up the tube of herbal cream still left lying nearby. He moves behind me and coats my anus with the powerful aphrodisiac, then slips his finger inside to lubricate the interior as well. When his finger is removed, it is replaced by the wide berth of his cock head pressing anxiously against my rear opening. His arms wrap around to hug me, his fingers settling into the folds of my pussy. Pushing past my tight barrier, he gasps out in pleasure, methodically enjoying all the taboo delights my ass has to offer. I sway in my bondage against him, two of his fingers rhythmically penetrating my pussy in sync with his precise thrusting into my bottom. His other hand rubs and massages my clit, until my toes are curling and I'm caught in the throes of another passionate orgasm. Russ is only moments behind me, releasing a flood of his seed deep into my irresistible ass.

"Would you find it exciting to exist as you are now, on a day to day basis, as nothing more than a sexy receptacle. . . . no worries, no cares, no responsibilities . . . your sole purpose being to bring me pleasure?"

Thank goodness he didn't ask me that question while wrapped in his embrace and smothered by his kisses.

"No, Russ . . . I wouldn't. I find it . . . exciting, to say the least . . . for the weekend. But as a way of life. . . . I would hate it."

Smiling good-naturedly, Russ responds with, "Hmmm . . . I'm not so sure. Weekends quickly blend into weeks . . . weeks into months . . . months into years . . . years into lifetimes. You'd be so engrossed that time would have no meaning for you. You'd be too busy *feeling* to bother with the passage of time."

"Russ . . ." I question, warily, "You're not thinking about reneging on your promise to return me home Monday morning, are you? Nick isn't stupid. He'll figure out where I am and come after you."

"No, no, no . . . just giving you food for thought."

"Thanks, but no thanks . . . I'm on a very strict diet."

Grinning, Russ shoots me a look that says, "Can't blame a guy for trying."

*　　*　　*

By nightfall, I am completely worn out. Russ has to physically drag me over to my bed, my limbs no longer able to hold my weight. He only attaches one ankle to the bottom of the bed, deciding that anything further won't be necessary, since he will be sleeping right beside me.

"Is it customary for kidnappers to sleep with their captives?" I ask him, with sarcastic innocence.

"Baby . . . I just do what feels good at the time. Right now I want nothing more than to snuggle up to your hot and inviting body and hold it against me all night long."

"Geesh. This is beginning to feel like a relationship . . ." I mutter, under my breath.

Morning arrives, and with it a rejuvenated Russ, eager to spring more of his surprises on me. I sit up on the bed and watch him as he prepares for my morning ritual, keeping a special eye out for the bottle containing the aphrodisiac herbs. I watch as he uses it, carefully measuring the powdered herbs before shaking them into the pink bags, relieved that I can now distinguish that bottle from the others. Russ wanders over to the seesaw ladder and hooks both bags up to pulleys, then hoists them way up near the ceiling. I look on with interest as my curiosity increases, never before being allowed to witness the time-consuming routine. Once everything is in place, Russ releases my ankle from the bondage bed and steers me over to the ladder.

I am placed lying face down again, only this time, Russ angles the ladder so that I am perpendicular to the floor, the top of my head aimed at the floor and my feet toward the ceiling.

"What are you doing? Why do you want me upside down?"

"I have something extra special in mind for you today. I want those herbs to stay put in that luscious pussy of yours for a while and not seep out. That cunt is going to need to be hungry and juicy."

"Jesus, Russ . . . what are you going to do to me?"

"Only time will tell, precious, now relax."

We complete the entire regime . . . the douche, the enema, the shower, and then Russ grabs the herb cream and walks back over to the bondage bed. With a sleepy, inviting smile, he pats the bed, indicating for me to join him.

"I thought you had something special in mind. What are we going to do, make out on the bed?"

"Have I lied to you yet? Come lay beside me."

Confused, I do as requested, lying flat on my back and looking up at him with suspicion. He simply grins as he undoes the cap to the tube and begins to massage the vilely wonderful cream onto my breasts and down into that sacred area between my legs. I shudder, knowing how the cream will affect me, combined with the added potency of my special douche. Russ tosses the tube aside and then leans down, pressing his body, off centered, to cover only the right half of mine.

He kisses me and tenderly strokes my body for almost a half an hour, never once touching my pussy in the process. My hips are bucking upward, my opening frothing with unquenched desire.

"My God, Russ . . . if you don't do something soon, I'm going to die! You're driving me crazy!"

As if on cue, Russ's hand slides down to nestle between my legs.

"Oh, baby . . . you're so wet, but I don't know if you're wet enough. I'll be right back."

The howl that follows him is pathetic as my own hands dive downward to help ease some of the torment. My fingers provide some relief, however temporary, until Russ returns, carrying with him a large container of petroleum jelly. His gaze is intense, and his eyes never waver from mine as he dips into the jar and begins to grease up his entire right hand. His look dares me to protest as he continues spreading the slippery substance up his forearm, stopping at his elbow. Certain that he is adequately covered, he lays back down and begins to taunt me.

"Ever been fisted, baby? Do you know what it feels like to have someone's entire hand and wrist buried to the hilt in your most intimate passages?"

I shake my head no, never breaking eye contact, frozen in awe at his suggestion. The thought all at once petrifies me, yet is responsible for another surge of moisture sent to saturate my already flooded sex. I groan with expectancy as Russ's fingers resume their position between my legs and attempt the improbable.

---

*　　*　　*

Russ easily slips three fingers inside and begins an in and out thrusting motion. I exhale slowly, drowning in the exquisite sensations, my feminine juices overflowing and mixing with the Vaseline. Encouraged by the ease in which the three fingers entered, Russ slyly slips in his pinky, making it four. Then tucking his thumb under, be begins to slowly gain entry using all five fingers. The process is painstakingly slow, the most difficult part of it being to get past the last knuckle on his thumb. Finally, after much kissing and coaxing on his part for me to relax, that obstacle is overcome and his hand begins to slowly disappear inside. Amazed, Russ sits up, needing to verify his success with his own two eyes.

I feel Russ's fingers curl as they make a fist inside, creating additional room for more of his arm to enter. I am thunderstruck, unable to speak, never undergoing such an intimidating and breathtaking experience. This feeling of total consummation and ultimate vulnerability exceed anything I have ever imagined. It is almost too personal, too giving of an emotion to happen with someone like Russ. This should be Nick's fist inside me. Too late to turn back, I give in, gasping as Russ slowly begins to plunge the entire first third of his arm in and out of me. I try to crawl out of my skin, arching backwards, the overwhelming sensations too much for my battered mind and body to handle. Russ holds fast, wriggling his fingers in an attempt to bring me more pleasure. I scream out in ecstasy as a catastrophic orgasm cruelly rips through me, the walls of my pussy clenching and suffocating Russ's invading fist.

*　　*　　*

When the spasms subside, I begin to worry irrationally . . . how in the world is he going to be able to remove his fist? He's going to rip me to shreds in the process. I begin to hyperventilate as this new fear nags at my consciousness.

"Baby . . . baby . . . it's okay . . . relax. You're okay. Take a deep breath and hold it. Shhhhhhhhhhh."

"Russ . . . I'm scared. . . . it's never going to come out. Your fist is going to be trapped inside. Oh my God . . . "

"Miranda, Miranda, Miranda. . . . calm down, baby. It'll come out, no problem, but you can't overreact and tense up on me like this. You have to relax, get all warm and gushy . . . like butta baby. . . . like butta."

His voice is like "butta," immediately lulling me back into a state of tranquil arousal, hypnotic, drugged. Something about being around Russ always makes me feel woozy, like I'm not in my right mind, under the influence of a powerful narcotic or something.

Before I am even aware that it has happened, he holds his wet and sloppy hand up for my inspection.

"See, I told you . . . nothing to worry about, darling."

"Hungry?"

"Famished. Finally going to feed me?"

Russ has the decency to blush. "Well, I kind of got sidetracked this morning. I'll be right back with some fruit. Don't you go anywhere, kitten."

Russ returns with a couple of bananas and a bowl of cut up melon. We devour the succulent slices of cantaloupe and honeydew first, and then Russ peels a banana and holds it up to my lips. I open my mouth to take a bite, but Russ pulls it away, content to lightly brush the tip of the banana across my bottom lip. Leaving my mouth partially held open, I hold still while he finishes playing out his current fantasy.

"Lick your lips and open them a little wider."

I do as he asks, and he immediately begins to penetrate my mouth with the top inch of the banana, slowly guiding it in and out. The simple act seems to fascinate him as he thrusts it in a little deeper.

"Fuck it. Fuck it with your mouth. Use your tongue. Get it squishy."

Russ is enthralled as he watches me take the banana as I would a penis. Soon the banana begins to soften and Russ's anxiety increases.

"Deep throat it. Keep your hands behind your back. Just take it as I give it to you."

Keeping my fingers tightly laced behind my back, I open up a little wider, expanding my throat and mentally psyching myself up to not gag. Soon I feel the persistent pressure, beyond my vocal cords, pressing further back and down. I begin to bite off mushy pieces of banana, not with my teeth, but with the contractions in my throat, quickly swallowing the tiny globs before I choke on them. Russ force feeds me most of the banana in this fashion, remaining very thoughtful throughout the whole process. He saves the last two inches of the banana for himself, chewing it down properly. Then Russ offers me a drink of orange juice, and I gulp it down gratefully.

"This just gave me an idea. Follow me."

Russ takes my hand and all but drags me back over into the white section of the room. He orders me up onto the white table on my hands and knees and then encases my head and arms in the white stockade. Then he flips up the side shackles and pins my legs to the table just below my knees, spreading my legs obscenely wide. I feel very defenseless in this doggy-style position, the stockade and shackles making it even more pronounced. But the herbs are still working, my body continuously craving attention, and my ass wiggles back at Russ in anticipation.

"That's my girl," he laughs, as he wanders back over to the bondage bed to retrieve the remaining banana.

My body immediately begins to tingle and my pussy clenches invitingly, certain that the banana will soon be finding its way inside. What is Russ going to do, insert it and then eat it out of me? The thought is definitely appealing, but my thoughts change instantly when Russ shows me the altered banana. Russ uses a knife to saw off the very top, leaving about a quarter-size opening. The rest of the banana remains securely in its peel, and then Russ makes a show out of coating it entirely with Vaseline. Next, Russ moves behind me, and I am held fast by the stockade, forced to look straight ahead into the wooden room.

I begin to struggle profusely as I feel the newly altered banana top pressing against my anal opening, but my efforts only succeed in amusing Russ.

"Baby, you can't go anywhere. You just have to kneel there and take it. Take whatever it is I want you to. And right now. . . . I want it to be this banana."

Gradually, Russ works the head of the banana past my tight barrier and slides it in deep, coating the walls of my rectum with the petroleum jelly. With exaggerated slowness he penetrates and then pulls it all the way back out, and then starts all over again, cruelly toying with my rear opening. The banana is fairly large, and I gasp as I try to relax enough to accommodate it comfortably. Russ picks up the tempo now, no longer removing it completely, thrusting into me deeply and quickly. My moans increase with intensity and are soon filling the room. Not quite ready to allow me another orgasm, Russ backs off, leaving only the first inch of the banana imbedded.

"Let me know when you feel something, baby."

Confused, I try to decipher his meaning, when all of a sudden I feel the walls of my ass expanding.

"Oh my God, Russ, what are you doing?"
"Just inserting a little lubricant, darling."

Mortified, I can do nothing but accept the fact that little by little, Russ is squeezing the entire banana out of its peel and into my ass. I cringe as I feel it filling my bottom, certain the end result will be nothing less than another unbearable humiliation. Russ leaves the peel hanging limply from my ass as he crawls up onto the table and situates himself on his knees between my outstretched thighs. He then simultaneously slips the peel out while pressing the head of his cock inside. I feel as if I'm going to burst as Russ penetrates my bottom and begins to slice through my banana coated interior. The moans coming from him tell me that the sensations for him are incredible, yet I continue to struggle with my own discomfort. Russ takes care of that immediately, reaching a hand around to manipulate my clit while he continues to fuck me from behind. The magic of his fingers quickly transforms me from passive victim to eager participant, and I begin to involuntarily thrust back.

"Oh yes, baby. Fuck me back. Take it all. You are such a sweet fuck . . . a sweet, receptive fuck. Come on . . . do me. . . . let's make some banana cream . . . fuck it."

Russ smacks my ass while urging me on via his erotic ranting, sending sizzling shivers throughout my body. The harder and longer Russ continues to plunge into me, the more liquefied the banana becomes, easing the bloated feeling I had initially. The rutting intensifies, our groans co-mingling, as the room begins to swirl and then constrict into a tiny dot of light. I feel my ears start to tingle and then go deaf, my nipples harden, and then suddenly I am there, immersed in feeling, every nerve the recipient of unparalleled ecstasy, as I miraculously climax at unimaginable heights, convulsing and shuddering into a pool of elated bliss. Two strokes later, Russ becomes lost in his own climactic spasms, collapsing in a heap across my back. It is sprawled out in this position that my husband walks in to find us.

■

CHAPTER 7

COMPLICATIONS

My eyes widen in shock, then horror as Nick steps out from behind a concealed door built into one of the mirrored walls.

"Ok . . . the party's over. Time for me to take her home."

"Hey, man. You said I could have her till Monday morning."

"I know what I said, but I've changed my mind. You've had plenty of time and enjoyed plenty of kink with my wife. No need to feel shortchanged."

I watch in bewilderment as Russ jumps down from the table and joins Nick on the other side of the room. My fury mounts as they begin to whisper.

"Will somebody get me down from this table and tell me what the FUCK is going on here?!!!!" I bellow, quickly gaining the attention of both men.

*   *   *

Russ guiltily races back to release me, while Nick stares me down, not at all daunted by the fact that I'm quite pissed off. I jump down off of the table, ready to do battle, when I am reminded that I still have banana oozing from my bottom and am in no condition to demand an explanation.

"I need to shower before I go anywhere. Are those clothes for me?"

Nick has a pair of sweats draped over his arm and tosses them in my direction. Then he and Russ leave the dungeon and head up the stairs to do some talking, leaving me with my privacy. Livid, I step into the shower and scrub myself clean, certain that my husband is the mastermind behind my abduction. How could he have done this to me? As I am getting dressed, I happen to spy the brown jar containing the special herbs sitting on Russ's counter. I quickly scan the room to make sure no one is around, then impulsively stuff the jar into the pocket of my hooded sweatshirt, not knowing what I intend to use them for, but confident they will come in handy someday. Then, taking the stairs two at a time, I enter Russ's kitchen ready for a confrontation.

Russ had the decency to at least get into a pair of sweatpants before I had to make eye contact with him again. I walk in to find he and Nick sitting, chatting amiably and drinking coffee at his kitchen table. Flabbergasted, I reiterate, "Does somebody want to tell me what's going on?"

*   *   *

"Sure," Russ offers, "Nick gave you to me for the week-end."

"You're not helping, buddy," Nick counters. "It's not quite that simple, Miranda. Have a seat and I'll fill you in."

Feeling unforgivably betrayed, I sit down with my arms crossed and wait for an explanation.

"As you know," Nick begins, "Russ has felt slighted ever since the poker game. It was beginning to affect our friendship, which wasn't something I had expected. In an effort to appease him, I suggested that he send you e-mails in an attempt to try and seduce you."

"You told him to write those creepy poems?" I ask, accusingly.

"No. I didn't tell him what to say. I just gave him your e-mail address. He came up with that tactic all on his own. Regardless, his initial poems didn't work, so he decided to mess with your head by using the *expect it when you least expect it* method. All that did was freak you out, but when you admitted to me that it turned you on, Russ and I got together and arranged the *rape*, so to speak."

"Nick! How could you? I'm your wife, for crying out loud. How could you do such a thing?"

"You're not letting me finish. I told Russ that I'd help to get you out to the baseball field, but that before he could take you by force, he had to get your permission. I never expected you to say, 'yes,' but I had no idea how cleverly Russ was going to manipulate the situation. Plain and simply, I underestimated him, and he out-smarted me. Once he had your 'ok,' all I could do was sit back and watch to make sure that he didn't get carried away."

"You watched us? The whole time? How?"

"Well, it was easy to watch while you were blindfolded, and then I just stood behind you after the blindfold was removed. When Russ decided to leave, I ran home and got the car and followed him. The room downstairs is surrounded by a corridor and a secret room. I stayed there all weekend. The mirrors are all two way mirrors, and Russ has the room wired for sound, so I could see and hear everything. By the way," he turns, pointing a finger at Russ, "you almost went too far with that candle thing. You have no idea how close I was to bursting in on you and slugging you square in the chops."

"Sorry, man. No harm, no foul."

"Miranda, I'm sorry, but I never expected you to say yes, to either the rape or the weekend in the dungeon. I may have set the stage, but honey, you made your own damn bed."

Well, he had me there. My anger slowly begins to subside, then evolves into embarrassment as I recall all of the degrading acts that Nick must have witnessed, and even worse, my reactions to them. Oh God. . . . I'm lucky that he's not the one feeling offended.

The ride home starts out uncomfortably quiet, neither one of us brave enough to break the ice. Lord knows, there is still plenty left unsaid, and once we get started, it has the potential of getting ugly in a hurry. Still, I sneak a look, heartbroken by his stony features. I am sooooo divorced.

*   *   *

"Mad?"

He smiles, in spite of himself, amazed that I'd even have the gumption to ask.

"Mad?. . . . No. . . . Hurt?. . . . maybe. But it's not anything I can't get over. I should have known. You are much too weak to resist the temptations of the flesh, my dear. I should never have put you in that position. I'm just as much to blame. I can't be mad just because it backfired on me. I just wish . . . "

"Wish what?"

"I didn't even think that you were attracted to Russ! What happened to he's a self-centered, egotistical, muscle bound jerk?"

"Uh . . . I think I was a little hasty with that opinion based only on my first impressions. I just never allowed myself to get to know him any better, preferring to stereotype him into a category of men that I have no respect for. I've found that I actually kind of like him."

"Yeah . . . well that is painfully obvious."

Again I wince, my conscience flooding with guilt and shame. Nick drops me off at the house, but doesn't exit the car with me.

"Aren't you coming in?"

"Nah, I think I'll drive around for a little while and do some thinking. This weekend has been just a little too weird for me. I'll be back by bedtime."

*   *   *

I watch dejectedly as Nick drives away. Damn. Don't tell me that I managed to salvage our marriage after a three month separation, only to lose it over a wild and depraved weekend. I wish I could add "meaningless" to the list as well, but it was far from that. Not only did I enjoy and thrive on Russ's control over me, but I also began to see him in another light . . . as a man, a sexy, compelling man, not just as "one of Nick's kinky friends." How is it that I always manage to get myself into these situations? One minute it's okay for me to explore and delve into my fantasies, while the next, it's not. Oh, God, I'm so confused. I need a friend.

Walking into the den, my gaze pauses on my ever faithful buddy, the computer, then settles on the VR suit and swing hanging suggestively nearby. Struggling to resist the urge of drowning my troubles in VR, I activate the computer to jump into the chat rooms hoping to find consolation there. Immediately, the VR software opens, the location icons glowing brightly to tease and tempt me. No, I can't. It may not be safe without Nick there. I haven't even contacted Antonio.

Even though I have several good reasons for not entering the land of make-believe, I hold my breath as I double click on the "Castle of Fantasies" icon. A short description of this Virtual World reveals that I will be entering an old, renovated castle built to satisfy any and all possibly conceived fantasies. The most basic ones can be satisfied immediately, where the more detailed ones need time to become intricately developed. Heck, I don't care. I'm not looking to fulfill a fantasy, just hoping for a little distraction from my current dilemma. Maybe, just maybe, I can even find someone else hanging out in the castle that I can talk to, but that is doubtful considering I haven't pre-arranged anything with Antonio, and only twenty or so people currently have access to these VR worlds. Smiling, I set the timer for one hour and change into my suit, attaching the "sex insert," just in case.

My entrance into the castle isn't nearly as dramatic as my flight onto the yacht. My vision is completely eliminated, leaving me shrouded in a tomb of inky darkness. Soon the black begins to fade into brown, and magically, I find myself standing in a room. It is a small room, constructed completely from stone, yet the comfort from the blazing fire creates a feeling of warmth and familiarity. The only other sights that greet me are first, a sign on a door saying, "Welcome to Castle Fantasy," and second, a bright red, fire alarm pull station. Without hesitation, I pull open the door that leads into the interior of the castle.

The door opens up into a long hallway to my right, and a solid stone wall to my left. The hallway is aligned with brightly glowing torches illuminating the entrances to several other doors, all which appear to be locked. I continue to walk down the corridor, trying each knob as I pass with the same results. Finally, the hallway opens into a huge room, well lit, with another fire burning reassuringly in the corner fireplace. To the right of the fireplace is a beautiful oak, roll-top desk, with a small figure bent over it, so thoroughly engrossed that my presence is not immediately detected.

"Hello!" I call out.

*   *   *
———

Immediately, the figure stands and turns, poised as if to fight. I continue to walk slowly closer, thrilled to find that I'm not alone, yet not wanting to startle my new-found friend. I get close enough to see that the figure is a woman, and notice her posture immediately begin to relax as she senses my lack of a threat.

"You startled me, Miranda. I thought I was alone."

Her voice is deep and throaty, and very, very seductive. Close enough now to make out her features, I am taken aback by the intensity and beauty of them. She is Oriental with long, straight, shiny, blue-black hair, falling easily to her waist. Her face is perfect, dark brown intelligent eyes, a small pert nose, and a pouty rosebud mouth. Her figure is just as exquisite . . . lean, muscular, controlled. She is wearing only a black, vinyl, bodysuit corset, and a pair of shiny black boots reaching to mid-thigh. She is also casually and fondly stroking the end of a very menacing-looking whip.

"How do you know me?"

"It's my business to know everyone who has access to the program. The real question is, what are you doing here? Antonio did not prepare me properly for your arrival, which causes me to assume that he has no knowledge of it."

"Oh, I'm really sorry. It was a spur of the moment decision. I wasn't aware that I had to let him know in advance. I was just going to explore the castle. I honestly didn't expect to find anyone here."

I stop walking as she begins to move toward me, her stride very determined and calculated. The look on her face is chilling, her eyes hard and cold, yet thoughtful, while her mouth remains in a soft, reassuring smile. Immediately, I know that this is not a woman to challenge. She exudes authority, power and confidence and appears to possess an uncanny ability to read people. I can feel her assessing me, easily summing up my chaotic personality and categorizing it effortlessly, filing it to later analyze and then effectively manipulate. I make my own mental note not to trust or underestimate her, at least not right away. She is dangerous and could be a formidable adversary. Despite my wariness, her smile remains hypnotic, transfixing me as she continues to move in closer, the tall, spiked heels allowing her to look me straight in the eye.

"My name is Raven. I am responsible for running the business aspects of Antonio's VR empire. I guess you can think of me as his secretary/treasurer. Personally, though, I prefer to be referred to as his partner."

Her breath smells sweet as it is blown across my nose for me to inhale. For some reason, I immediately like this woman, knowing that earning her respect will be of utmost importance. I smile back at her, keeping my composure and never losing eye contact.

"Well, Raven. I am very pleased to meet you. Shall I call you Raven, or do you prefer. . . . Mistress?"

Smiling, she takes the flexible end of her whip and places it at the hollow of my throat, then gradually wraps the entire length of the whip around my neck, until there is just a short distance between the handle and my throat. Pulling at the handle, she commands, "Follow me."

Somewhat frightened by the constricting feeling around my neck, I clutch at my throat as she pulls me along.

"Where are you taking me?"

"Just on a mini tour of the castle. I can't have you wandering alone and getting lost, can I?"

Raven guides me back down the same hallway from which I entered, and randomly begins to unlock doors, allowing me a peak inside. Each room is a pre-staged setting based on the most popular and basic fantasies of the human psyche. They are all very elaborate and realistic, almost too realistic.

"Here we have an outdoor cave setting. This is for people, mostly men, who fantasize about living back in the caveman era and enjoy dragging their women around by the hair. It's a very macho fantasy, ready to satisfy the male chauvinist side of any man. Of course, there are also women that request this fantasy, and those are the women that crave a strong man and don't mind being used on that primitive a level."

Raven smiles and then winks at me as she closes the door and leads me over to the next one.

"This here is your classic schoolroom fantasy, and covers areas ranging from a teacher/student fantasy, to finally getting the cheerleader that always turned you down. Of course, if that doesn't apply to the female client, well then, I'm sure there was an elusive football player in her past. We can create the identities of the players to closely match any descriptions given, or if a picture can be provided, that's even better. There are so many possibilities in VR, only limited by one's own imagination."

I find my body tingling as I listen to Raven's alluring voice, momentarily transporting myself into each of the fantasies as she's describing them. Only the impatient tug on my neck snaps me out of my reverie, returning me to the present as we continue on the erotic journey.

She quickly shows me several other basic rooms; a hotel room, a pool hall and bar, a strip club, a gym full of weights and workout equipment, an office, a jail, a library, a doctor's office, you name it. Every imaginable setting is accounted for, even the more difficult ones simulating the outdoors. Raven shows me a deserted island, complete with palm trees and sunshine. The whole concept is so overwhelming that I just gape in awe, suddenly very eager to try one of them out.

"Now this is a fun room," Raven explains, as she unlocks yet another door. She takes me inside and I feel as if I've just stepped into the body of a Boeing 747 airplane. I look down the entire length of the aisle, spotting the cockpit at one end and the restrooms at the other.

"This set also satisfies many fantasies, starting simply at always wanting to pilot a plane, to overcoming a fear of flying, having sex with the stewardess, or meeting an enticing stranger and finally becoming a member of the 'Mile High Club.' We anticipate this to be an extremely

---

168

popular room once the general public has access. In the meantime, we can fill empty seats with the flip of a switch, immediately crowding the airplane with holograms."

"Wow, this is mind boggling, Raven. How long does it take to set one of these fantasies up?"

"Well, it's always best to give us at least a twenty-four hour notice, but some of the less intricate ones can usually be ready almost immediately, as long as there is at least one other 'real' person available to interact with. Depends on what you're requesting."

"Like, for instance, if I wanted to meet a stranger on this airplane right now, could I do it?"

Raven grins, almost as if she had expected me to ask that. Leading me back into the main room, still controlling my movements by her trusty whip, she forces me to have a seat in a throne-like chair.

"Be a good girl and stay put, and I'll see if there's anybody available to play with right now."

Raven wanders back over to her amazing desk and accesses her computer. In the interim, I make myself comfortable as I analyze the unique chair I find myself occupying. The throne is very strange and appears almost as if it is built for two. Just below where I'm sitting, maybe only an inch lower, is another padded seat, nestled up close to the higher one. There are also distinctive grooves, spread widely apart, for two pair of legs to be cradled in. Also not escaping my notice are several straps conveniently located to helplessly bind someone to this erotic bondage throne. I smile wishfully as I run my hand along the lush red velvet material covering the exquisite chair.

"You're in luck, doll," Raven whispers enticingly into my ear. "I found somebody eager to join you."

I jump, almost falling out of the chair, surprised by her stealthy reappearance.

"Jesus, Raven. You scared me to death."
    Grinning seductively, she replies, "Now we're even."

I cover my heart with my hands, trying to still the erratic beating as Raven takes this opportunity to ask me a few questions.

"Just a couple little details to work out, Miranda. What would you like to be wearing on your flight, or shall I pick out an outfit for you myself?"

Wearing? Geeze, that never occurred to me. What am I wearing right now? I can't believe I hadn't even bothered to check.
    "Um, something sexy of course, easily accessible. What would you wear in the same fantasy, Raven?"
    "I'll take care of you, doll. Have no worries. Sit tight while I work out the details, and then we'll have to wait about fifteen minutes for it to be ready. We can take that time to get to know one another a little better."

*　　*　　*
_____

She practically purrs that last sentence, again sending tingles throughout my body. I look down curiously to see what my current outfit consists of noticing that it is nothing special, just a cute little sundress and a pair of comfortable sandals. Hmmmm, must be a "default" outfit for any female guest entering the castle unannounced. Raven returns, positioning herself standing between the widespread legs of the throne. She leans over, looking me suggestively in the eyes.

"All set. Now, whatever shall we do with our time?"

I watch, sucking in my breath, as her hand reaches out, presumably for my breast. Instead, she grins wickedly as she grasps the handle of the whip, somewhat forgotten as it was left to dangle in the comfort of my cleavage. She pulls it out and toward her, dragging me along with it, until my bottom slides off of the upper level of the throne to plop unceremoniously down onto the lower padded seat. Then she proceeds to fasten my legs into the innermost grooves of the chair, seemingly leaving the outer ones for her own legs to nestle into. Once my legs are immobile, she stands facing me once again and pulls on the whip handle until I am looking up at her.

"Do you ever fantasize about making love with another woman, Miranda, or are all the figures in your fantasy world built with a penis?"

"I try to keep my fantasy world open to all possibilities, Raven, completely uninhibited. Some things even carry over into my 'real' world," I answer, thoughtfully . . . breathlessly.

* * *

"Mmmm, good answer. It's not very often that I meet a woman who possesses as much sex appeal as me, Miranda. You have potential, and I find you extremely arousing."

Raven then lowers her head until her lips are within a millimeter of touching my own, and I feel her breath tickle my nose and mouth as she asks, "Would you like for me to kiss you?"

"Yes," I whisper, almost too eagerly.
"Yes, what?" Raven asks, smiling.
"Yes, please?"
"No, try again."

I struggle, trying to decipher what it is that she wants me to say. She still has a grip on the whip handle, and pushes it up between our mouths, seductively licking the side facing her.
"Lick the handle while you think."

I begin to lick and suck on the other side of the leather device, while searching her eyes for the answer. Raven is careful not to let our tongues co-mingle. Almost immediately, a thought comes to me, and I am almost certain that I now know what she's looking for. I pull my lips away just long enough to say, "Yes, Mistress."

Raven rewards me with a huge smile, and then snakes her tongue around to graze my own before removing the handle completely and covering my mouth with her intoxicating kiss. I melt into the incredible softness of her lips, then yelp as she changes her tactic and starts to nip and bite at me instead. Satisfied, she pulls away and unravels the whip from my throat. Then she climbs up onto the throne to sit behind me.

My back is immediately enveloped in the warmth of her chest, and she playfully kisses the back of my neck as her nose snuggles into the fragrant softness of my hair. Next, I watch as she situates her legs to rest comfortably in the outer grooves of the chair, her legs now even more widely spread than my own. Her arms reach around to clasp me tightly to her body, while her hands work on softly caressing the material of my dress, stimulating my breasts underneath. I can also feel her pubic bone grinding into my lower back and tailbone. Mmmmmm. I relax into her while she continues her slow seduction.

"So tell me, Miranda. Why are you here?"
I try to answer her as best as possible, finding it very difficult to concentrate on speech when all I can do is focus on her roving hands. They are gently caressing my entire torso, awakening all my nerve endings, and then softly touching the tops of my exposed legs. I shiver as she uses her long, manicured nails, and rakes them up the insides of my thighs, stopping at my dampened panties.

"I'm waiting," she demands, impatiently, now stroking and rubbing my crotch expertly while continuing to kiss the back of my neck.

"Ahhhh . . . um . . . my husband, Nick . . . and I had a little . . . confrontation . . . of sorts. He . . . he's off driving . . . to think, so I, I . . . decided to look, ah, for my own . . . distraction. Ohhh, Raven."

173

"Mmmmm, I see. Nothing like a little sex to take your mind off of your problems, huh?"

"Ah, I think . . . think . . . that's what got, uh, ohhhh . . . got me in this . . . into trouble . . . in the first place."

"Mmmmm, I do recall hearing somewhere that you are quite insatiable. One of these days, you and I will have to play. Are you brave enough to trust me?"

"Why would I need to be brave to. . . . ? OH GOD . . ."

"Don't worry, doll. I'm not going to make you cum. I'm just getting you all worked up for your airplane encounter. It's almost time."

Raven slips one of her tapered nails into my crease and then inserts it deep into my sopping interior. Slowly she pumps it in and out, taking away the clitoral stimulation and any threat of an unintentional climax. The feeling is exquisite, and it is impossible to comprehend that it is not really happening, that I'm actually reclining comfortably in my swing at home. Finally, she removes her finger and asks me to wash it off for her. I take it into my mouth and suck it clean. Then, jumping down from the throne, she releases my legs and announces that it is last call for boarding.

Raven ushers me inside the room, then closes the door behind me. I turn to ask her one more question, only to find that the door is gone, replaced by the interior wall of an airplane. Suddenly panicked, I wonder how on earth I'll be able to get out if I don't like what happens. I scan the interior until I discover the fire alarm, breathing a huge sigh of relief. Ok, ok. Settle down, Miranda.

Next I check to see what interesting outfit Raven has
chosen for me. I am wearing tight, shiny black pants that
look like they are made from leather, but they're not.
They are much lighter, almost that "wet look" fabric.
Silently, I thank Raven for selecting the easy access
clothing I requested. I should have known that she'd try
to make this interesting. I look down to see that I am
wearing high, black platform shoes and also a pink,
crop-top, angora sweater. It has short sleeves and nestles
snuggly against my rib cage, accentuating my breasts to
their best advantage.

"May I show you to your seat? I'll just need to have a
look at your boarding pass." Startled, I look up to see a
very friendly and very attractive stewardess holding her
hand out. Is she real? I resist the urge to touch her and
wonder where in the heck my ticket is supposed to be.
I start to frisk my own pockets, then realize that I have
a purse slung over my right shoulder. Praying that Raven
has taken care of this little glitch, I open the purse to
find the elusive boarding pass. Smiling, I hand it to the
patient stewardess.

"First class. Right this way, Miranda."

I start to follow her, becoming immediately aware that
the interior of the plane is now a bustle of activity. There
are people walking up and down the aisle, tucking away
luggage in the overhead storage bins and scouting for
extra pillows and blankets. All the same activities you
would expect to see on a real flight. Again, it's so hard
to convince my brain that this is all a simulation.

*   *   *

The stewardess guides me over to a window seat in the lush and roomy accommodations of the first class section, then reaches behind to close the curtain separating first class from the rest of the airplane. There are a total of twelve seats now remaining in my vision, all currently occupied, all that is, except for the aisle seat directly next to me. I glance at each person, wondering at first if it's a real person or a hologram, and next, if that is the person with whom I'm supposed to have an erotic encounter with. Eager to proceed, I scoot on over into the aisle seat for a closer look.

"I believe that you're in my seat."
   "Oh, I apolo. . . . Lucas?!"
   "Ah, we meet again, lovely Miranda."
   In shock, I slip back on over into my own seat, suddenly uncomfortable that Raven has set me up with Lucas. Hmmmm, this is not what I expected, not what I was hoping for at all. I wanted a stranger. No names, no connections, just a wild "wham, bam, thank you ma'am" encounter.

Lucas sits down and then turns to me saying, "You're not very happy to see me, are you?" Then he reaches a finger across to brush a stray lock of hair away from my face. "What is it about me that you don't like?"

I close my eyes, trying to ignore the electrical charge that radiates throughout my face and scalp from his simple touch. I visualize his sinfully handsome face . . . those incredible teal eyes, the jet black hair, the sun-kissed skin. My God, what's *not* to like? Maybe that's the problem. Maybe I feel inferior, that he has the upper hand . . . that he has the *control*. Ah, not good to not be in control of your own fantasy. Certain that I have pinpointed the reason for my discomfort, I once again open my eyes and focus in on him.

Just as I'm about to answer his question, the captain's voice comes booming over the intercom for all passengers to fasten their safety belts and prepare for takeoff. The stewardess returns and assists Lucas and me with our buckles, then prepares the safety demonstration. I look out the window, amazed to see an airport ramp area, complete with baggage-toting vehicles and line men. Then I actually feel the vibrations of the engine and the airplane start to move as it taxies down the runway. Within minutes, we are airborne. Suddenly playful, I look over at Lucas and smile. "Do *you* have any idea where we are going? I forgot to ask."

He just winks in response and says, "Does it really matter?"

"Guess not." Okay, now what?

"You never answered my question, Miranda. Why don't you like me?"

I look at him thoughtfully, momentarily mesmerized by his incredible eyes, then ask my own question.

"Not many women say 'no' to you, do they?"

"No. But I don't imagine many men turn you away, either. Is that what this is about? You think that I'm a womanizer?"

*　　*　　*

I shrug my shoulders and then change the subject. "Do they serve refreshments on this flight? I could use a cocktail."

Lucas shakes his head in amusement. "Sorry, baby. That's one aspect of VR that Antonio hasn't quite perfected, eating and drinking. He can get the texture and flavor to the lips and tongue, but hasn't quite mastered the art of swallowing. Screws up a good blow job, too."

I laugh, and then hesitantly ask Lucas the dreaded question that's been nagging at me since the flight began. "So, what exactly did Raven say to you? I mean, why did you decide to meet up with me here?"

"Oh, Miranda, please. Don't be coy. We both know why I'm here."

Lucas leans closer, whispering lustfully into my ear. "Now, the only thing we have to worry about is *where* you want me to fuck you."

"No! No! Oh my God, Lucas. It's not supposed to be like this. It's supposed to be ... spontaneous, not planned."

"Nothing's planned, baby. It's like we've just met and felt an immediate attraction to one another. And now you are playing the indignant female pretending to be insulted by my blatant invitation, when what you'd really like to do is tear my clothes off and have your way with me. Suit yourself."

"That's it. I'm not going to sit here and listen to you puff your feathers. Please excuse me."

I stand up, destination unknown, but determined that I will no longer subject myself to his arrogance. As I pass by him and out into the isle, Lucas reaches up and grabs my ass, the final straw. I turn around, furious at his nerve, and slap him soundly across his smug face. "Go fuck yourself, you self-centered ass." Extremely pleased that I did not allow him to get away with manhandling me, I strut down the isle until I spy an unoccupied restroom and seek temporary refuge within. Just as I'm about to slide the lock in place, the door comes bursting open, throwing me backwards and onto the closed toilet lid.

"What the . . . ?"

Lucas barges in, even more incensed over my slap than I was about his unwanted groping. Oh God. I'm so dead. Slamming and locking the door behind him, he quickly turns to me, appearing absolutely livid, obviously struggling to get his anger under control.

Pointing a threatening finger at me, he utters through clenched teeth, "Don't you *ever* slap me again. EVER!"

I cringe and scoot back, certain that he's going to rip my head off, but instead, he just stands next to the door, continuing to breathe erratically.

"Get up!"
  "Wha . . . what? Why?"
  "I said, stand the fuck up . . . now!"

Terrified, I jump to my feet, and start to try and calm him down.

"I'm sorry, Lucas. I don't know what came over me. I . . ."

My words are cut short as he grabs hold of my hair and pulls me smack into his chest, kissing me viciously, bruising my mouth. Immediately, every thought and every feeling disappears except for intense lust and passion . . . and . . . need. Greedily, I kiss him back, not at all intimidated by the punishing kiss. Starting deep within the pit of my belly, I feel liquid heat rapidly spread through my veins, setting my entire body on fire. I feel animal, primitive and can focus on nothing but Lucas's presence. My God. I want to fuck him. I want to fuck him hard. I want to fuck him fast. I want to scream.

With disgust, Lucas pushes me from him so that I'm standing just in front of the toilet again. The desire and lust clearly visible in his eyes is scary, yet excites me. We stare at each other, unable to catch our breath, quickly becoming lightheaded as we fill the small cabin with carbon monoxide. Lucas takes the back of his hand and swipes it across his lips, as if to remove the memory of my kiss, and becomes even more angry when the simple gesture only heightens his arousal.

"Take off your pants."

I meet his gaze, rising to his challenge, and begin to remove my pants slowly, my eyes never leaving his. No way am I going to allow him to reduce me to a cowering, pathetic, whimpering frightened schoolgirl. He wants a fight, well he's going to get a fight. Finally, I wriggle the pants down from my hips until they fall into a heap around my ankles. I try to step out of them, but cannot get beyond the barrier provided by the clunky shoes. Beaten, I just stand there and wait for his next move, eyes still locked with his, daring him.

"All the way."

"I . . . can't . . . get . . . them . . . past . . . my . . . shoes," I practically spit out through clenched teeth.

Lucas walks over to me, my bravado slipping momentarily as he takes hold of my thong panties. In one powerful jerk, he rips them from my body, causing me to gasp in surprise. The act is almost painful, yet the excitement immediately following, overshadows, then suffocates any physical hurt I felt initially. All it serves to do is reinforce my desire not to cringe before him, and issue my own unspoken challenge. Is that all you've got, fucker?

Lucas grabs my hair again and pulls backward until I cry out.

"I said, take off your pants, not pull them down. I meant it. Now, do what you have to do, but get them off. I am running out of patience with you."

I am pushed back into a sitting position as Lucas releases his hold on my hair, finding myself once again warming the lid of the pot. Never have I ever felt such murderous thoughts, the urge to fling myself at him and scratch his eyes out very hard to ignore. Luckily, I manage to stifle them as I work on first removing my shoes, then my pants. After kicking them aside, I stand proudly, only to witness Lucas in the process of hurriedly removing his own constricting clothing.

In no time at all, Lucas is completely nude, and I am held utterly spellbound. He is beautiful, muscular, built quite similarly to Russ, only darker, and shiny with sweat. Somehow, seeing his body covered with perspiration makes him only more desirable, irresistible, magnetic. And his cock is magnificent . . . rigidly standing out, straining against the confines of its own skin, deepening to an angry purple. I can't help but imagine it thrusting aggressively into me, practically collapsing against my weakened knees at the thought. Oh my God. I could cum just thinking about it. Lucas's next command saves me from embarrassing myself any further.

"Now your shirt."

Ready, wanting nothing more than to wildly fuck this man, I pull the sweater up and over my head, and quickly remove the satin bra hidden underneath. Standing as gloriously naked as he, I watch as he repositions himself in the cramped quarters. He leans against the wall opposite the sink and then slowly lowers himself until his bare feet are braced against the foot of the sink, then turns to look at me.

"Ride it, bitch."

I smile and straddle him seductively, positioning myself just above his throbbing member.

"Gladly," I whisper back, as I let my full weight fall and envelope him in one fell swoop.

*   *   *

Two distinctly different sounds are wrenched from us, his an animalistic groan, mine a scream of intense pleasure combined with a sigh. Lucas grabs hold of my hips and then prepares to take me on the ride of my life, repeatedly lifting me up, then slamming me back down the full length of his ultimately aroused cock. Each thrust is overwhelming, ears tingling while my eyes fill with unshed tears of pure ecstasy. Just when I think I can take no more of the punishing encounter, Lucas drives home one more time then releases himself inside me, flooding me with several spurts of his thick, creamy cum and marking me with his own individualized masculine scent. Seconds behind him, I too get caught up in the throes of my own orgasm, collapsing and falling across his chest. Breathlessly, I open my mouth to speak, but never have the opportunity to utter the words. Magically, I am transported back into my basement as my hour comes to a close, the preset timer impeccably reliable.

CHAPTER 8

■

CONFRONTATIONS

Monday morning comes much too quickly as I swat at the snooze button somewhat annoyed. Oh God, I don't want to go to work today, with the events of the weekend still plaguing me. Well, at least Nick decided to come home last night. That's a good sign, I guess. I had already gone to bed, quite depressed and loaded, opting to drown my sorrows with wine after the VR experience failed to lighten my mood. If anything, I was even more confused after my confrontation with Lucas. I have to admit, it was quite thrilling. He must have gotten so pissed when I just disappeared after the timer went off. Well, at least he "got off" before that happened. Two minutes earlier and we would have both been left extremely frustrated. I might have had to go back in a second time. As it was, Lucas probably expected me to reappear, irking him further when I didn't.

Moaning, I turn to look at Nick who has just begun to stir. "Morning, hon."

Groaning, he replies, "Already? Feels like I just fell asleep."

"Well, maybe you did. When did you get home last night?"

"Mmmmm, right around midnight, I think."

"Ah, you've had plenty of sleep, but I think I'm going to blow off going to work today. I'm seriously hung over."

"Well, unfortunately, I don't have that luxury. I have to go in. A world run by computers has no tolerance or compassion for their human counterparts. They'll crash, despite how much sleep I've had. Now, Lois, hand me my cape."

Giggling, I reach out my hand and lovingly stroke Nick's face. "We're okay?"

"Yeah, baby, we're okay."

Nick pulls me over to him and kisses me leisurely, gently, thoroughly. Then he flops me over so that my back is cradled against his stomach, both of us resting on our right sides. Slowly, he enters me, tenderly melting away the ice crystals that had begun to form around my heart in self-preservation. Ah, the coupling is sweet, magical, healing, and both Nick and I feel quite back to normal when it's over. With one final kiss to the tip of my nose, Nick hops out of bed and into the shower. I quickly call work and leave a message for Beau telling him that I am not feeling well enough to join him at the office today, then fall back into a blissful sleep.

When next I awaken, it's just after 10 AM, and I'm feeling wonderfully refreshed. Headache and hangover gone, I quickly decide that I am quite capable of putting in a few hours at Handymans after all. No sense wasting all this newfound energy just sitting around the house. By 11:30 AM, I am out the door and whistling my way to work.

The lobby is lifeless when I enter, not a soul in sight. Even Wesley has made himself scarce, almost as if Mr. Miller had given everyone the day off in my absence. Checking my appointment book, I realize that today is solidly booked for the guys, and that they are all probably out on calls. Feeling somewhat guilty for the bind I left Beau in, and on such a busy day, I quickly brew a fresh pot of coffee and then take him a cup.

The door to his office is closed, and I hesitate just long enough before knocking to identify a very feminine squeal coming from within. Pausing, I strain to listen more closely, almost certain that he is sexually "entertaining" a lady friend. The bastard! All this time he led me to believe that he remains celibate, that he is too offensive for women to find sexually attractive. He even had me feeling so sorry for him, that I dressed kinky and masturbated to appease his voyeuristic fantasies. I can't believe he had me so fooled! And, and, if he's not really disfigured, not really unattractive, why doesn't he want me? There were times when I begged him to take me, to fuck me, to use me, but never once did he seem interested in anything but watching. What does "she" have that I don't have?

Confused by the irrational feelings flooding my emotions, I move away and race back to my desk, trying to come to grips with my hurt. I feel so naive, knowing now that's he's been using me, *toying* with me, probably even laughing at me. How could he do that to me? All I ever wanted was to help him with his burden. I didn't deserve this.

Reaching blindly into my purse, I yank out my stash of tissues and start dabbing at my eyes, hoping to quickly quell the flow of my tears. Then, of course, I try to rationalize. Why do I care? I have a husband I adore who allows me to pursue any and all fantasies I feel comfortable going after. I have a virtual world to explore all the ones I'm not so at ease with. Why does it bother me so to discover that Mr. Miller has no sexual interest in me? "It's not that, Miranda, it's the fact that he made a fool out of you. That's what's really upsetting you. Don't be hurt. Don't get mad. Get even," persuades the tiny voice inside.

Sniffling, my tears subsiding as my anger increases, I start to stuff the remaining tissues back into my purse when my fingers close around a hard, cool object. Smiling again, I lift the bottle out and hold it up as I begin to create my own form of revenge. Ah, Russ's herbs, the aphrodisiac herbs. I had almost completely forgotten about them, thoughtlessly tossing them into my purse as my sweatshirt unceremoniously joined the neglected piles of laundry on the basement floor. Oh, I couldn't think of a more perfect way to get back at him.

Grinning now, I begin to stir a small amount of the herbs into Beau's cup of coffee, until no trace of them remain, then meander back to his office door. Boldly, I knock on the door and then twist the knob, surprised when it swings wide open. Pretending not to suspect anything amiss, I begin to address Mr. Miller.

"Good morning, Beau. Sorry I'm late. I woke up feeling terrible this morning, but after a few more hours rest, I felt like a whole new person. I decided to surprise you with a fresh cup of coffee and the promise of at least a half a day's work."

The silence behind the curtain, as well as the lack of movement, is almost comical as I wait for a response. Finally, Beau clears his throat.

"Ah, Miranda. What a . . . a nice surprise. Of course I'm glad that you could make it after all. Um, you can just set the coffee down on the edge of my desk and I'll get to it in just a moment. I'm in the middle of something rather critical, unfortunately demanding my full attention."

I bet it does. I place the coffee on the desk as requested, but rather than take the cue and leave, I close the door and have a seat in the chair opposite his desk.

"Oh, come on, Beau. I've had the most incredible, wild weekend I've ever had. You just have to let me tell you all about it while you drink up. I'm just bursting, and I know you'll get a kick out of it."

With all of his blood rushed to the "other head," Beau is unable to come up with a plausible excuse quickly enough to make me leave, and succumbs gracefully. Again, I have to stifle a giggle as I watch his finger slip up under the curtain and begin to drag the coffee cup toward him.

"By all means, then, Miranda, please, enlighten me regarding your weekend activities."

I spend the next fifteen minutes describing my encounter after work on Friday night. Beau apologizes for keeping me so late, convinced that it was his fault that I landed in the predicament I had. I explained to him that I eventually ended up enjoying it thoroughly, and that he shouldn't blame himself. After a slight pause in my story, his empty coffee cup is slid back to the edge of his desk.

"We need to invest in a different brand of coffee. That cup tasted pretty stale."

"No problem. I'll take care of that this afternoon."

For the next fifteen minutes, I explain how Russ convinced me into agreeing to spend the weekend in his dungeon and all the fine tortures that I exposed myself to as a result. Beau is pretty quiet for most of the verbal dissertation, then out of the blue, gets on the intercom.

"Dante, I need you in my office immediately."

"Yes, sir."

In less than twenty seconds, "Dante" is knocking on the office door and Beau invites him in. Oh my God. I hope I didn't just get him into trouble. That certainly wasn't my intent.

* * *

He walks in, a bit surprised to see me, then asks, "What's wrong? Your page sounded urgent."

"Please close the door and then block it. I don't want Miranda to be able to leave."

Russ and I look at one another, completely befuddled. What the hell is going on?

"Beau?" I venture. "I don't understand."

Beau's voice sounds positively icy when he finally speaks. "What was in the coffee, Miranda?"

Oh my God, so busted.

"Uh, just a little cream and sugar. Why?"

The sound of his fist slamming into his desk causes both Russ and I to jump simultaneously.

"Don't screw with me, Miranda. I've got a raging hard-on right now that I can't account for. My veins feel like they've got lava flowing through them, and I have an uncontrollable urge to fuck my chia-pet. What was in the God-damn coffee!"

I wince at the full-blown rage I hear in his voice, then reel backwards even more as Russ joins in and double teams me.

"You bitch! You stole them, didn't you? I've been looking all over for them. I can't believe you just up and took them!"

"What? What'd she take? Did she poison me? For God's sake, tell me what I just drank!"

"Calm down. Just some herbs. You're not going to die. You're just going to be insatiably horny for the next eight hours or so."

Oh my. I am soooo backed into a corner. What am I going to do? Well, denying it seems pointless, plus I'm sure the expression on my face has already given me away. With no other option available, I extend my claws and get ready for battle.

"Well . . . Beau. . . . if you hadn't been back there fucking some floozy when I got to work, I never would have used them on you. And you," I screech, as I turn to face Russ, "had no right to use those herbs on me in the first place. Serves you right, you cock-sucking bastard!"

Russ looks momentarily shocked by my vulgar misuse of the English language, while Beau mellows out some, probably a little embarrassed over getting caught.

"I apologize for my little indiscretion, but that didn't give you the right to drug me. Where are the herbs now?"

"None of your damn business."

For the next several moments, a lot of shuffling about and whispering goes on behind Mr. Miller's curtain. Then finally, a creamy chocolate leg appears, soon followed by the rest of an extremely exotic female body. From behind the curtain steps a very tall, very regal, and very beautiful black woman. Her gaze immediately settles on me, then narrows, accusingly. Her hair is long and bound in corn rows, exquisitely decorated with colorful designer beads. Her skin is creamy and flawless, accentuated by a short, bright yellow leather dress and a pair of yellow heels. She continues to stare at me, as if waiting.

"I'll ask you one more time. Where are the herbs?"

Before I can answer, Russ interjects. "They've got to be here somewhere, or she wouldn't have been able to use them on you. They're probably in her purse or something. Maybe on her desk somewhere."

"Ah, I bet you're right, Russ. Janelle, my sweet, would you mind searching Miranda's personal belongings and around her desk for them?"

"Not at all, love."

She has an English accent! Not at all what I would have expected her voice to sound like.

"Russ, what do they look like?"

"Well, they should be in a small brown glass bottle."

"Janelle, if you should find them, please bring them back here to me. Oh, and would you mind getting me another cup of coffee?"

"Consider it done."

Gracefully, she confiscates the empty cup and exits the office. In less than five minutes, she returns, a shiny brown bottle in her grasp, as well as another cup of fresh coffee.

"Thank you darling. Please give those to Russ and have a seat next to Miranda. Russ, I want you to mix up a very potent amount of those herbs into that coffee and then supervise Miranda as she drinks it."

"What if she won't drink it? What if she spits it out at me?"

"Oh, she'll drink it, because if she doesn't, we'll take her out into the parking lot and force feed it to her, enema style."

Russ grins from ear to ear, I'm sure visualizing me draped over the hood of a car while the warm coffee is pumped slowly into my unwilling ass.

"I'll drink it, I'll drink it! No need to resort to violence, but why? Why do you want me horny? I mean . . ."

"You mean, you're always horny, so why do I feel the need to increase your sex drive?" Beau asks, maliciously. "I'll tell you why. Because, if I'm going to suffer through the afternoon in this state, so are you, baby."

"Ah, so maybe now, you'll want to fuck me."

"What?! Jesus Christ, Miranda. Is that why you did this? Because you wanted me to fuck you?! I can't believe this."

Russ hands me the drugged coffee, and I reluctantly sip it while I give Beau the rest of my explanation.

"For weeks, you've led me to believe that you were incapable of sex, always thwarting any advance or invitation I made in your direction. I thought it was because of your 'condition,' whatever that's supposed to be. And then I find you here . . . with her, obviously quite capable of pleasing a woman. I was hurt that you never thought of me in that way, and were probably laughing at my lame attempts at seducing you. This was the perfect way to get back at you. Give you the herbs, get you so incredibly horny that you'd stoop so low as to even fuck me, and then I'd turn *you* down."

Beau can't resist chuckling, despite the feeling of betrayal. "Miranda, Janelle is not a married woman. You are. I make it a point not to mess with married women. I wouldn't like having to look over my shoulders all the time wondering if there is an enraged husband following me, ready to strike me down. Resisting you has been the greatest challenge of my lifetime. As it is, I've let things get too far, but I had to have something. Watching you, listening to you recap your sexual adventures are all at once heaven and hell. God, I thought you knew that."

I finish the last sip of my coffee wondering how on Earth I managed to once again misinterpret a situation, therefore creating an even worse one. Will I never learn? What is wrong with me?

"Oh God, Beau. I'm so sorry. Please don't hate me."
"I don't hate you, Miranda, but you win. There's no way I can deny my desire for you under these conditions. I'm *going* to fuck you. And then I'm going to fuck you again. And again, and again, and again. For a solid eight hours, or until this drug wears off, I'm going to pound into your treacherous little body. I'm going to make you scream. I'm going to make you beg. I'm going to make you cry. I'm going to make you sigh. I'm. . . . going . . . to. . . . make . . . *you*! Be careful what you wish for, Miranda. It just might come true. Russ, can you get the blindfold out of my bottom file drawer? I think it only

appropriate that since she stole from you, you should be the one responsible for taking away her sense of sight."

"Ah, let the games begin." Russ announces, much too enthusiastically.

"I also have some silk scarves in that drawer. Use them to tie Miranda's hands behind her back."

"You're the boss."

Russ takes his time placing the blindfold over my eyes and securing it in place, eliminating any chance that it will slip and reward me with any insight into what's in store for me. Next he binds my hands behind my back, using a scarf not only at my wrists, but another at my elbows as well. By now, the aphrodisiac has already entered my bloodstream and is beginning to wreak some havoc with my mind, raising my body temperature several degrees as well as heightening the rest of my senses. My breathing quickens as my anticipation intensifies, my body eager to live up to the challenge of nonstop sex. Please . . . hurry.

The wait is interminable, and the three of them are exceptionally quiet, hardly making a sound. Just when I think they're going to leave me standing there, I begin to feel hands touching several parts of my body concurrently. One pair of hands is working on the buttons of my blouse, another is removing my shoes and thigh highs, while the last pair is working on the zipper of my skirt. Someone is kissing my lips, but I can't tell who. The lips are soft, so I assume they're Janelle's. I also feel lips on the inside of my thigh, and more kisses being pressed into the small of my back Oh God, I'm in heaven.

Soon my blouse and bra are unclasped and pulled back over my shoulders to drape across my bound arms. The person behind me begins to wind the excess material around the silk scarves, utilizing my own clothing for further bondage purposes. My skirt and panties quickly follow the removal of my stockings and shoes, until I am left standing completely naked. Then the true assault begins. Lips, fingers, hands, tongues, mouths . . . all licking and sucking and biting and touching and groping and probing and pinching. At one point, I have mouths and tongues lapping away at my pussy, ass and nipples all at the same time. Lost in glorious bliss, I succumb to the first of many orgasms I'm certain to experience this afternoon.

Next I find myself being pushed to my knees, then encouraged to sit on a waiting face. Immediately, an eager tongue begins to clean up the mess from my climax, while a persistent cock coaxes my mouth open and commences to thoroughly use it. Back and forth it glides, in and out, hitting the back of my throat on one stroke, then dueling with the tip of my tongue on the next. Not to be left out, the person behind me, now also on his knees, takes the bottom half of my hair, being careful not to upset the blindfold, and wraps it around his cock. Once it is completely surrounded by my silky tresses, he begins to masturbate, using my hair as a form of lubrication. Luckily for me, the two men have their rhythm in sync, one pulling in one direction while the other pushes in the opposite.

We maintain this position until the man behind me spews his seed into my hair just as Janelle beneath me brings about my second orgasm. The man currently ravaging my mouth quickly removes his still throbbing cock, and then pushes me over forward, until my face is smashed into Janelle's crotch, her delectable feminine scent taunting me.

Unable to brace myself with my arms, she is forced to accept the full brunt of my weight, but her squeals indicate that she's not too terribly upset. I begin to lick and suck at her, praying that they don't let me suffocate in the process, while I feel someone entering my upraised pussy from behind. Oh God.

The thrusting is relentless, powerful, potent, exquisite. I am unable to shout out my ecstasy as my face remains buried in the juices of Janelle, however, the man who made the mess in my hair is now alternating between pinching my nipples and pulling back on my head so that I can catch an occasional breath. Still, nobody says a thing, as if the entire encounter had been previously choreographed and practiced to perfection. Everybody just *knows* what they are supposed to do, myself included. Finally, the man behind me groans out his release, flooding me with his sperm, then changes places with whoever is tormenting my nipples.

Again, I feel myself being entered from behind, only much more slowly, calculating. He is swirling his cock around, almost as if trying to completely cover it in the mixture of my and the other man's cum. Then he withdraws, and the light comes on. It has to be Russ, and he's going for my ass. My anal violation is momentarily delayed as Janelle finally lets herself go and climaxes, squirting her fragrant nectar all over my face. Beau pulls my head back in the nick of time, saving me from an imminent drowning, obviously familiar with her sexual responses. I gasp for air, then suddenly gasp for another reason all together, as Russ begins to enter my ass and fuck it as relentlessly as he had in his dungeon.

Janelle squeezes her thighs tightly together, allowing my head a resting place while Russ continues to plunge into my ass. Somebody's fingers begin to tease and tantalize my clit, while another finger slides unobstructed into my pussy. I never knew it could feel like this. I don't want it to ever end.

But end it does. Janelle is the first to speak up that she'd love to stick around, but that she has a previous engagement that she can't ignore. Russ also had to bow out, sheepishly stating that unfortunately, he hadn't consumed any of the drug and is out of commission for a while. Somehow, I don't think that Beau is overly upset, probably relishing in the knowledge that he can finally make good on his earlier threats.

Somebody helps me to stand so that Janelle can get up off the floor and get herself together. Soon the office door closes for the last time, leaving me solely at the mercy of Beau's imagination and his artificially increased sex drive. Still, the thought is arousing to me, that I'm finally going to be ravaged by my mysterious boss. Who is he? To know him, yet not know him at all, only intensifies this cat and mouse game. What's he doing right now? How close is he standing to me? Is that his breath I'm feeling on my shoulder? What's he thinking?

I stand waiting, afraid to even move a muscle, then hear him sit in the chair directly behind me. Grasping my hips, he pulls me stumbling backwards until my legs are straddling his, then eases me downward. Oh, yes, right onto a magnificent cock. The cock that will no doubt ease the fire raging out of control within. He steadies and controls my movements, lifting me up, pulling me down . . . sometimes slowly, other times maniacally. Once, he even holds me up, poised at the tip of his cock, and just waits. I begin to wriggle, trying to squirm my way down, but he doesn't let me. It's not until I beg and grovel and promise him unconditional devotion that I'm finally allowed to slide back down and lose myself in the splendor of his rigid thickness. We both climax again, but the release doesn't even begin to assuage the burning desire and ache we feel coursing through our bodies. Again and again we fuck, against the wall, arched backwards across his desk, draped over the back of a chair, on the floor, on his lap, to finally end under a torrid stream of hot water from his bathroom shower. Several hours have gone by, and I know that Nick must be sick with worry, not even aware that I changed my mind and went to work today. Oh, God, how am I going to explain this one to him?

Beau unties my hands and then exits the bathroom before I have a chance to remove my blindfold. Damn, I was so close. I finish the shower and delighted, spot some fresh clothing on the counter. Not what I arrived in, but at least they are warm, comfy and dry. As I walk

back into Beau's office, I can't help but notice the dis-
array. Furniture knocked over, clothing scattered about
. . . mostly mine, I come to determine, and office supplies strewn in all directions, obviously disturbed by the
wild coupling on top of his desk. I pause in front of his
curtain, sure that he's sitting behind it.

"Now what?" I ask, hesitantly. "Do you need my resignation?"

"I'd have to say that my trust has been somewhat
shattered. It'll be a while before I can accept a cup of
coffee that you've prepared."

"It's probably best if I just gather my things and we
go our separate ways. Everything's different now. The
office is set up and running smoothly. If you hire someone right away, there shouldn't be any repercussions."

"Goodnight, Miranda."

"Goodbye, Beau."

I gather up my meager belongings quickly and head out
the door, halfway home before I realize that I left my
purse behind. Damn it. That's what I get for being in
such a hurry. Nick is going to be so upset when I finally
get home. It's already dark, probably after 9 PM. I turn
around and start heading back to the office, thankful that
I at least have the keys to the door on my person.

The building is completely dark and empty upon my
return. As I enter, I have the uneasy feeling that I'm
trespassing, and that I'm under heavy surveillance.

Don't be ridiculous, Miranda. You have a perfectly valid
reason for being here.

———————

I find my purse and start to head back to the lobby door, when my inquisitiveness gets the better of me. This may be my one and only chance at ever finding out what's behind Mr. Miller's curtain. I may not learn anything more about him, but at least my curiosity will be satisfied. Against my better judgement, I head in the direction of Beau's office.

I try the handle, expecting to find it locked, then smile in surprise as it opens effortlessly. The office is dark and vacated, no sign that Beau is anywhere nearby. Cringing somewhat, I flip on the light switch then hold my breath, expecting bells and whistles to notify all of my intrusion. When nothing happens, I step inside and shut the door behind me. Eagerly, I head for the curtain.

What I find is astonishing, a veritable control panel of switches and monitors. I feel like I'm behind the security guard's desk at Fort Knox or something. Anxious to see what all the switches are responsible for, I seat myself in the comfortable chair, still warm from Beau's backside. I begin flipping levers and buttons, watching in amazement as the monitors come to life. Beau has cameras placed all over this building, and I play with the one located in the lobby, zooming in on my very own desk, or what used to be my desk. Man, this thing is so powerful, one could easily see straight down my blouse from this angle. Another monitor shows his dark and empty bathroom, just slightly illuminated by the light seeping in from his office. Two more monitors show additional offices, but it's too dark to be able to ascertain which ones.

With another flip of a toggle, all four monitors momentarily go dark, then begin to light up slowly. Curiously, I watch as four new rooms come into sight, then open my mouth in bewilderment as I recognize the rooms. Oh my God. These cameras are in my *house!!* I can clearly identify my bedroom, my bathroom, my kitchen and the computer area of my basement. How can this be? Who is Mr. Miller, and how did he get into my house to install hidden cameras? Oh my God, am I in danger? Is Nick in danger?

Just as this thought passes through my confused brain, I see Nick come into view on the kitchen monitor. He has his coat on, as if he just got home. Oh, no. He's been out looking for me, I'm sure of it. I have to call him. I look down searching for the phone, only to notice that there are two phones sitting side by side on his techno console. One looks just like the phone at my desk, with several different incoming and outgoing lines, and the other is a red, superhero phone, just like the one in all the Batman movies. Totally befuddled, I pick up the familiar phone and quickly dial my home number.

I watch Nick's head turn in the direction of the phone as it rings, jumping when the "bat phone" also starts ringing. Knowing that I'm taking an awfully big risk, I answer it and hold it up to my ear, hearing nothing but heavy breathing. Oh God. He knows. He knows that I'm here.

"Hello?"

I screech and then drop both phones as my own voice rings loud and clear through the ear piece of the "bat phone." I just called myself! I dialed my home number and it rang in here. What in heaven's name is going on? I hang up both phones and continue to watch Nick as a very unpleasant concept crosses my mind. No, it couldn't be. Could it? Nick, Mr. Miller? No . . .

Nick picks up the phone and begins pressing buttons, then hangs it back up again with a thoughtful expression. Oh, please, don't let it be so. The more I think about the possibility, the more it makes sense. No wonder he has never let me see him. But what about his voice? Beau and Nick sound nothing alike. I search the control panel looking for some more clues, and find them. Sure enough, there is a microphone protruding from the console. I lean forward and speak into it. Nothing happens. I look around until I find an on/off switch, and try again. My world quickly begins to crumble as I hear my words broadcast out into the office, cleverly disguised. Oh, the bastard.

Still suspecting, but not yet positive, I decide to try out one more test. Picking up the phone a the second time, I again dial my home number. This time it rings at the house, but not in the office. Nick answers the phone, the call forwarding obviously deactivated.

"Hello."

"Hi, baby." I respond, with higher spirits than I actually feel.

"Miranda! Where are you, honey? I've been worried to death."

I bet you have.

"I felt better after my little nap this morning and decided to come into the office after all. Beau had tons of work for me to do, so I stayed until it was all done."

Nick casually asks, "Oh, so are you still at the office?"

"Yes. I was halfway home and then realized I had forgotten my purse, so I came back for it. I should be home pretty soon."

I watch Nick look directly into the camera, then move toward it as he says, "Okay, baby. I'll be waiting for you." Next, his hand comes up and the screen goes black.

"See you soon."

Oh, I can't believe it, but the proof is right there in front of me as I follow him from room to room, systematically disabling all four of the cameras. He *is* Mr. Miller! How could I not have known about his double life? And why all of this? Just to spy on me? Does he trust me so little that he has to know my every move? Is he afraid and trying to protect me? And from what, myself? How long has this been going on, since my return home?

I begin to feel nauseated as everything comes together with stunning clarity. My own husband, obsessed. Just like Russ had been, maybe still is. Russ . . . he has to know the truth. Those two have been in cahoots since the start. God damn, do I feel duped. What am I going to do?

Nothing, Miranda. You're going to go home and act like nothing is wrong. Then tomorrow, you're going to have the house re-keyed!

Reluctantly, I listen to the voice of reason . . . or is it?

CHAPTER 9

■

REALIZATIONS

Pretending not to know is very difficult, especially when all I want to do is shake Nick and ask him, "why?" As soon as he leaves for the office, I quickly call the locksmith and request that all my locks be changed. He informs me that he can be here in an hour. Nervously, I chomp on my nails. What am I doing? I can't just lock him out of his own home, keep him from his things. Eventually I'm going to have to face him. Eventually, but not now. He can just stay at a motel for a few days, buy some new clothes to get by on, a new toothbrush. I'll call him at the office as soon as we have new locks and tell him that I don't want to see him for a few days, maybe ever again. God, it's still so inconceivable that Nick could deceive me so thoroughly.

With time to kill, I sit down at the computer and e-mail both Angela and Antonio that I'd like to hook back up with them again in VR, preferably around noon today at the Castle. Then, I sit back and watch as the locksmith does his thing. It is almost noon when he leaves, assuring me that no one can enter uninvited, providing me with both sets of keys. I thank him as I usher him out the door, anxious to barricade myself within. Convinced that all the locks are bolted and secure, I race to the basement to make the fated phone call. As luck would have it, he doesn't answer, and I am routed to the voice mail box of "Beau Miller."

"Hello, Beau, or should I say . . . Nick? Your secret is out. I know who you are, and I know what you've been doing. I am so disgusted, that I can't even face you right now. All the locks have been changed at the house, so don't even try to contact me for the next several days. I can't believe that you would stoop to something this low, Nick. I'll contact you when I feel that we can talk about this. Goodbye."

The ache in my heart as I hang up the phone is suffocating. I can barely breathe. It is with tears in my eyes that I read Angela's reply that she and Antonio will gladly meet me at the Castle at noon. Checking the time, I realize that I'm already late. Quickly, I don the suit and insert, click on the Castle icon, then fasten the helmet to my head as I situate myself comfortably in the swing. Then, with the turn of a knob, I'm standing in the foyer of the Castle.

Angela and Antonio aren't there waiting for me, so I enter the castle and head in the direction of Raven's desk, and what I assume to be, the reception area. Raven greets me with a cat-like smile, then invites me to sit on a stunning leather couch while I wait for the others.

*   *   *

"How've you been, doll? You don't look very happy."

"I'm not. Things have gone from bad to worse with my husband. I'm afraid it may be over for good."

"Aw, sweetie, I'm sorry. That's too bad. I know he means the world to you."

Raven tries to comfort me, stroking my forehead and whispering soothing and encouraging words, but I remain pouting miserably. Finally, I see Antonio and Angela entering hand in hand, and can't help but shiver at Antonio's image. He looks just like Lucas, and Lucas gives me the creeps. Joyous to see Angela, however, I jump up and race to greet her.

"Oh, I've missed you so much." I exclaim, as I squeeze her in an incapacitating hug.

"Well, I guess so." She laughs, when she is able to catch her breath. "Guess what, Randi? I have the best news!"

"What?" I ask, excitedly, my mood already beginning to lighten.

"Antonio and I are getting married in June. I want you to be my Matron of Honor."

"Oh my God, you guys! That's wonderful! Of course I'll be your Matron of Honor! Uh, just one quick question, though."

"Yes?"

"Have you guys actually met in person yet, or is this going to be a 'virtual wedding'?"

Both Angela and Antonio start bursting out laughing, then finally get a hold of themselves.

*   *   *

"Of course we've met. We've actually been living together for the past month. Guess I haven't kept you up
to date. It happened so fast that even I'm having trouble
keeping up."

"Well, I'm so happy for you, and even happier to be
a part of it."

Antonio must have sensed my reluctance to speak intimately with Angela in his presence, and chivalrously
offers to excuse himself so that we can talk freely. Then
Raven offers us the use of any room that strikes our
fancy to become reacquainted in. Without hesitation, we
both immediately request the "strip club" location and
then laugh over our respective sentimentality. Raven
smiles knowingly, then leads us into the room to have a
seat. She warns us that it will take approximately ten
minutes for any type of atmosphere to be incorporated,
but to be patient. Angela and I scarcely notice, so
wrapped up in our own conversation.

Before long we are chatting again like the old friends
we are, and I heartbreakingly tell her about my situation
with Nick. She is disappointed, knowing all that we've
gone through to stay together, and offers me some sound
advice.

"Randi, you've got to give him a chance to explain.
Maybe there's something you don't know. Look at all
the things he's overlooked and forgiven you for. Even
if he has no excuse, and just temporarily lost his mind,
it's not anything worse than what you've done. But you
shouldn't just push him away. Let him come home and
discuss it with him. I would love to discover that An-

tonio loves me so much that he may lose his mind a time or two and do something crazy like that."

"Yeah, I suppose you're right, Angela. But where do you draw the line between love and obsession? Are they one and the same?"

"Good question. I know you don't need to be in love to be obsessed, but do you become obsessed if you are truly in love? Hmmmm, definitely a point to think about. You and Nick have both done some awfully crazy things in the name of love. I think you're both a little obsessed with one another."

"Oh, Angela. I knew you were the right person to come to about this. How did you become so wise?"

Smiling, she pats my hand in understanding, then gets up quickly. "Oh, shoot. I have to use the little ladies' room, but I don't know if that's possible in VR! I may have to exit the program and then come back in. Wait for me here, Randi. I'll be back in a flash. Mr. Swivel Hips up there can keep you company while I'm gone."

I glance up to see a very handsome male dancer gyrating on the stage, slowly removing what's left of his skimpy costume. Geeze, how long has he been up there, and how could I not have noticed? Happy with the distraction, I sit back and continue to watch the show as Angela hurriedly leaves the room.

Within five minutes, Antonio is poking his head in the door and crooking a finger at me to follow him. Sighing to be leaving such an enjoyable companion, I wave goodbye and follow Antonio out the door. I silently giggle as I wonder if I had just waved goodbye to a hologram.

* * *

Antonio picks up the pace as he wanders into a section of the castle that I'm not familiar with, and I find myself almost jogging to keep up.

"What's wrong, Antonio? Why the urgency? Did something happen to Angela?"

Antonio doesn't respond, just quickly ushers me into a room at the end of the hall. I walk in expecting to see Angela, and am taken aback by the sight before me. I feel like I've just re-entered Russ's dungeon, only with brand new toys! I look back at Antonio for an explanation, just in time to witness him locking us in, then turn to face me with an evil grin. Oh, no. Too late I realize my mistake.

"Lucas, what are you doing?"

Leaning against the door lazily, he takes his time assessing me, giving my body the full once-over.

"We have some unfinished business, baby. It wasn't very nice the way you just up and disappeared on me last time."

"Sorry, it wasn't intentional. I had the timer preset for an hour. The hour was up. Just think how mad you'd be if it had turned off five minutes earlier."

Lucas glares at me and then asks, "So what's the timer set for this time?"

"I . . . uh . . ." Oh my God. I *forgot* to set the timer!

Lucas watches as the panicked expression crosses my face, and then my eyes desperately scan the walls for a life-saving pull station. Not immediately locating one, I turn to Lucas for reassurance.

"Where's the pull station, Lucas?"

"You didn't set the timer this time, did you? And I can assume from your alarmed expression, that hubby is not nearby to rescue you. Oh the fates are smiling upon me right now."

"You can't do this to me, Lucas. It's not safe. You have to let me out of here."

"All in good time, Miranda. All in good time. Let's have a little fun, first."

After a fifteen minute struggle where I invariably emerge the loser, I find myself stark naked with my arms yanked painfully above my head and fastened to the ceiling. For now, I remain standing flat on the floor with my back pressed into a smooth, wooden post. Sweating and panting from exertion, Lucas holds up a one by four wooden plank with metal tabs protruding from one end, and asks me to stand on my tip toes. Knowing that to disobey him in my current situation will only result in pain, I comply.

Lucas spreads my legs so that I'm straddling the wooden plank, narrow sides facing up and down, and inserts the metal tabs into pre-made notches cut into the wooden post behind me. Satisfied, he backs away and gives me permission to relax, no longer being required to remain on my tip toes. As soon as I lower myself, I catch my breath as the hard edges of the wooden plank separate my nether lips and press uncomfortably into my pussy. Lucas just smiles.

---

*   *   *

"Ever ridden a wooden horse, Miranda? I can't wait to watch you giddy on up."

"Lucas, you're mad. What did I ever do to you to inspire such contempt?"

"Hmmm, that would be confusing to you, wouldn't it? This should clear things up some."

Lucas turns around and faces the wall, when suddenly my vision begins to blur and waver. But no, everything else is remaining in focus but Lucas. He is blurring. My crotch starts to burn from the constant pressure of the inflexible wooden plank, knowing that I'll soon have to raise up on tiptoes again to help alleviate the pain. I look down as best I can in my current trussed up state to see if it's possible to wriggle free, but discover there is no escaping. I'm stuck here until Lucas decides otherwise. I look up to try and reason with him and scream in terror at the vision before me. No longer am I gazing at Lucas, but another, more frightening apparition. Wit. Oh my God. Lucas is really Wit.

Immediately, I am catapulted back in time and to memories I'd thought long dead and buried. Wit. Back to the first time we had spoken in the chat rooms. Wit. Back to his irresistible opening line, "I know what a woman wants. I know what a woman needs." Wit. Back to that fateful day when I relinquished control and allowed him to call, an encounter that both sickened and thrilled me. Wit. Back to the Vegas elevator, and how he overpowered and took me captive, to be used solely as a plaything, not only for his amusement, but his lovely companion, Rachel's, as well. Wit. Back to how I es-

212

caped, physically and emotionally. Wit. Back to all of those conflicting feelings . . . terror . . . acceptance . . . intrigue . . . resistance . . . excitement . . . unrest . . . acquiescence . . . stubbornness . . . enlightenment . . . mystification . . . freedom . . . confinement . . . awareness . . . degradation . . . strength . . . weakness . . . but above all, fright.

I fear his power and control over me. I fear what I'm capable of at his hands. I fear what I become when in his presence. Oh God. And now I find myself right back in his clutches.

"Why?" I croak out. "Why can't you just leave me alone?"

Wit approaches me carrying a latex hood, complete with eyes and nose areas cut open, and a double-ended penis protruding from the mouth portion. Lewdly stroking the outer phallus, Wit explains, "Nobody bests me, Miranda. And nobody disappears from me . . . for very long, that is. You and I have so much more to experience."

"But, Antonio? How?"

"Oh, Antonio really is my brother, just not my twin. That's one of the beauties of VR. You can program the computer to portray your image however you'd like. Antonio has no idea what he's helped me to accomplish. Originally, I used him to search for you, but he found Angela instead. Ultimately, that led me back to you."

Frozen, I can only gape as he inserts the smaller end of the dildo into my mouth, then covers my head with the rest of the hood, zipping it tightly closed in back. Unable to resist, he runs his tongue along the tip of the large appendage protruding from my mouth, mocking me. Suddenly, the horror of the wooden horse has lessened, being eclipsed by the menacing figure standing before me.

"Who would you like to fuck with your face first, Miranda? Raven? Perhaps you'd even like to take *me* for a ride? Wouldn't you like to stick those eight inches right up my ass?"

The last sound I can remember hearing before I pass out and blissfully succumb to the darkness, is his endless evil laughter, "Ha, Ha, Ha, Ha, Ha, Ha, Ha!!!!!!"

CHAPTER 10

■

VALIDATIONS

"Honey, you can't end it with her trapped in VR! The readers will go nuts!"

"You think? They all know that Miranda has a guardian angel following her around. No real harm ever comes to her, just difficult situations."

"Ok, wife, but if you ask me, that's just plain mean."

"Oh really? Has my husband developed a soft spot for her?"

"Uh . . . well . . . maybe."

"Don't worry, darling. I'm sure Nick breaks down the door and rescues her from Wit's clutches in plenty of time."

"Well, as long as you're sure," he says with a wink. "Oh by the way, a letter came for you today."

"Really, from who?"

"Doesn't say. Open it and let's see."

The blood drains from my face as I read the letter:

Someday I will come for you, and you shall experience
each and every page of your novels.

ME

Romance of Lust
Anonymous

The Romance of Lust is that rare combination of graphic sensuality, literary success, and historical importance that is loved by critics and readers alike.—*The Times*

"Truly remarkable. All the pleasure of fine historical fiction combined with the most intimate descriptions of explicit lovemaking."
—*Herald Tribune*

"This justly famous novel has been a secret bestseller for a hundred years."

The Altar of Venus
Anonymous

Our author, a gentleman of wealth and privilege, is introduced to desire's delights at a tender age, and then and there commits himself to a life-long sensual expedition. As he enters manhood, he progresses from schoolgirls' charms to older women's enticements, especially those of acquaintances' mothers and wives. Later, he moves beyond common London brothels to sophisticated entertainments available only in Paris. Truly, he has become a lord among libertines.

Caning Able
Stan Kent

Caning Able is a modern-day version of the melodramatic tales of Victorian erotica. Full of dastardly villains, regimented discipline, corporal punishment and forbidden sexual liaisons, the novel features the brilliant and beautiful Jasmine, a seemingly helpless heroine who reigns triumphant despite dire peril. By mixing libidinous prose with a changing business world, Caning Able gives treasured plots a welcome twist: women who are definitely not the weaker sex.

The Blue Moon Erotic Reader III

Once again, Blue Moon presents its unique collection of stories of passion, desire, and experimentation

A testimonial to the publication of quality erotica, The Blue Moon Erotic Reader III presents more than twenty-five romantic and exciting excerpts from selections spanning a variety of periods and themes. This is a historical compilation that combines generous extracts from the finest forbidden books with the most extravagant samplings that the modern erotic imagination has created. The result is a collection that is evocative and entertaining, perhaps even enlightening. It encompasses memorable scenes of youthful initiations into the mysteries of sex, notorious confessions, and scandalous adventures of the powerful, wealthy, and notable. The Blue Moon Erotic Reader III is a stirring complement to the senses. Good taste, and passion, and an exalted desire are all here, making for a union of sex and sensibility that is available only once in a Blue Moon.

Beauty in the Birch
Anonymous

Beauty in the Birch is a remarkable description of exotic Victorian sexual episodes. Reportedly first published in Paris in 1905, the letters reveal the exploits of the handsome thirty-year-old rake Charles, who finds employment in a country mansion for wayward girls, and the impetuous and mischievous Lizzie, who, as the daughter of Britannia's plenipotentiary in an Arabian territory, makes herself privy to all the pleasures and punishments of the royal harem.